Slaves, Masters
and Traders

Also by H. Ann Ackroyd
 Colonial Adventure and Other Stories - novella and short
 stories in rhythmic prose
 Across the Rift - novel in rhythmic prose

To order, contact ackroydhelen049@gmail.com.

Slaves, Masters and Traders

Historical Fiction

H. Ann Ackroyd

Copyright © 2020 by H. Ann Ackroyd.

Library of Congress Control Number:		2020902388
ISBN:	Hardcover	978-1-7960-8662-1
	Softcover	978-1-7960-8661-4
	eBook	978-1-7960-8672-0

All rights reserved. No part of this book may be reproduced or transmitted in any form or by any means, electronic or mechanical, including photocopying, recording, or by any information storage and retrieval system, without permission in writing from the copyright owner.

This is a work of fiction. Names, characters, places and incidents either are the product of the author's imagination or are used fictitiously, and any resemblance to any actual persons, living or dead, events, or locales is entirely coincidental.

Any people depicted in stock imagery provided by Getty Images are models, and such images are being used for illustrative purposes only.
Certain stock imagery © Getty Images.

Print information available on the last page.

Rev. date: 02/04/220

To order additional copies of this book, contact:
Xlibris
1-888-795-4274
www.Xlibris.com
Orders@Xlibris.com
779080

CONTENTS

Preface xiii

First Week of January 1800 1
  Engagement 1
  The Barber-Surgeon 3
  The Laird of Glen Orm 5
  The Angus Herd 8
  The New Club 11
  Child of the Forest 15
  Big Baba 18
  Banyan Village 21
  Thimba Teaches 24

Second Week of January 1800 27
  Jemima Manifesto 27
  Bagpipes 29
  The Old Earl of Gryphon 32
  Camel and Trader 35

Third Week of January 1800 37
  Broomstick Wedding 37
  Ethnology 42
  Afternoon Tea 44
  Ne'er-Do-Well and a Dog 46
  Breakfast in Leith 49
  Nightcap 53
  Thimba and His Loa 55
  Breakfast in Banyan Village 62
  Event on the Beach 65

Fourth Week of January 1800 70
    The Lawyer 70
    A Friend at Last...75
    Rabbie Burns Night 78
    Foreigner in Leith...80
    The Trade Winds...82
    Fall of the Earl..87
    Skirting Confrontation...89
    Fable 91

First Half of April 1800...93
    The Chevalier..93
    The Wife..96
    The Slave Mother..98
    André on Horseback..101
    The Storeroom 105
    Wandering Mind...108
    Cécile's Prayer...111
    Ignorance 115
    Stanley Spring Cleans...117
    Inconvenient Conscience...120
    An Earl in Sight..122
    Conundrum 124
    Thimba Sharpens His Spearhead..127

Second Half of April 1800...129
    You Are Mine! 129
    On the Job 131
    Elusive Voice 134
    Caledonian Forest 137
    Plans for London...140
    Staircase Talk..143
    Neophyte 145
    Outing...147
    Efia and the Arabs 149

Fifth Week of April 1800 152
    Longing for Escape...152

Still on the Job 156
Desperation 158
Albatross and Pencil 162
Awkward Conversation 166
Not an Illusion 168
Pontefract's Place of Work 170
Lord Richard Warns 173
Honey, Infana, and the Bad Boys 175

First Week of May 1800 178
Betrayal 178
Tom in London 180
The Medallion 183
The Bookshop 186
Improved Plan 188
Mayday 190
The White Hart 193
Action Needed 196
Misguided 198
Mask and Costume Store 201

Second Week of May 1800 206
From Job to Sickroom 206
Hyde Park 210
Better State of Mind 214
Fright 216

Third Week of May 1800 219
Forgetfulness 219
Increase the Dosage? 221
Rouge Stain 224
The Kahve Bean 227
Salmon Beat 231
Banishment 233
Interesting Encounter 236
The Young Dandy 238
Émile's Transformation 240
Pretty as a Picture 245

Surprise for Tom..247
Lord Richard and William in Liverpool................250
Alternative Plan for Tom 252
Preparations for Gran Legbwa 254
Hairdresser...258
Palm Walking..260
Laying the Fires 262
Falling Coconut 265
Gran Legbwa Celebration...................................267

Fourth Week of May 1800 271
Danger in the Bayou 271
"Stop Interfering, Maman!"................................274
Phony Academic 276
New Mother...278
New Plan 280
Champagne in the Garden 281
Betta's Discomfort...284
New Worries 286

Fifth Week of May 1800 288
Monsieur le Docteur 288
Opening Up..293
Double Confession...295
Encounter on Princes Street 298
Hunters Depart...300
Outward Trek...303
Stolen Dinner...305
En Route...308

First Week of June 1800 310
The Jetty 310
The Real Sons 317
Too Far Left? 322
Back in Circulation 324
Schools...327
Weaning of the Young Earl.................................329
The Giant Eland Hunt......................................331

Second Week of June 1800 333
    Revelation 333
    Change of Guard 337
    Calton Hill 339
    Betta in Bed 342
    Returning to the Camp 344
    Shamwari Follows 346
    Family to Feed 348
    Sequel 349
    Return to the Village 350
    Jacques Explains 352

Beginning of the Third Week of June 1800 355
    Adieu, Mon Père 355
    Smiles 357
    Whipping 360
    Opening the House 365
    Outlandish Ideas 367
    Christening 369
    Fulfillment 371
    What Next? 372
    Kwame in Trouble 375
    Ackees 377
    Babalawo and Kwame 380

Last Night of Third Week of June 1800 385
    Strangers on the Pry 385
    Kwame on His Own 387
    Bad Start 390
    Tears of an Old Warrior 393

Fourth Week of June 1800 395
    Rip Current 395
    Stagecoach Terminal 399
    Émile at Glen Orm 401
    Tom's Arrival 404

Beginning of the Fourth Week of June 1800 406
    Goodbye, Betta 406

First Day of the Fourth Week of June 1800 408
    Schooner 408
    Babalawo 410
    Abena 412
    Efia 414
    Indaba 418
    Masimbarashe 420
    Kwame to the Rescue 422
    Instructions 424
    Final Thoughts 427

Second Day of the Fourth Week of June 1800 429
    Circle of the Dead 429

Fifth Week of June 1800 431
    André Scores 431
    Nascent Plans 435
    On the Way 438
    Another Barber-Surgeon 440
    Lamb to the Slaughter 442
    Efia on Board I 444

Second Week of July 1800 446
    Vodun Dolls I 446
    Old Methods and New Allegiances 448
    First Letter to Ambrose 453
    Tea with the Countess 456
    Efia on Board II 458

Third Week of July 1800 461
    Good Riddance 461
    Absolution 463
    Second Letter to Ambrose 465
    Abebi on Board 467
    Abena on Board 469

Fourth Week of July 1800 471
    Post-Jacques 471
    Third Letter to Ambrose 473

First Week of August 1800 475
    Vodun Dolls II 475
    Fourth Letter to Ambrose...................................479

Second Week of August 1800....................................481
    Proposal 481
    New Horizons..483
    Fifth Letter to Ambrose.....................................487

Third Week of August 1800......................................488
    Arrival..488
    Slave Auction 495
    Foreign Contraption 497

Fourth Week of August 1800 499
    The Voice..499
    Decision..502

Thirty-First of October 1800 504
    Sixth Letter to Ambrose 504
    Inauguration Day..507
    Slave Chapel..511
    Eureka Moment 514

Vodun Vocabulary 519
African and Louisiana Words.....................................521
French Words and Phrases...523
West African Vegetation..525
Fictional Characters 527

Preface

Some readers might find the description of an African village life at times too detailed, but I believe those details are justified in that many African Americans are not aware of the way their ancestors had lived prior to enslavement.

It might disturb some readers that I use Standard English to convey the thinking and communications of Africans, both in their West African homeland prior to enslavement and in Louisiana after enslavement. In that until recently, African languages were passed on exclusively by word of mouth. It is impossible from the point of view of the twenty-first century to know how people living in West Africa in the early nineteenth century would have expressed themselves, especially as countless different languages existed then as they do now. Likewise, it is impossible to know exactly how the African slave patois used in Louisiana - prior to the Louisiana Purchase (1803) - would have sounded. It, too, was an oral tradition and never documented. It would most likely have been a mixture of a little Spanish, much French, and words from one or another of the African languages depending on the origins of the slaves. In addition, in the course of time, each plantation is meant to have developed its own patois.

To bypass these problems, I use Standard English to convey the essence of my characters' thought processes and do not attempt to second-guess how they would have spoken in reality. The universality of human nature is the intent and not language as used in a specific location at a specific time.

With regard to the parts of the story line that play out in Britain, modern English is used to express the intent ontent and not the language of the day. Although English as spoken in AD 1800 is amply documented, it can be tiresome to the modern ear.

First Week of January 1800

Engagement

Plantation, Louisiana

André has always known that when a slave with whom the chevalier has chosen to breed miscarries, he will ban her from his bed. While replacing her with a nubile virgin, he will assign a suitable slave partner to the girl he is dismissing.

André most recent bed companion Andréa, a high-cheeked Choctaw[1] beauty, has recently miscarried. However, he is not thinking of the matter as he crosses the farmyard heading toward the stables. On the way, he finds the chevalier striding toward him. The chevalier, not only André's master but also his father by the black slave Agathe, is dressed in the formal attire of the ancien régime[2]: high heels, silk stockings, breeches, a brocade jacket, and as a crowning glory, the riotous curls of a top-heavy wig. To be thus attired indicates he is en route to a prestigious event in Baton Rouge where emphasis on French superiority is necessary.

---

[1] Native tribe of the southeast of North America
[2] Social and political system used in France prior to the Revolution

As André salutes him, the chevalier says without preamble, "I was thinking, son, Andréa might be a good match for you. What do you think?"

André knows, in spite of the question, that this is an order - his father is assigning Andréa to him as a *broomstick wife*.[3] Refusing is not an option. It is lucky therefore that he has no inclination to refuse; none at all! A burst of ecstasy has set his heart racing. Beaming, he blurts out, "Thank you, Master! Thank you!"

With a wry twist of the lip, the chevalier remarks, "I thought you'd be pleased, son!" Giving André a fatherly pat on the shoulder, he turns back toward the Big House where the coachman and a carriage wait. André knows his father would prefer to ride and wonders what the occasion might be that requires a show of status; he also knows he is unlikely to find out. A slave, even if that slave is a favorite son, is never privy to such information.

---

[3]   African ceremony that involves jumping over a broomstick

The Barber-Surgeon

Liverpool, England

With his left arm amputated above the elbow and the hospital experience in New Orleans behind him, Tom is renting an attic and looking for a new way to earn a living. Due to the injury he sustained on *Spirit-of-Clyde* during a storm in the Gulf of Mexico, work on a slave schooner is no longer an option. After juggling a number of unrealistic alternatives, he has concluded he needs a better education. He has always had a craving for knowledge, but meager finances never allowed for formal studies. Now he has learned that society offers an alternative means to education: the coffeehouse. As a result, he spends his time at the Merchants' Coffeehouse, which lies within the precincts of the Port of Liverpool, there where the River Mersey meets the Irish Sea.

Like many before him, he is discovering that coffeehouses, at their best, are egalitarian institutions that can help a person pursue a path to learning, if such is the intent. Although some might scoff at the *riffraff* poring over papers and chin-wagging about politics, he is delighted to pay his penny for a bowl of coffee and - armed with pencil and notebook - to sit for hours reading broadsheets and magazines. When he tires, he is able to listen to the learned discussions of his betters at nearby tables.

Today he sits alone at a table in a corner by the window. Having just finished reading the most recent edition of the *Spectator*, he gives a snort of satisfaction. He now understands the word *libertarianism*, a word he has often overheard in discussions. It means "rejecting institutional authority and replacing it with trust in individual judgment." It means that the upper-class toffs that form the *Spirit of the Clyde* consortium are - in their intrinsic humanity - no better than is he, Tom Brown. Even if they have titles, even if they are physical and financial titans like Aaron Migu, Tom Brown - a mere barber-surgeon of small stature and nondescript appearance - is their equal! Nor is he inferior to *proper* naval surgeons. Proper naval surgeons are his bête noire. They think it is their God-given right to belittle barber-surgeons, especially those who work on slave schooners and whose only training is an apprenticeship to another barber-surgeon. Proper naval surgeons do not serve apprenticeships and do not work on slave schooners. They train at colleges and universities inaccessible to men of Tom's background.

He feels forming within him an ironclad determination to prove to the outside world that even *nobodies* count. He hauls out his pipe, and he fills, tamps, and lights it. Tilting back his head, he ejects a stream of smoke as he has seen his betters do. That his eyes already smart from tobacco smoke and that the view of the Mersey is lost in a miasma is the price he gladly pays for the knowledge he is acquiring. For the first time, thanks to the article in the *Spectator*, he feels confident enough to join a discussion group at another table.

Sitting back in his chair, he surveys the scene. Clustered around tables, men from all walks of life discuss issues of the day. The topic at the first table is the two assassination attempts on the life of His Majesty King George III: one in Hyde Park and one in Drury Lane. At the second table, the discussion concerns the upcoming union of the kingdoms of Ireland and Great Britain. Tom will not join that group; he still has to bone up on the subject. If he wishes to express opinions, his pride requires that he be well informed. At the third table, he discovers the gentlemen are discussing his subject - libertarianism!

He rises, takes *The Spectator* back to its appointed place, and - with confidence still intact - approaches the table, and asks in a polite but not subservient manner, "Would you mind, sirs, if I joined you?" As he knows from observation, this is the way to proceed, and he soon finds himself participating in the discussion, obeying all the requirements for civil discourse and mannerly behavior. He has watched and learned, and although in the presence of his superiors, he has expressed valid opinions on a meaningful subject. He is proud of himself.

The Laird of Glen Orm

Aberdeenshire, Scotland

In the crisp morning air, the old laird stands at the front door surveying his domain. At seventy-nine, he is fierce and lean with bushy white eyebrows and tufts of gray hair sprouting from ear and nostril. His hooded eyes and beaked nose - now pinched from the cold - rival those of a golden eagle that circles overhead. Both he and the eagle, by virtue of the generations that precede them, belong in this place. Yet the new industrial age threatens their survival. The feudal system under which the laird's class always thrived is in a state of collapse, while the eagle's habitat - the Caledonian Forest - is vanishing before their very eyes.

Twenty-four years earlier, in order to save the struggling lairdship from bankruptcy, the old man had stooped and allowed his only child, Frances, to marry beneath herself. As a result, Pontefract Staymann, a financial tycoon but of lower social standing, has provided funds to keep the estate flourishing. In addition, he has fathered Stanley, providing the lairdship with an heir.

From his present position at the front door, the old man sees the craggy cliffs where the eagle nests and which at present is topped by a sprinkling of snow. He allows his eyes to follow the thick swathes of boreal forest that sweep down the sides of the glen to the pastures and stream below. It might not be much in the greater scheme of things, but it is better than the stumps of trees that elsewhere have fallen prey to the prodigious appetite of Britain's ship-building industry.

The old man's eyes - they are still as sharp as the eagle's - seek out a clump of Scots pines with their flaking orange barks and flattened clusters of blue-green needles. They shelter a stone chapel that serves as a repository for the history of the laird's family. It is a family that has owned the estate uninterrupted since the Middle Ages and has documentation and graves to prove it. That the laird had been forced to accept Pontefract Staymann into the heart of his illustrious family has remained a thorn in his side for over two decades. He knows that criticism of Pontefract is curmudgeonly, but he cannot help it. Even though Frances and Stanley both love Pontefract, it does not make him less vulgar. Even though Pontefract has not made his money through the slave trade - thank God - he remains the son of a merchant.

Now indoors again, the laird's thoughts turn to the subject of breakfast. It's usually something to which he looks forward, but today, along with Frances and Stanley, Pontefract will be present, probably the reason for the unwanted resurgence of his grievances. Heading for the gentleman's water closet to wash his hands - the closet is one of Frances' modern additions to the ancestral home - he resolves to put himself into a better mood and think of Frances. Although a lovely lassie, she is incapable of seeing failings in another, least of all in her husband whom she refers to as *the kindest and sweetest of men*.

As the old laird dries his hands, he grins at the fierce image he sees in the mirror. Being *the kindest and sweetest of men* does not seem like a masculine thing to say of a man and is luckily not something anyone would be likely to say of him!

As he wend his way through the narrow corridors that lead to the new breakfast room, the laird's thoughts move on to Stanley. The lad would be a suitable heir for the lairdship if he were not obsessed with all the newfangled nonsense so prevalent in present-day agriculture. The laird wishes Pontefract and Frances had managed to have more children - boys of course - then there might have been one more like himself!

He cannot blame Pontefract for the lack of children because Frances has often been with child, but - since having given birth to Stanley - she has never carried her bairns to term. She is expecting again now, and the old man's hopes are running high that this time it will be different. She has overstepped several danger points, and the baby is still alive.

The old man has now arrived at the breakfast room, and as he is early, he stands in the doorway admiring the south-facing chamber that now graces his austere ancestral home. To his chagrin, someone had once referred to his home as grim, but no one could say that about this room decorated with Frances's exquisite watercolors. He had, as with all Frances's other modernizations, fought the breakfast-room issue tooth and claw but had succumbed, when she assured him that servants would still serve them as in the great hall. The idea of serving himself at the sideboard appalls him, yet that's what happens even in families who should know better. They say they don't like servants hovering but that's daft. There's no need to notice servants provided they are doing their job.

Ah, he hears the family approach! All three are laughing. Between his wife's death and Pontefract's appearance, he and Frances never laughed. She now laughs a lot, but he still never laughs. He is too beset by problems. All three of them - Frances, Pontefract, and Stanley - are so lighthearted that he fears none of them care about the lairdship the way he does. Now though is not the time to brood. Breakfast smells good.

The Angus Herd

Aberdeenshire, Scotland

Pontefract having had his fill of porridge is content to sit back and luxuriate in the pleasant atmosphere of the new breakfast room. Breakfasts here are more leisurely affairs than they are in the cavernous great hall where comfort is not a consideration. As Pontefract knows from Frances, the new open-backed chairs with their graceful lines and delicate inlays are characteristics of the neoclassical style as practiced by the cabinetmaker George Hepplewhite. Pontefract's favorite aspect is the upholstered seats, which invite lingering unlike those in the great hall.

The laird and Stanley also seem content to sit around the breakfast table longer than they ever did in the great hall. *Stanley, dressed in his everyday plaids, is a handsome and personable boy,* thinks Pontefract. He feels proud of his son and proud that, when the time comes, he will make a good laird. He turns to Frances hoping to catch her eye, but she is listening to Stanley and the laird, who are conversing amicably. Thank God! It isn't always the case. Stanley is impatient and forward-thinking, whereas the old man holds fast to the old ways.

Stanley is now saying, "Gramps, while you were visiting Aunt Rachel" - the laird had visited an ailing sister after Christmas - "I visited Keillor in the Vale of Strathmore."

"Ah yes," says the laird, helping himself to an oatcake. "Mr. Watson was here a while back - you were away at the time - and wanted to look at our Angus doddies.[4] He was accompanied by a precocious wee laddie who knew a lot about selective breeding. It seemed like an unsuitable area of learning for a child!"

---

[4] Naturally hornless cattle native to Angus and Aberdeenshire

Both grandfather and grandson share a brief moment of laughter, something Pontefract doubted he had seen before and liked. He always likes to see people get on.

"The laddie's name is Hugh," says Stanley. "He is eleven, and he filled me in on all the desirable traits for the new Angus breed that he and his father intend creating. At eleven years old! When I asked how he pictured his personal input in the venture, he had it all figured out! He told me that when he was old enough, he would start as a tenant farmer with a good black bull, with six black heifers from his father and as many suitable doddies as he could find at the cattle markets. All must be black and have broad chests and well-padded rumps. In ten years, he told me, he would have his own registered herd of polled[5] black Angus cattle that would outstrip any other breed in Great Britain for high quality carcass beef."

Pontefract is wondering where all this is leading. The laird is probably wondering, too, when Stanley asks, "What do you think, Gramps? Might this be an area with potential for Glen Orm? We have the same temperate climate as Keillor - reliable rainfall, good pastures, plenty of grass."

He waits for a reply, but as Pontefract notes, the laird remains sunk in thought, his face inscrutable.

Stanley continues, "Gramps, would it not be possible for us to breed a handful of good black bulls with our blackest female doddies, and within a decade, we, too, could have a pedigree herd of polled black Angus cattle to rival anything in England."

Pontefract clenches his jaw and waits for the axe to fall. For Glen Orm to start breeding Angus pedigree cattle would involve the new science of selective breeding: anathema to the old man.

---

5   Hornless

The laird replies in measured tone, "On the one hand, it would be nice to have something truly Scottish with which to poke the English in the eye. On the other hand, one has to remember it is never wise to tamper with nature, and this new science has already produced unthinkable aberrations such as sheep with bodies so large their legs can't support their weight."

Pontefract scrunches up his eyes as his worst fears are realized; without saying a word, Stanley abandons his breakfast, gets up, and leaves the table.

The next day, despite the cold, Stanley is up early and out riding. Returning home, he is famished. Striding toward the breakfast room, he is looking forward to the meal. He is about to enter the room when he stops in the doorway unable to immediately process what he is seeing. On the walls of the room, several large grotesque etchings of badly deformed sheep have replaced his mother's delicate watercolors. Gathering his senses, he sees his mother has her head bowed and looks down at her lap in mortification. His father isn't even present, and his grandfather is watching his grandson from under hooded eyelids and sporting a smug little smile.

Stanley swings around on his heels and leaves; he'll do without breakfast today. From now on, he will be putting all his energy into finding a sponsor for a New World adventure of any kind. He does not care what. He just knows he has to get away from Glen Orm and an intractable old bigot.

The New Club

Edinburgh, Scotland

Swashbuckling and huge, with drink in hand, Aaron Migu is in his Edinburgh club sprawled out on a comfortable leather chair by the fireplace. Although only addressing his companion Pontefract Staymann, the booming voice - redolent of the streets of Leith[6] - resounds throughout the room.

The others present in the room - they sit in small groups speaking sotto voce - look up aghast, when Migu proclaims, "We will not have *Spirit* ready to sail again until the end of May." To be admitting - in this hallowed space - an association with the infamous slave schooner *Spirit of the Clyde* is inexcusably vulgar. Those present start to rise and leave.

The New Club is a members-only private club with upper-class leanings. As such, it is symptomatic of a backlash against the coffeehouses where classes mingle to discuss issues of the day. True gentlemen have now had enough of rubbing shoulders with the hoi polloi. They want to be with their peers in a home away from home and away from both commoners and the women in their households. The retreat must resemble their own establishments in its grandeur of architecture, furnishings, and decor. Thus, the New Club features a study, smoking room, dining hall, drawing room, and library as well as bedrooms, bathrooms, and water closets. Although gambling is illegal, members-only establishments are an exception. Hence, the club also features an entertainment room.

Clubability is a prerequisite for membership of the New Club. With wealth dating back for generations, members must belong to the leisure class and have no need to work. Certain standards of dress, speech, and behavior apply. Aaron Migu meets none of these requirements. Nonetheless, he sits in the study as a bona fide club member.

---

[6] Port city that serves Edinburgh

Among those leaving the premises are Lord Richard Castleton and Sir George McCallum - one tall and scrawny; the other, small and nondescript. As they move toward the foyer, Lord Richard - eyes fierce and black - looks down on his companion and growls, "We must get rid of that oaf! He doesn't belong."

"Not possible," Sir George reminds his lordship. "Without him, the *Spirit of the Clyde* consortium would collapse. Remember how - all those years ago - we agreed to make him a member in exchange for financial backing? We hoped he would never use the membership, and he never has until now."

Lord Richard gives a snort, then excuses himself, and goes off to inspect the club's new water closet. Alexander Cumming, a homegrown talent with a number of inventions to his name, has also applied himself to the area of plumbing and came up with an ingenious improvement: a flushable toilet that, although not yet in common use, should soon feature in all respectable households.

Sir George, who has always been interested in how things work, is in awe of such inventions and wishes he had received training in mechanical engineering - or something of the kind - but alas, that wasn't possible for a gentleman of his standing. Oxford and Cambridge - they set the educational standards for Britain - have determined in their greater wisdom that science is best suited to the lower classes and does not require schools for dedicated training. Apprenticeships suffice. Sir George becomes hot under the collar just thinking of the stupidity of it. Even the University of Edinburgh, more open in its approach to science than most, still fails woefully when it comes to education in the sciences.

Waiting for Lord Richard, Sir George thinks of the one area of scientific education in which the University of Edinburgh has excelled: the medical school. It is renowned everywhere for its hands-on approach. In contrast, the medical faculties of Oxford and Cambridge offer no practical experience. Their students graduate without ever having seen either a real patient or the inside of a hospital!

As Sir George ponders the establishment's attitude to science, a club member who is also fleeing Migu asks Sir George, "Who is that obnoxious lout? He's surely not a member."

Sir George answers, "Aaron Migu *is* a club member, although he rarely appears. Today is an exception."

"And the other fellow, who is he?"

"Pontefract Staymann. Like Migu, he is nouveau riche, but unlike Migu, he has a pleasant personality and is a talented engineer. While Migu takes pleasure in mocking us, Staymann conforms."

The gentleman, taking his hat from serving hands, comments, "People like that can never become clubbable." Then before heading to the door, he turns back and asks, "How did this Migu wiggle his way into our midst?"

"Who knows?" replies Sir George with a shrug.

The gentleman leaves as Lord Richard reappears. "Discussing the lout, were you?" he asks, as white-gloved hands help him into his overcoat and bring his top hat.

Sir George feels the familiar discomfort at Lord Richard's words. He dislikes being reminded of the skewed priorities of his class. On the one hand, he and his fellow slave traders find Migu's vulgarity objectionable; on the other hand, they find it acceptable to trade slaves - provided no one finds out - as though they were textiles, factory goods, or pig iron. Although Sir George conforms outwardly to the attitude, his dependence on the slave trade is a matter of deep shame to him, and he hates seeing his slave-trading peers masquerading as models of propriety and rectitude.

His lordship, stickler for correctness, looks in the mirror to adjust the angle of his silk cylinder - it must be *just so* - and then examines his tasteful cravat, saying, "The awfulness of the lout's cravat alone is a reason to blackball him."

Sir George cringes at the mention of Migu's cravat, but bans the item from his mind as an obsequious presence opens the door for them, and they descend the steps to Lord Richard's waiting carriage. Sir George, who lives close at hand and prefers to walk, stands aside as a footman helps Lord Richard into his vehicle. From there, he pontificates through the open window, "Someone should tell the oaf that a gentleman must never attract attention by dress or behavior."

Sir George wants to say *Aaron Migu prides himself in* not *being a gentleman* but remains silent. He also wants to say that Beau Brummell - inventor of dandyism - might decry flashy jewelry and bright colors as attention-getters, but his own tight-fitting shirts, tailored bespoke jackets, and trousers attract as much attention, albeit to his trim physique.

The lord's black eyes are boring into Sir George, demanding a reaction to the mention of blackballing, so Sir George says, "In spite of his cravats, the *Spirit* consortium needs Aaron Migu and his money."

As the coachman prepares to set the matched bays into motion, his lordship looks down his long-barreled nose, saying, "*Money* is a word that should never pass a gentleman's lips! We hire lesser beings to handle such matters. Our hands must remain clean."

If only that were possible! Sir George thinks, as he watches the coach speed away scattering peeved pedestrians, who shout and shake their fists. Changing his mind about going home, Sir George does an about-face and reenters the club for a game of poker. It is not something he enjoys but something he does to prove to those with whom he consorts that he is truly one of them. He wishes he did not care about their opinions, but he does.

Child of the Forest

West Coast of Africa

On jungle fringe, five-year-old Abebi - naked but for ornamentation at the neck, wrist, and ankle - crouches on a branch high above a pool in whose mirrored depths she sees her own upside-down image. She sees her hair is a shock of wiry black curls; it makes her look top-heavy. She also doesn't like it but won't have it cut anytime soon; she is letting it grow. She wants a cornrow hairstyle like her mother Efia's, and Zainia, a village hairdresser, says it is impossible until her hair gets longer.

Abebi loves this place! That's why she chose a nearby tree to make an altar to her own little *loa*,[7] Baby Infana. It's close to the place where Mammi has an altar to her loa - Twenty-Seventh Wife, Abebi's grandmother. Baba Thimba, Abebi's father, has his shrine to Masimbarashe among the aerial roots of a nearby mahogany. Masimbarashe is a scary loa, which suits Baba Thimba. Unlike her grandfather Big Baba, Baba Thimba is also scary. Big Baba's loa is *his* grandfather, Mkulu. Big Baba hasn't made a shrine for Mkulu. He says Mkulu doesn't need a shrine because he and Mkulu are together all day anyway under the banyan.[8] They are like a single person, and an altar and offerings in such a case would make no sense.

Adjusting her position on the branch, Abebi thinks that she must remember to bring Baby Infana a couple of slices of mango. When he was still her young brother, before he became a spirit, he loved sucking on bits of ripe mango. He'd get it all over his face and naked body, and Abebi and Mammi would have to sluice him off on the edge of this very pond while they would pretend to scold him, and he would gurgle in delight. He was a tubby, happy little boy until he ate the ackee[9] seeds, died, and became a spirit. Now he's her happy little loa.

---

[7] Spirit, in this case the equivalent of a guardian angel

[8] Large tropical tree related to the fig; features aerial prop roots

[9] Fruit with toxic seeds

Swaying on the branch, Abebi giggles at the thought of him. Her peers, sitting on sturdier branches near the trunk of the tree, set up an agitated twitter, "Ooowh, Abebi! Come back! That branch isn't safe!"

Abebi grins at them over her shoulder. The whites of their eyes and their dangling legs are all that betray their presence. With the interaction of sun, leaf, and shadow, their camouflage is perfect. If Abebi didn't not know better, she'd think they were young parakeets, bush babies,[10] or even ravens.

"Abebi, stop! Turn around! Come back!"

The more they protest, the more Abebi enjoys herself. What fun! She loves teasing and having an ability that her peers don't have, albeit an ability for which she paid heavily. She'd never want *that* to happen again, but for now, the side benefits serve her well.

A few years back, while accompanying her mother to this very stream, she stepped on the silken burrow of a baboon spider. With hair sticking out in all directions, the fat-bodied horror had shot out of its lair and reared up on its back legs, and showing a gaping red mouth, it launched an attack on her naked toes.

She spent days conscious of nothing but pain, which not even Babalawo's[11] chants, dances, herbs, and salves could control. On the second day - although dizzy and vomiting - she heard Babalawo say to Mammi, "If we don't cut off those two toes, she'll soon be dead."

While Abebi was shrieking, Mammi and Auntie Abena had held her down and Babalawo, who was wielding a sharp-bladed knife, had done the necessary. She needed throat *mutis*[12] for weeks afterward. Despite the agony, the event had given her an advantage - bywith missing two

---

[10] Small African lemurs
[11] Healer, medicine man
[12] Medication

middle toes on her left foot, she can now grip a branch in a manner impossible for normal human toes. That's why she can hover, as she now does, in the *skies* above a pond riddled with reptiles, snails, and aquatic worms.

Gloriously at home in her world, Abebi bubbles with laughter at the thought of her unusual ability. Meanwhile, she hears her companions in the tree behind her exchanging worried words, "What should we do? We mustn't frighten her. Will she fall? It's a long way down. She can't swim. The branch is thin, might break. Should we fetch Efia?"

At the mention of her mother, Abebi begins to doubt the wisdom of her actions. She knows from experience that Mammi's intervention is best avoided. She turns on the wobbling branch and returns to her friends.

Big Baba

West Coast of Africa

Banyan Village is named after the tree situated down the hill midway to the beach. It is an autonomous village, and Big Baba is the most senior member of the Council of Elders. Dignity and an air of authority - along with impressive adornments of fang, claw, and copper - testify to the fact. At present, he is inspecting the communal areas of the village. It is a weekly duty that - amidst the hubbub of village life - he now performs with Abebi and his dog Inja frolicking at his side.

It's been a duty that Baba has performed ever since he became an elder, but the job - although he doesn't like to admit it - takes more out of him than before. His hair - black and wiry a few years back - is now white, and his body, once that of a top-ranking warrior, is sinew and bone with folds of excess skin hiding his tribal markings.

Baba knows that Abebi sees him as permanent and unchanging and therefore doesn't want to tell her he needs a rest. How could she understand that peering into storage bins full of bulbs, corms, rhizomes, tubers, and roots exhausts him? How could anyone understand that listening to a child singing out words like *shallot, taro, ginger, yam, lotus,* and *cassava* tires a warrior? Yet these things have exhausted him, and he must rest.

He says, "Abebi, we're now going back to Mammi."

Abebi stops in her tracks and stares up at him in shock. "But, Baba, what about the spears? You promised! Ple-e-ase!"

Children are rarely allowed into the arsenal, so it was a treat when he mentioned the matter earlier saying that she could help him count the longswords, pangas,[13] spears, shields, daggers, bows, quivers, and arrows. It was a mistake to promise, but now he has no option but to renege. Putting on his stern warrior mien, he says, "No, child! I'm taking you home."

He sees the animation drain from Abebi's body, and as she walks beside him, he sees how she droops her head, sucks her finger, and kicks at the dust. She does not even look over to the nearby group of women - with babies tied to their backs - grinding millet with stones on a flat area of rock. Normally, she would stop and comment, but not today. In silence - except for Baba's heavy breathing - they negotiate the distance to Efia's hut. It isn't far, but to Baba, it might as well be as far as Mbaleki Village. Inja, with tail pointing down, senses Abebi's dejection and doesn't bother - as he wants to do - to chase the bellicose cockerel with its yellow legs and lethal spurs.

In spite of his exhaustion, Big Baba notices Efia is crushing the cassava - or is it perhaps hot peppers and ginger? - using the pestle and knee-high mortar, which he made decades earlier for Twenty-Seventh Wife, Efia's mother. Wood carving is another ability of which age has deprived him. His fingers are now crooked and weak.

To his relief, Big Baba sees that Efia's friend Abena has just arrived from the women's work shelter and has her infant son Abinti tied to her back. That will help Abebi forget her disappointment; she loves babies.

Barely managing the last few steps, Baba flops into the throne that Efia keeps under the eaves of the thatch. It takes him a while before he can catch his breath, but with Efia, Abena, and Abebi otherwise engaged, he is able to regain his equanimity without anyone fussing. Filled with self-loathing at his feebleness, he distracts himself by looking out toward the plains, where Thimba - in his capacity as leader of the warrior-hunter corps - is holding a training session for the adolescent

---

[13] A large, broad-bladed knife; both weapon and implement for cutting through jungle growth

boys. Judging from the boys' movements, Thimba has them stamping barefoot on thorns of the most aggressive variety - those that women use as sewing needles.

There is no lack of thorn bushes on the savanna given that plants need protection from the herds of antelope, eland, buffalo, giraffes, and elephants. Some thorns though are easier on adolescents' feet than others, and Thimba could have chosen a smaller and less resilient type for training, but he has not done so. Baba, in his younger years - when doing the same job that Thimba is now doing - never pampered trainees either. He had drummed into the lads' heads that enduring pain is the bedrock of warrior identity and needs practice.

The youngsters know that their ability to tolerate pain will later be tested during an initiation rite that marks the transition from boyhood into adulthood. Any boy that fails the test cannot be trusted to defend the tribe. Although he can be called upon to serve as a warrior, he will never enjoy the veneration and social status of a top-ranking warrior.

Looking at Thimba from the distance, Baba knows he is seeing what he himself once was - the quintessential warrior. As never before, he marvels at the nature of warriorship so pivotal to the tribe's survival. Like Thimba, Baba's courage was legendary. Like Thimba at the initiation rites, he had endured circumcision in full view of the entire village without once flinching or batting an eyelid. (Such details are monitored by a committee set up for the purpose.) Like Thimba, Baba was a role model for every young boy in the village. Now though, he can't even keep up with a five-year-old child - a girl-child at that!

Shifting on his throne, Baba suddenly understands the humor in the situation and sees how stupid it is not to recognize and accept the aging process. Self-loathing has no place in the thinking of someone renowned for wisdom!

Banyan Village

West Coast of Africa

After resting at Efia's, Big Baba takes his leave and with Inja in tow, he heads downhill to the Banyan. Stopping to rest, he turns his back to the ocean and looks up toward the village. Leaning on his staff and sheltering his eyes from the sun, he studies the place of his birth as a stranger might. He notes how it lies between the tropical savanna to the south and jungle to the east and north.

The ocean lies to the west. Even without seeing it, Baba senses its presence by the muted sound of the crashing breakers and the reverberations they generate beneath the soles of his naked feet. On the hunt, he could always sense with his feet the approach of a stampeding herd long before hearing or seeing it.

Both forest and ocean protect the village from enemies, and as an added bonus, the forest protects the village from the Harmattan - a northeasterly trade wind that blows in from the desert and during the dry season plagues the plains with stinging sand. A disadvantage of the jungle is that while deterring predatory tribes, it also deprives Banyan Village of desirable contacts such as the itinerant Arab traders. In the past, Banyan villagers by having to visit the markets on the plains meant exposing themselves to aggressive tribesmen. Luckily, that is now no longer an issue thanks to the cooperation between Big Baba and his friend Mbaleki from the eponymous village on the savanna. Fifteen years ago, the two men were able to broker peace among the tribes of the region; something that Big Baba remembers with pride.

Resuming his trek to the Banyan, Baba reminisces on the details of the *indabas*[14] that were instrumental in achieving the peace. They always took place in the open and under the special tree - usually an acacia - that stood in the heart of each village. Baba marvels at how he

---

[14]   Meetings

and Mbaleki handled the complexities of the negotiations and has to smile at how gifts of kola nuts[15] had helped. Kola trees only grow in the forest, and thus, Banyan Village has always had easy access to a desirable product that is scarce on the plains.

At his next pause, Baba turns his eyes back to the village and concentrates on the structures: communal work shelters, storage huts, family groupings of huts, burial mounds, vegetable patches, and a cleared circular area around the *poto mitan*.[16] These features are distributed among scattered palms like coconut and plantain. In the case of the savanna villages, the structures, if not the vegetation, are similar, but the main tree is usually located in the center unlike the peripheral banyan in Baba's village.

In Banyan Village, the three biggest shelters are situated toward the northeast of the clearing. The first is the butchery, surrounded by the paraphernalia needed for hanging meat and for stretching and treating skins. The second is a work shelter where men, when not out hunting, practice a craft - whether leather work, woodwork, or the fashioning of tools and weaponry. The third shelter is for women and is used for basketry, pottery, and needlework. The village market has a separate setup and looks out onto the plains. It's the only side from which outsiders can approach with ease.

The open-sided shelters can offer protection from rain by the use of woven mats and leather curtains. All Banyan villagers are grateful that it is only rain from which they need protection and not from the hot blasts of driving desert sand as is the case in Mbaleki Village.

Most of the storehouses - thirteen of them - are modest in size and lie scattered between the family units. Each has a designated purpose.

---

[15] The fruit of the kola tree contain more stimulants than Arabica coffee and are chewed, used in beverages, and also as a currency.

[16] Wooden pole in the center of the ritual dance circle, where, during a ceremony, the Spirit takes up residence.

One is for tools, grinding stones, axes, hammers, and shovels. Another is for communal cooking utensils and metal serving dishes. A third is for animal cages of irregular shape and made of bark, branch, and thong. The others are for clay vessels, baskets, and carved furniture, including Big Baba's various thrones. The three biggest store houses are reserved for masks, drums, and weaponry.

Big Baba continues his trek down to the Banyan, which, like all old banyans, has spread out laterally using aerial prop roots for support. These grow down from horizontal branches and take root in the ground beneath. They eventually look like a forest of individual trees but are attached to the parent plant. The multitude of prop roots create interconnected spaces. Baba can sit on his own, partly looking out over the ocean while others can use different sections without bothering him. Two sculptors are the only others present that day.

Reaching the banyan's protective shade, Baba looks forward to a session of silent interaction with his grandfather Mkulu, who, as a spirit, resides in the tree. He is as present to Baba as he was in life. Allowing his eyes to adjust to the shade, Baba moves toward his throne but stops suddenly seeing that the throne is already occupied, not by a human - no human would show Baba such disrespect - but by the old billy goat who refuses to budge. It takes yipping and a serious nip from Inja to restore the seat to its rightful occupant.

Thimba Teaches

West Coast of Africa

On the savanna-side of the village, Thimba is holding another of his daily training sessions for the thirteen-to-fourteen-year-old age range. The continued existence of their tribe depends on them, so it pleases Thimba that the present group appears to be one with potential. It includes his younger brother Kwame and Kwame's best friend, Assimbola.

As Thimba knows all too well, training adolescents is a daunting task. Until the onset of adolescence, boys are subjected to precious little discipline. They spend most of their time amusing themselves by playing in the ocean, roughhousing on the beach and hunting small edible animals using traps, slings, and bows.

At the onset of adolescence, the boys' lives change dramatically. They have to leave their family compounds, and from then on, live, play, and learn together. They sleep together in one bunkhouse, eat together around one fire, and are encouraged to think of themselves as a team and a fraternity to which at initiation they will swear allegiance and remain loyal until death.

It now falls to Thimba to shape the present crop of young rowdies into disciplined warriors capable of annihilating all enemies. He must also turn them into consummate hunters capable of bringing down even the biggest game: elephants, lions, giraffes, and eland.

Trained by Big Baba, Thimba often uses Baba's methods to pass on raiding techniques as well as the different strategies for attack and defense. When it comes to developing expertise in the use of spears, shields, axes, knives, and the lateral, circular, and oval parries of longswords, he draws on help from his fellow warriors to offer one-on-one training.

He has also thought up a number of role-playing games himself. Today's game uses sticks in lieu of real spears and is designed to awake in adolescents the aggressive spirit of their heritage - the spear culture. Even though they will only receive their first proper spears from fathers or older brothers after initiation, it is never too early to inculcate the need for aggression.

At present, the boys crowd around Thimba as he hands out the sticks. Wide-eyed, they listen as he tells them, "I'll match up each of you with an opponent. Using the techniques with which you are already familiar, you will fight each other as though in mortal combat. If you get hurt, it is your own fault. You weren't good enough."

Before he lets them loose, he makes them recite a tribal chant that he taught them the previous week:

> We carry spears as symbols of our courage. We'll fight to death and will never succumb; never desert our comrades.

There are other verses, too, pertaining to keeping the upper hand and to being true men, but those can wait.

Standing to the side, Thimba watches as the boys battle it out. Only when the possibility for real damage surfaces he does interfere. For the most part, he monitors how each boy performs and keeps in mind suggestions for improvement. When he sees that the boys are starting to tire, he calls a halt and allows them to take turns to drink by dipping a halved coconut shell into a clay pot of water. The respite is brief. Endurance, too, is a lesson that needs teaching.

The next item on today's agenda is to practice the dance moves that the warriors use in Gran Legbwa celebrations - the Grand Leap, the stamping of feet and the vigorous movements of the body. He notices that Kwame is especially good at the Grand Leap; he leaps higher than any of his comrades. *He will be as big and strong as I am,* thinks Thimba with a self-deprecating smile. *I'll have to be careful he doesn't overtake me!*

For the time being, Thimba only teaches the boys those dance moves that are exclusively militaristic in nature omitting those that are overtly sexual. There are many as seeing that virility and warriorship go hand in hand.

Having run through the gamut of dance moves, he goes on to the abilities needed for a good hunter. In the past, he has taught the boys to move with the stealth of the big cats and to pick up scents and follow spoor like canines. He still must teach them how to interpret trampled undergrowth, bent stalks, and the differing messages inherent in the sounds of birds and insects. The ability to mimic these sounds is an art of its own and will take a long time, a lot of listening, and a lot of practice. He won't start on that now; instead, he moves on to something the boys much enjoy, mimicking the behavior of a top-ranking male gorilla. He gets them to stride along, kicking at everything in their path, scowling, elbowing others, and growling. It is necessary that they become proficient in behaviors designed to instill fear and compliance in everyone they meet.

"Remember," he tells them, "when you act like that, you must have the right things in your head. You must remind yourselves that you are not afraid and that no one can challenge you without dire consequences."

The last item of today's session is designed to fill his pupils with bloodlust. He leads them in the cry for bloodletting and shouts with them at full volume, "Kill! Kill! Only with blood on our spears are we men!" He then sends them down to the beach for a swim.

Second Week of January 1800

Jemima Manifesto

Liverpool, England

Tom is not going out today; he's staying at home. He is upset. Instead of spending the day at the coffeehouse studying broadsheets, pamphlets, and magazines and instead of listening and participating in discussions, he feels the need to cope with the fact that his only friend - his kitten Jemima - is dying. He decides that writing a poem might be what an educated person would do in such circumstances. Although he has never written his own material before - not even a letter - there is no harm in trying. He writes as follows:

Jemima, you are dying,
leaving without me.
Why? I feel betrayed.
If you loved me,
you'd stay,
not leave me alone
in a place
that without you
is no longer a home.

Sitting back and appraising his work, he likes the shape the lines form on the page. Yet he has to wonder if what he has written is a real poem. Real poems use meter, rhyme, rhythm, and stanzas. His effort seems to hint at some of those requirements, but it is obviously not what tradition demands. Does that matter?

Maybe not, but nonetheless he continues in prose:

> Can it be wrong to love a kitten? The church says animals have no souls, but I don't believe it. Libertarianism tells me I have as much right to my opinions as do my superiors. Like them, I carry within me a spark of the deity. Like them, my beliefs respond to my requirements just as their beliefs respond to theirs. If I believe Jemima has a soul, so be it!

Rereading his words, he feels that what he has written might be a manifesto - a statement of his beliefs. It seems like a ridiculous aspiration for an ignoramus, but if he manages to educate himself, he could end up with a *real* voice.

Turning his attention back to Jemima - she lies stretched out and unconscious on her mat - he sees that her breathing is shallower and less regular. He thinks how she chose him not vice versa. On the day he had moved into this attic, she had tried to squeeze in through the window - it was only open a tad - and had become stuck. She has been with him ever since and is now dying. Today, when he got up and saw that she was scarcely breathing, he'd been peeved - he has no other friend - but now is no longer irked. He'll miss her but feels she has helped him formulate his beliefs and helped him establish a goal.

Bagpipes

Aberdeenshire, Scotland

Stanley braces himself for the cold and throws aside the thick plaid that kept him warm throughout the night. He hopes the water by the washstand has not frozen. With his feet encased in thick knitted socks, he pads over to look but stops in his tracks. Bagpipes! So early in the morning! To hear better, he holds his breath and cocks his head. His ears have not deceived him; a piper is practicing somewhere.

He goes to the window. There is not much to see. It's misty, and the window - set in the alcove of a thick stonewall - is small. Nonetheless, he establishes that the piper is probably practicing for the Rabbie Burns festivity. The degree of competence also indicates that the piper is most likely wee Johnny's father - an estate manager - who taught both Wee Johnny and Stanley how to play. As soon as their fingers were big enough to cover the holes, he started them on practice chanters. By the time they were thirteen, each possessed a full stand of pipes provided by Stanley's father, Pontefract Staymann. Throughout their teens, Stanley and Wee Johnny played at various cèilidhs,[17] dances, Highland games, funerals, and weddings.

As Stanley sloshes himself with cold water at the washstand, he thinks how it must be nearly four years since he used his pipes. His life had become too busy. He had discovered the miraculous new era of science and research and also was making headway with the piano, so he pursued that avenue instead of the pipes. Wee Johnny stuck with the pipes and is now a good Pibroch[18] player.

---

[17] Social gatherings

[18] Classical genre of Scottish music, originally created for the harp, then adapted for the bagpipes; often of a brisk marching character.

As Stanley dries himself and gets into his trews,[19] he feels a yen for his piping days. He has his pipes stored at the back of his wardrobe, and now fully dressed, he fishes them out and takes the case downstairs to the drawing room, where the servants already have the fire going and Angus McCorm - his old deerhound - waits for him. Angus is now too old for stairs and spends his nights in the kitchen.

On the table by the window, Stanley carefully unpacks the bagpipe set by removing toweling and examining the disjointed pieces: drones, blowpipe, chanter, and mouthpiece. All seem to be in good order, so the humidity and temperature must have been right. He resists the temptation to blow into anything because he doesn't want to be drying away the moisture afterward. Also, he first needs to make new reeds for the drones, chanter, and practice chanter - a labor-intensive job not to mention deciding whether to use Elder or something else. He repacks the pieces, resolving not to allow the matter to slide again.

Despite having given up the bagpipes in favor of other interests, they still exert an atavistic hold on him. At their sound, he pictures himself on the battlefield wielding his claymore against the enemy. He knows that - even if he travels to distant places, something he longs to do - he'll always take his pipes. In the past week since Gramps nixed his suggestion for developing a new breed of Angus cattle, the dream of the New World has been taking a firmer hold. He often envisages himself on some distant plantation celebrating Rabbie Burns' Night with his guests. Black slaves would pipe in the haggis not only with "Ode to the Haggis" and "Auld Lang Syne," but also with a couple of Wee Johnny's Pidroch marches!

Returning upstairs to replace his pipes in the wardrobe, he dwells on a repeating vision of himself on his plantation. In the vision, there is always a vacant chair at the dining room table. It is for the hostess. Who will she be? All he knows is that she will *not* be Rose Migu to whom he is supposedly betrothed; she might even be black!

---

[19]   Close-fitting pants made of plaid cloth

Seeing Stanley was only six years old at the time that Pops and Uncle Aaron dreamed up their Betrothal Agreement, the matter has always been a nonissue for Stanley. To him, Rose was never more than spoilled brat. Although he hasn't seen her in years and does not want to see her, he squirms at the constant parental reminders that Rose is now of marriageable age.

He doesn't like the thought of gainsaying either Pops or Uncle Aaron; nonetheless, he will make his own decisions. First of all, he needs to get himself across the ocean, away from Gramps and Glen Orm. How he will do that, he doesn't know. He needs a backer with deep pockets, and it's unlikely to be Pops, who wants him to inherit the lairdship. One way or the other, though, he'll find someone. He is determined.

The Old Earl of Gryphon

Edinburgh, Scotland

Despite himself, Sir George, who disapproves of gambling, has almost become a habitué in the New Club's entertainment room. It helps him retain his status in the circle in which he chooses to move. Tonight, upon leaving, he spots the Earl of Gryphon in the lobby. Having seen the old gentleman place a bet of thousands of guineas on a single hand and lose, Sir George commiserates, "The cards did not treat us kindly tonight, did they?"

"I hate losing!" the earl grumbles before adding, "So you lost too?"

Luckily no reply is necessary as the lackey helping the earl into his outdoors attire distracts the ancient. Sir George has lost a mere pittance at the tables but will not be admitting it. He never gambles with more than a pittance; he hates using slave-trade money on frivolities. Slave-trade money should only be used on things of lasting benefit to king and country.

While another club member commiserates with the earl, Sir George - he is still waiting for his coat and hat - remembers how he had checked the accounts of his own household regularly and had always found the amounts spent providing for his family deeply shocking. He couldn't reconcile needing the slave trade to support his family with the conviction that slave-trade money must benefit Great Britain. He would have preferred to have spent those funds on the railway industry - his pet project at the time.

In those years, a patchwork of privately owned railways outside Edinburgh needed to amalgamate to become more efficient but had lacked the means. He felt that providing the means would contribute to the advancement of the nation and cancel out the whiff of unethicality in a way that another house and new winter wardrobes for his family could ever do.

However, he has long since saved himself that type of irritation by refusing to look at the accounts. He merely hands over the bills to an accountant, who pays them without question. Sir George can then use what remains - ever increasing amounts as the slave trade flourishes - on what is of most interest to him at the given moment. He has a tendency to move from one project to another, but knows he should be more systematic in his approach to charitable undertakings. His donations will have more impact if he chooses a specific area and hold to it, although he has never decided what that area should be apart from being of a scientific nature.

As he waits for his coat, hat, scarf, and gloves, Sir George thinks of the strain he endured before hiring the accountant. He remembers one specific area of family expenses that had infuriated him to a degree that he had become ill. It had concerned the purchase of numerous large works of art - Gainsboroughs among them - which portray not only his wife and the girls but also his in-laws along with their homes, horses, dogs, and a pet monkey!

Once in his winter gear, Sir George takes off to join the earl again. The two gentlemen wend their way through the crowd and then step out into the cold.

Sir George comments, "I sometimes wonder what my family would say if they knew what I spent on gambling."

"The gaming tables have nothing to do with family!" counters the old gentleman with unexpected verve. "My family has everything they need without nibbling into what enables my gambling." He stops at the top of the steps to catch his breath, then wheezes, "The original patrimony remains untouched. My grandson William will inherit what I did. I don't use inherited wealth for gambling."

Sir George thinks, *The new wealth he uses is a slave-trade fortune that would be many times greater than the patrimony!* He says, though, "Some gentlemen here tell their families about the *Spirit* consortium, but I don't."

"Nor do I and nor should anyone else!" the earl opines. "Business, trade, and money should only be mentioned between those of us as compromised as you and I are. I've heard that the oaf Migu has no compunction about advertising his participation in the consortium."

"True, but in spite of his offensive vulgarity, he is unlikely to start mentioning names."

Sir George, snugly bundled up and heading homeward through the night on foot, feels the familiar gratitude to modern technology for the new street lighting. In his early slave-trading years, he had invested in that area and now feels smug that his funds have been put to the use for the benefit of the public at large. He cannot imagine why anyone would forfeit this type of satisfaction in favor of gambling the way the old earl does.

Camel and Trader

West Coast of Africa

Abebi has accompanied her mother Efia and a group of women to a market on the savanna. She is fed up after a long day. She stands swathed in a length of cotton cloth wound tightly around her head and body to protect her from the high wind and stinging sands of the Harmattan. She keeps her arms wrapped around herself to stop the wind from ripping the cloth from her body. Although she turns her back to the wind, her eyes sting and her nose is clogged with dust.

Mammi crouches on the ground in a shelter protected by camel-skin curtains. She inspects wares spread out on a mat, while in the dust-laden air a hawk-nosed Arab stands with his camel. In the middle distance among the ghostly shapes of the milling crowd, a venerable *madala* (old man) sits protected from the driving sands by his hut. His face is worn and furrowed much like Baba's, and Abebi knows that his name is Mbaleki. He's a friend of Baba's, and Baba gave Mammi a bagful of kola nuts to pass on to Mbaleki.

Tired and not looking forward to the long hike home, Abebi says to Efia, "Mammi, why can't traders come to us so we don't have to walk so far."

Efia looks up from the pot that she is examining and explains, "They can't come to us, Abebi, because the feet of camels are made for desert sand not for forests."

The Arab trader, who understands Mammi, says, "You're right, ma'am." He lifts the wide foot of his camel to reveal two big toes, the nails of which are joined by webbing, with a ball of fat in the center. Prodding the fat, the trader explains, "This acts like a cushion."

Abebi - given her fixation with toes - also wants to prod the cushion of fat and does so, which does not please the camel. It registers its protest by turning its head and spitting at its owner. The gob of slime catches the trader on the side of his face and dribbles down onto his white robe. Hand to her mouth, Abebi wants to giggle, but doesn't dare, when she sees the thunderous expression on the man's fierce face and hears the fury in his voice. Lambasting the creature, he reaches for his whip.

Luckily, he doesn't follow through with the whipping because Mammi intervenes by telling him that she has decided on her purchase: a family-size cooking pot for which she pays with cowrie shells earned with her baskets. The trader suddenly becomes all smiles. As Mammi explains afterward, she had grossly overpaid the man feeling she had to make amends for Abebi interfering with his camel. While no longer feeling tired, Abebi giggles to herself all the way home.

Third Week of January 1800

Broomstick Wedding

Sugar Plantation, Louisiana

Regardless of age, the chevalier refers to his mixed-race progeny as coffee-colored kiddies. André, as the favorite and most competent of the kiddies, was made chief overseer a number of years previously and occupies the best-appointed slave cabin. It is here where Agathe now sits with a roomful of people waiting for the wedding to commence. André went to fetch his bride from her cabin a while back and hasn't reappeared. Whatever has caused the delay, it is not because the bride is adorning herself; adornment is reserved for white folk. All female house and farmyard slaves must always wear the regulation long dark dress, white pinny and cap, even if it's their wedding day.

Hands demurely folded on her lap, Agathe looks around her. Cooking utensils hang on the walls, and a fire crackles in the hearth. By slave standards, this is indeed a fine cabin - bigger and better than others. It is almost a house and even has floorboards and curtains. Apart from the large main room where the wedding is now to take place, there are two bedrooms and a small private porch at the back that looks out over a vegetable patch. A larger porch across the front is open to the view of the occupants of lesser cabins down the road.

No one sits out on either porch tonight. Instead, family and friends are crowded into the main room for warmth. As Master informed Agathe earlier, the outside temperature is ten degrees centigrade. It amuses her that he cannot leave the house without checking the thermometer that hangs on the wall by the *pendule*.[20] He is obsessed with measurements. She shrugs at the strange obsession but knows it is not for slaves to reason why.

Agathe - as the bridegroom's mother - is the only person in the room with a chair. Adrienne and André's four coffee-colored siblings stand behind her. Adrienne is Agathe's only pure black child and - as her youngest - is not fathered by the chevalier but by a newly acquired slave husband, whom Master had assigned to her after she miscarried Master's sixth child sixteen years earlier.

Agathe rarely thinks of her broomstick husband, but now hearing Adrienne laugh, she gives him a passing thought: there is something irresistibly African about Adrienne's laugh; something that she must have inherited from her father. Pity he had not lived longer. If Agathe had gotten to know him better, she might have grown to love him. A week into their marriage, he had died under the wheels of a cart in a harvesting accident. The tragedy though had soon lost its import for Agathe when she discovered she was pregnant with Adrienne. She had always longed for a pure black child.

Master, too, had been pleased about the pregnancy because - having given up on Agathe as a breeder - it was a pleasant surprise to discover he would be gaining a new slave of good parentage without spending money at the auctions. Agathe notes how her thoughts center on Master - even here amidst her own family and friends. He is always in her mind; she can't escape him any more than the kiddies can who share his bloodlines.

---

[20]   Grandfather clock

Aah! Andréa is standing in the doorway and looks beautiful even in her slave attire. Yet how much more beautiful she'd look if the master had allowed her to use a pair of earrings that she Andréa and her trainees make for the market in Baton Rouge.

Andréa is inspecting the new besom.[21] It is made from fresh sage twigs tied to a pole and has a pungent aroma that tickles Agathe's nostrils. She wants to sneeze but suppresses the urge knowing that the besom with its invasive tang will soon be put outside for more natural uses.

André has now appeared behind Andréa, and by his look, Agathe realizes that something is not to his liking. Stunned, she watches as he turns his bride to face him and removes her slave cap. As a result, Andréa's hair - gleaming straight black - cascades down her back.

A collective gasp arises from the bystanders not only because André has defied the master's rules by removing the slave cap but also because most slaves never leave their master's plantations and do not know that a Choctaw and natives of the land - as is Andréa - would have a different type of hair to those of African descent. Agathe - as the chief house-slave - has seen Andréa with her hair down in the master's bedroom, but most of those present now have never had the privilege.

Elise - Agathe's daughter with the chevalier - is standing behind her mother and says in an awed whisper, "Her hair is as sleek and shiny as a crow's wing!"

Stepping around to see his bride from behind, André's face brightens. "That's the way it should be! Now we can start."

Even though the broomstick is held in the air at each end by two of André's coffee-colored siblings, he could easily have stepped over it. Instead, he leaps into the air, head nearly touching the rafters.

---

[21]   Broom

Landing on the other side of the broom, he grins and straightens his clothing - the master's castoffs. They are not any old castoffs; they are the stockings, silk breeches, and brocade waistcoat of the ancien régime. Only the wig and high-heeled shoes are missing. *Grr*! Agathe finds the master's inconsistency intolerable! He is contravening his own rule by providing André with showy clothes yet not thinking to allow Andréa even earrings!

The swaying, singing, and clapping that accompany André's leap gain momentum. Such things are also a breach of the master's rules; slaves are only allowed to sing *civilized* songs and even those must be sotto voce. However, seeing the master is having dinner with Master Olivier at the neighboring plantation, he is unlikely to find out. Not having to hold back, the wedding guests let loose with the full-throated glory of their true voices. Even though the drums are missing, walls and shackles fall as these diminished people transport themselves to where they are free to be what they are.

Agathe, eyes closed, remains seated but allows herself a rare visit to an ancestral nook still stubbornly alive in her soul. Then - opening her eyes - she sees André holding out his hand to receive Andréa who is now taking her turn to jump the broom. She jumps every bit as high as André did, even though her style differs. While he was all flailing limbs, Andréa has drawn her legs up into her skirt and is waving her arms over her head as her hair flies around her in glorious disarray.

As she lands with the help of her new husband, Elise bends and whispers to her mother, "They are a handsome couple, and he looks every bit as fine as any Frenchman!"

"True, except for the color of his skin," Agathe whispers back. She has known the chevalier all her life, and it shocks her to see how André resembles not merely *any Frenchman* but his father as he was in his younger years. Not only do André's bearing, features, and size resemble the master's but he also uses the master's mannerisms, facial expressions, and laugh. It is not right. André is a slave, not a master! Doesn't the master realize the damage he is doing by confusing the issue in André's mind?

Agathe can't believe the master would want to harm André for she knows that the chevalier loves him - loves him more than his two legitimate sons by his absentee wife Cécile. Agathe knows this because she has heard the master in his cups say as much. Since childhood, he has treated André differently from the other coffee-colored kiddies. He has educated him better, has taught him how to read and write, has shown him how to run the plantation on his own, and has showered him with privileges, giving him a taste for things that as a slave can never be his.

Sniffing and giving herself a vigorous shake, Agathe hopes that anyone who sees she is crying will assume that her tears are tears of joy. The truth though is that in her divided soul - alongside resentment - an element of gratitude toward the master genuinely exists. After all, the master did put thought into his choice for André's bride and has also provided the wherewithal for a feast to celebrate the present event. The enticing smell of roast pork and chitterlings[22] is starting to drift through the room.

---

[22] Made from the small intestines of a pig

Ethnology

Liverpool, England

At the coffeehouse, Tom studies an article that is of interest to him. He has always wondered about the lives - prior to their capture - of the *blackamoors*[23] who were his patients in the holds of the *Spirit of the Clyde*. He has always wished he had a language in common with these people so he could learn about their backgrounds and know how they spent their days in their villages. He had acquired a few words from this or that African language - depending on those in *Spirit*'s holds - but only rarely was it of help in understanding conversation.

Now from the broadsheet Tom has spread out in front of him, he has learned certain interesting facts. The article is written by an ethnologist who seems to be a person who analyzes the characteristics of different peoples. Luckily for Tom - in this specific article - the people in question are those who interest him most: blacks from the west coast of Africa, but not those of the type sold by their kings to agents and marched to coastal forts in *koffles*.[24] The article deals with the type in which the *Spirit of the Clyde* consortium specializes, i.e., those who are lured and kidnapped directly from their coastal villages.

He reads now that these coastal villages are small and autonomous as opposed to the powerful kingdoms prevalent inland. The villages have no political connection to their neighbors, only trade links. They have no hereditary king; instead they are governed by a Council of Elders that controls the social, economic, and political affairs of the village. The Council settles disputes, distributes land and food, punishes the intransigent, and regulates trade with other autonomous villages. They also elect a headman, who is changed every few years. It is the headman who implements the Council's decisions and mediates between the tribe and the Council.

---

[23] A word commonly used for all people with dark skins
[24] A line of slaves chained together

To Tom, this information is an eye-opener. Who would have thought that primitive people could have such a sophisticated form of governance?

"One lives and learns," he mumbles to himself as he returns the broadsheet to its appointed place.

If he later spots someone else reading the same article, he may be able to exchange a few ideas with that person. He has to wonder though if anyone can be as interested in the subject as he is.

Afternoon Tea

Aberdeenshire, Scotland

Pontefract is at home taking a rest from business in Edinburgh. The laird has just arrived back after a visit to his ailing sister, and even Stanley is present and again on speaking terms with the old *bodach*.[25]

All four of us! How wonderful! thinks Frances as the family sits gathered by the fireplace in the drawing room, enjoying tea, sandwiches, and Scottish shortbread.

Frances's son and father have had set-tos before, but the last one - the changing the pictures in the breakfast room - was the worst. Stanley had refused to speak to his grandfather for days and eaten only in the kitchen. Then Pontefract - the consummate peacemaker - had brokered a peace by persuading the contestants that the tension was bad for Frances's unborn child. Thereupon, the laird had restored the breakfast room to its former state and patted Stanley on the shoulder, saying, "Sorry, lad. I got carried away."

The old man usually so fierce - beak of a nose, hooded eyes, bristling brows, and white hair sprouting from ear and nostril - now sits silent and content sipping his tea.

Poor dear is probably tired, thinks Frances. *The Great North Road is no place for the elderly in the middle of winter.*

She can't deny though how pleasant it is to find him nonconfrontational and sneaking a treat - a corner of his shortbread - to Angus McCorm. Smiling at the sight, she looks away quickly knowing her father wouldn't want her to catch him feeding human food to a dog. She moves her gaze to Stanley and watches him wolfing down the shortbread.

---

[25] Affectionate term for an old man

Seeing his mother looking at him, he says, "I like this new idea of afternoon tea, Mums!"

The remark pleases Frances. Until today, four o'clock has not been a time for eating and gathering, but having read in a magazine about afternoon tea becoming a fad in England, she thought she would give it a try. Initially apprehensive about how the family would react, she now sees there was no need to worry.

Having just returned from a meeting, Stanley is still in traditional garb - plaid belted at the waist with one end over the shoulder, sporran,[26] brogues,[27] and hose to midcalf held up by garters. Frances feels he cuts a fine figure, every bit the laird. Yet that role no longer seems to be the given that it always has been in the family. Since the episode with ugly etchings of distorted sheep, Stanley has distanced himself from the affairs of Glen Orm and instead immerses himself in matters pertaining to the New World. It seems to have become an obsession, and that's not right. He needs a distraction, and marrying Rose - sooner rather than later - would fit the bill and put paid to his unseemly fantasies of slavery and plantations. Yet marrying Rose doesn't seem to be on his agenda at the moment. Maybe Pontefract should give him another prod.

As the baby kicks in her womb, Frances - trying to get more comfortable - ponders Stanley's fascination with slaves and sugar production. She believes it started with an illustration on the sacks of sugar that came from the village grocery. They showed black laborers - slaves - working in endless rows of sugarcane. The image obviously insinuated itself into Stanley's young mind and remained lodged there. She remembers an incident when, trying to limit his intake of sugar, she had forbidden him a sweet treat and he had said he would like the ability to produce sugar like those *black people on the sugar bags*.

Could it really be that such a silly little thing managed to embed itself in an otherwise rational mind?

---

[26]   Leather pouch worn around the waist
[27]   Traditional thick-soled shoes with no tongues and with long laces

Ne'er-Do-Well and a Dog

Edinburgh, Scotland

Sir George proceeds homeward, turning off onto Fredrick Street from Princes Street. It is late, cold, and icy, but there's no snow. His nose drips, and the tingling in his hands tells him that, despite fur-lined gloves, his fingers are white and bloodless. He almost wishes he had used a carriage, but that would be pampering himself.

He is glad no one is waiting up for him in his terrace house[28] on Queen Street. His family and the servants are staying in his Glasgow house so as to be close to his aging in-laws - a situation that suits Sir George well. He prefers living alone, prefers it to family life. It's therefore fortunate that his wife and five daughters enjoy spending winter in Glasgow and summer in his North Berwick house. Next year, though, with his eldest daughter Isobel coming of age, London will be the preferred venue. Although he is not keen on the idea, he will need to buy a suitable property in England's capital. He'll attend to the matter in spring.

No matter how many residences he may be forced to acquire for the family, the Queen Street address is the only one he can regard as a home for himself. It matters not that the drapes are closed both day and night, that dust sheets swathe the furniture, and that only old Ms. Young is there to attend to his needs. Being unobtrusive and not of the hovering kind, he finds her presence preferable to the armies of swarming servants that families require.

As he plods on, he thinks that although he is fond of his wife and children, he prefers not to see too much of them. They are a token family - something necessary if he wishes to find acceptance among his upper-class friends.

---

[28] A three-story sandstone structure that shares a wall with the neighboring house. The two have corresponding fronts and heights to form a stylish architectural unit.

As a boy - being small, nondescript, and of a retiring nature - the masters at Eton ignored him while his fellow students teased and belittled him. Sometimes they would even throw rocks at him and, once, set fire to his spare shirts - all twelve of them - along with his waistcoats and cravats. They left him with nothing but a pair of breeches, stockings, and his high heels. The humiliation had scarred him, and as he approached adulthood, he realized that in order to prevent future victimization from his peers, he needed what they expected of those in their ranks - an income sufficient to provide for a big family in style. That income must be generated by never-to-be-mentioned inherited wealth.

Although he realized as a youngster that his own family - because of an industrializing world - had run into hard times, it was only on reaching the age of majority that he understood that he needed access to greater financial resources than those available. While recognizing the slave trade as sleazy, he made the decision to invest in it anyway. No other investment delivered such high returns. Financially it was a decision that exceeded all expectations, and thanks to his covert involvement, he had managed to achieve the approbation he craved.

Nonetheless, in spite of achieving his goal, he is unhappy and tortured by guilt. He cannot come to terms with the expenses attached to his family's luxurious living. He is - as he sees it - a decent man with a deep-seated insecurity that forces him to do what is wrong. It's a sorry state. The unpleasant thought causes him to stumble on the icy pavement, and he lands on his knees. Scrambling to his feet, he looks around. It is lucky no one saw.

He is dusting himself off when he realizes that there was a witness. From between the pools of light around the streetlamps, a dark figure has appeared - a man in scruffy attire, most likely a pickpocket. Sir George thinks that - seeing he was destined to lose his hundred guineas anyway - it's better to have already lost them gambling. Nonetheless, he could still get thumped and considers running, but not being a runner, he stands his ground.

He and the potential thief are eyeing each other when he hears ringing footsteps and gets a glimpse of another dark figure - this one dressed respectably - materializing behind the thief. The pickpocket turns to look before scurrying away. Continuing toward Queen Street, Sir George comments to his rescuer in passing, "I wish those scalawags would stay away. They don't belong here!"

The stranger walks on without comment. Pondering the unfriendly reaction, Sir George thinks, *Perhaps he didn't hear me. Perhaps I mumbled my words. Perhaps he doesn't speak to strangers. Perhaps if I hadn't had a drink or two, I wouldn't have spoken to him either. Ah well, no hard feelings. He helped me.*

As Sir Gorge reaches his house, a stray dog follows him up the steps and - rubbing its mange-ridden body against his leg - it wags its scrawny tail. He knows it is hungry and means no harm, but wanting it to go away, he turns and gives it a kick in the ribs. Tumbling down the steps, it lands at the bottom, where - yelping in pain - it manages to get itself onto three legs, and with tail crooked and dangling, it limps off into the dark. He stares after it, hating himself for what he did, but then reasons, *It's just a dog. Like slaves, it doesn't feel pain the way we do.* Besides, strays don't belong in the New Town no more than pickpockets or the noxious traders now banned by law.

Breakfast in Leith[29]

Leith, Scotland

Rose Migu, after taking a sip of tea, carefully replaces the Wedgwood cup on its saucer and, with a refined gesture, dabs her mouth, saying to Betta, "Mother, I intend to inform Father today that I'll not be marrying Stanley Staymann."

Betta's cup clatters back into the saucer. "Not marry Stanley! What do you mean?"

Rose of alarming beauty gives a pretty smile and says, "Mother, please be careful with that cup. Such items must be treated with respect."

Betta stares at her daughter wondering, *Is she mocking me?* Betta knows that Rose - wanting to gentrify the household to suit her newly acquired upper-class tastes - is genuinely protective of her acquisitions. On the other hand, Rose has inherited her father's streak of devilry and who can tell what game the child now plays?

Choosing to ignore the remark about the cup, Betta says, "According to the legally binding agreement made by your father and Pontefract Staymann, it's your obligation to marry Stanley. Should you refuse, penalties and social stigma will result."

"I know, Ma," Rose counters, "but I've been told that if both parties agree to annul the agreement, that will not be the case."

"Why should Pa and Pontefract agree to annulment when they want the marriage to go ahead?"

Rose's eyes bore into her mother's as she answers pronouncing every word slowly and with precision. "They will annul, Mother, because *I* do

---

[29] Port near Edinburgh

not wish to marry Stanley. Regardless of Father's wishes, it will be his job to persuade Uncle Pontefract an annulment is necessary."

Looking at her daughter, Betta wonders at this strange creature that she and Aaron - with all his bluster and swagger - have produced between them. The lassie is ridiculously decorative with dark curls framing a small triangular face and with skin as translucent as the fine porcelain that she has started to buy for her family home. Everything about Rose is exquisite, even her morning gown that has long, detachable sleeves for warmth, and over them were thin puffy ones for looks.

Betta sometimes wonders if this sophisticated apparition can actually be her daughter. Might there have been a mix-up at birth? Yet this speculation - as always - ends with the certainty that Rose *is* her daughter and that it isn't right that she, Betta, should find her own daughter intimidating. She blames Aaron that it's so.

Although always scornful of everything pertaining to the upper classes, Aaron allowed Pontefract to persuade him that Rose should be educated as if she belonged to an upper-class family. She had heard Pontefract say - she was listening at the keyhole - "You can better afford a good education for her, Aaron, than can many of those upper-class snobs." Hence Greek, Latin, French, history, the arts, culture, propriety, decorum, manners, and so on have always featured and continue to feature in Rose's schoolroom.

Fancy governesses from highborn families that have hit on hard times come and go by the dozen. They terrify Betta, and she tries to keep out of their way without always succeeding. One of them once told her that Rose was an excellent student and would soon become "capable of gracing any of the noblest homes in the land."

Betta wants to finish her tea but not daring to pick up the Wedgwood cup, she decides against it. She also starts out hungry, but is no longer so, even though the table is laden with delicacies: oatcakes, rolls, breads, butter, cheese, and confects. Rose for her part is staring at the window coverings. Perhaps - so Betta speculates with dread - they might become the next *target* in Rose's campaign to gentrify the household. (She is able to do such things thanks to the very generous allowance her father gives her monthly for clothing and whatever else she desires.

Suddenly, the humor of the situation strikes Betta. She throws back her head and laughs. Rose turns her gaze from the window, raising an exquisitely plucked eyebrow in query. Betta tries to shake off the laughter, but looking at her daughter, she finds the situation even funnier. This is not the daughter of some upper-class toff who happens to sit in their breakfast room. This is Rose whom she carried in her womb.

That Rose should now choose to present a different face to the world is neither here nor there; it's a mask beneath which the real Rose still exists and can still be as loud and bawdy as Aaron. The point is proved when Rose drops the mask and joins her mother in laughter. When they tire, Betta wipes her eyes and nose with her serviette, noting Rose refrains from her usual comment, "Use your hanky, Ma, not your napkin." According to Rose, *serviette* is a low-class word.

Her napkin now back on her lap, Betta says, "Tell me, Rose, is a laird no longer good enough for you?"

Rose replies in a cultured drawl, "You understand perfectly, Mother. I want an earl. Lairds own land and classify as upper class but have no title. By the way, please note that I'll now be calling you Mother not Ma." She dips an elegant finger into the strawberry confect and licks it.

Betta stares at the finger, aghast. Even in her *tradesman's* upbringing, such behavior is not acceptable; nonetheless, she overlooks the point and says, "Given the way your pa feels about the upper classes, he will never consent to an earl!"

Rose replies, "You're discounting feminine wiles, Mother!"

Betta feels that Rose might be right. Aaron dotes on Rose and has overindulged her ever since they lost their baby son to an infection. Eyeing her daughter - pink tongue licking delicately around her manicured forefinger - Betta resists the temptation to dip her own finger into the jam. Instead she reaches for a brioche.

Nightcap

Leith, Scotland

Migu and Betta sit by the hearth in their bedroom. It is their habit to enjoy a nightcap before bed. Betta is wearing her flannel nightdress with a plaid wrap over her shoulders; Migu, with his black bush of hair blending into the encroaching shadows, is still in day clothes. Placing his huge slipper-clad feet on the footstool, he holds his tumbler up to the fire.

Noting the play of light through the cut glass, he says, "I see our Rose has been shopping again. I wonder when she'll realize we cannot be gentrified. Don't tell her that I recognize this glass is Waterford. It might spoil her fun!"

Giggling, Betta takes a sip from her glass and makes a face.

"You don't like it?" he asks. "I don't think it's bad at all. It's from a distillery near Glen Orm, which Pontefract is helping to finance. It's a wise move on his part. In spite of the powerful London gin-merchants' lobby and taxes placed on Scotch, Scotch is catching on south of the border." After a brief pause, he adds, "Seeing Rose is providing the household with these fine tumblers, I hope she doesn't feel the need to sample the intended contents."

Shock registers on Betta's homely face. "Of course not! That would be improper for the future wife of a nobleman!"

Migu says, "The behavior of some of those SOBs is far less proper than anything our kind can imagine, but leaving that aside, I'm dreading telling Pontefract that his son isn't good enough for Rose and that she wants me to find someone better."

"Is that how she phrased it?"

"That's what it boiled down to, and I caved in. She looks at me with those huge dark eyes, and as always, I promise whatever she wants."

"Even a nobleman?"

"Yes, but I'm hoping to find someone more attractive than a run-of-the-mill aristocrat; someone who might change her mind."

Migu gets to his feet, yawns, and stretches, his huge form now a smudge in the darkness. Then taking Betta's hand, he helps her to her feet; she has difficulty getting up nowadays. He says as they go, "I wonder if Baby Aaron had lived if he'd have been as difficult to handle as our Rose."

Thimba and His Loa

West Coast of Africa

Thimba moves through a twilight zone where sunlight only penetrates when a tree falls and leaves a hole in the canopy. Although he is a huge man, he makes barely a sound. In one hand he carries the roasted haunch of a small antelope; in the other, a pierced coconut shell filled with ale. He wears no clothing, but necklaces, bracelets, and anklets adorn his limbs and neck. He carries a fire-making kit in a pouch on his back and a knife in a holster at the waist. Both his body and the braids of his cornrow hairstyle are covered in the red-ochre clay he uses as a mosquito repellent. Although his dark figure blends into the speckled gloom and is difficult to spot, the creatures of the forest sense his presence and remain eerily silent.

Thimba's senses pick up sights, sounds, and odors from which he extrapolates whatever information might prove useful. In this case, it's a smell - not an unpleasant one - which tells him that a rosewood tree has fallen. He veers off his path to look and locates the fallen giant by the shafts of sunlight that now reach to the forest floor. He makes a mental note to mention the matter to the village carpenters, sculptors, and drummers for whom the fallen tree will be a valuable resource. They wouldn't know about it yet as it would only have fallen recently. The red flowers of the liana that pulled it down are only now starting to wilt.

Returning to the path, he fixes his attention to the ground beneath his feet: fungi, herbs, and moss flourish in the dampness; insects scuttle about in the leaf mold. He also sees a colony of interesting spiders with shiny black bodies and long legs striped in yellow and black. He watches one capturing a moth and encapsulating it in silk. He hopes Kwame and Assimbola don't discover the creatures; if they did, they'd use them to scare Abebi! Lifting his gaze, he catches glimpses of the most colorful sights of the forest: noisy birds high in the canopy and orchids closer to the ground. Marmosets, too, are present, but he can't spot them; merely hears their chatter.

Nowadays, Thimba only feels content in the natural world away from humanity. The sense of belonging that he knew as a child dissipated after his formal initiation into manhood. Since then he feels nothing but bitterness toward his fellow tribesmen. That is why he is now in the forest heading toward the shrine for his loa Masimbarashe. He needs guidance, and the ale and meat he carries are an offering. All offerings to Masimbarashe must include meat seeing that in life, like Thimba, Masimbarashe was a top-ranking hunter.

As Thimba approaches the shrine, he brings his thoughts to bear on Masimbarashe and the bond they share. He knows that by merely thinking of Masimbarashe, he is informing the spirit that he will soon be at the shrine and would like a consultation.

Thimba has a disfigurement that dates back to his encounter with the incarnated Masimbarashe at the time of his initiation into manhood. Killing a lion single-handedly with a spear was and remains the most demanding requirement placed on the candidates. Thimba's lion - a black-maned male in his prime - had fought fiercely, but finally Thimba managed to deliver a mortal wound. Filled with pride at his accomplishment and wanting to show off, he had approached the dying creature and tried to pull out a whisker. The lion with its last reserve had lashed out and a claw caught in the metal hoop of Thimba's earring. The action ripped the external ear from Thimba's head, leaving only a dark hole.

Later Thimba had consulted with Babalawo[30], who had little sympathy. He had told Thimba that what had happened was a rightful punishment for adolescent posturing and that trying to tweak out a whisker was an act of disrespect to a dying and noble creature. Babalawo's words had struck a chord in Thimba, and his head had

---

[30] Medicine man, healer of mind and body

drooped in shame. Noticing remorse, Babalawo had said, "Seeing you are sorry, I suggest you beg forgiveness from the spirit and ask if he would be willing to become your loa."

"How do I know I'm forgiven?" Thimba had wanted to know.

Babalawo had told him he'd know inside himself, but if he was still uncertain, he should ask for a sign. Thimba had asked for a sign, and Masimbarashe had delivered it in a dream in the form of the full-throated purr of a satisfied lion! Since then, Masimbarashe has been Thimba's guardian spirit. Thus, that inappropriate example of adolescent behavior had been resolved. There is, though, another example of inappropriate adolescent behavior that still needs resolving, which - if it were to become common knowledge - would lead to the death of both Thimba and Shamwari - his lover, friend, and fellow warrior.

They live in a homophobic society, and while homoerotic behavior is tolerated between adolescents until the time of initiation, it then becomes taboo. Child mortality is high, and the tribe needs a high birthrate to survive. Hence, it is a man's duty, especially that of a top-ranking warrior, to take as many wives and have as many children as is humanly possible. This expectation does *not* suit Thimba, and he and Shamwari continue in the homosexual relationship they developed in their adolescent years.

Were the truth to become public knowledge, Big Baba, as the head of the Council of Elders, would have to unleash hired assassins from the savanna. That is what the tribe would expect and what has happened in the past. Meanwhile, with the case of Thimba and Shamwari, no one yet suspects that anything is amiss, but with the passage of time, the danger of discovery increases. Shamwari has been successful in camouflaging the truth by acquiring a number of wives and by fathering nine children.

This is as it should be and places Shamwari beyond suspicion. Until now, his friend's situation has helped Thimba, who still only has one wife and one child: Efia and Abebi. People would take into account that he had fathered not only Abebi but also Baby Infana, who died from eating ackee seeds. Yet that excuse is now wearing thin.

If he wants to remain a hero, save his family from shame, and escape the assassins' knives, he has no option but to overcome his aversion to women and do what Shamwari has done. Nonetheless, he finds it impossible. He hates the idea of having to service countless wives. He only manages doing what he has to do with Efia every now and then and even that is only with the aid of aphrodisiacs.

He has never been able to relate to women regardless of who they might be. He even feels uncomfortable with his own mother, let alone his stepmothers, aunties, sisters, grandmothers, and now with his daughter Abebi. He doesn't know how to treat Efia either if she doesn't tell him what she expects of him. From their earliest days, she had him in her sights and had tagged along behind him regardless of what he was doing. She was insistent, and he hadn't known how to get rid of her without being nasty. Over the years, he almost grew accustomed to her, and for that reason, when it came time for courting, he chose her.

Courting, like everything in tribal life, has its rituals. It involves a literal chase in which the newly minted warriors chase the eligible girls around the village. When a girl is caught - if she favors her captor - she gives him a copper ring. The chase goes on for days with the young men accumulating rings from different girls, which then gives them options for their first wife. Thimba had chased the girls, as he was meant to - that part did not bother him - and had a ring from every eligible girl. That meant he had first choice and had chosen Efia as the girl he feared least.

Thimba has now reached the site he uses for his altar. It is at the base of the tallest mahogany in the forest: a tree that uses aerial buttress roots to stabilize itself in the unstable terrain. These aerial roots resemble low wooden walls that define spaces of different sizes and shapes. It is one of these spaces that Thimba has chosen to use for his shrine to Masimbarashe. Like rosewood, mahogany is a valuable resource for the village and especially prized by drummers for making *djembes*.[31] The tree though has to fall first to make that possible, and for Thimba's mahogany to fall would be the worst of omens. Luckily neither disease nor heavy vines threaten it.

On arrival, Thimba sets to rights the altar - a low table on sturdy legs - then lays the haunch on top and the coconut-shell on the ground to the side. Next he pulls out from his hidey-hole (a hollow in a nearby stump) a small woven mat on which he arranges objects of spiritual significance: a chunk of quartz with a streak of gold, a large irregular pearl, the jawbone of a shark, and the skull of an eagle. The newest item is a lion-faced carving of Masimbarashe with his full moon emblem carved into the pedestal.

Standing back, Thimba eyes the display and makes small adjustments before picking up a stick and scratching Masimbarashe's *vévé*[32] onto ground. Then shaking his fire-making kit out of its pouch, he establishes that it contains everything it should: a small fireboard, a long spindle, a bit of bark, and some dry grass for the tinder nest. He thinks how that very morning his younger brother Kwame had successfully used the hand-drill method for the first time. He feels proud of the boy. He has potential.

Crouching on the ground, Thimba twiddles the spindle and soon has smoke and an ember that he is able to transfer into the tinder-nest. Blowing gently, he brings the spark to life and holds the flame to the wick of one of his beeswax candles that belong in his trove. Facing the altar, he joins his hands at his chest, and bending his head, he acknowledges Gran Legbwa, the highest accessible authority of the

---

[31]   Type of drum

[32]   A loa's symbol

spirit world. He asks Gran Legbwa for a blessing and then, as required by the ritual, says out aloud, "As your humble servant, I call on you, Gran Legbwa, to draw back the curtain to the world of the spirits and grant Masimbarashe passage."

As he waits, he knows he must define in his mind the nature of his problem so that Masimbarashe can pick it up from there when he arrives. Eyes closed, head bent, and his braids falling forward, Thimba formulates his problem as best he can. He then empties his mind and waits.

As he stands immobile among the towering trees, the creatures of the forest lose interest in him and continue their normal activities. Monkeys squabble, and the insects again embark on their deafening chorus of clicks, pops, and taps. Feeling himself to be an integral part of his surroundings, he loses all sense of time until he feels the arrival of a presence, and knowing it is Masimbarashe, experiences a rush of pleasure. He says in their silent language, *I've brought you meat and ale, Masimbarashe, and need your advice. The pettiness and bigotry of tribal thinking threatens to destroy me. I need an honorable escape from a life in which I no longer find pleasure.* As he speaks these silent words, it occurs to him that what he says is not quite accurate. It is with pleasure that he anticipates the two-week annual giant eland hunt. It is the highpoint of the hunters' calendar and will take place at the beginning of June.

With the thought of the giant eland hunt, something unexpected pops into his mind - a feasible plan for escape from life! Masimbarashe has delivered; he has given him an idea that has never occurred to him before! Out of nowhere, he suddenly has a clear picture of how the giant eland hunt can provide an opportunity for the escape that he yearns. Filled with gratitude, he thanks Masimbarashe, and the presence withdraws.

Feeling something tickling his naked foot, he looks down and is glad he does! It's a snake - seven-foot-long with lustrous skin, a sinuous black body, and a big flat head. It is examining his foot with a flickering tongue, and as Thimba knows, he only has one option: to stand still and wait until the creature leaves of its own accord. Although he can't see the wide cross-stripes under the chin and across the gullet, he knows they exist. He knows, too, that this is a forest cobra and that its venom is lethal.

Standing immobile for another ten minutes as the cobra does a thorough investigation of his feet, Thimba concludes that Masimbarashe has sent the cobra as a warning. Although the giant eland hunt will offer Thimba the opportunity he needs, the hunt is still over four months away. In the interim, there is danger of discovery, and extreme caution will be needed, if both he and Shamwari are to survive.

No sooner has Thimba come to this conclusion than squabbling marmosets distract the reptile, and it slithers away.

Breakfast in Banyan Village

West Coast of Africa

Efia was up before dawn plying Thimba and Big Baba with their kola-nut drink along with the remains of last night's *fufu*[33] and berries. One of Big Baba's younger wives normally provides his breakfast at his own compound, but today, Baba has joined Thimba at Efia's. Both men have now gone about their ways, and in the burgeoning daylight, Efia and Abebi settle down for their own breakfast. Efia notes that the endless gray of a featureless ocean is slowly brightening and turning to silver. The shrieks of the forest's parakeets, joined by a handful of village cockerels, tell the world that the sun will soon appear. Already its radiance penetrates the trees to the east.

Crouched on a reed mat in front of their hut, Efia with deft fingers makes a small ball of the sticky fufu and feeds it to Abebi, who holds open her mouth open like a young bird. After savoring the offering and swallowing, Abebi, too, makes a ball - her fingers less deft than her mother's - and giggling at the sheer joy of life pops it into Efia's mouth. Both then help themselves to berries with Abebi managing to get the juice all over her face and body.

Laughing at the sight her little skellum,[34] Efia reaches for a damp cloth and wipes off the naked body of her child, including the necklace that Abebi wears. It is a bit of wood that Infana chewed, when still alive and teething. As a fetish, it now hangs around Abebi's neck on a leather thong, threaded through a string of beads spaced with inserts of silver, copper, and ivory. Efia and Abebi had made the necklace after Infana died. It was at the same time that Infana changed from being her baby brother to being her invisible loa, a capacity in which he was supposed to offer her protection in exchange for respect, not something that

---

[33]   Mash made with flour from yams, cassavas, or other starches

[34]   A bug, but also used as a term of affection, equivalent to rascal

features in Abebi's everyday life! However, for better or worse, Infana is now her loa.

As Efia wipes off the fetish, she feels a longing for her young son but refuses to brood; she does not want to spoil this shared breakfast with Abebi by remembering her struggle to remove the poisonous seeds from the back of Infana's throat.

When both have had their fill, Efia makes a big ball of the remaining fufu, which she holds up saying, "I don't think Infana would be happy with this as an offering!" Abebi squeals in delight at the joke because Infana always spat out fufu! With the job done, Efia stands up noticing that down at the Banyan, Kayefi, a sculptor, is trying unsuccessfully to oust Old Billy from Baba's throne. She clicks her tongue and hands Abebi the ball of fufu with the words, "Take this down for Old Billy. It might get him off Baba's seat." She then watches Abebi silhouetted against the ocean barreling off toward the Banyan.

When Efia has finished sweeping and it's time for the women to get going on their foraging trip, she sets out to fetch Abebi. The little skellum should accompany them, seeing her chatter tires Baba and also because the bad boys are now collected in a noisy group outside their bunkhouse, and it's best for cheeky little girls like Abebi to stay well clear of them. Efia has noticed how - among the adolescent boys - the bond among one another is needed for an effective warrior-hunter corps, which often translates into a gang mentality.

As Efia approaches the Banyan, she sees that Abebi is sitting on her grandfather's lap playing with his warrior necklace, composed of fang, claw, bead, and bone. It is the fearsome trapping of a tribal leader; yet it doesn't frighten Abebi, who has been acquainted with it since birth. As Efia draws closer, she notices that with her finger, Abebi is following the lines of the striations on Baba's ancient cheeks. He smiles down at her with an indulgent smile, and then as Efia comes into hearing range, she hears Abebi say "I love you, Baba!" and sees the child bury her face in his chest.

This intimate scene surprises Efia. Although Abebi has always been an affectionate child, she would never behave like this with Thimba, her own father. Abebi is frightened of Thimba; never says a word in his presence. As a warrior-hunter in his prime, Thimba is too big and too intimidating for her. He is also too humorless, although he wasn't like that when he was younger. After his initiation, he changed.

Efia doesn't blame Thimba for not knowing what to do with a miniscule scrap of humanity like Abebi, who isn't even a boy but a girl! The continued existence of the tribe depends on warriors like Thimba, and the skills required to do the job are not of the gentler kind appropriate for little girls. That doesn't make Thimba less than perfect in Efia's eyes. This being the case, when the tribe so badly needs a new headman, Big Baba should nominate Thimba. Why isn't he doing so?

Event on the Beach

West Coast of Africa

After Abebi climbs down from Big Baba's lap and trots off after her mother, Big Baba settles into the stillness that is normal for this time of day. With the workday in progress, the village is quiet. The hunter-warriors are up at the butchery, where they still have a backlog of hides needing attention. Removing flesh, fat, and hair is no mean feat, not to mention stretching. The fishermen are out at the fishing grounds; he can see their dugouts, if not necessarily identify them. The women are now assembling under Efia's guidance for a foraging expedition on the plains. Everyone is busy, yet he is sitting around doing nothing.

Kayefi breaks into the stillness by huffing and puffing, as he drags over a massive wood carving and places it upright in front of Baba on the ground.

"Ah, Gran Legbwa!" exclaims Big Baba, recognizing the seated figure - fierce, horned, and phallic. He has forgotten that the Council of Elders has commissioned the work, but he now praises the boy with the words, "You are almost as good a sculptor as your father! The Council will be reimbursing you appropriately." He then continues by sharing with the young man memories of the lad's sculptor father who met his demise during the time of tribal warfare, a time that few, apart from Baba, remember.

Face wreathed in smiles, Kayefi returns with his awkward load to his area of the Banyan. Baba thinks how in his younger years he used to secretly scoff at the way old men would sit on their thrones doing little beyond reminiscing. He realizes now though that by reminiscing in the presence of others they were performing a vital role in preserving tribal history - something that can only be passed on by word of mouth.

Baba thinks he must remind himself of this consoling fact when next afflicted by one of his periodic attacks of guilt for spending his time doing nothing. The problem is that warriors aren't trained to place the same value on cerebral matters as on physical prowess.

Relaxing, Baba allows the breeze to caress his cheeks while his farsighted eyes scan the sky and ocean, noting cloud types and bird activity. They register wave formations and color, but finding nothing unusual, he shuts his eyes and listens to the gulls and the swoosh of the surf. His mind stops wandering when he realizes that the changes in himself - the physical weakness and feelings of uselessness - are his body preparing him for his transition into the spirit world. They are telling him that his ancestors will soon be calling him. That is all right with him. He doesn't fear death, but he doesn't want to leave behind a mess. He must resolve all unresolved issues now.

Under his watch, the Council of Elders has done well catering to the social, commercial, and political well-being of the village. Now that peace reigns among the neighboring tribes, the most common issues brought to Council at indabas concern the resolution of disputes, the punishing of the intransigent, and the distribution of land and food. These matters are always handled equitably. If it were only these matters for which he must answer, he would be happy to join his ancestors right away.

An important matter, though, still remains unresolved: the nomination and election of a new headman. The job of headman is to enforce Council's decisions and to act as intermediary between Council and the tribe at large. Not having a headman means Council and the people no longer communicate as they should, and the results can have serious consequences, especially as the post has been vacant for months.

The obvious candidate for the headman's post is Thimba and, as much as Efia - his daughter by Twenty-Seventh Wife - wants him to nominate Thimba, Baba has reservations, which even he does not fully understand. Outwardly Thimba is qualified. He is the tribe's top warrior-hunter outperforming all others in an area where peak physical performance and athleticism trump all else. He is also intelligent and dutiful; characteristics not always applicable to warrior-hunters! Yet . . .

Needing help with his thinking, Baba extracts the long-stemmed pipe that he keeps tucked into the top of his loincloth. He fills the bowl with tobacco and tamps it down with his thumb. Then getting up and hobbling over to the embers of the sculptors' fire, he uses a taper to light the tobacco.

Back in his seat, he takes a puff before forcing his thinking back to the headman issue. What bothers him about Thimba is that he never says more than is essential, never relaxes, and never laughs or jokes. It is unnatural, and as a boy, he wasn't like that. He was as outgoing and as bubbly as Abebi, who gets her exuberance from him because Efia could never be described as bubbly! Something must have happened to Thimba during adolescence.

Eyes fixed unseeingly on the distant divide between ocean and sky, Big Baba - in an attempt to pinpoint the problem - compares Thimba to the stereotypical warrior-hunter. The typical warrior lifestyle tends toward excess when it comes to food, alcohol, bloodletting, and sexual conduct. As Baba's mind touches on the latter, he realizes that while Thimba doesn't go overboard when it comes to food, alcohol, and bloodletting, he still fits in the pattern. Sex is the only area where he definitely doesn't fit into the pattern!

Shifting uncomfortably in his seat, Baba chastises himself for not picking up on this issue earlier. Obviously, Thimba should be taking more wives and procreating like other healthy males. That he isn't doing so should have rung an alarm much earlier. Seeing others enjoy fulfilling their sexual duties, why then not Thimba? The explanation can only be that the homosexual behavior tolerated in adolescence has persisted beyond the cut-off point of initiation. Baba shakes his head. It's bad news and can only lead to catastrophe.

Before Baba can follow through with his unpleasant insight, he is distracted by the sight of one of the fishing boats, which has turned homeward, although it is still too early. It is also making slow progress. As Baba waits to find out why, he continues to puff on his pipe. Having pinpointed the Thimba problem, he must now decide how to act. What solution would least harm the tribe, the family, and Thimba himself? Baba is too old and has seen too much of human nature to condemn Thimba but knows that to keep damage to a minimum he has to act. The longer the matter continues unchecked, the greater the risk of discovery. He needs to speak to Thimba alone and in a nonconfrontational manner.

Happy to have pinpointed the problem and to have decided on action, he becomes curious about the dugout, which - because the ridge obstructs his view of the beach - he can no longer see the beach. Old Billy is biffing at his arm trying to persuade him to leave, and he decides he will do just that but will not allow himself to take orders from a goat! He therefore fills his lungs with smoke and blows it into the goat's face. Old Billy closes his eyes, lifts his head, and inhales with a look of ecstasy on his face! With a chuckle, Big Baba takes a last puff and bangs out the dottle on the leg of his throne. Taking his staff to hand and rising, he joins the stream of villagers that are streaming past on their way down to the beach. Someone will help him negotiate the slithery path down the embankment when they get there.

When Baba finally reaches the beach, the sight that meets his eyes strikes terror into his heart. The dugout has dragged back the naked and bloated corpse of a warrior. Incised on his chest are the tribal markings of Mbaleki's village. The sexual organs are missing; they have been chopped off.

All those gathered - Thimba among them - know what this outrage means. Baba also knows that Mbaleki would not have wanted to unleash the hired assassins - that is obviously what has happened - but he was forced to comply with his tribe's requirements.

Fourth Week of January 1800

The Lawyer

New Orleans, Louisiana

The chevalier often wonders what will happen to his coffee-colored kiddies - adults and children - when he dies. He suspects they will not fare well under his legitimate son and heir Jacques or under any other new owner. At the best, they will be treated as regular slaves and subjected to the cruelty and indignity, which is the fate of millions of slaves throughout the Americas and the Caribbean. He wouldn't want that to happen to his kiddies. They carry his superior bloodlines and are therefore special. Besides, he loves them, or at least, he loves those who are loyal to him. He sends those who are disloyal to the slave auctions.

Although the issue of the kiddies' fate after his death has haunted him for years, the recent celebration of his seventieth birthday has spurred him into action. He realizes he has reached the three-score-and-ten mark, which according to the Bible is the measure of man's God-given span on earth. Although he does not believe that he will be dying any time soon, he doesn't want to presume on the Almighty. It behooves him therefore to address the kiddies' future while he is still capable. With this in mind, he makes an appointment with Olivier Girrard - his friend, lawyer, and neighbor both on the plantation and here in New Orleans.

With a bottle of cognac and a humidor between them, the two Frenchmen sit opposite each other at the Louis Quatorze desk in the chevalier's office. The chevalier opens the conversation with the words "*Mon ami*, I'm worrying about the fate of André and his siblings after my death. I'd like them to have a better future than most mixed-race kiddies have after their father's demise."

Olivier, who is of an uncompromising disposition, does not reply immediately. While the chevalier waits, sipping his drink, he watches his friend take his time choosing a corona[35] from the humidor. He watches the precision with which Olivier uses the guillotine to chop off the rounded head. As he taps the cigar on the desk, lights it, and turns it around to blow gently at the glow of orange, the chevalier starts to get impatient. They don't have all day! Curbing his impatience, he waits as Olivier - holding the cigar to his mouth and angling his head up to the ceiling draws in the smoke, rolls it around in his cheeks, and blows it out again. It reminds the chevalier of how years ago, when he taught André how to smoke cigars, it had taken *le gar*[36] a while to understand that unlike cigarette smoke one must never inhale cigar smoke. Poor lad had to endure several paroxysms of coughing before he mastered the technique!

Finally Olivier speaks, "Guillaume, you should have thought about your mixed-race offspring before you set out on your mission to improve the black race. It's now too late. Your kiddies are slaves, and they and their children will remain so ad infinitum."

The chevalier doesn't like the implied criticism and fires back, "All of us slave owners, including you, met the challenge of improving an inferior race with our bloodlines."

"True, but you've ignored a basic rule, which is never to become emotionally involved with your slave children. I don't regard mine as

---

[35]   Type of cigar with an open foot and rounded head
[36]   The lad

anything other than slaves. The point is to create better slaves, not uppity savages wanting wages and fancy accommodation! Remember, too, they could turn on us! Given how they outnumber us, we'd be dogs' meat if they did."

While listening with half an ear, the chevalier replenishes his cognac and picks out a Torpedo from the humidor. Olivier is telling him nothing new - nothing that doesn't belong in the slave owner's credo. Nonetheless, he allows him to ramble on, "Slaves should never be educated and never acquire a taste for nice things. They have to realize they are slaves in perpetuity . . ."

Only when Olivier moves from banalities to matters specifically aimed at the chevalier himself does the chevalier pay more attention. Olivier is now saying, "Don't go soft on us, Guillaume! You are not a sans culotte[37] by nature or upbringing. We have something good going here, so don't break ranks and upset it! Don't forget that your kiddies, in spite of your input, are still negroid. Even your André is a *nigger*."

The chevalier snaps to attention and - sitting forward in his chair - glares at Olivier. "That, mon ami, goes too far!" he snaps. "Who do you think you are to lecture me with your platitudes?"

Startled, Olivier stops and stutters, "S-s-sorry, Guillaume."

Olivier is small in stature, and although he is unlikely to admit it, the chevalier suspects he feels intimidated by larger men. Therefore, seeing he has made his point but still needs legal advice, the chevalier decides to revert to his normal tone, saying, "It is not your opinions that interest me, Olivier. Given you are au fait with the laws of the land, I need to know how best to circumvent them."

---

[37] Partisans of the French Revolution. *Culottes* refers to "the fashionable silk knee-breeches of the upper classes." *Sansculottes*, meaning "those without silk breeches," refers to "the lower classes who wore *pantaloons* (trousers) instead"

"What, specifically, do you want to know?"

"I'd like to leave André enough land for him to make a living for himself and give employment to his siblings. He and they are capable of making the scheme a success."

Olivier clicks his tongue and says. "No, no, mon ami, stop dreaming! You know as well as I do that by law no slave is allowed to own property."

The chevalier persists, "I heard of a slave owner who gave a sloughed-off *placée*[38] and her Creole children a tract of land to use for themselves."

"I know of the case, but it is one in thousands, and it took years to free each family member individually before it could happen. The owner also became a pariah in a community that did not want freed slaves owning land in their midst."

With his head down, the chevalier sinks into himself. He doesn't like to think of the vitality and affectionate nature of his kiddies trampled or of their eagerness to learn beaten down by the drudgery of the cane fields. He squirms at the thought of their innate abilities remaining unfulfilled and of their unconditional trust in him betrayed.

Lifting his head, he says, "The kiddies give me more pleasure than either Jacques or Jean. Surely there has to be a way to resolve the issue?"

"The only way is for you to initiate the lengthy procedure of freeing each kiddie individually, and you probably don't want to do that."

"No, I wouldn't do that," says the chevalier, knowing he won't be making any further headway with Olivier, but also knowing there has to be a way around the problem. There is always a way around such matters for those of his kind. To find it though, he'll need another lawyer. He'll look into the matter later. Dealing with the law is a long and frustrating

---

[38] Common-law slave wife

procedure, and he doesn't look forward to it, but he has time. He won't be dying any time soon.

Meanwhile, Olivier is starting to opine again and is saying, "Give up, Guillaume! Remember your kiddies are *darkies* and will accept whatever treatment Jacques or anyone else metes out to them. They don't feel pain the way we do."

A Friend at Last

Liverpool, England

Tom sits in the corner at the Merchants' Coffeehouse reading *The Observer*, the world's first Sunday newspaper. As always, he jots down pertinent points. Between reading and note-taking, he sips at his penny's worth of gritty coffee. He feels it sharpens his mind and helps him process the learned article that he now reads on the relationship between cleanliness and health.

In his work as medico among slaves in the holds of the *Spirit of the Clyde*, he had often suspected a connection between filth and sickness and wished he'd been able to use scientific methodology - experiments, evidence, causes, and research - to prove the theory. As a mere barber-surgeon, though, he didn't have the training. For the parish school he'd attended, science might as well not have existed. However, now reading the present article in *The Observer*, he feels proud that, although he doesn't have the scientific training, his personal experience and observations match the facts as supplied by someone with suitable credentials.

Tapping the top of his pencil against his teeth, he thinks how pleasant it would be to find someone with whom he could discuss his medical observations. A proper naval surgeon would be ideal if proper naval surgeons were not so darned arrogant! Yet it's possible that he is being unnecessarily judgmental; perhaps, not all naval surgeons conform to the stereotype. One person, who obviously doesn't conform and who sometimes participates in discussions is a huge gentleman with curly red hair, whom others refer to as Ambrose.

Perhaps, if he picks the right moment, he could approach Ambrose and manage to talk to him without becoming tongue-tied and red in the face. When Ambrose next puts in an appearance, he resolves to put the matter to the test. In the meantime, he must get on with his reading.

The article has moved from dirt and disease to the link between a poor diet and the type of disorders that Tom experienced daily among the slaves on *Spirit*: scurvy, cholera, dehydration, gangrene, leprosy, flux, and dysentery. The article starts with scurvy and James Lind, who maintained that fresh fruit and vegetables could prevent the disorder. Seeing the slaves on board never received any type of fresh fruit or vegetables - discounting the odd bits of African vegetable-matter floating in a loathsome gruel - it is no wonder scurvy was so prevalent.

Tom is pondering the stupidity of allowing valuable *cargo* to perish - captured blackamoors are considered cargo - when a polite voice at his side asks, "May I join you? I see you are reading the article I read yesterday."

Shocked, Tom looks up. It's the proper naval surgeon - the big, red-haired Ambrose! Flustered, Tom indicates an empty chair, says, "Please, sir, sit. I should like to hear your opinion."

"And I, yours. You don't look happy!"

Tom blurts out, "I was thinking of the foolishness of slave-schooner owners treating valuable *property* so poorly. I read here," - he jabs his finger at the article - "and also know from my own experience as medico on *Spirit*," - he doesn't notice Ambrose's eyebrows rise in surprise -"that slave-deaths could be prevented if owners budgeted for clean water, sanitation, fresh air, and good food."

Ambrose nods in encouragement, so Tom continues, "You have no idea, sir, what it is like in the holds of *Spirit*. Chained together, the men spend the entire journey in sweltering heat without ventilation or sanitation. Sick and starving, they live and sleep in their own filth. It's no wonder so many die!"

"It certainly would seem stupid to treat valuable *cargo* in such a cavalier manner," Ambrose agrees. "One can only assume that Aaron

Migu and his kind have no inkling of conditions on their schooners and feel that their astronomical profits indicate no changes are needed. Only those like you who have experienced life on board a slave ship are truly aware of the facts. The rest of us remain in blissful ignorance." He gives Tom a speculative look, before adding, "Have you ever thought of informing the public yourself?"

"I have," says Tom, "but no one capable of changing the situation would listen to the babblings of a crippled, out-of-work barber-surgeon. To have a voice, one needs a proper education."

Rabbie Burns Night

Aberdeenshire, Scotland

In the cold gray light of dawn, Stanley hears the sounds of slaughter, pipes, and panic. Alongside his comrades-in-arms, he leans low over the neck of his horse and thunders into battle - breathless and sweating - only to wake in his own bed.

Slowly it dawns on him that while the sounds of death, pipes, and terrified animals would be similar to those of the battlefields of yore, in the present they originate from the farmyard. There preparations for Rabbie Burns Night are finally afoot, and sheep are being led to the slaughter to make haggis.[39] Liver, heart, lungs, and giblets will all be chopped and stuffed into sheep's stomachs and boiled. In the great hall, tonight not only the family will be enjoying a dinner of haggis, tatties, and neeps[40] but all the neighbors, villagers, employees, and tenants will also be present.

Rabbie Burns Night is a new event that promises to become an annual occurrence. Last year's celebration was a resounding success. Held in the great hall with the guests seated, the mind-numbing blast of pipes had heralded the arrival of the Great Chieftain o' the Pudding. Held high on a salver by a servant, the aromas had filled the hall. Then placed in front of Gramps - the pipes now silent - Gramps had recited by heart Burns' "Address to the Haggis." Much impressed, Stanley - at that stage he'd still wanted to become laird - had learned the poem himself.

Although he has forgotten bits, he remembers the part about *Old Scotland* not wanting any *watery stuff* and preferring *gushing entrails . . .* Good, too, is the part about the earth trembling at the tread of the *haggis-fed* Scot cutting off human heads and arms with his claymore, as if he were deadheading thistles!

---

[39] Savory Scottish dish

[40] Mashed potatoes and pureed turnips

Stanley feels that when he gets across the Atlantic, he will become more Scottish than he is now. He can picture himself in his own great hall among his own guests. A slave in fancy garb holding high the silver salver would be accompanied by pipers; they would be slaves taught by him, who would parade around the table in kilts.

After the slave places the *Great Chieftain* in front of him, he hears himself delivering in a sonorous voice the recitation and following it by lifting his glass of Scotch in a toast to the haggis. He can even feel the ceremonial knife in his hand as he cuts into the sheep's stomach. He can see the juices flow - *warm, reeking,* and *rich* . . . He pulls himself together. It is time to get up.

Foreigner in Leith

Leith, Scotland

David opens the front door of a terrace house in Leith. David's employer - Aaron Migu - is leaving for work not in a carriage but on foot. Migu enjoys walking; he walks to work daily regardless of the weather.

David - his footman's attire immaculate - stands to the side watching Migu pausing to survey the scene from the top of the steps. Usually at this time of year, the view is of a busy street swathed in a blanket of fog. Carriages and those hurrying to work are reduced to blurs in a world without substance. That is not the case today. With a shout of jubilation, Migu - a man of huge proportions - spreads his arms exulting, "Sun, Davey, sun! Today will be a good day!"

David knows that in the presence of a gentleman, a footman's face must remain rigid. Yet he can't resist a twitch of a smile at Migu's ebullience and - knowing no one sees - he forgives himself for his breach in etiquette. Besides, in spite of having more money than a mere footman can even imagine, David knows Migu is not a true gentleman, and rules can be broken.

Lingering a moment at the open door, he watches Migu stride down the street. With his top hat at a rakish angle, Migu swings his cane and shouts greetings to those he knows. Although Migu's clothing - cloak, waistcoat, frockcoat, breeches, and stockings - is of best quality, although he lives in a fine house, and although he has servants galore, no one can mistake Migu for a gentleman; true gentlemen are understated, not loud and flashy. Whether Migu flaunts the conventions deliberately or not, David can't decide, but his employer's behavior is always good for a laugh, and he pays well.

Before reentering the house, David checks the fittings on the front door. The new maid from a croft in the Lothian countryside is not always as careful as she should be with polishing. As he inspects the doorbell, the sound of hooves distracts him, and he straightens to see a hired cabriolet pulling to a halt. The occupant bundled up and driving himself - groom on the rear platform - calls to David in a foreign voice, "I look for Aaron Migu."

David replies at his formal best, "Mr. Migu is at work, sir."

"I shall go to his office then," says the foreigner, "I have the address." With a flick of the whip, he sets the horse back into motion, and they clop off down the street.

Odd, thinks David, bolting the door from the inside. *That man could be Aaron Migu himself or, at least, an identical twin in French clothing!*

The Trade Winds

Leith, Scotland

Not wanting to talk to the foreigner at his office, Migu is taking him on foot to the local pub that has a sign that shows a slave schooner - sails bulging - as it skims across the ocean. The *Frog* claims he's a cousin. Huh! Migu has never had a French cousin and does not want one. Britain's at war with France and *Frogs* - even civilians - aren't popular. He would have rejected the Frenchman's claims right away except this person is the spitting image of what he sees in the mirror!

He has always thought of himself as unique - bushy black hair, big build, and big personality. Yet as they walk together to the pub, the *cousin* - he says his name is Émile - claims a whole tribe of them exists in Bordeaux; and despite anti-Semitism and persecution, they have been there since the Middle Ages.

"Many of us have this family look," Émile says. "It's a badge of our pride. We recognize one another wherever we might be, and believe me, we've spread! I have had contact with a cousin in Norway, another in Odessa, and even a chevalier and his son across the Atlantic."

"Why do you hound us?" Migu asks with a belligerent thrust of the chin.

Unfazed, Cousin Émile explains, "For business reasons. These are good times for the mercantile fraternity, and the best way to widen our reach is with our own kin. As I mentioned in a recent letter to the chevalier's son, Jacques, our family has excelled at business and trade since biblical times. Jacques says that his father is not long for this world and that on his demise, the family will want to sell his sugar plantation lock, stock, and barrel, slaves included. I'm therefore looking for a buyer."

On arrival at the pub, Émile disappears in the direction of the facilities while Migu finds them seats in a small, secluded room known as the *snug*. As he waits, he winds up his pocket watch; it helps him think. What should he do about this so-called cousin? Pondering, he comes to the conclusion that while the business aspect might prove interesting, he wants nothing to do with the family aspect.

Émile reappears rubbing his hands and says, "I look forward to the ale you promised!"

"I, too," says Migu, "I'll fetch it - there is no service in the snug - but first, I need to establish some ground rules. While I'll be glad to talk business with you, I like being a dyed-in-the-wool Scot and don't need a lost tribe of Israel hanging around my neck!"

Émile tries to comment, but Migu presses ahead saying, "I also want to admit that as a teenager I found out - from a document in a box in the attic - that an ancestor, a Sephardic Jew from Bordeaux, appealed to authorities for merchant status in Leith and received it. That is all I know, and all I want to know. This person must have assimilated quickly because nothing of him has filtered down through the generations."

"Nothing except his looks," Émile teases.

Migu chooses not to hear because he has more to say. "I've never spoken of or thought of this ancestor in thirty years. Neither my wife nor daughter knows he existed, nor do they need to know. I'm a Scottish businessman, and that's it."

To Migu's surprise, Émile throws back his head and bellows with laughter. "I liked it best," Émile says through laughter, "when you spoke of the *lost tribe of Israel*. Do you realize you use the term out of its biblical context?"

"I realize no such thing," huffs Migu. "Neither do I give a damn!"

That he has set Migu off balance enhances Émile's amusement, and he explodes into a new bout of raucous laughter. Migu, recovering his equanimity, joins in the laughter. The uproar and backslapping that follow bring the landlord rushing to the door. The snug is a place for the genteel.

"Mr. Migu, please!" he begs.

Contrite, Migu says, "Sorry, Bill!" and with expansive gesture, he introduces Émile, "This is my new friend from Bordeaux. We got carried away, and you are right to reprimand us."

"Oh no, Mr. Migu," the landlord assures him. "I don't wish to reprimand you, but was wondering if you'd like me to serve you, or will you come to the bar yourself?"

"I'll come myself, Bill! Of course! That's the rule for the snug, and I don't want to be an exception."

As Migu rises, he says to Émile, "You, mon ami, stay here while I attend to the ale. You're in for a treat. Bill's Schooner Ale is the best in the land." With a heavy arm around Bill's shoulders, Migu guides him back through the door that separates the snug from the public taproom - a place where sawdust covers the floor and customers sit on wooden benches. It is used by the hoi polloi and is rougher in character than the snug.

Returning from the bar in the taproom, Migu wends his way back through the hubbub clutching two tankards of ale with towering heads. As he goes, he sees Stanley Staymann, Rose's supposed betrothed. He hasn't yet spoken to Pontefract about canceling the Betrothal Agreement. He dreads doing it, he but has given himself until March, so there's no hurry.

Stanley entering the pub from the street is accompanied by a group of foreign mariners. Busy establishing his guests at a suitable table, he doesn't see Migu, so Migu, with a voice bigger than any foghorn, bellows across the room, "Stanley! I hope you're not snubbing your uncle Aaron!"

For a moment, the taproom turns silent, as Stanley - looking over the upturned faces - grins and waves. Migu acknowledges the greeting with a nod before he pushes back through the door into the snug.

"I heard you shouting out there," says Émile, "Était-il un problème?"

"Pas de tout!" Migu assures his cousin, as they clink tankards and enter into a discussion on the power of *new money* and how the upper classes - while resenting the *new money* - need that money to remain relevant. As Émile probably does not understand how the system works in Britain, Migu elucidates, "We give the pompous asses our daughters in marriage and provide the money they need. They in turn give our daughters and our grandchildren titles. Meanwhile, they enjoy occupying the moral high ground believing they are better than we are. They see us as an underclass whose job it is to run the businesses they pretend to despise yet which generate their wealth."

"Will you give your daughter in marriage to a *pompous ass*?"

Migu chuckles. "*Touché,* mon ami*!* The answer is I should hate to do so, but who knows? Pragmatism is the name of the game." He pauses before adding, "It might be difficult finding a suitable snoot seeing that I enjoy mocking upper-class sensibilities with bad behavior."

Eyebrows raised, Émile stares at him asking, "You behave badly on purpose?"

"Bien sûr!"

"We *Frogs* are too polite. We like good manners," comments Émile, his tone mildly censorious.

"I can well believe it, but I need to express my contempt, although I wouldn't go as far as exposing any of the clandestine highborn slave traders that I know. It would damage my own interests. The *Spirit* consortium has served me well." Émile gives him a questioning look, so he elucidates, *Spirit of the Clyde* is the flagship of a consortium that owns a fleet of slave vessels."

"*Ah, très intéressant!*" Émile leans forward, eyes ablaze.

Migu becomes more cautious. Taking a gulp of ale, he moves onto safer ground and says, "Out in the taproom, I saw Stanley Staymann, future Laird of Glen Orm, or so his parents hope. The lad himself is champing at the bit, doesn't want to wait for the lairdship. He fantasizes about distant lands, plantations, and slaves. I'm willing to wager, he is out there now picking the brains of sailors who ply the oceans and know about such matters. It worries the hell out of his old man, but luckily, the lad needs financial backing, which he doesn't have at the moment."

Émile's florid face lights up. "You say a plantation with slaves? I have one to offer as I told you on the way here!"

"Slow down, mon ami!" Migu protests. "As I told you, Stanley doesn't have the finances."

"Aaron, but *you* have the finances!" Émile fires back. "You have been presented with a unique combination of circumstances: the opportunity to buy a flourishing estate from a reliable source. At the same time, you know of a suitable person to run it for you. You should jump at the opportunity to gain a foothold - as a landowner - in a new market with a brilliant future. The United States will not rest until they acquire Louisiana, and when they do, you'll be there ready to expand in all directions!"

Recovering from his shock, Migu feels a growing excitement. Noticing Émile studying him with amusement, he says without rancor, "*Bâtard!* You know you've hooked me, don't you?"

Fall of the Earl

Edinburgh, Scotland

Sir George hasn't been to the New Club since the evening of the pickpocket and the dog. It left a bad taste in his mouth. However, seeing he can't stay away from the club forever, he decides lunching there today would give him some distance from his brooding. Lord Richard might now have recovered from his dyspepsia and refrain from delivering tiresome tirades concerning Aaron Migu. Such displays of displeasure, so Sir George believes, play into Migu's hands.

With ice sparkling on skeletal young trees in Charlotte Square - as yet unfinished - Sir George feels he has chosen a good time to escape his self-imposed isolation. A sunny day at this time of year is unusual. As he approaches the club - slowly and with care because of the ice - he sees Aaron Migu on the other side of the street. He is about to turn away and find somewhere else for lunch when the flamboyant style of dress of the person he sees strikes him as a different type of vulgarity to Aaron Migu's. While equally appalling, what he sees has a continental flair. Aaron Migu's vulgarity is of the homegrown variety.

As he continues to watch from a distance, the door opens from the inside the club, and the Migu-double marches in. The door though remains open, and the old Earl of Gryphon emerges to coincide with the appearance of his coach. As the old man starts to totter down the steps - he refuses assistance from the doorman - he spots Sir George, stops, and - jowls quivering - calls, "Did you see what I saw?"

"I thought I saw a second Migu!" Sir George - now at the bottom of the steps - replies. He still can't believe his eyes upon seeing a second Migu!

"The original is upstairs," the earl huffs. "These people multiply like bloody toadstools! First, we had one. Now there are two. Heaven knows where it will end!"

A sudden contortion disfigures the old man's face; he gasps and - dropping his cane -grabs for his chest. As Sir George starts up the steps to help, the earl collapses and tumbles down toward him. Sir George throws himself to the side allowing the avalanche of cane, hat, and flailing limb to land at the bottom of the steps on the pavement.

Gathering his wits, Sir George stares down in confusion at the mound of black clothing on the glittering ice. As others rush to the scene, Sir George's inconvenient conscience tells him that he might have broken the earl's fall had he not jumped out of the way to save himself.

Skirting Confrontation

West Coast of Africa

On that day when the fishermen had dragged the mutilated corpse onto the beach, Big Baba had seen that Thimba was badly disturbed and gave him a few days to regain his equilibrium. Now Baba has sent him a message that he would like to see him, and Thimba has complied.

Having greeted Baba with the respect traditionally accorded an elder, the big warrior stands in front of Baba and waits. Baba acknowledges the greeting with a gracious nod, then says, "Thimba, I'm sorry to take you away from your duties, but *my* duty requires that I ask you a personal question to which I trust you will reply truthfully. Are you in a sexual relationship with Shamwari?"

Thimba takes a breath, looks Baba in the eye, and says in a steady voice, "Yes, Baba, I am."

Big Baba, liking the honesty, says in kindly tone, "You must know, son, that that is wrong."

His face showing no emotion and his tone even, Thimba replies, "Yes, Baba, I know."

"And you know the consequences?"

"Yes, Baba, I've always known and - if I hadn't - the beach event would have taught me."

"You know, too, that it is I, as senior elder, who would be expected to arrange for punishment?"

"Yes, Baba, I know."

"And you realize the shame that discovery would bring on Efia, Abebi, and myself?"

"Yes, Baba."

"Do you, our hero, want to die a shameful death at the hands of hired assassins?"

"No, Baba, and I told Shamwari our relationship must end, and it has."

Relief sweeps over Baba. "Thank you!" he mutters to his loa Mkulu. To Thimba, he says, "Well done, son. That will decrease the chances of discovery. What remains is the issue of acquiring more wives and fathering children."

A flicker of discomfort crosses Thimba's face. He says, "Baba, would you give me a little time to adjust before I start courting?"

Baba ponders, then says, "Very well, but don't delay too long."

Fable

West Coast of Africa

The women sit on mats in their work shelter. Today is basketry day. All manner of cane-like materials lie in neat piles on the ground around them: papyri, vines, reeds, rattan, and the long fibers of raffia palms. Wickerwork is a favorite in the hardworking lives of the village women. Along with the companionship, storytelling, laughter, and singing, they also produce items of beauty and usefulness: baskets, mats, blinds, and hangings, most of which are destined for the market at Mbaleki Village.

Abebi, who sits next to her mother playing with a length of vine, thinks of the day the camel spat in its owner's face and giggles.

"What's so funny, little one?" Efia wants to know, as her deft fingers twine material gleaned from roots and tree bark. When Abebi tells her, Efia, with mock severity, says, "I hope you learned your lesson. I can't afford a repeat! Meanwhile, you'd do better to look at what I'm doing. It's a technique my grandmother taught me, and I'll pass it on to you. You in turn will pass it on to your daughters and granddaughters."

Abebi likes to hear Mammi talk like this. It makes her feel as though she has a definite place in an established order. At the given moment though, it is not wickerwork that interests her. She is waiting for Mammi's story that she hopes will come when Auntie Abena finishes talking about a warrior-shield made from wicker instead of leather.

As the subject runs its course and winds down, Abebi perks up. *Now! Please, Mammi, it's storytime,* she begs silently. It works!

Efia announces, "Today's story will be about Anansi - the patron loa of storytelling. As a freewheeling spirit of mischief, he precipitates events that appeal to his taste for upheaval. In today's story, Anansi will take the form of a spider with many eyes and eight legs striped in purple, red, black, and white."

Abebi feels a frisson of anticipatory pleasure.

"Deep in a den," Efia begins, "close to earth's magma, Anansi grooms himself, uses a deodorant, and flexes his legs. Then with malevolent grin, he sets out for Banyan Village."

Abebi cannot believe what she is hearing. Mammi will be using Abebi's own encounter with a spider in today's story. That's not right! Anansi stories should be fun and not serious! She shouts out, "No, Mammi!" Efia looks up in surprise as Abebi glowers at her and repeats, "No, Mammi!"

Unfazed, Efia says, "Well, I'll tell you then how at the beginning of the world, Anansi cheats Crow out of his paints."

Abebi's scowl turns to smiles. She jumps up and claps; she loves that story!

First Half of April 1800

The Chevalier

Plantation, Louisiana

The chevalier and his wife, Cécile, have just arrived from New Orleans by carriage. They sit on the porch of the Big House supposedly relaxing in the breeze that drifts up from the Mississippi. Cécile on her high-backed chair has dropped off to sleep. Eyes closed and head sunk into the frills under her chin, she breathes to a soft but audible rhythm. Looking at her, the chevalier envies her, wishing he could summon sleep the way she does. She does it so often that he sometimes wonders if she fakes it.

In the past few weeks, he has lost the capacity for sleep, feels ill, gets headaches, and lacks energy. In New Orleans on Monday, in an unprecedented event in, he had to come home from his office during the day. That is why - when Cécile said he might feel better on the plantation - he had readily agreed; he loves the plantation. It was however a bad shock to hear she would accompany him. Neither she nor their two adult sons have ever set foot on the plantation in all the decades that he has owned it!

He extracts a large handkerchief from his pocket and wipes his face; he is sweating profusely. Seeing that the thermometer in the vestibule registered only twenty degrees Celsius, he must have a fever, which isn't surprising given the way he feels. Carelessly stuffing the drenched bit of cloth back into the pocket of his breeches, he returns his thought to Cécile; there must be an ulterior motive for her presence. Whatever it is, it has caused him considerable inconvenience. He has tried to send a message ahead instructing André to keep himself and the other coffee-colored kiddies out of the way of the Big House, but it obviously didn't arrive in time. His daughter Elise is among the welcoming party of house slaves assembled on the front steps, and she is now on the porch.

Cécile has never known about his slave family, and he would have liked her to remain in ignorance, but now the cat is out of the bag. She has eyes in her head and does not need to be Blaise Pascal to divine the origin of so many coffee-colored slaves!

He shifts in his chair, is feeling worse, and cannot get comfortable. He used to think of these cushioned, high-backed wicker chairs as luxurious, but now feels they need replacement. He doesn't even have the energy to move and try some other chair. His thoughts remain, sticking to Cécile like leeches. Why has she accompanied him? When he asked her in the carriage earlier in the day, she had replied, "You're unwell, and I wish to keep an eye on you." She has never before shown that type of concern. He has also noticed that for the past few days in New Orleans, she had fussed over his breakfast insisting she pour his coffee when a slave has always performed the duty perfectly well.

He doesn't pursue the subject; he can't concentrate. The headache centered behind his eyes is worsening. He has never before experienced the like. On arrival at the gates of the plantation, he would normally get out of the carriage and stride up the alley between the evergreen oaks. He never gets tired of the view of the Big House with its sturdy classical pillars and steps sweeping up to the porch. Today he'd stayed in the carriage, and on alighting at the porch steps had had to ask Agathe to help him.

His eyes now wander over to the grouping of female slaves who - after serving a tepid fruit drink - remain in the background waiting to do his bidding. He is pleased to note that Agathe - now that she knows about Cécile's presence - has sensibly placed the beautiful Elise in the shadows and out of Cécile's line of vision. He will have to find a suitable husband for Elise soon, but that's a problem for another day.

His gaze now lingers on Agathe herself. She wears the uniform of every house slave: long dark dress, white pinafore, and cap. Nonetheless, she stands out from the others because of a certain *hauteur* - a pride in bearing unusual in a slave - some would say inappropriate. Her back is straight, her neck long, and her head held high. Yet today there is something different in her stance. Ah! She is trying to hide someone behind her back! Interesting!

He cranes his neck and, *voilà*, recognizes the gorgeous creature as Adrienne - Agathe's pure black daughter by her broomstick husband. Since he last saw the girl, she has blossomed. That is why Agathe tries to hide her! *Too late, Agathe*, he tells her inwardly. *Now I've seen what you have. I'll claim what is rightfully mine - Adrienne's virginity.*

Neither mother nor daughter will like the situation, but he'll sweeten the pill for both. He always does in such cases. That's why those affected tolerate his actions. (In truth, they have no other option if they don't want to work in the cane fields.) For Agathe seeing he never uses his own daughters for breeding, it will be a new situation. He knows though she can't afford to fuss. When masters demand, slaves must obey.

Unfortunately, he does not feel capable of claiming his right to Adrienne now, but he will be better soon, and she will not be going anywhere in the meantime. Besides, if he did take Adrienne now, Cécile would have to receive some sort of potion to keep her asleep in her room, and he wouldn't like doing that. Also, Agathe, who would provide the sleeping potion, and in this case, she might not do her best!

The Wife

Plantation, Louisiana

Cécile pretends to sleep. She has mastered the art. She knows how to keep her eyes open a slit and knows, too, how to keep her breathing steady, rhythmic, and marginally audible. The mouth must be open a little, but certainly not gaping. While her slumber must be credible, she must take care not to exaggerate and make a fool of herself. It's a delicate balance.

She has adopted the ruse in order to watch her husband without him knowing. His mien and mannerisms will always tell her what she needs to know, provided he doesn't realize she is faking sleep and is watching him. Whether dressed in the costuming of the ancien régime or whether sitting with his shiny, bald pate in his dressing room, she can always read his mind.

From this afternoon's subterfuge, she has learned, which voluptuous young slave girl will be his next victim. That a seventy-year-old nobleman should lust after a black teenage slave appalls her. That his superior bloodlines should run in the veins of slaves is an unconscionable betrayal of his nobility!

Although her husband doesn't realize it, Cécile has always known about the coffee-colored kiddies, and their ever-increasing numbers turn her mind into a raging inferno. Although he never speaks of the plantation's house slaves and although she has never seen any of them until today, she knows their names. She now, too, also knows the names of his next victim and of her mother; they are Adrienne and Agathe. She also knows the name of her husband's eldest daughter with Agathe; it's Elise. No one can miss the girl even though she is supposedly hidden in the background. She towers over the others, and albeit coffee-colored and female, she is the image of the chevalier. *Grrr!*

Cécile acquires her knowledge of the house slaves and everything that happens on the plantation from the wife of her husband's friend and lawyer, Olivier Girrard. The knowledge that causes her most grief pertains to Agathe's eldest child with her husband - André. He is supposedly her husband's favorite - a person whom he treats better than either Jacques or Jean and who has grown into a big handsome man, who (except for the color of his skin) looks like her husband. Her Jacques and Jean are both small men, who don't stand out even in the attire of the ancien régime.

Suddenly Cécile notices through the slits of her half-closed eyes that her husband is pale, sweating, and . . . *oops*! He is now watching her with humiliating distaste. Maybe she has allowed her mouth to go too slack or allowed her breathing to become too loud.

The Slave Mother

Plantation, Louisiana

Agathe has never seen Mrs. Cécile until now, yet she has always known of her existence and of the existence of her two sons. She has often wondered about the mistress and pictured her with the pointed nose and beady eyes of a shrew. Now - witnessing the haughtiness and stupid pretense of sleep - she sees no reason to think kindlier thoughts.

The fact that the mistress wears rouge on her cheeks and lips means, or so Agathe believes, that she is trying to mask an innate nastiness. Agathe gets the idea from a stock-figure in African mythology - an evil stepmother who tries to hide her malice behind a painted face. This stereotype also reminds Agathe of a French story that the master sometimes reads to his younger coffee-colored kiddies. It features a girl called Cendrillon[41] and a wicked stepmother whose sneering lips, according to the accompanying illustration, are painted as bright and shiny as blood. Thinking of the victimized girl in that tale brings Agathe's focus back to where it should be: protecting Adrienne from the master.

Although Agathe herself spent years in the master's bed - bore him five beautiful, coffee-colored kiddies - she cannot tolerate the thought of her daughter having to follow suit. Since Adrienne started turning from a gangly teenager into a voluptuous young woman, Agathe has suspected that with the master's next visit - the present one - Adrienne would catch his eye no longer as a cute little girl to pat on the head and stuff with *bonbons* but as a candidate for his bed. That's why she is trying to hide Adrienne behind her back, but the wile isn't working. She sees the master craning his neck, and - *Oh mon Dieu!*[42] - his eyes have found their prey! What will happen now? As she waits, Agathe chastises herself for believing her attempt to shield Adrienne had a chance of

---

[41] Cinderella

[42] Oh dear!

succeeding. *I'm pathetic,* she thinks, *even more pathetic than the mistress with her phony sleep!*

After waiting for the master's next move, she realizes with a surge of relief that nothing will be happening. His skin has turned white. He's sweating, and best of all, his mind - *Grâce à Dieu* - appears to occupy a place in which Adrienne no longer features. He is obviously ill, which will give her family time to try to cope with him in a manner that leaves him impotent but otherwise undamaged. "Le diable on sait vaut mieux que le diable on ne sait pas."[43] Regrettably, though, death is sometimes an unwanted side effect of the potions for impotency.

The mistress is now exaggerating her phony sleep with gaping mouth and snoring. As Agathe waits for the next development, she runs through her old standbys for coping with the master's lechery: poison, spiders, or a Verdun curse. She could try placing a curse on him, although curses only work on those who believe in them. The master as a practicing Catholic does not believe in them. Yet who knows? She'll have to consult André and Adrienne, although André has always refused to support action against the master. Now, though, with Adrienne's virginity at stake, his attitude might change. She and Adrienne can't cope with the job on their own.

There's another problem. Agathe worries that Adrienne does not understand the danger. The child knows that on reaching maturity, many of the master's female slaves must endure stints in his bed; it is an accepted rite of passage from which they emerge with several coffee-colored kiddies. Yet Adrienne seems to believe that this only happens to other slave girls, not to those of her family. She doesn't realize that the master only considers his own daughters *hors des limites*[44] because he doesn't believe in *consanguinité*.[45] Adrienne, as a pure black child though, is not related to him and is therefore not *hors des limites*. (Agathe

---

[43]   The devil one knows is better than the devil one doesn't know.

[44]   Out of bounds

[45]   Interbreeding; consanguinity

learned about consanguinity one night when she eavesdropped on the master and his friends in the gentlemen's study.)

Adrienne is now whispering in Agathe's ear. "I don't want to go on standing behind you, Mammi. It's stupid! I want to see what is happening."

"Nothing is happening," Agathe tells her. "If you prefer, you could make yourself useful in the scullery. The cruets need filling and remember to align the cup handles."

As Adrienne leaves, Agathe thinks she should also have told Adrienne not to sing. Although the master likes to hear Adrienne and Elise sing as they work - he has taught them a number of French folk songs - the mistress might think differently. Both girls have a compulsion to sing, but Adrienne more so than Elise. While Elise has a good voice, Adrienne's voice is special.

André on Horseback

Plantation, Louisiana

Before taking off for the cane fields, André embarks on his morning rounds in the yard. Whip in hand and mounted on Pégasse, he proceeds sedately from one area of activity to the next. As he goes, he greets by name those he meets: carriage driver, barber, gardener, blacksmith, butcher, weaver . . .

Like his father the chevalier, he knows he presents an imposing figure. Pégasse - a difficult-to-handle breeding stallion assigned to him by the master - is a bay with compact body, broad chest, and powerful hindquarters. André loves Pégasse; he feels they belong together. For Pégasse, he is the master, the role for which *Le Bon Dieu* created him. That he should be ensnared in slavery is a situation that never ceases to rankle.

As a reckless teenager, he had smuggled onto the plantation a broadsheet acquired at a market day in Baton Rouge, and it had given him hope that slavery might one day end. He has never repeated the folly with the newspaper but is glad he did it that once; the paper had contained an article that gave him hope for the future. It had explained how at the beginning of America's War of Independence all thirteen British colonies had legalized slavery, but just thirteen years later, five states abolished the practice. This proved to André that slavery was not necessarily permanent and might one day cease to exist.

Equally important to André was a second insight gleaned from the broadsheet. Until then, he had held his father in high esteem, loving and admiring him unconditionally. After the broadsheet incident, he realized that while he had been able to read the paper - the master had allowed him to learn his letters - the average slave was not given that opportunity. In other words, the master was using the intentional deprivation of education and contact with the outside world as a means of oppression. For reasons of personal greed, the master was preventing his fellow human beings the right to fulfill their potential. He had never seen the chevalier in that light before.

This clear-sighted understanding of the master's failings - added to André's own pre-existing resentment - started to nibble into his love for his father. Nonetheless, he has not yet lost that love completely. Indeed many of the chevalier's gifts to him fill him with such gratitude that he knows he could never bring himself to betray the master. Of those gifts, three rank above all others: Andréa, literacy, and permission to ride Pégasse. Galloping across the land on Pégasse gives him a taste for the freedom he hopes will one day be his.

Pégasse, too, loves to gallop, and finding their present pace too slow tosses his head and triples; but seeing they have not yet finished their morning rounds, André keeps him on a tight rein, as he exchanges pleasantries with the tailor, wheelwright, wagoner, carpenter, cooper, and thresher.

At the crafts section - a large shelter open on all sides - Andréa, now pregnant, stands at a table in her work apron. She sorts through piles of reeds and grasses for use in basketry. In this public setting, André gives her no special treatment, except *there's a glow in his face* whenever he sees her. These are words André once overheard Elise use.

Pégasse - if left to his own devices - would head straight for the orchard and vegetable garden, but André is still not ready. He is inspecting the barrels of corn, early ripening apples, dried fish, and pork that are being loaded onto a wagon and are destined for the market in Baton Rouge.

When they finally head in the right direction, Pégasse neighs and tries to break into a trot, but André continues to keep him on a tight rein while he casts a practiced eye over the patches of pumpkins, okra, peppers, melons, and yams.

Thanks to the master, André knows a lot about vegetables and fruits. He knows that white folks used to believe tomatoes were poisonous and that corn and pumpkins are native to Louisiana; *our kind of food,* a slave of Choctaw origin had once said. André also knows that okra, red peppers, watermelons, and yams came with the early slave ships from Africa. This is information often passed on by Agathe in her attempt to keep alive all things African.

Pégasse has spotted his special friend in the beans. He is a retired field hand with shock of gray hair and a one-toothed grin. Born in Africa, he possesses an unusual affinity for manifestations of the natural world and loves Pégasse, who does not need André to steer him down the right row. He greets the old man with a nicker knowing he has a treat in store - normally a carrot, but not today. A bright green apple appears from the tattered pocket. *Probably too tart,* thinks André, but Pégasse, slobbering and chewing with big square teeth, likes the change, and nuzzling the old man for more nearly knocks him over.

"Woho, boy!" André protests. "You forget your strength!"

Leaving the old man, they head toward a track that leads to the cane fields. While en route, André sees admiration in the eyes of the under-ten youngsters who stopped their play to wave. They want to grow up to be like André, but alas, they will soon be spending the rest of their lives in the mind-numbing drudgery and murderous heat of the cane fields. He sees the same esteem in the washerwomen gathered around a huge wooden tub brimming with froth and suds. Sleeves rolled up on strong black arms, they straighten and give him a grin, calling across the distance, *Bonjour, André!*

Although now out of the yard, galloping is still not an option. The track - muddy from last night's rain - has turned into a quagmire from horse-drawn wagons carrying harvested cane to the mill. The mill lies adjacent to the farmyard and features a soaring chimney that belches out sickly, malodorous smoke. Finally reaching drier ground, André is able to give Pégasse his head. To the pounding of hooves and the rush of air, they fly with the wind across the land.

The Storeroom

Plantation, Louisiana

With both the master and mistress in residence, the scullery is a busy place with some slaves washing, drying, and storing dishes; others were scouring kettles, pots, and pans. At present though, Agathe finds Adrienne temporarily alone and says, "Adrienne, you and I need to talk. Come with me, while I check the store room." She shepherds a reluctant Adrienne ahead of her toward the storeroom, which is connected to the back porch by a narrow path. Rarely does anyone enter the room. Its only purpose is to store old kitchen utensils that had fallen into disuse decades ago.

Following Adrienne along the path, Agathe cannot help but notice Adrienne's recently acquired female attributes: the seductive walk and the pleasing curve of hip and derrière. Added to those are the lovely smile, the perfect teeth, and a chest that is no longer flat: all constitute the perfect recipe for everything that pleases the aster most.

Agathe has to battle with the key before the heavy door creaks open. When it does, they are hit with the intolerable heat and stuffiness of the room. Hand at her nose, Agathe goes ahead and sees that the room not only needs ventilation, but that rats have again taken up residence. In the dimness, she hears rustling and fleetingly catches a glimpse of a shadow disappear behind the cupboard. *Créatures misérables!*

Seeing there is nothing she can do about it at present, she ignores the matter and casts a practiced eye over the contents of the room: old dough scrapers, toast racks, graters, a roasting oven with a handle, grease lamps that use animal fat, and snuffers, along with a host of unidentifiable objects. She must set aside time for this hellhole, but now other matters must be given priority.

She retreats toward Adrienne, who hovers in the doorway her hands over nose and mouth. As they move out into the fresh air of the back porch, Agathe says, "Child, we must decide what to do about the master. I have a few suggestions."

Adrienne removes her hands from her face and exclaims, "No, Mammi, please! Snakes and spiders in the master's bed aren't an option."

Agathe suspects Adrienne is mocking her because she hasn't yet mentioned snakes and spiders but often has in the past and was about to do so again! On the defensive, she asks, "Well, what's wrong with snakes, spiders, or for that matter, rats? Even a dead one would not go amiss."

Adrienne, looking to the heavens in mock despair, says, "Mammi, rats whether dead or alive will not *rob the master of his masculinity* to use your words."

"No rat then!" replies Agathe suddenly finding humor in the situation and adding "He would probably die from a heart attack!"

When both have finished laughing, Adrienne turns serious, saying, "Mammi, please understand, we can't use the methods you always suggest."

Agathe sniffs, says, "I know, child, but I was hoping that we could find some way to prevent him from abusing you whether it is with . . ." Her voice trails off. She has nothing better to suggest than her old standbys.

Adrienne, with face blank, says, "I've discussed the issue with André and know what has to happen."

Agathe draws back in shock, "You spoke to André! You know how he dotes on his father."

"You misunderstand, Mammi. Together, André and I have decided to allow the matter to proceed as it has proceeded for those before me including you, Mammi! I'll survive just as you have."

Agathe glares at Adrienne and exclaims with all the passion of her conviction, "No! I will not allow it! You are a child and do not understand!"

Adrienne, with eyes downcast and hands clasped in front, says in an even voice, "I have an idea of what to expect, Mammi, and shall try not to mind. I've spoken to those who know, and they say it's best to go with the flow, turn off the mind, and think of something lovely like a mango or Pégasse."

As Agathe gasps for breath, Adrienne abandons the feigned nonchalance and, with eyes blazing, challenges her mother, "*You*, Mammi, did what I now have to do. *You* sacrificed yourself for the sake of your family, and I will do the same. Besides, it'll be nice for us to have a beautiful *bébé* in the cabin."

Agathe lets out a howl and, with hands to her head, injects the intensity of her feelings into the only French swearword she knows, *Merde!* She likes the sound, and it helps, so she repeats it, Merde!

Adrienne gathers her mother into her arms, where Agathe continues to babble her word into her daughter's shoulder. "*Shh,* Mammi!" Adrienne warns. "We don't want anyone to hear you."

Agathe pulls herself together, knowing she has to get back to the porch to keep her eyes on events there. Like an animal at the slaughter, she feels like bellowing in pain but instead consoles herself by silently repeating her miracle word *Merde! Merde!*

Wandering Mind

Plantation, Louisiana

The chevalier feels twinges in his stomach and throbbing in his head. His thinking, too, is jumping around. It bothers him that Agathe and Adrienne won't be happy about his designs on Adrienne. He feels it is unreasonable that - as slaves - they should resent and not fully recognize the prerogative of a master to use - as he pleases - those women who belong to him.

When he picks the girls, whom he considers suitable recipients for his superior bloodlines, he would like them to feel privileged and to perform their duty with pleasure. Although this is rarely the case, he notices that most of the girls do enjoy the resulting coffee-colored kiddies as much as he does. He realizes that the girls' pleasure derives to no small extent from the benefits that accrue from bearing a coffee-colored kiddie, but he doesn't brood on that aspect. His mind is now fixed on Agathe.

Agathe was the first slave born on his plantation after he bought it. The year? He can't remember. He is not accustomed to forgetting things. He was always a quick thinker. He tries to work it out; it was the year that France handed over West Louisiana to the Spanish and East Louisiana to the British. The arrangement split Baton Rouge down the middle, and it meant his plantation has been under Spanish jurisdiction until the present. However - with Napoleon now in charge in France - France is in the process of reappropriating the territory.

The chevalier feels encouraged that these complicated events in Louisiana's history are clear in his mind, but the exact date - it must have been nearly forty years ago - still eludes him. He would ask Cécile, but she continues to sleep - almost snoring - but not quite.

His thoughts move back to Agathe. Looking over at her - she has just returned to the porch from somewhere - he ascertains that Agathe is a much pleasanter sight than Cécile. Agathe's neck is long and slender like the delicate stem of a flower. Most of the coffee-colored kiddies have the same attractive feature. In contrast, his *real* sons - Jacques and Jean - are *sans cou*,[46] a condition more exaggerated in Jacques, whose head sits on his shoulders without transition. The chevalier feels sorry that Cécile only provided him with two puny sons. If they had had more sons, there would have been a greater chance that one or the other might have looked more like André.

His thoughts are now with Jacques and Jean. He feels that while Jean has a more pleasant personality than Jacques, he has an unfortunate problem - he is unable to stand up to Jacques, who, as a bully by nature, reduces his brother to a stuttering moron. Many consider Jean half-witted, although away from Jacques, he is normal. He even achieved academic success in Boston writing an acclaimed doctoral thesis - albeit in the ludicrous field of ethnomusicology. (It was also in Boston that he adopted the libertarian ideas so unsuitable for one of his class.)

A shooting pain behind the eyes leaves the chevalier gasping for a moment, then departs as inexplicably as it came. Eyeing Cécile, he notices her breathing has become stentorian, and something pulses in her double chin. The few centimeters of neck she once had have long since yielded to fat.

Trying to escape the revulsion he feels for his wife, he tells himself that she looks better now than when she experimented with the egalitarian fashions of the French Revolution. They allowed women more freedom of movement - so he was told - although he never understood why decorative objects like women needed to move much anyway. In the end, he had insisted that Cécile return to the style of the *ancien régime* from which - *Grâce à Dieu* - she has never since strayed. He should be

---

[46] Without neck

less curmudgeonly, but his mind is full of jabs and voids, and reason no longer finds a footing.

The only thing he knows is that he must get himself to bed somehow, but while trying to rise, he falls back into the chair. At that point, Cécile opens her eyes and lifts her head. Speaking in a hoarse whisper, he asks, "Cécile, do you remember when I bought the plantation?"

"Of course," she chirps. "It was 1763, the year Spain took over from France. You needed land grants from both the French and Spanish authorities and had to draw up the contract in French, not Spanish, because Spain hadn't yet set up a civil service. Surely you remember!" She waits for a reply, but receiving none says in disparaging tone, "I can't believe that you should have forgotten something so basic."

He manages a grunt. Let her think what she will. Through the burning in his head, he feels a stab of envy at her mental agility. Again, trying to rise and failing, he looks over to Agathe pleading for help. As she approaches, he feels a surge of relief. She is reliable, will get him up the stairs to bed, will look after him, and give him muti[47]. He'll feel better tomorrow.

---

[47] African word for medicinal compound.

Cécile's Prayer

Plantation, Louisiana

Cécile watches Agathe help her husband to his feet; she knows that a good wife would probably have lent a hand, but she doesn't feel like it. Through the open door from the porch into the house, she sees Agathe steer her master across the hall toward the divided staircase. As they start the ascent, he has an arm over her shoulders and leans on her; she has one arm around his waist and grips the bannister with the other hand. He has lost weight in the past week and although Cécile can see that Agathe is a strong woman, she is still much smaller than the chevalier, and it wouldn't be surprising to see them both tumble down the steps to the bottom. *If they should meet their demise on this very day,* Cécile thinks, *it would suit me fine!* Yet it doesn't happen. With ongoing encouragement from Agathe, "You can do it, Master!" the disparate couple reaches the top step and disappears into the corridor.

Disappointed, Cécile gets up, goes to the porch steps, and looks down toward the river. She has only just arrived, but already longs for the boat that, when the arsenic has done its job, will carry her back to New Orleans. She crosses herself, closes her eyes, and wishing to ensure the wait will not be long, she prays to the *Vierge Marie*[48] to intercede on her behalf with the *Seigneur Jésus*. She promises to pray all the Mysteries of the Rosary and to give Father Joseph - the parish priest - a sizeable donation if her husband should die in the coming week.

Returning to her seat, she contemplates summonsing one of the slaves to turn her chair to face the river but thinks better of it. Sinking into herself, she reviews her most recent conversation with her husband. She sees his loss of mental acuity as a proof that the arsenic is working. On another level, it shocks her that he does not remember life-defining events. His mind was always as agile as a whip snake. (Whip snakes featured in her childhood spent in a chateau in southern France.)

---

[48]   The Virgin Mary

Cécile herself remembers the dates all too well; she remembers how her husband bought the plantation on a whim. He saw the sale advertised in a local New Orleans broadsheet, and the idea of a self-supporting operation appealed to him. As a French nobleman - albeit of lower ranking - he felt that owning swathes of land and countless slaves would enhance his status, and he was right.

Another factor that appealed to him was having the Mississippi at his doorstep. It's a river that for him has near-mythical status. He spoke about it often, and she remembers him once telling her about rip currents that could whip up out of nowhere making the waters unpredictable and treacherous. He offered explanations: the shape of the shoreline, sandbars, underwater channels, wave actions, and other factors she can't remember. He said that such currents could even pull strong swimmers out into the middle of the river and create serious problems for boats. "One should never underestimate the Mississippi" were his words. For her part, she would be happy never to hear that stupid name again and does not understand why no one has given such a major river a decent Christian name. Like it or not, though the river will be the quickest way to get her back to New Orleans when the time comes.

She turns her thoughts back to the time her husband acquired this godforsaken plantation. At the time, he was a successful merchant but knew little about agriculture. However, as a quick learner, he soon picked up what he needed to know. He comes from an entrepreneurial family based in Bordeaux but had lost touch until recently when a certain Émile, claiming he was a cousin, wanted to establish business ties.

It seems that - although of Jewish ancestry - those of the chevalier's immediate family had drifted away from Judaism, assimilated to French ways, and became Catholics. To the outside world, the chevalier has always presented himself as a Frenchman of noble lineage. No mention has ever been made of Judaism. She wonders how this Émile person might change the situation, but one way or the other, it won't affect her seeing she will soon be a widow living in France. Jacques can cope with any new situation as he sees fit.

From the back of the house, an astonishing sound interrupts her musings. Someone is singing a French folk song, one of her husband's favorites. Quite beautiful! Who can it be? She snorts as the realization hits her that her husband must have taught that song to one of the house slaves! She feels the gall rise. Her husband is unconscionable! Does he not realize, no matter how strong and beautiful the voice might be, it is not something to encourage in a slave? In addition, it is not something her son Jean with his obsession for ethnic music should ever hear. He might fall in love with the owner of that voice!

She resolves that the best way to stop the singing will be to wait for Agathe to reappear and get her to put an end to it not just for now but forever. The incident reminds her of the Choctaw slave, who looked after Jean as a young child and taught him the heathen songs of her own people. When Cécile discovered what was happening, she had stormed into the nursery and had the girl locked away until the next slave auction. She told Jean he was never to sing her songs again. Yet even though he obeyed, he had retained a fixation for primitive music whether native Indian or African.

The singing stops, but Cécile's thoughts remain with Jean. Poor Jean! He is a lovely boy, intelligent, too, but without a practical bone in his body. He always had an academic flare but allowed Jacques to bully him and make him appear like an idiot when he is not. For some reason, he is petrified of Jacques; he bumbles in his presence and makes himself look as stupid as Jacques says he is.

Cécile flinches as she thinks how Jean's fear of Jacques might have something to do with Jacques dropping him when he was a baby. The incident is shrouded in mystery, but the slave present at the time maintained that Jacques actually threw the baby to the ground. Whether that is true or not, Cécile knows that Jacques *was* jealous of the *intruder* who received more attention than he did. He might indeed have taken what he considered suitable action.

The clamor of a pack of barking dogs interrupts Cécile's musings. She is not accustomed to such things. In New Orleans, dogs come in singles, not in frightening numbers. She turns to the slaves standing in the shadows, beckons to the one her husband was eyeing earlier - Adrienne. The girl appears to have just returned from somewhere. Perhaps she was the one singing.

"Why are the dogs making such a noise?" she demands of the girl in the haughty voice she has tailored for lesser beings.

Demure, eyes to the ground, the girl replies, "It is time for their food, Mistress. They are fed every day at this time."

The answer surprises Cécile. She has often heard that plantation owners keep packs of dogs to chase down runaway slaves and has heard too that those dogs should not be fed regularly. That makes them vicious, a desirable trait for slave catching. When Jacques takes over - it shouldn't be that long now - it will be a nasty surprise for both slaves and dogs! She smiles, which - because of her rotting teeth - she rarely does in the presence of others.

Ignorance

Liverpool, England

Tom and Ambrose have met at the corner table in the Merchants' Coffeehouse. It is early in the day. The density of tobacco smoke is not yet as thick as it will become, and the traffic on the Mersey is still visible. The two men are a mismatched pair: one red-haired, big, and burly; the other, small and timid with the lower part of his sleeve pinned over his stump.

Tom is saying. "Ambrose, you once mentioned how little the educated public knows about the treatment of slaves in transit, so I've been testing the matter and find out they know nothing! Worse they aren't even interested!"

"I suspected as much. They probably say rumors of squalid conditions are lies put out by abolitionists and - even if conditions are squalid - it wouldn't matter because blackamoors aren't human and don't suffer or have emotions like we do."

"Exactly!" Tom burst out. "That is exactly what they say! It's outrageous! In my years of service on *Spirit*, I have seen black women comfort their children. I have seen them sing dirges and heard them tell stories and communicate with mime when they have no language in common with their fellow slaves. These are things humans do and not animals."

Ambrose, who has been half-listening to an exchange at another table, nods in the direction, saying, "That group is discussing that very subject."

Tuning in, Tom hears a gentleman say in an educated drawl, "Blackamoors are another species. They run around naked; worship demons; don't have libraries, coffeehouses, machines, or canals like we have. Even the best of them can't read or write."

Listening in, Tom feels let down by those, to whose ranks he aspires. None would have set foot on a slave schooner, and few would have seen a black other than as a woman's pet or in a freak show. Yet they feel it is their God-given right to judge and inflict those judgments on others. He longs to castigate this ignorant stance, but how?

As he looks across at the table in question, the sight of so many big, well-dressed men is too much for his still fragile ego, and his righteous anger fizzles away. He wonders if puny, shy, and self-effacing Tom Brown will ever be able to swim against the current even though, as a libertarian, he knows he is a person of value. Perhaps he will have to give up on his dream of acquiring a voice that will force others to listen.

Stanley Spring Cleans

Aberdeenshire, Scotland

Stanley is up early and clad for the outdoors. He needs to find Wee Johnny, who should be in the farmyard. Servants move around in the house, but he manages to yank open the hall door and to slip out unnoticed - even without waking Angus McCorm, who now has a bed in the drawing room. Standing outside, Stanley stretches and looks around. With the last remnants of snow gone from the glen, the stream is a mere thread of silver gleaming through the morning mist.

Stanley loves the land with its heather, crags, and bracken and always fancied the idea of becoming laird. However, as his discontent has continued to grow, the yearning for that overseas plantation has become more insistent. The prospect of realizing the dream, thanks to Émile and Uncle Aaron, has been a godsent, and he has been eagerly awaiting a reply to Migu's Offer of Purchase. However, now standing in front of his ancestral home watching the eagle seeking out the thermals, the scene leaves him wondering if given the opportunity, he might not forfeit the plantation in favor of his ancestral home.

There is still something in him that wants to put into practice those new ideas of James Anderson, Scottish agriculturist and major figure in the Scottish Enlightenment. Stanley admires Anderson, who applies scientific principles - research, evidence, personal experience, and causation - to every subject including religion. Anderson has a farm of 1,300 acres here in Aberdeenshire, and by applying scientific methodology to agriculture has achieved exceptional results. He has also invented a small two-horse plough to replace its predecessor, which was a monstrous engine drawn by a string of oxen. Surely, Gramps would see the benefits, but alas . . .

Turning away from the scene, Stanley starts out toward the farmyard. As he goes, he reminds himself that Gramps' pigheaded refusal to consider *newfangled nonsense* is so deeply ingrained that, while he is still at the helm, innovation can never succeed. It would be a mistake to succumb to the temptation to give up on the Louisiana plan.

Turning his thoughts to Wee Johnny, his eyes scan the bustling farmyard without finding any sign of the lad. Stanley and Wee Johnny have known each other since they were bairns; they learned the bagpipes together, and vied with one another at Highland dancing. Stanley though was and is boss; he gives the orders.

As he heads for the farmyard, he passes the family chapel and the tiny graves of his stillborn siblings that nestle beneath an old Scots pine with orange bark and blue-green needles. There is a bench here on which his mother often sits communing with the tiny personages that no one knew but she, who had carried them in her body. Stanley for his part never lingers.

Passing icehouse and smokehouse, giving a brief greeting to those he sees en route, he stops at the stables, a place where he wouldn't mind lingering with the big-bodied Clydesdales that nuzzle at his arm and cheek. He needs to find Wee Johnny though. The groom suggests he try the smithy.

As he takes the shortcut through heather and bracken, Stanley begins to suspect Johnny is intentionally avoiding him and tells himself that if any of his slaves behave like this, they will regret it! While his parents disapprove of slavery, he has always liked the idea of having people cater to his every whim. He thinks of the words of the poet William Cowper who wrote that the moment a slave takes his first breath of British air, he is free and his shackles fall. It sounds noble, but Stanley feels ideals put into practice are often tiresome.

Reaching the smithy, he sees the attendants trying to soothe the irascible stallion but sees Wee Johnny isn't among them, Stanley carries on to the cart shed. It's a place where antiquated farm equipment is stored and where - to get the noise out of the house - his mother used to make him practice the bagpipes. An ancient beech stands nearby and - when it leafs out - the leaves will hide the shed entirely. That suits Stanley because in the milder weather, he uses the shed as a love nest. Last year, he was even there with a lassie at the end of September.

The walls of the shed are three-foot thick and date back several centuries. They are made from rough-hewn local stone pierced in front by two great arches. More important for Stanley's purposes are the wooden stairs at the back, which lead to a loft originally used for grain but now are only used by Stanley. With local lassies coming into bloom every spring, it has proved idyllic.

Stanley does sometimes worry about the consequences of these trysts, but so far has considered himself lucky that no bairn has put in an appearance. It now occurs to him, though, that if Mums again miscarries and a bairn should result from one of Stanley's trysts, that bairn might be useful to Gramps, who would have an heir of his own flesh and blood to replace Stanley.

As Stanley wrestles with the heavy door, he is starting to feel things are falling into place. If he could provide the family with a backup candidate for the lairdship, he would feel less guilty about abandoning Glen Orm for Louisiana. He hopes Mums will not miscarry again, but the odds aren't good.

Inconvenient Conscience

Edinburgh, Scotland

Mounting the steps to his front door, Sir George remembers the time in January when he kicked the dog. The wretched creature pops into his mind every time he comes home. He even thinks he has seen it a couple of times but has never been sure; he suspects it might be a mechanism that his mind has chosen to shame him.

Glad to be home, he fits his key into the latch and enters. Shutting the door quickly behind him, he says in a stern voice, "Stay outside, dog!" Having spoken and having left the cool and damp behind, he starts to feel better, especially as the light from one of the new oil-filled streetlamps streams in through the transom lighting the entire hallway.

As he rids himself of his damp overcoat, his elation at the miraculous age in which he lives banishes all vexing thoughts. Alleviating the unrelenting tyranny of darkness is something earlier generations could never have imagined. He feels like letting out a whoop of jubilation the way Aaron Migu did at the original launching of *Spirit*. However, as Sir George now reminds himself, he's a gentleman and gentlemen don't wake their housekeepers in the middle of the night with whoops of jubilation about streetlamps! Sir George regards it as his duty to set a high standard for the lower classes.

Once in bed and again subjected to the tyranny of darkness, his elation dissipates. The bogey inside him is again asking, "What sort of person are you to allow yourself to flourish on the fruits of evil?" He tosses and turns, losing his nightcap, which falls to the floor. He wonders what makes him feel guilty about things that don't bother others. That is especially the case seeing that, beyond supporting his extravagant family, every penny of his slave-trade money benefits the king and country! It's unfair that he, such a pleasant little fellow, should be plagued by shame and guilt.

With nothing he can do about the situation, he swings his legs over the side of the bed, scrabbles around in the dark for his nightcap, finds it, and pulls it over his head. Then feeling his way to the chest at the end of the bed, he extracts the bottle of Jamaican rum that he has hidden there. It's a nightcap that will serve him better than the one on his head.

An Earl in Sight

Leith, Scotland

Rose settles in a chair opposite her mother, Betta. They are upstairs in the bay window that looks down onto their little garden.

Rose says, "Ma, I wish Pa would finally tell Uncle Pontefract that Stanley and I will not be marrying each other. I want to be looking into suitable substitutes, and nothing can happen until that previous agreement is officially canceled. Lady Abigail tells me that she knows of a suitable earl."

Betta interrupts, "Who is Lady Abigail?"

"Ma, for heaven's sake!" Rose exclaims in a voice of genuine shock. "Lady Abigail is in this house every day teaching me etiquette, French, and Italian. She's a lovely person and has told me about a suitably titled young man whom she feels might suit me. I'm wondering if Pa might know the family."

"He does know members of certain upper-class families. The other members of the *Spirit* consortium are of that ilk. However, seeing that he has so little respect for the upper classes and enjoys heckling them, it would reduce the chance of any of them accepting you!"

Rose, in the voice that she has perfected under the direction of her governesses, says, "Mother, as I've said before, I want a husband with a title and won't back down. As to Father's heckling, that must stop. As to me being rejected because of past heckling, you'll find that money in the quantities Father can provide will smooth many a ruffled feather!"

"You might have difficulty persuading Pa to cooperate."

"Ma, Pa is a pragmatist and will adapt."

Betta sighs. When it comes to assessing her father, as always, Rose is right; Aaron will adapt. He has no problem doing an about-face if circumstances so require. She, Betta, is the one who would have difficulty adapting. She knows she would not manage well in the elitist circles to which Rose aspires. She is too shy and self-conscious to interact with those of noble birth. Even the various governesses frighten her. All are from highborn families, albeit families with financial difficulties.

Feeling a now familiar pain in her side, Betta thinks it might benefit her family if the malignant thing she feels growing inside her should prove lethal. A graceless mother would only be a liability to Rose.

Rose is watching her mother with a curious expression on her face. Betta must make sure the little vixen doesn't start "reading" her the way she reads her father!

Conundrum

West Coast of Africa

As so often, Big Baba sits under the banyan mulling over the Thimba/headman issue. Two months have passed since he gave Thimba what he felt would be a *short* respite, and for weeks now, he has been expecting the warrior to declare his readiness to court. Yet it hasn't happened, and Baba is having nightmares about unleashing the hired hitmen. Ever the optimist, he had initially hoped that if Thimba had made the necessary adjustments right away - taken a new wife and impregnated her - Baba would have been justified in nominating him as headman, but alas . . .

Today Big Baba's throne faces the village instead of the ocean, and he's grateful for a minor distraction - Efia in the distance organizing the women and their paraphernalia for an outing to the clay deposits. It is a long trek, but the red-ochre clay found on the savanna can be used for pottery, as a mosquito repellant, as a warrior war paint, and as a hair fixative.

Efia as always has been quick and efficient in getting everyone organized, and the party is already setting out. Baba watches as the women and their children wend their way along a path through grass that is starting to sprout at the bottom. All have containers on their heads and are probably singing, but are too far away for Baba to hear.

With both Efia and the headman issue on his mind at the same time, Big Baba has a strange thought, *I can nominate Efia for the job of headman! She always is a good organizer and has authority.* His lips twitch in amusement that such foolishness should enter a man's head - a woman as headman! Women give birth and nurture families; they grow crops, forage, and provide marketable goods. They don't have time for other things.

Although Big Baba has heard itinerant traders speak of matriarchal societies, it is not something he can imagine. In his tribe, those with authority - head of a family and members of the Elders' Council - have always been men. A headwoman is unthinkable! However, because of a lack of a headman, certain matters are starting to slip; matters that Efia could easily remedy.

Council allots every family a piece of land to grow food and keep small livestock. In return, they must share a certain amount of their produce with the community as well as lend tools, work together on one another's land, participate in one another's hunts and fishing forays. Now though without a headman to perform routine checks, several families are taking advantage of the situation and shirking their communal duties. Big Baba has been receiving complaints. Such matters should not be allowed to slip, and Efia would have no trouble setting them back on track.

There is, though, a problem with appointing Efia even on a temporary basis as an interim headman. It would be a slap in the face for Thimba. Baba shakes his head. It's absurd to even imagine that Thimba would tolerate such a loss of status, yet if he doesn't behave in the manner expected of him, Baba sees no option. Virility in all its facets, especially in the ability to father countless children, is a kingpin of warriorship. It would be much simpler if Thimba just did what needs doing, whether he likes it or not. Surely it can't be that hard for him!

Another distraction! He is glad for any respite, even if the distraction is the *bad boys* kicking around something unspeakable. They are throwing bits of it at one another and onto the roofs of the huts. It seems to be the rotting corpse of an animal. Baba clicks his tongue. With Kwame as their ringleader, this group of adolescents is proving harder to handle than most. Kwame, as Thimba's younger brother, should know better. Instead, he is more creative in the mischief he instigates than any other teen rebel Big Baba has known. It's lucky that Thimba is the one training him.

No sooner have Big Baba's thoughts returned to Thimba than the massive form of the warrior materializes, storming down from the butchery and bellowing from a distance. The boys stop what they are doing, cringe as Thimba thunders into their midst, doles out blows, and bashes a few heads together. Then manhandling the petrified miscreants into single file, he marches them up to the butchery, where he'll give them the nastiest job he can find. It's usually one that requires the use of urine and feces to soften leather.

Baba is full of admiration for how Thimba has handled those skellums. Not many would manage as well. The tribe can't afford to lose him! *He is one of our most valuable assets,* Big Baba tells himself, not for the first time. Putting Efia in as a substitute, regardless of the capacity, would not be a satisfactory solution.

Thimba Sharpens His Spearhead

West Coast of Africa

Today guilt has gained the upper hand, and Thimba knows he has to speak to Baba. He goes down to the shade of the banyan to sharpen a twenty-inch metal spearhead. It is something warriors do when wanting an informal chat with the senior elder.

Crouching on the ground, while Big Baba - in the company of Inja, the *hookoos*,[49] and goats - watches from a distance, Thimba extracts his sharpening stones from their leather pouch and starts on the job. Holding the spearhead steady and first using the grittiest of the three small pebbles, he makes small circular motions along the metal edge. He must make sure he keeps the spearhead at the correct angle and that he uses only the flat part of the pebble.

It is not easy, and although his concentration is on the job, he is still marginally conscious of his surroundings - the sounds of hammering and chipping from the sculptors' area and the pounding of the surf from the unseen beach. Meanwhile, Big Baba sits silently and watchfully, as Thimba swops pebbles moving on to the one of medium grittiness and ending with the smoothest.

Blowing dust off the edge of the spearhead, he tests it with his forefinger; it is it should be. Getting to his feet, he rubs his hands to rid them of dust. As he does so, he closes his eyes and asks Masimbarashe to help him with the coming encounter. Although Masimbarashe gave him a plan to solve his problem, he needs the giant eland hunt to fulfil it and that hunt does not take place until the beginning of June. Meanwhile, Big Baba wants action *now*.

Going over to where Big Baba sits, he bows his head as tradition requires and says, "Baba, as is my duty, I'm ready to begin courting. I

---

[49] Chickens

should though like to request that you allow me to delay until after the giant eland hunt. It wouldn't seem right to have just acquired a new wife and then to leave so soon."

Big Baba does not reply, so Thimba carries on, "I know you've been patient with me, Baba, but I want to get it right. After the hunt, I'll start courting. I've already . . ." Before getting himself into deeper water, he stops.

Baba, who has had his eyes focused on the horizon, returns his gaze to Thimba. Staring him straight in the eye, he says, "Son, as you know, I was hoping for an earlier resolution, but seeing that you came here of your own volition and are showing good will, I'll give you the time you request. You must realize though that people are already asking me why you aren't taking more wives, and I can't keep them at bay much longer."

Second Half of April 1800

You Are Mine!

Plantation

Drifting in and out of consciousness, the chevalier lies in his canopied bed facing the open window. A pleasant breeze wafts up from the Mississippi and against the light. He sees Agathe sitting and knitting him a nightcap. He likes having her in the room; her presence comforts him. She has featured in his life since the day of her birth. She was the first African slave born on the plantation. It was at the time he had decided to use black slaves instead of the native Choctaws, who delighted in flaunting his authority. Besides, they belonged to the land and knew it so well that they escaped with ease.

When the chevalier poured out his woes about the Choctaws to a visiting Spanish administrator, the Spaniard had told him that blacks being in a foreign land made better plantation slaves than the locals. He remembers the conversation well. He and the Spaniard, who had a pointy beard as was the Spanish fashion, had been sitting on the rickety porch, which predated the building of the Big House. By the light of a half moon, they had drunk rum and kept the mosquitoes at bay with Cuban cigars. Meanwhile, the guest had described the confusion black slaves felt on arriving in a distant land across the ocean. It was something that worked in a plantation owner's favor.

The chevalier had listened as the Spaniard speaking in flawless French had said, "Each slave is deliberately sold apart from his tribal members. This means that when he arrives on a plantation, there is no one with whom he has a language in common. Each slave is an island unto himself and is severed from everything he has ever known. He doesn't know where he is, what has happened to him, what he is meant to be doing, or what the future might hold. Beaten, abused, and starved, he has no one with whom to share his anguish. In other words, he has become the perfect slave."

The chevalier was apprehensive about the switch to blacks, but the words that clinched the matter came as the Spaniard - swigging back the last of the rum - said, "Blacks are the best breeders and will provide you with more future slaves than the natives."

The chevalier had attended the next slave auction and purchased a handful of blacks newly arrived from West Africa. Due to difficulties of capture and transport, they cost more than Choctaws, but with the first birth, the purchase started to bear fruit. Advised of the birth, he had hurried down the path to the slave quarters and arriving at the cabin, he remembers the midwife holding up the tiny scrap of humanity for his inspection. He had placed his hand on the infant's head and said, "You are mine, child. I name you Agathe."

On the Job

Plantation, Louisiana

Riding along the side of the field, André sits high on Pégasse and checks the slaves who harvest the cane. He has done the harvester's job himself and knows the issues. The master had insisted, before making him chief overseer, that he try all the jobs himself.

Slogging along in unrelenting heat, the cutter armed with a machete[50] must work through rows of twenty-foot cane. He must slash through stalks as thick as his arm, then chop off their plumes and strip them of leaves, the edges of which are as sharp as razors and slice into flesh. There is no respite; sweat pours from the body, stings the eyes, and etches paths through dust-clogged skin. There is no guard against mosquitoes or flies and no protection from the vengeance of ousted spiders or snakes. A whip-wielding overseer strides alongside and, always on the lookout for loafers, yells and curses.

An alternative method the chevalier had sometimes used to harvest the cane was to burn a field, so as to free the stalks of their plumes and razor-edged leaves. That though meant smoke and soot wreaking havoc over the rest of the plantation.

Doing the harvester's job, André had always felt he would have lost both sanity and his humanity had he not known that for him the drudgery of the cane fields was temporary. For those he now sees working their way along the rows with their machetes, this - and equally objectionable jobs - is the only type of work they will ever know for nine hours a day and seven days a week right through their lives. To hope for anything different either for themselves or for their children is unrealistic.

---

[50] Large cane knife

The overseer in the present instance has become expert at cracking his whip above the heads of the slaves but without touching them. André suspects the explosive sound of the cracking whip might damage human hearing, but it is an improvement over using the whip on flesh as used to be the case. The present overseer - like André - is one of the master's coffee-colored kiddies, but he is one with a different mother and one who hasn't met with either the master's full approval or with his full disapproval.

Pégasse is swishing his tail against the flies and wants to move along faster, but André is not yet ready and keeps him in check, so they don't outpace the reapers. Meanwhile, he wonders how resentful his coffee-colored half brothers are about the master having chosen him, André, from their ranks and vested more power in him than in any other of the coffee-colored kiddies. Outwardly, he sees no signs of envy or resentment, but who knows what festers beneath the surface?

Reaching the end of the row, André sweeps a practiced eye over the entire scene, noticing that the horse-drawn cart, which carries the cauldrons for the midday meal has pulled up at the far end of the field. From noon to one, the field hands will have a break for their midday meal, often their only meal of the day. It is usually of the stew type with meat, vegetables, gravy, and some sort of starch, such as hominy,[51] or grits.[52] The cooks ladle the meal into waist-high troughs around which the field slaves stand and eat with spoons. While the quantity is usually sufficient, the quality is often wanting.

André consults his pocket watch and is glad nothing more needs his attention. It means he can get back to the yard and attend to the dogs. They are fed once daily with the same food as the field slaves. It is André though who ladles the stew into the dog troughs, not the cooks. He must be the one who feeds them so they know that he is the master and that they must obey him and no other. He is the only one who can

---

[51]   Grits that uses a treated type of corn

[52]   Cornmeal

give the order to attack. Not even the chevalier, who is not a regular presence in their lives, has that type of control over the pack. The master only visits the plantation periodically whereas André is a constant.

With respect to the dogs, the chevalier only uses the pack for hunting. André knows though from his mother, Agathe, who knows from conversations at dinner parties that Master Girrard uses his dogs to hunt down runaway slaves. The chevalier uses bounty hunters for that purpose, and instead of punishing the returned fugitives with the amputation of a limb, whipping, or branding, he sends them off to the slave auctions. He feels that incapacitating a slave makes the slave unmarketable, whereas able-bodied slaves fetch good money.

Cantering back toward the farmyard, André passes through the field slaves' quarters, which are far larger and more meager than the house slave's quarters. Seen from the main thoroughfare, the ornate forms of the whipping post, pillory, and stocks stand out against the darkness of the bayou. Although they have rarely been used since André became chief overseer, the chevalier insists the instruments of punishment remain in pristine condition. He believes they then serve as a deterrent better.

With respect to punishment, the chevalier doesn't mind what methods André uses to control the slaves. Delivering good results is what matters, and André has been doing that although he has been using less corporal punishment than in earlier times. Under André's watch, the sugarcane production, raison d'être for the plantation, is showing a rise in productivity while the general farm not only keeps the plantation self-sufficient but also provides excess for the market in Baton Rouge.

Elusive Voice

Liverpool, England

At the coffeehouse seated as part of the group in which Tom and Ambrose have become regulars, Ambrose jumps into the fray. Sitting forward in his seat, he says to an elderly gentleman, his tone respectful, "I've heard you say, sir, that blacks aren't human, that they are a species of ape. It is an interesting statement, given that some scientists maintain that the entire human species evolved from apes. That would mean all of us have apes in our family trees."

Tom thrills at the audacity of such thinking, but others don't share his enthusiasm. Cries of outrage follow Ambrose's words. A stranger from a nearby table jumps to his feet and without a *by-your-leave* or *may-I-join-you,* approaches the table and declares in a strident voice, "The theory of evolving species is nonsense and warrants nothing less than burning at the stake! God created animals, and God created humans. The way they are is the way they were at the time of Creation. That's what the Bible says. To say otherwise is blasphemous and a violation of God's Word!" With jutting chin and bulging eyes, he challenges his audience.

A reporter from a local paper finally breaks the awkward silence by saying, "According to Bishop James Ussher, the first day of Creation took place at 9:00 a.m. on October 23, 4004 BC."

"How could he have arrived at that bizarre conclusion?" asks a curious bystander for whom there is no longer space at the table.

The reporter explains, "The worthy gentleman counted the generations listed in the Bible from Adam and Eve, then added them to modern history thus fixing the date with precision."

"Impressive!" murmurs a teacher.

SLAVES, MASTERS AND TRADERS   135

Tom remains silent as opinions flow fast and thick concerning the world as a specific act of divine and instantaneous creation that happened literally in the six days mentioned in Genesis. He notes, too, that no one has taken up Ambrose's exciting idea of the human species having evolved from apes. Everyone remains within the biblical framework as taught by the church for the past eighteen hundred years. The status of Adam and Eve as the literal originators of the human species remains uncontested, and no one uses the words *metaphor* or *symbolism*.

Tom has only recently discovered the importance of such words, and the idea of using concrete images to explain abstract ideas thrills him. He wishes he could speak up against the literal interpretation of the Bible. Yet when even great minds balk at expressing ideas that contradict church dogma, he wonders if he will ever be able to say what he truly thinks. It seems unlikely that he'll be able to cultivate a real voice when the Establishment, whose approval he courts, is as dictatorial and intolerant as is the church. Vilification is not the type of attention he needs.

Tom does not have long to brood on the depressing situation because Ambrose is reentering the debate.

He says, "A biologist, Erasmus Darwin, thinks the earth and life were evolving for millions of years before the existence of humankind."

"Heresy!" shrieks an apoplectic old-timer. "He should be excommunicated!"

"That, sir, is happening," Ambrose counters.

Tom notices for the second time how Ambrose expresses his own controversial opinions without drawing anger to himself. With his first intervention, he had said, "Some scientists now maintain . . ." and now he has said, "The biologist Erasmus Darwin thinks . . ." never intimating that he himself subscribes also to these theories.

Tom would like to try Ambrose's tactic and say, "Some people believe blacks are human, and it behooves us to treat them with dignity and help them advance." Yet he does not. He suspects that the words of a small, insignificant person with only half an arm would not carry the same weight as those of the big, handsome Ambrose. He hangs his head in dejection.

Back at their table, Ambrose stretches out his long legs and says, "You, Tom, were quiet, but I know you have opinions on the matters discussed. Why didn't you speak?"

Tom blurts out the problem. "I would like to have spoken, but my words would never carry the same weight as yours. I don't think I can ever develop a voice that anyone will take seriously."

Puffing on his pipe, Ambrose says after a while, "*Words* and *voice* do not necessarily involve speech. You should set your sights on becoming a writer. Robert Burton, a sixteenth-seventeenth century scholar, wrote, 'the written word strikes deeper than a sword.'"

After another pause, Ambrose suddenly flicks his fingers and says, "I've got it! You must become a writer who uses a pseudonym. That way you can express your opinions in print without anyone considering you a heretic. I realize though that it would take a while, but a concrete goal can never harm and you can start practicing getting your thoughts onto paper right now. In fact, I'll be looking forward to seeing how you have made out, when we meet again next week."

Tom gives his friend a broad grin. That someone like Ambrose should believe in him is well-nigh miraculous!

Caledonian Forest

Aberdeenshire, Scotland

With afternoon tea now a firmly established routine in the household, Frances, the old laird, Pontefract, and Stanley sit by the fire in the drawing room; Angus McCorm lies stretched out on his rug snoring softly.

As is often the case, the old laird intones, "Afternoon tea is a most civilized break in the day even though the idea originated south of the border."

"Hear! Hear!" echoes Stanley, scoffing down his third triangle of shortbread.

Pontefract, too, expresses his approval with a vigorous nod. Frances feels that, if she were a cat, she would be purring. Having Stanley and her father agreeing with one another, even if it is only about shortbread, is a pleasant change from the bickering.

She finds it surprising that small, homely details can make a difference in family life. When she read in the Glasgow paper that enjoying a snack and a pot of midafternoon tea was becoming fashionable in England, she liked the idea. To that point, like everyone else, the family had only eaten morning and evening. Frances had always found the twelve-hour gap too long, especially when, as now, she was with child; yet it had never occurred to her to have a snack between meals. That would have been a sign of weakness, decadence, and greed.

She ponders the stupidity of the attitude. At Glen Orm, they are among those fortunate enough to afford whatever food they want. Only recently has it occurred to her that voluntarily depriving her body of nutrition could be the reason for her miscarrying so often. She always assumed the reason was the stress of her father's expectations, but perhaps all along, she was the one at fault. With any luck, she has now rectified the problem, and this bairn will arrive hale and hearty.

The contentment that Frances feels is suddenly shattered by a potential bone of contention that she hadn't foreseen. It seems her father had sent Stanley off to a meeting, which he had not wanted to attend but to which he had finally agreed to please his grandfather. It concerned the endangered Scots pine, the principal feature of the Caledonian Forest that is succumbing to the ever-increasing demands of the ship-building industry. It is a subject about which Frances, the laird, and Pontefract feel strongly, and she has always assumed that Stanley agreed with them. Yet here is her father asking if anything came of the meeting, and Stanley is only replying with a disinterested shrug. The reaction shocks her.

In the awkward pause that follows the unanswered question, Pontefract comes to the rescue filling the void with the words, "Although it isn't much publicized, I've been told that our shipbuilders are bringing in lumber suitable for masts from as far afield as Canada."

Frances feels a surge of gratitude to her husband for skewing the subject away from Stanley's strange behavior. Thanks to the intervention, the discussion has turned to the different types of wood used for masts. Relaxing back into her chair, Frances thinks how Pontefract's conciliatory nature averts many a confrontation. He shows the same tact with Stanley when it comes to the subject of slavery, something that Pontefract strongly opposes. Frances has always been proud of him for amassing a fortune without reverting to the slave trade.

Sighing, Frances thinks it is not easy for people like her and Pontefract - those who believe in balance and respect for others - to live with those who don't share their views. It fills her with horror that their son should feel that slavery is fine and good. A further blow is now to discover that he doesn't care either about the thoughtless clear-cutting that is wiping out the Scots pine and with it the nine-thousand-year-old Caledonian Forest.

At this last thought, she suddenly sits upright in her chair. She is remembering how earlier in the afternoon - at the time of the meeting - she had seen Stanley from an upstairs window walking in the direction of the old cart house. Ergo, he had not attended the meeting at all! This would explain his noncommittal attitude to his grandfather's question. The young devil! She can't help an indulgent smile, although heaven knows what he would be doing in the old cart shed. He used to practice the bagpipes there, but he wasn't carrying them this afternoon, and besides, he hasn't played since his teenage years.

Plans for London

Edinburgh, Scotland

Along with the *Daily Universal Register* and the mail, old Ms. Young has just brought a breakfast tray up to Sir George's bedroom and withdrawn again. She never lingers. Now sitting at the table under the window, he sprinkles salt over his steaming oatmeal. He feels he needs a break after another abysmal night dreaming that mounds of dark clothing lay strewn over his front step. The night before it was a slave woman sitting at the end of his bed singing a lullaby to a dead child, and two nights ago, it was the dog limping behind him and wanting to humiliate him by sneaking into the club with him.

He wonders if he may be losing his mind, but as hot porridge starts to fill his stomach, he concludes that that is probably not the case. The dreams are just fragmented images created by a guilty conscience. Nonetheless, it might be a good time to take the London trip he has been resisting. A change of scene might put an end to the nightmares and obsessive brooding.

He needs to look at the London properties that Aunt Stella has lined up for his inspection and feels he could arrange the trip to coincide with the relaunching of the *Spirit of the Clyde* in Liverpool. For some perverse reason, he feels the need to attend that event. The vessel has become emblematic for the course his life has taken. He knows he will not be feeling the same urge to attend events pertaining to the *launching* of his eldest daughter Isobel into society next year, this being the reason for needing a fashionable address in London.

He is dreading the string of social events that his family will need to host every summer for years to come. Seeing he has five daughters and each in turn will need time in the limelight, his wife Lady McCallum - Jessica to her friends - has impressed on him that nothing but the grandest London address will do. The grandness of the house - so she tells him - will be commensurate with the nobility of the suitors that will appear at the door. Bearing this in mind, he has asked Aunt Stella to look into the matter of a suitable house and - as a dowager countess with time on her hands - she has been pursuing the matter with verve. In her last missive, she wrote that it was time for him to come and scrutinize the properties that she considers best.

Across the room where old Ms. Young left the mail on his dresser, he sees from the distinctive envelope that another of Aunt Stella's missives has arrived with today's mail. He'll open it when he's finished his breakfast. He scrapes the remnants of his porridge from the bowl and sets it aside, giving himself space to cut off a generous slab of the fresh loaf Ms. Young bakes every morning. As he does so, he reaches for the newspaper but rejects it again when an article on Wilberforce catches his eye. He is not going to spoil his breakfast with antislavery propaganda! With grim determination, he slathers more butter and honey on his bread than normal.

His thoughts turn back to the London trip. If it weren't for the balls, dinner parties, private concerts, and God knows what else that his family will be hosting, he would enjoy London between April and July. It is the time when the royal family is in the city and corresponds to a time when Parliament is in session. The gentlemen parliamentarians having left their country estates to be in London demand entertainment. Hence, all types of cultural events are featured at that time. It's the private events that his family must host - and for which he must pay - that bother him.

As he chomps on his bread, he thinks how it is not normal for people of his kind to feel such a disinclination toward events that are part of their given lifestyle, yet that's the way it is with him, and Jessica knows it. If he's lucky, she might allow him to stay in Edinburgh. Let her scoff - good naturedly - all she wants at his preference for perennially closed drapes, furniture shrouded in dustcovers, and the service of no one but old Ms. Young!

Wiping his hands and mouth on a napkin, he thinks - with a self-deprecatory chuckle - that his present line of thought has been just as disagreeable as reading about child labor, Wilberforce, and the working poor - subjects that so often are featured in the *Register*.

He gets up and retrieves Aunt Stella's letter from the dresser and, bringing it back to the table, picks up the bread knife to open it. He notices in the process that he hasn't yet had his second slab of Ms. Young's excellent loaf, but seeing he no longer feels like it, he hopes old Ms. Young finds good use for it; wastefulness is not a Scottish trait.

Staircase Talk

Leith, Scotland

With the household asleep - Rose tucked up in bed and the servants retired to their quarters - Migu and Betta mount the staircase to the bedroom floor. Their distorted shadows play on the walls as he holds up an oil lamp to light their way.

"Have you spoken yet to Pontefract about the Betrothal Agreement?" Betta wants to know as they go.

Although in the flickering light she can't gauge his facial expression, she guesses he doesn't like the question. After a pause, he says, "It's not easy telling one's best friend that our daughter would prefer to marry an earl instead of that friend's son. Nonetheless, I have made an appointment with Pontefract at his office for next week and shall do the necessary."

Stopping on the next step to rest, Betta sympathizes saying, "I understand. I wouldn't want to tell the Staymanns either. I do wish our Rose weren't so strong-minded - in that she takes after you, dear - but she is as she is and is getting fretful about you procrastinating. She now refers to you as Father not Pa, which shows her state of mind."

"Seeing we don't have a replacement for Stanley, I don't see why we have to rush, but as I said already, I'll be canceling next week," Migu replies.

"She'll be happy and start calling you Pa again and will also tell you that she already has a Stanley-substitute in mind," Betta informs him.

"I was hoping to line up some suitable substitutes, before we rush headlong into the matter," he replies. "Canceling the agreement is enough for now."

"Would your substitutes be earls?" Betta wants to know.

"Of course not! They would be suitable and personable young men from good backgrounds. She'll come around to my way of thinking when she meets a couple of them."

Betta, feeling a dagger-like pain in her side, stumbles at the top step. Migu has to grab her arm to prevent her toppling down the stairs. Holding up the lamp, he peers into her face with concern. "What's wrong, dear?"

"Nothing, except I should look where I'm going!" She knows though that something is seriously wrong with her health and embraces it, but needs to see Rose happily settled first. If it takes an earl to reach that goal, Aaron should not be raising barriers!

Neophyte

Leith, Scotland

Young William - the only boy in a family of girls - has inherited the title from his grandfather, the old Earl of Gryphon. He is twenty-one years old and now sits in the snug at the Trade Winds with Lord Richard. It is still early, and the pair has the snug to themselves.

Lord Richard likes a *wee dram* of Scotch after breakfast, and William - although not yet having acquired a taste for his country's national drink - has followed suit. He is feigning pleasure because he wants to stay in his lordship's good graces, for now anyway. Therefore, when Lord Richard asks William if he is ready for a refill, William pretends he is and offers to go out into the main area of the pub to fetch the drinks.

As he pushes through the door into the taproom with its noise, sawdust, and benches, William marvels at how - having reached the age of majority and inheriting the title of earl - his life has changed so drastically. The likes of Lord Richard now treat him as an adult and an equal, which makes it easier for him to find out about the covert slave trade. He is still uncertain what he should do about his grandfather's investments in the area. Should he hold on to the controversial assets or take the high road and ditch them? Lord Richard is obviously well-versed in matters pertaining to the secret slave trade but only speaks to those whom he likes and trusts.

Back in the snug, William has managed to empty most of his drink under the table, without Lord Richard noticing. His lordship now well-oiled is answering William's question about how the blackamoors react when they discover they have been conned and taken captive. He is saying, "I'm not sure how they feel about the situation, but one would assume that - like all wild animals - they resist tooth and claw."

William, thinking he would not much like being kidnapped himself, makes a face. Lord Richard notices and says, "We mustn't allow ourselves to overdramatize or assume blackamoors are like us. They are not like us. Even the lowest among the British lower classes wear clothes and balk at eating human flesh. While any form of trade is appalling, the slave trade is like trading cattle and horses. It's unfortunate that our class can no longer survive without involving ourselves in such things."

"I've never seen a black man," William says, "but I've heard of a lady who keeps a wee black laddie as a pet. He has a diamond-studded collar, and she leads him around on a leash."

"Ah!" comments his lordship. "I know the lady well! I gave her *Blackie* as a gift."

Outing

West Coast of Africa

Upon returning home to the family compound, Abebi throws herself onto the ground, pedals furiously with her legs in the air, and giggles. She likes the way her new anklets rattle.

"You seem to have enjoyed yourself," comments Efia, who sits outside the hut using a thorn needle and reed fiber to repair a kapok pillow. Big Baba - pipe in hand - sits nearby watching Abebi with an indulgent smile.

Abebi did enjoy the outing with an insect-gathering group led by Auntie Abena and now gurgles like a bird that she had just heard in the forest. She would have preferred to go deeper into the forest to explore on her own, but that's forbidden. That never deterred her in the past, but a few months ago, a boy of her age went too far, must have gotten lost, and has never been seen again. That frightened Abebi, and now she sticks with the group, which she still enjoys except for the excess of adult supervision.

Efia, using her teeth, cuts her thread and puffs the pillow back into shape, saying, "Why don't you tell Big Baba and me in a language we can understand what you did and what you saw?"

Complying with her mother's request, Abebi tells of a marching column of stinging ants. "They were like a river, Mammi!" she enthuses. "We also saw a pangolin that had climbed out of a tree to eat them, but when it saw us, it rolled up like a ball covered with blades!"

Baba puts away his pipe, and as he gets up and prepares to leave, he tells her, "Pangolins roll up like that when they are frightened. The *blades* are sharp scales. I hope you left the blighter well alone!"

"Yes!" Abebi wrinkled her nose. "He let out a bad smell, so I didn't want to stay!"

"He did that to chase you away," says Baba. "Ants are his favorite food, and you disturbed him."

"I'm glad she was with Abena," Efia comments to Baba. "The child never looks where she is going and might have stepped into the midst of those ants, and they could have killed her."

Abebi is now babbling away about the insect larvae they had collected and how it makes her sad that those larvae have to be starved in order to eliminate their gut content before they die. Efia doesn't comment; she knows if she tells Abebi that the larvae are one of the main components of Abebi's favorite stews - along with ginger, onion, melon, tomatoes, and salt - Abebi would never eat that stew again.

Efia and the Arabs

West Coast of Africa

Taking wares to the Mbaleki Village market - as those who have embarked on the present outing are now doing - takes a full day. The men have already set out ahead - sculptors with their carvings and fishermen with smoked and salted fish. Warrior-hunters, too, with pelts and hides are part of today's group. Thimba is among them, but he takes no goods for sale. Instead, accompanied by his adolescent trainees, he carries the obligatory gift of kola nuts for Big Baba's friend Mbaleki, senior elder of the eponymous village.

The women led by Efia - Abebi remains at home - are half an hour behind the men. They walk single file along a path through grass that is still short, but with the onset of the rainy season will soon reach their shoulders. Baskets on their heads and their hips swinging, they sing as they go. Efia for her part is enjoying herself. She loves these market days, especially as the high winds and stinging sands of the *harmattan* are over for the season. The women no longer need the long lengths of cotton cloth for protection and have reverted to their normal manner of dress - a brightly colored cloth around the loins.

Since Big Baba and Mbaleki brokered peace between the tribes, access to the markets on the plains has made a major difference to life in Banyan Village. It has made their world bigger and given them access to a wider range of nature's bounty. Efia loves the varieties of colorful produce more common on the savanna than in the forests: papayas, avocadoes, mangoes, huge starchy plantains, and small sweet bananas.

A greater attraction than the produce, though, is the presence of the Arab traders. Ingrained in Efia's memory is her first sight of them - she was still a young girl - as they appeared on the horizon. They started as tiny dots with strange silhouettes that as they got closer resolved into robed men with fierce faces and laden beasts called camels. These men brought with them wondrous metal wares: spearheads, axes, shovels, utensils, and platters, which they laid out on mats among the local produce.

However, the greatest attraction of the savanna markets was and still is the tales the Arabs tell around the fires at night; at those times, the Banyan villagers have to stay overnight on the plains. It is something that won't happen tonight but will be happening several times during the coming rainy season. These tales have exposed Efia to knowledge of worlds that she had not known existed. She would listen open-mouthed as the strangers told of vast distant kingdoms ruled by kings of untold wealth. Big Baba was always unimpressed by such tales, wanted no truck with the like. He felt that Banyan Village's small clan is better served governing themselves than depending on a single authority like a king.

Feeling that the basket that she carries on her head is slipping, Efia, without slowing her pace, reaches up with her naked arms - bangles glistening in the sun - and adjusts the coil on which the basket rests. As she makes the necessary adjustment, she recalls another tale that pertains to a great city that used to flourish on the edge of the desert to the north. Featuring high buildings made with mud, it became a center of learning where wise men recorded events and preserved the spoken word in signs called *writing*. She often thinks of that.

Something else that often occupies her mind is that the Arab traders have different beliefs to her people. She had always assumed that all humans were born with the knowledge that the world of the spirits exists alongside that of the living, yet the Arabs don't believe in spirits. While she can't get her mind around that aspect, she has no such problem with the mainstays of the traders' beliefs. Allah seems to correspond to Bondye, while the Prophet Muhammad seems to equate to Gran Legbwa. Yet without the mediation of the loas so intimately connected to an individual's life, Efia cannot imagine that a person like herself could ever mean anything to such grand personages as Allah or the Prophet. How could she feel as much at ease with them - so distant and impersonal - as she does with her loa, who is her own mother? How could she trust those distant entities, who when incarnated would never have seen the beach or banyan nor ever walked across the plains?

She feels a sudden impetus to see what will happen if she tries to speak directly to Allah. If she were seeking contact with a loa, she would do it in her mind by focusing on that loa and thinking of her problem of the moment. However, seeing that Allah is the equivalent of Bondye and one never addresses Bondye directly, she does not know how best to approach the matter. She decides it will be best to use her voice - her magnificent voice - and cries out, "Allah! A-a-llah! A-a-ll-a-h!" The sound reverberates across the plains while Efia waits to see what will happen.

All that happens is that Abena - her forehead creased in concern - comes scuttling forward from behind and asks, "What's wrong, Efia? Are you ill?"

Fifth Week of April 1800

Longing for Escape

Plantation, Louisiana

Cécile is passing another of those days that never end on the porch of this hellhole of a plantation. Reading the papers brought by the mounted courier from New Orleans has heightened her longing to get back to civilization. Never did she imagine there would be a time when she'd regard New Orleans as *civilization*! She is tempted to leave right now in the hope that the arsenic already administered has done enough damage to kill her husband.

Off and on through the decades, Cécile has wanted to take revenge for the humiliation accorded her by the slave mistresses and their half-breed brats, but she has never known how. Now though, she has found support from an unlikely source - her son Jacques. He has come up with a plan that will dispose of her husband and - Jacques doesn't know about this aspect - will allow her to return to France; something she has longed to do for the past forty years.

The chevalier has always had a low opinion of Jacques's abilities and has systematically kept him out of the New Orleans business. As a result, Jacques has seethed with resentment and frittered away his time while waiting for his father to die in order to inherit his substantial estate. On turning forty, Jacques had decided he'd waited long enough and would take action. When he told Cécile, she wanted to know how he would go about the deed. "With your help, *ma chère Maman,*" he had announced breezily."

It turned out that her role was to do what she is now doing - add a daily dose of arsenic to the chevalier's morning coffee. She had administered the first doses in New Orleans, and they are already having an effect - even if not as quickly as she would like. Jacques had, though, said that a gradual decline would look less suspicious than the sudden demise of a healthy man. Also as a safeguard against discovery, he'd decided the plantation was the best place for the poisoning to play out. It was sufficiently remote to prevent family and friends from poking their noses into the matter. Besides, the doctor in Baton Rouge was likely to be less competent than the doctor in New Orleans and less likely to relate the causes of the illness to its symptoms.

Cécile gets up and paces back and forth along the front of the porch. She hates thinking of all these unsavory details and of the circumstances that have put her in this position. She should never have married the chevalier and can't believe how naive she was back in 1760 when the chevalier - all bravura and charm - had come courting, and she had fallen in love with him and accompanied him to this hellish land. She'd believed that with him at her side, she could tolerate anything. *Hélas,* the moment she'd set foot in the new continent, she'd realized love was no match for the mosquito-infested hothouse of New Orleans. Ever since, she has had to live in the company of puffed-up colonials with their outrageous placées and Creole[53] retinues. There has never been a moment when she would not have preferred to be in France. She hates the New Orleans hodgepodge of races! Now though an escape is within her grasp.

She is not sufficiently naive to believe that France is still the place she knew in 1760. Revolution has since swept away the monarchy, but

---

[53]   Colored common-law partners and mixed race

with the young hero Napoleon now in charge, it will be safe for her to return home and live in a manner to which her noble birth entitles her. Life can never again be as it was under King Louis - at the thought of him, she crosses herself and mutters, "Que son âme repose en paix"[54] - but she'll be where she belongs and free of the provincialism of New Orleans.

Cécile still lives in the shade of the guillotine that stripped His Most Christian Majesty Louis XVI and Queen Marie Antoinette of their dignity and turned them into common criminals. Although seven years have elapsed, the scene as described by witnesses of the king's beheading still haunts her. She replays it now. Behind closed eyelids, she feels the whoosh of air as the blade falls, sees the blood gush as the head tumbles to the boards, and begins to roll before the executioner grabs it by the hair and holds it up to the masses. She hears the crowd roar as blood drips from the executioner's elbow.

The beheading of Queen Marie Antoinette - it took place several months after her husband's - occupies a place of equal prominence in Cécile's mind. She hears - as though she were there - the guards instruct the queen to undress in their presence. She sees how those guards shave her and dress her in sacking. She sees how the queen retains her regal bearing and how she holds her head high, as guards place her on a leash and lead her to the guillotine. As the crowd whoops, bellows and jeers, as they shout, "*Salope!*"[55] Her Majesty mounts the steps of the scaffold, and Cécile hears her speak her last words. She says to the executioner, "*Pardonne, Monsieur!*[56] It was not my intention." She had stepped on his toes by mistake.

Although still overwhelmed by the events that irreparably damaged her class, Cécile suddenly realizes - perversely - that the beheading of the king and queen are proof that the high and mighty can fall. That is

---

[54]   May his soul rest in peace.
[55]   Bitch!
[56]   Forgive me, sir.

what is now happening to her husband. He though deserves what she is doing to him, while Their Majesties did not deserve their fate. The thought convinces her that she should not risk the possibility of her husband recovering by leaving the plantation before he is dead. After all, the wait shouldn't be that much longer.

Still on the Job

Plantation, Louisiana

André, having checked on the harvesting, leaves Pégasse in the hands of the stable slaves and feeds the dogs now and turns his thoughts to his father. Baring his upper body and washing himself outside the kitchen at the tub provided by the house slaves, he grimaces at the thought that the chevalier's condition is not improving. His father hasn't left his bed since the day he and the mistress arrived weeks ago. In the meantime, the old man asks daily for André's presence at his bedside. According to André's mother, he keeps his eyes fixed on the door expecting André to step in at any moment. It seems unkind to keep him waiting and owning his father's old watch. André keeps it in his waistcoat pocket. He is able to arrive at the time Agathe stipulates.

The watch is an impressive timepiece featuring a heavy gold chain that curves across his stomach. The chevalier passed the watch on to him when he himself received something even more impressive - not only heavy gold but also bejeweled - in recognition of the services rendered to the Spanish authorities of *Nueva Orleans*. André recognizing the watch as a powerful status symbol consults it more often than necessary.

As he makes his way to the backstairs, he thinks of the expression on the faces of the field slaves when they see sun reflected by the gold. They seem to think that a Vodun deity has taken up residence. André rather hopes that will never be the case! He is frightened of Vodun deities, who can be nasty in the extreme.

When still a child at the time, Father Joseph came to the plantation regularly to preach and say mass. André would think that praying to the Catholic saints to intercede with the Almighty was the same as asking favors of Gran Legbwa. According to his mother Agathe - she only knows such things secondhand from her parents - Gran Legbwa and his cohorts serve Bondye the Great Unknown just as the saints serve the master's three-in-one God: Father, Son, and Holy Spirit. The two belief systems - Vodun and Roman Catholicism - sounded similar to André in his childhood and still do at times, but for himself, he prefers the master's system to Vodun. Saints seem kinder, more approachable, and less demanding than loas. That Christianity is a white man's religion is unfortunate.

Climbing the backstairs, André thinks how he would like to discuss these matters with the master and have him clarify certain issues, but he knows that Vodun is taboo, something he must never mention.

Desperation

Liverpool, England

Tom sits at his regular table in the corner by the window, the one that would have a view if the glass were clean and had not turned the Mersey into a dirty smudge.

He is at the coffeehouse today for an arranged meeting with Ambrose, who has not yet arrived. Tom has intended on showing his friend what he has written since they last met, yet he now sits at their table empty-handed. Reading through the work earlier, it had hit him that he would never amount to anything. What was he thinking by believing that he could be a player in a field dominated by true intellectuals? Delusion! How had he not understood that his God-given place in the world is to remain a nothing?

Filled with shame, he groans and holds his face in his hands. He can't face Ambrose, who believes in him. He must hide. Looking around like a furtive rabbit, he realizes it would be best just to leave and never to return. He still has a few minutes to spare before Ambrose is due. In a rush, he swigs back the contents of his half-full cup of coffee, returns an unread broadsheet to its place, and - with head down and notebook clasped to his chest - he makes for the door. There he bumps headlong into Ambrose, who being much bigger than Tom has to put up his hands to steady the distraught young man.

"Whoa, my friend!" he exclaims. "What's the hurry? I'm looking forward to seeing what you've written."

Tom blurts out, "I haven't brought anything, Ambrose! What I wrote is no good. I should be ashamed to show you."

"Oh dear! I see we have a crisis. Let's go and sit." Ambrose steers Tom by the elbow to their table, settles him in his seat, and before going to get coffee, says, "Now tell me what happened."

Sniffing, Tom explains, "I was researching the muses of Greek mythology: Erato, Clio, and Urania. Being so high-minded and pure, they intimidated me and made me feel like scum."

"They aren't meant to be like us. They're personified ideals. They are goddesses intended to guide and assist us in our creative endeavors. The idea is for us to appeal to them for divine inspiration. Erato would probably be the one you would need."

In a tone of disdain, Tom exclaims, "I wouldn't dream of appealing to any one of them for anything! You say they are goddesses, but I know nothing about goddesses. The church only teaches about God and the saints, and they don't run around naked like the goddesses I once saw in an art gallery painting!"

Tom is too absorbed in his own misery to see Ambrose suppressing amusement, but does hear him say, "Don't take these things too seriously, my friend. If you can't relate to them, ignore them, send them packing!"

Tom starts to feel better. He thought goddesses needed respect; now here is Ambrose telling him to send them packing!

He says, "I'd never be able to write a word with one of those arrogant dames hanging over me. I'd rather call to mind Sister Angélique's kindness and smile, but I fear I might tarnish her light with my drivel."

Ambrose holds up his hand, saying, "Stop! That's enough self-pity for one day! You need to get away. I have to go to the Royal Naval Hospital in Greenwich next week and shall be taking the mail coach to London on Monday. You could travel with me and visit your folks. Think about it."

Might be an idea, thinks Tom, as Ambrose goes to the counter for coffee. He has been feeling guilty about his folks and needs to visit. The journey is now easier than it used to be. Money from turnpikes is helping maintain the roads, and there are fewer bumps, ruts, and potholes than previously. Besides, as opposed to the lumbering stagecoaches, mail coaches only carry four passengers and can travel at speeds of ten miles per hour!

When Ambrose returns to the table, Tom says he would like to travel with him, adding, "I'd need to return here to Liverpool by the third week in May for *Spirit*'s departure."

"That gives you time to catch up with your folks, to check out speakers in Hyde Park, and find out what's doing the rounds in London's coffeehouses. It should get you out of the doldrums."

"I don't know about that," says Tom. "My folks tend to drag me down. It's not because they mean to. It's because of the poverty they have to endure."

"I hope you realize that if you battle on with your writing, when you become a proper writer, you will be able to give a voice not only to the slaves' problems, but also to those of your kith and kin."

This Ambrose, thinks Tom, *always tries to push me beyond my limits!*

Ambrose though has not finished and is saying, "If you'd start seeing yourself as a writer-in-training instead of an ill-bred cripple, in the course of time, you'll be able to save enough money to help your family and also to start thinking of marriage."

When Tom recovers from this outrageous suggestion, he hears his friend saying, "I'll miss seeing *Spirit* sail, but you could write it up for me."

When Tom gives him a dubious look, he adds, "But if you don't want to do that, try writing a few lines on something simple like the pencil - symbol of the writer's trade - or maybe about the albatross that is a good luck symbol for mariners. Such neutral topics might help you get started."

Albatross and Pencil

Liverpool, England

A few days later as darkness settles, Tom, careful to avoid street detritus, wends his way homeward. Although it was a beautiful day, he now feels cool night air nibbling at his neck and cheeks and longs to be back in his attic and to get going on his writing. He has recovered from his despair, feels confident, and is ready to go.

Reaching his street, he notices the lamplighter across the road. He carries a flame at the end of a pole and moves from post to post igniting oil in the lamps as he goes. His work makes the streets safer. Tom likes that idea. Could he use the image as a metaphor? He is hung up on metaphors!

Up in his attic, he lights his lamp and settles at the desk, which is one of his three bits of furniture along with a bed and chair. He likes his little garret. It resembles his cabin on *Spirit*, which he always regarded as a safe place away from the horrors of the holds. Thinking of it now reminds him of the good things about his life at sea and closing his eyes, he hears again in his mind the cries of albatross and gull; of buffeting wind, waves, and creaking hull; of jangling in halyard and rigging. He feels again the vessel moving underfoot like a live creature and . . . He pulls himself together. Enough is enough. He has a job to do. A page a night of his own written material is the task he set himself.

To celebrate the new beginning, he bought himself a new pencil and will now be using it for the first time. Unlike the regular graphite he uses for his daily note-taking, the graphite in the new pencil is encased in wood and will keep his fingers clean. He extracts it from its wrapping and opens his notebook at the place where he took notes on his research into pencils and albatrosses.

SLAVES, MASTERS AND TRADERS 163

Starting with pencils, he begins to review the materials, but his writing is so small and neat that his eyes begin to tire. Nonetheless, he persists and reads,

> *Pencil* - word from Middle English *pense,* from Anglo-French *pincel*, from Vulgar Latin . . .

Rubbing his eyes, he questions the usefulness of such information and concludes it has none. No metaphor springs to mind, and he cannot imagine such facts interesting to anyone.

Remembering a cube of caoutchouc that Ambrose had given him, he brightens. Ambrose had said at the time, "Use this as much as your pencil. Erasing all but the essential is the key to good writing." Tom dutifully erases the list but still hopes to find useable material in his pencil research and reads,

> Graphite - black lead - discovered before 1563 in Cumberland - storm uprooted oak, and shepherds discovered black substance they used to mark sheep.

This tidbit at least has some good organic images and a story line, but he still doesn't know how best to use them, so this information and what follows also falls victim to the caoutchouc.

Abandoning the pencils, he moves on his albatross notes. He always loved watching the huge birds as they followed in *Spirit*'s wake. He reads,

> The albatross uses feathers, muscle, and bone to harness the wind, which propels its body forward like a projectile. On land, it is clumsy, but in the air, it is a magnificent machine with the widest wingspan in nature of up to twelve feet. It glides better than it flies. By locking its wings in an open position, it catches the wind and without flapping can glide in long

undulations for hundreds of miles. It crosses oceans, circumnavigates the planet, and on occasion, will travel thousands of miles with a delicacy for its chick. It is possible that during a lifespan of fifty years, an albatross can clock up several million miles.

This information thrills him. He feels sure he can use it to write something good, but what? Could he use the facts as metaphors and weld them into a piece that includes Sister Angélique?

He had become hopelessly infatuated with this young nun, who had nursed him back to health in the New Orleans hospital run by the Sisters of the Ursuline Order. He was too shy to say anything to her about it and heaven knows what she felt. Perhaps, her kindness was merely an act of Christian charity, but with time, he has come to realize that her motivation isn't important. What he feels for her now is a love uncontaminated by the jealousies and possessiveness of carnal love.

His new pencil hovering over the blank sheet of paper, it occurs to him that he shouldn't be attempting to write about the ineffable. It would be like nailing an albatross to the deck to see how it flies. The albatross material therefore also falls victim to the caoutchouc, which is getting smaller. He will soon have to start using white breadcrumbs, which Ambrose says also work.

Seeing he is tired but refuses to go to bed until he gets something onto paper, he makes a snap decision. He will write about the accident on *Spirit* that got him into the hospital in the first place. He forgets about his notes, metaphors, and articles for the *Observer* and allows pencil to meet paper and thinks of nothing but his story.

He had been in the women's hold attending to a slave child when the storm blew up out of nowhere. He knew he had to get out of the hold in a hurry because crew members would be slamming closed the hatch to prevent water from entering. He packed up his kit as fast as he could and began scrambling up the ladder to the deck. He was nearly at the top when the heavy wooden hatch slammed down on top of him. His last memory was of his scream as he fell.

He heard afterward that he had been in the hold with the slave women and children all the following night and part of the next day. The wretched creatures would have had no love for their captors and because - unlike the men in the neighboring hold - the women were unfettered. They could have torn him apart, yet they didn't. Through the ravages of the storm, they had cared for him as best they could.

After the hatch crashed down, his next memory was of waking several months later to the glorious welcome of Sister Angélique's smile. That same smile still greets him on waking every morning and assures him that alongside evil much good exists in the world.

Putting down his pencil, he rubs his eyes and feels he might one day well end up with a tool that will allow him to fight for that good.

Awkward Conversation

Aberdeenshire, Scotland

As the family minus Pontefract wait for their porridge, Frances and Stanley sit in silence as the laird regales them with his recent sojourn in a friend's country house near Newcastle. He is saying how he didn't feel comfortable there because the servants laid out everything on the sideboard and then retreated, allowing the family to help themselves.

The subject being one of the old man's pet peeves, he harps on it all too frequently. Frances doesn't let it bother her, but knowing it bores and irritates Stanley, she tries to steer her father onto a subject of more interest by asking if his friend does any foxhunting. The effort badly misfires. Instead of talking about foxhunting, the laird begins holding forth about the type of farming practiced on the estate. At first, the new subject goes smoothly with Stanley perking up the moment the laird mentions the agriculturist Robert Bakewell, who by inbreeding his livestock and exaggerating desirable traits achieved spectacular results.

"Andrew," - the laird is speaking of his friend - "tells me that the weight of cattle sold at Smithfield has risen from three hundred and seventy pounds per animal to eight hundred pounds and that is on half the amount of feed. His sheep too are much larger."

Stanley speaks for the first time, saying, "In the Bakewell system, animals only have one purpose. For sheep, it is either meat, milk, or wool, never all three. For cattle, it is either beef or milk, never both. Did you try their beef, Gramps?"

"Yes, and it was good, but I also saw the type of cattle that provided those roasts. They have monstrous bodies, small heads, spindly legs, and a malevolent look in their eyes. Good roasts don't justify meddling with nature."

Frances watches in anguish as Stanley pushes his chair from the table and standing, says, "If you'll excuse me, Mums, I have things to do." He leaves the room as the steaming porridge is carried through the double doors from the kitchen.

Not an Illusion

Edinburgh, Scotland

In his spacious bedroom - it is the only room in the house without dustcovers and without permanently closed drapes - Sir George has finished his breakfast, and old Ms. Young has removed the tray and left. He sits at a small desk by the window preparing to write to Aunt Stella about dates and plans for his London trip.

He has prepared the pen he needs - it is from the flight feather of a goose - with a special knife and has angled the nib to produce a line of medium thickness. Pen in hand, inkwell open, and paper correctly placed, he leans back a moment to collect his thoughts. As he does so, he hears an unusual sound from the open window that looks out over Queen Street, named after Her Majesty Queen Charlotte. He loves the view but sees nothing out of the ordinary. Then the noise comes again, and he looks directly downward into the area of his own house, two floors below.

A sudden jolt passes through his body, and he straightens. What is that, which he sees poking its head through the area railings? Unbelievable! It can't be, yet it is the dog that he had kicked down the steps in late January! He had always assumed it was dead, but here it is now in broad daylight and no chance that this is his imagination or that he has had a drink or two too many. He has not had alcohol since before dinner yesterday.

He is still trying to assemble his thoughts when Ms. Young hobbles into view below carrying something from inside the house. She is whispering sweet nothings to the creature that is now wagging its broken tail and yipping a greeting. She breaks off a hunk of what turns out to be his leftover breakfast loaf and feeds the creature by hand.

It takes the offering delicately and chews as she waits until it is ready for more.

Sir George doesn't know what to do. He feels like blabbering; instead, he sets down the pen, closes his inkwell, and descends the stairs where he puts on his coat and hat and leaves for the New Club.

Pontefract's Place of Work

Leith, Scotland

Migu rarely visits Pontefract's place of work but is doing so today to cancel the Betrothal Agreement. Although the agreement is not of the type that has full legal standing, a formal cancelation is the correct way to release the parties involved.

Pontefract is poring over a blueprint with one of his engineers and has signaled to Migu that he will be coming out shortly. Migu meanwhile paces the waiting area that looks down onto a space where draftsmen and engineers work at tables. It's an environment very different to Migu's places of work, which are vast brick textile factories of the type referred to by William Blake as *dark satanic mills*.

In Pontefract's space, the atmosphere is one of tranquility in which professional men determine materials, specifications, and dimensions for bridges, roads, sewage systems, and flood-control projects. Migu's workforce comprises not only men but also women and children - thousands of them - who work day in and day out in airless machine halls exposed to the ceaseless and deafening clatter of heavy machinery.

As Migu takes a seat, he wonders if Pontefract's equanimity might be a product of the tranquility of his workplace. He has to wonder, too, what damage machine halls do to his employees. He himself cannot tolerate the conditions in his factories for any length of time but assumes that those who spend their working lives in such places become accustomed to them. Whether they do or don't, it doesn't pay to dwell on the matter, just as it doesn't pay to dwell on the rights and wrongs of the slave trade. He didn't invent these things. He merely takes advantage of what exists and will continue to exist with or without him.

Pontefract doesn't agree with this laissez-faire attitude; Stanley though thinks like Migu, and it is a blow to Migu that Rose rejects the laddie, but seeing he can't change her mind, he can only hope Pontefract who is now ready for him won't overreact. Now in Pontefract's office, Migu blurts out without preamble, "As per our long-ago agreement, I would have liked your Stanley as a son-in-law, but Rose has other plans, and I don't have the gumption to force my will on her. How do you and Frances see the matter?" Having said his piece, Migu - fearing his friend's reaction - keeps his gaze fixed on an engraving on the wall of what he assumes to be a Roman viaduct.

When his comment meets with silence and he sneaks a look at Pontefract, what he sees in his friend's face is more than he ever dared to hope for - an expression of the greatest relief!

"I, too," Pontefract confesses, "have been worrying about the matter but have procrastinated thinking you might be offended if we canceled."

Both burst into the uninhibited laughter of their childhood.

"What fools we are!" says Pontefract. "We should always say what's on our minds!"

Migu feels uncomfortable with that remark knowing he and Stanley should be confessing something far worse than the cancelation of the Betrothal Agreement. Neither though wants to give Pontefract the opportunity to nix the Louisiana deal before Migu's Agreement of Purchase has been accepted and become legal.

As he leaves the building, Migu resolves not to dwell on the negatives. He has canceled the Betrothal Agreement, and that's enough for the time being. He can worry about the Louisiana deal later. Besides, the Rose saga isn't over yet; he still has to try to persuade Rose that the Simmonds boy would be a better substitute for Stanley than the earl that she seems to have unearthed from somewhere.

Walking home, Migu finds the warm air invigorating. Bogged down in worries, he has not noticed that in the front gardens along his route, the pussy willow catkins, anemones, and bluebells are putting on a show.

"Vive le présent!" he says aloud before realizing he is talking French to himself! He clicks his tongue in disbelief. Amazing how that bâtard Émile - appellation Migu uses with affection - has the ability to worm his way into every facet of a person's life.

Lord Richard Warns

Edinburgh. Scotland

Young William, who is the new Earl of Gryphon, and Lord Richard Castleton have met in the lobby of the New Club and move toward the smoking room. As they go, Lord Richard inquires, "Are you still interested in accompanying me to Liverpool to see *Spirit* sail?"

Young William's response is immediate and enthusiastic, "Very much so, Lord Richard!"

Lord Richard looks pleased and replies, "It'll be in the third week of May."

"Will we see Mr. Migu there?" William wants to know as they enter the wood-paneled room with its coffered ceiling and leather chairs.

"He'll certainly be there, but we'll avoid him," replies Lord Richard, nodding a greeting at the only other occupant of the room, an elderly gentleman half-hidden in a cloud of cigar smoke.

"I've heard that Mr. Migu has an attractive daughter," comments William.

Lord Richard's expression transforms from benign to peevish. "If she is like her father," he snaps, "you would do well to give her a wide berth! I have plenty of better suggestions."

William backpedals and says in a conciliatory tone, "I meant nothing by the remark, Lord Richard. It just happens that family friends have been forced to allow their daughter Lady Abigail to earn a living as a governess. In that capacity - so Abigail has told us - she coaches the Migu daughter in etiquette, French, Italian, and music. She seems to like the girl - her name is Rose - and they have become friends. She says

Rose has a voracious appetite for everything her highborn governesses have to teach her."

Lord Richard gives his trademark snort and says, "I can only repeat. Keep well away from her!"

"Thank you for the warning, Lord Richard," says William, his manner suitably meek.

The truth is, he has had several *chance* meetings with Rose arranged by Lady Abigail on Princes Street and is now head over heels in love with her. Rose's blinding beauty combined with correctness - thanks to the governesses - a sharp mind, and a down-to-earth practicality are irresistible. Apart from the fortune that accompanies her, he feels he would do well by Rose. First, though, he'll have to work out how best to get around her father, who by all accounts has a poor opinion of the upper classes and would therefore not lay value on William's title. The title is the usual bargaining chip for this type of marriage, but he'll think up something that will suit this situation better.

Honey, Infana, and the Bad Boys

West Coast of Africa

At the Banyan Village market, Abebi stands near her mother watching Efia swop one of her coil baskets for honey. The young woman - Adjoa is her name - has just harvested it from a rock crevice in the wild. Abebi loves honey and can't take her eyes off the item; she sees nothing else.

Judging from the amount of honey Efia is receiving, Abebi knows her mother is exchanging a bigger basket than she normally would and wonders why. Mammi is no amateur when it comes to making the best deal for her family. The ensuing conversation reveals the reason. Mammi feels sorry for Adjoa and is asking if she has a papaya at home to cope with the problem. As Adjoa admits to not having a handy papaya, Abebi wonders what problem Mammi thinks a papaya might solve.

Only then does Abebi take her eyes off the dripping honeycomb and sees that the person in front of her is not Adjoa, who has a pretty face. This is an evil spirit with a bulbous visage that is uglier and scarier than anything in the mask store! With a yelp of horror, she hides behind her mother clinging to her hips.

Irritated, Efia takes a swat at her child, "Stop that nonsense, Abebi! What's wrong with you?"

Between sniffs and sobs, Abebi nods in the direction of the apparition that is examining Efia's basket. The eyelids are so swollen it is difficult to imagine the monster can see anything. "Mammi," she whispers, "is that thing a zombie?"

"Don't be so stupid, child!" Efia exclaims. "Adjoa has not become a *thing* or a *zombie* just because she's been stung by bees." Turning her attention back to Adjoa, she says kindly, "When I get home, dear, I'll bring you a papaya."[57]

As Abebi recovers her equilibrium and helps Efia pack up, she says, "I didn't know, Mammi, that bees are dangerous and that I must now hate them like I hate spiders and ants. I thought that because they make honey, they must be good bugs."

"They are good bugs, just don't steal the food they make for their babies! Remember, too, there is no honey without bees, so don't think we should go around killing them!" Efia is speaking in her preaching voice, which worries Abebi. She fears Mammi might be preparing for another attempt at *education*.

Fortunately, this is not the case. Efia settles down in front of the hut, and with Abebi crouching at her side, she carefully opens the banyan leaf that Adjoa had used for packaging. With a knife Mammi cuts off a small corner from the comb and pops the dripping offering into Abebi's mouth; she then cuts off another piece for herself. As they delight in the treat and lick their fingers, Efia says. "Should we cut off a piece for Infana and you can take it to his altar?"

Abebi purses her lips; she is not sure what to say. Her baby brother had loved honey, and she wouldn't want to deprive him of a treat, but he's no longer her baby brother. He's her loa, and she is not happy with his service. He doesn't obey her. She has told him several times what to do with the Bad Boy, but he doesn't listen. He doesn't deserve honey, yet she doesn't want to say that outright to Mammi, so she says instead, "Mammi, now that Infana is a spirit and doesn't have a body, he can't eat, so the ants would eat the honey."

Efia sighs, but cuts off a piece for Infana anyway. As she wraps it in a fresh plantain leaf, she says, "What you say is true, Abebi, but it is important to Infana that you sacrifice something that you like.

---

[57] Applications of papaya flesh are used for bee stings.

I'm not sure what happens to the offerings we leave for our loas, but I suspect Kwame and his friends might have something to do with their disappearance." Realizing her mistake - stoking Abebi's antagonism toward the bad boys is never a good idea - she stops midstream, but it's too late.

Abebi's chest swells in indignation as she splutters, "I've *told* Infana they are a *shooper*[58] and that he must *chaia*[59] them" - she pummels the air with her fists - "but he does nothing. He's useless!"

Efia, eyes wide, stares at her daughter in shock, says, "Abebi, you should *never* tell your loa what to do and *never* speak about a loa like that!"

Abebi doesn't understand why she should kowtow to her younger brother, whom in life she loved dearly. He for his part adored her and was always happy to recognize her as boss. Why then, now he's a spirit, should it be any different? She has never said anything about it because Mammi is touchy when it comes to Infana. Now though with her blood boiling at the outrage of Infana allowing the bad boys to eat his honey, she doesn't care. Glaring at her mother, she exclaims, "I want a new loa, one who listens to me and knows how to chaia bad people." She again pummels the air with her fists.

---

[58] Menace

[59] Hit someone

First Week of May 1800

Betrayal

Plantation, Louisiana

Today André is later than usual, and on arrival at the Big House finds his father asleep. He is about to return to his duties, but Agathe asks him to stay and to keep watch over his father while she checks on the household.

Standing at the bedside, André looks down at the frail figure barely delineated beneath the sheet. The head - it is engulfed in a nightcap - has so little substance that it barely dents the pillow. If his father had been awake, André had planned to tell him how improvements to the stables were now complete and how the body of a slave baby from upstream was found tangled in debris at the plantation's jetty. However, given that the chevalier now sleeps, André finds himself at a loose end. Not knowing what else to do, he settles on the chair by the bed.

Listening to his father's breathing is hypnotic and shifts him briefly to another plane. He sees the scene of which he is part as a third party might see it. He sees an old man asleep and a young man sitting at his side. They seem small, diminished by the size and height of the room and by the light streaming in through tall windows. It is obvious to André - now the viewer - that these two men belong together, yet it is equally obvious that a barrier separates them. The skin of one is the only darkness in a room where all else is light.

Shifting back into his regular mind-set, André pinpoints the bond that binds him to his father - love. He thinks of the toothless grin with which the chevalier always greets him. That grin, so Agathe tells him, is reserved only for her and for him.

As gratifying as this might be, André knows the master's love does not translate into anything material. He feels the gall rising to think that on his father's death, the two *real* sons will inherit the plantation and will rid themselves immediately of their coffee-colored siblings. The families will be separated one from another and sold individually at the slave auctions. This is what happens, so André was told by a young coffee-colored slave, whom the master once bought at the auctions and came from a similar situation to André's. The unfortunate youth did not last long, was desperately unhappy, ran away, and fell victim to the dogs of a hired slave catcher.

As André looks at his sleeping father, he wants to rant and hurl accusations at him. Then seeing that the chevalier's sleep is troubled and the groans are turning to sobs, the gall dissipates. He caresses the blue-veined hand and, at the same time, becomes aware of Adrienne singing in a nearby room. For some unfathomable reason, it cheers André even though he knows the mistress has forbidden all singing.

Tom in London

London, England

While glad to be among his kin, provided it is only for a week or two, Tom despises the squalid conditions in which the family must live: overcrowding, dirty, bad odors, and lack of fresh air. Each morning he feels the need to escape the neighborhood and frequent the parts of London that display the miracles of modern technology: new street lighting, innovative methods of paving, and above all, the revolutionary manner of delivering water to individual buildings. The West End is a case in point.

Today he manages to let himself out of the family home without anyone noticing and steps into the alley. Filthy and malodorous, an open sewer carrying human waste and all types of unspeakable refuse runs down its entire length. He barely escapes the contents of a chamber pot thrown from an upstairs window and has to walk through the blood of a recently slaughtered ox.

He heads in the direction of the Kahve Bean, a coffeehouse, located, thank God, in a better area. He has a way to go yet though before getting there. Meanwhile, in his own neighborhood, he picks his path through the hustle and bustle of porters, needlewomen, and street hawkers, who go about their daily business in spaces already clogged with the pony carts of coal merchants and those selling flyblown meat and other comestibles. Given that the wheat crop failed last year, bread is not among the foods offered. There is no bread in London, which is an added hardship for those like his folks for whom bread is the staple.

Moving into a slum area of a different character to his own, Tom threads his way through a rabbit warren of alleys and mews where milkmaids, orange sellers, fishwives and piemen walk the streets crying out their wares and where knife grinders and furniture repairmen stake out territory at the corners. Then the streets start to widen and horse-drawn carts carrying goods and hackneys[60] carrying passengers must vie for space not only with pedestrians but also with sedan chairs.[61]

Finally, Tom emerges from a dark, narrow alley into the brightness of a formal square that features fine paving and decorative gas lamps. Ah! He feels his spirits soar. What a sight - urban palaces with their chains, iron railings, and gates! All is elegance and sophistication. The carriages are a wonder to behold; the horses, majestic; and the people dressed as works of art.

He knows better than to stand gawping; he knows he must move back into his own environment so as not to attract attention. Having stepped out of a squalid alley into the startling splendor of the square, he now steps back into another squalid alley different to the one from which he emerged. The grandeur of new developments all too often exists cheek by jowl with slums.

For Tom, the chief attraction of the homes of the wealthy is that he knows they all have running water. That means indoor taps, bathrooms, and water closets! In most areas of London, the population is dependent on ground water from unsavory public wells. The existence of a solution to the water problems excites him even though, for now, only the wealthiest can afford it. Over Tom's years as medic on *Spirit*, water has become an obsession, a matter he has not yet discussed with Ambrose but will. He has formulated theories on the subject; unfortunately, theories as yet unsupported by scientific facts.

His theory concerning water stems from his observations of the rapid spread of disease among the slaves in the holds of *Spirit*. Although he could pinpoint many possible reasons, the foul-smelling water that slaves must drink seems like a major contributing factor to the high death rate on board. For one thing, rats often drown in the water barrels and remain there throughout the journey.

---

[60] Carriages for hire
[61] Enclosed chairs carried between horizontal poles by two porters

Armed with his suspicions of the connection between impure water and disease, he now understands that the same problem applies to the disease-ridden slums of his upbringing. However, unlike the slaves in the holds of *Spirit*, Britain's poor have *small ale*[62] as a substitute, although that, too, though has its problems. Because of *small ale* - this is another of Tom's unproven theories - the populations of Britain's slums, including children, are permanently drunk and therefore incapable of bettering themselves.

He would dearly love to weld the power of the pen to the power of the fact, but alas, he'll have to wait until he has educated himself better.

---

[62] Diluted ale

The Medallion

Aberdeenshire, Scotland

Frances is at home alone closing the piano when her friend the Reverend Neil McKenzie drops in unexpectedly. He's a retired cleric with an angelic pink face and a fringe of gray hair. He comes once a month to hold a service attended by the family, along with the estate's employees and its tenant farmers in the Glen Orm chapel. Apart from fulfilling his religious obligations, the old priest also enjoys the odd social visit like today's. He remembers Frances from the time she was a toddler, as he never tires of telling her.

"I didn't realize you still played the piano," he says, as she gets up and busses him on the cheek.

"I barely play nowadays," she tells him, "and we don't even have sing-alongs anymore."

"Pity! Remembering back to the old days, when Glen Orm had a choir, you all sing well."

"Doesn't everyone?" Frances queries in reply. "Isn't singing a human attribute like walking and talking, something that comes with one's birth kit?" As he gives an amused chuckle, she asks, "Do you have time for tea?"

"Tea would be lovely if it won't be holding you up." As she goes to the bellpull to place the order, he delves into his pocket and hands her a small package, saying, "This came my way recently, and I'd like you to have it. It's a Wedgwood antislavery medallion."

Frances is excited by the thought of finally seeing one of the medallions about which she has read but never seen. As they settle down in the niche by the window, she says, "I've heard they are quite the rage among antislavery supporters in the United States. Some men have them inlaid in gold on the lids of snuffboxes, while women wear them as bracelets and hairpins."

As she removes the medallion from its packaging, he says, "The reason for their popularity is that Wedgwood's friend Clarkson sent a packet of them to Benjamin Franklin, and Franklin's enthusiasm was such that the medallion became an instant success. He wrote to Wedgwood saying the image was as effective as any written pamphlet!"

Frances, holding the medallion in the palm of her hand, examines it in the light of the afternoon sun that streams through the window. "*Brèaghach!*"[63] she says to herself as the old cleric fills her in with the details most of which she knows already but doesn't want to deflate him by saying so.

"Wedgwood engaged the sculptor Henry Webber to create the design of the kneeling slave," the Reverend McKenzie lectures, "and it's a figure based on the cameo gemstones of antiquity. The modeler prepared the medallion for production in black jasper against a white ground of the same ceramic paste. As you can see, the words arching over the figure read: *Am I not a man and a brother?* As you probably know, that's the motto also used by the Society for the Abolition of the Slave Trade."

Acknowledging the comment with a nod, she says, "I also read that the image references the literary figure of the *noble savage.*"

"I didn't know that," the Reverend McKenzie replies, "but it did occur to me that the use of black and white is symbolic and that the figure could either be pleading to his white master or to our Lord Jesus. I'm glad to say many slaves have abandoned their heathen beliefs for Christianity."

---

[63] *Beautiful* in Gaelic

Frances remains silent not wanting to spoil his obvious pleasure by mentioning the likelihood of converting to Christianity as probably being obligatory. Instead, she pours the tea and offers her friend some shortbread.

As he munches happily on his triangle, he says, "This is a treat for me. Shortbread doesn't come my way too often."

Again, Frances doesn't comment knowing that although her family eats shortbread every day, it is out of reach for many. She remembers when Stanley as a child had asked why *shortbread* had that name, although it was neither *short* nor *bread*. She would tell him about a baker calling it *bread* to avoid the tax on pastry, about the *short* coming from *shortening* - butter - and about the triangular shape being that of the shape used for Elizabethan petticoats. Stanley likes the explanation so much that he told his playmates - the children of farm workers. She remembers them standing around gawping and not having any idea what he was saying. They had never heard of shortbread. She smiles at the memory. That was before Stanley understood about class distinctions. He understands well enough now!

She turns back to the Reverend McKenzie, who is speaking about his personal encounters with blacks, which, like her own, are minimal. Her only experience was in London, where she once witnessed ex-slaves performing strange music on the street.

"Londoners are more familiar with blacks than we are," the Reverend McKenzie comments. "Many live there, and streets are named for them like Black Boy Lane and Blackmore Alley.

As Frances accompanies her friend to the door and thanks him for the medallion, she knows she won't be showing it to Stanley. Antislavery sentiments irritate him.

The Bookshop

Edinburgh, Scotland

Sir George should have been finalizing his plans for the dreaded London trip. Instead, he has spent days mulling over the issue of science education, which is excluded from the curricula of reputable schools because of the stranglehold Oxford and Cambridge have over education in Britain. To escape the irksome issue, he decides to walk over to the New Club and see what is happening there.

En route, he stops at the new bookshop on George Street and, to his surprise, makes a serendipitous discovery - a slender volume that touches on the paucity of educational facilities dedicated to the sciences. He suspects the author has liberal leanings, and although he doesn't like agreeing with liberal thinkers, he doesn't have other options. He pages through the work and becomes caught up in the author's approach to what he refers to as a *curricular stasis*.

Sir George spends longer than he intended paging through the work, and when he next looks up, he is the only customer in the shop, and the owner is coming over to him to ask if he needs help.

"I'm paging through a book that I won't buy but about which I'm curious," Sir George says.

"Don't worry about it, sir. For us bibliophiles, seeing a book is wanting to know its contents."

"You have your work cut out for you if that applies to every book here!" comments Sir George.

The man chuckles and says, "I became a bookseller to ensure I'd never run out of reading matter. Books are my passion."

As the man retreats, Sir George wishes that, as a youngster, he could have nurtured his passion, albeit not for books but for science. Had it been an option, his life would have followed a different trajectory. He would not have spent his time pretending to be like everyone else in his surroundings. He would not have had to resort to the slave trade and would not have cared about the opinions of Lord Richard or of the old Earl of Gryphon. He might have been happy!

Leaving the store, he now knows what he has to do. He must use a chunk of his ever-increasing profits from the slave trade for the endowment of a science faculty at a major university. He will not allow others to miss their calling like he has.

Improved Plan

Edinburgh, Scotland

It's midday, but if Sir George did not know that, he would have thought it was dusk. Since the incident with Ms. Young feeding the dog, he keeps the drapes closed both day and night. During the day, he lets in light by leaving open the door to the landing, which in spite of good-sized windows is not sufficient. He how feels a need to escape the gloom, but first, he must finalize the details pertaining to his London trip.

Without further ado, he writes to Aunt Stella confirming his time of arrival and agreeing to all her suggestions. Looking through the agenda that she has laid out for him, he sees that there will be enough time for him to seek out forward-looking educators in southern England to help him think through the idea of endowing a science faculty - as an anonymous donor - at a university yet to be determined. By being anonymous, he can continue to maintain his public persona as a member of the ultraconservative elite while giving material support to his true convictions.

Suddenly the London trip looks more promising. Excited, he jots down the requirements for the new faculty that would promote training for the needs of the new industrial era. All the tools of scientific methodology would come into play: laboratories, research, observation, experiments, measurements, cause and effect . . .

Reading what he has written, he sees how the items fly in the face of what Oxford and Cambridge maintain constitutes a good education - the classics. He himself had tutors until the age of thirteen, then went to Eton until he was eighteen, and on to Oxford after that. At Eton, the curriculum featured classical studies, writing, arithmetic, Euclid, Greek, Alexander Pope, and antiquities, i.e., subjects that have snob value by supposedly nurturing good taste, intellect, and morality but are of no use to society in the industrial era. At Oxford, it was no different.

One decision remains: which university should he choose for his bequest? Scotland in the past, thanks to the Scottish Enlightenment, outstripped England in many fields of scientific endeavor; the universities in Glasgow and Edinburgh featured then - and still feature - chairs for mathematics, astronomy, chemistry, and economics. They also became respected centers for medical education. These attempts to meet contemporary needs made Scotland into an intellectual center and a major player in the European Enlightenment. That was then. Now nothing is happening to ensure that education keeps pace with the needs of the modern age. He can help change the situation though by choosing Edinburgh University for his new faculty.

All that now clear in his mind, he goes to the window, opens the curtains, and lets in air and light.

Mayday

Leith, Scotland

It's a holiday, and Migu is having breakfast with Betta and Rose. Rose tells her parents that she got up at dawn to wash her face in the morning dew.

"Why, dear?" Migu, ever-curious, wants to know.

"Father!" Rose exclaims. "Surely you know that all girls of marriageable age want to be more beautiful and must, therefore, wash their faces in the morning dew on Mayday."

Migu throws back his head and roars with laughter. Betta chokes on her chocolate drink, and Rose has to get up and pat her mother on the back. She says with an impish smile, "If I'd realized my activities would cause such a stir, I'd have kept them to myself!"

With order restored, Migu rises from the table, saying, "I must get going on my Mayday job. You, Betta, might want to sit in the garden watching me. I'm assuming Rose will need to catch up on her beauty sleep after her strenuous dawn outing."

Rose wags an elegant finger, saying, "Now, now, Father! No mockery. Today is your day to tend roses, and I being one such rose means finding me an earl!"

"Give me a break, child!" her father exclaims, "I only canceled the Betrothal Agreement a couple of days ago."

Rose looks at him with affection and says, "I know, Pa, but you must realize that the cancelation should have been done in January."

He tries to excuse the delay with the words, "I was hoping to line up an array of suitable *beaus*. There is the Simmonds boy, for instance, and . . ."

Studying his sheepish expression with an amused smile, Rose looks him in the eye and says in a gentle voice that he knows masks a will of steel, "Pa, the Simmonds boy doesn't pass muster. I want an earl, but if you don't want to do the footwork, Lady Abigail can help. She can arrange a *coincidental* encounter for you with a suitable candidate. That would allow you to make an assessment without committing yourself."

"Huh!" is all Migu can say before fleeing. His Mayday pruning of the roses is his one and only gardening job and has been his practice since Rose's birth fifteen years earlier. "Prune after the final frost and just before the plant breaks its dormancy" is the wisdom he follows. Arming himself with snippers, gloves, and a leather apron, he embarks on the job, which he hopes will prove easier than the daughter job! He pulls away the dry leaves so he can see what he is doing, and with some judicious snipping, he takes out the dead and diseased shoots to open the center of the plant. He has to ensure no stems cross and to prune at a forty-five-degree angle above and away from the buds.

As he works, memories intrude of his pathetic attempts to present the Simmonds boy in a good light. He remembers saying, "He is personable and competent, and his father's stables are worth millions."

Rose had looked at him - her dark eyes, unfathomable pools - and replied in a sweet tone, "Father, the Simmonds boy is not an earl. I need an earl."

Migu hates the thought of an earl, of hobnobbing with the nobility, and of conforming to their niceties and pretentious cultural blab. It looks though as if he will have to grin and bear it. At least, Rose has thrown him a lifeline by saying Lady Abigail could arrange a coincidental encounter with a suitable candidate.

He should perhaps take her up on the offer. It would save him a lot of trouble if Rose had already vetted the person in question while still leaving Migu with the option of rejecting the candidate.

The White Hart[64]

Edinburgh, Scotland

Young William - the new Earl of Gryphon - and Lord Richard sit in the White Hart, each with a tankard of ale in hand. Situated at the foot of the castle at 34 Grass Market, the pub is, if one is to believe what the sign says, the oldest such establishment in Edinburgh. Its founding date is 1516. William, not having had much exposure to pubs, finds it pleasant enough with its front windows made up of small panes and Toby jugs hanging from a low ceiling. Being of average height, William passes beneath those jugs without a problem, but Lord Richard, a tall man, has to stoop to reach the secluded table at the back, which he has chosen for their tête-à-tête. William surmises that people must have been shorter in 1516,

Today's lecture on William's initiation into the world of the slave trader starts where Lord Richard left off a few days earlier, the place where the *Spirit of the Clyde* consortium captures its slaves.

His lordship explains, "It's that area of West Africa that lies just north of the equator, an area that is not used as much by other companies whose agents buy *products* supplied by the kings and chiefs of the interior. The agents then have to march their purchases to the coast in coffles[65] and, once there, keep their captives imprisoned until they are ready to ship them. It is a long and tedious procedure. We, in the *Spirit* consortium avoid those expenses by operating farther south where the villagers have had little exposure to the outside world and are easy to kidnap. Many are so naive they can be lured on board with cheap factory-made goods."

---

64 Adult male deer; especially a red deer over five
65 A group of slaves chained together

William chips in by asking if these goods are from Mr. Migu's factories. With a sharp tone, Lord Richard replies, "I never speak of our unfortunate liaison with Aaron Migu and neither should you."

Swigging back the last of his ale, his lordship catches the server's eye and orders coffee, then says to William, "Before winding up the first leg of the journey, I should like to point out that the long strings of fort-like holding pens that exist north of *Spirit*'s area occupy entire islands off the coast. With our methods, we don't need to own either forts or islands! Providing the goods is a lot cheaper for us." After a brief period of rumination, he says "Perhaps we should leave the Middle Passage until next time. We might enjoy our coffee more!"

William welcomes the announcement. Although he feels he should learn as much as he can about this lucrative source of income, he doesn't enjoy the details. He is beginning to suspect that most slave traders make a point of *not* delving into detail.

Their coffee arrives, and as Lord Richard spoons sugar into his mug, he says, "By the way, it's the third leg of the journey that brings this sugar to our table." He holds up a heaped teaspoon to illustrate the point. "Once emptied of slaves, the holds of the schooners are loaded with sugar, and the vessels ride the westerlies[66] home to our British markets."

William stares at the glittering crystals in the spoon hovering over his own mug and says, "I've never thought about where these come from. Are you saying, Lord Richard, that they might have crossed the Atlantic in the holds of *Spirit*?"

Lord Richard grins and says, "Not in the holds of *Spirit* - it has been in dry docks since last year - but possibly in one of our other schooners."

---

[66] Winds that blow from west to east across the Atlantic

William returns his spoonful of sugar to the bowl. He has heard from Lady Abigail - she is a clandestine Wilberforce adherent - about conditions in which slaves are transported during the Middle Passage and cannot imagine that the holds could ever be cleaned well enough for him to again enjoy sugar that has traveled in those same filth-ridden holds!

Action Needed

West Coast of Africa

Today Efia and Abebi have just returned from a short foray into the forest, where a plant used for a medicinal compound is in flower. Efia needs to stock up on those flowers before it is too late. The compound - used for crudities of the stomach and fumes in the head - sells well at the market, and she doesn't want to interrupt the supply.

She lifts down the basket from her head and tips the contents onto the drying rack. Barely has she shaken out the last blossom when she is interrupted by shrieks from behind a nearby hut. Abandoning her basket, she rushes to the scene to find Kwame, Assimbola, and another of Thimba's trainees holding down Abebi and smearing her with what appears to be goat dung. In a flaming rage, Efia yells at them, and they bolt, leaving Abebi shrieking in anger at the indignity.

Efia grabs her child by her filthy arm, gives her a slap on the bottom, and marches her downhill to wash in the ocean. "How often have I told you *not* to incite those boys?" she chastises. "Your baba trains them for aggression, and they could hurt you. Your disobedience will one day get us all into a lot of trouble."

A few hours later, thinking of their evening meal, Efia fetches a knife and cuts off a couple of plantains from the bunch hanging under the overhang of the thatch. Abebi, having finished sorting through her shells, eyes the plantains and asks, "Mammi, can I take one of those for Infana?"

Given the incident with the bad boys, Efia suspects Abebi will again place inappropriate demands on poor little Infana. "Let's give Infana a rest," she suggests. "Why don't we make an altar for Gran Legbwa instead? He'll like a plantain and some sundried giraffe."

Abebi pouts, and her eyes start to glaze over as they do when she anticipates boredom. "It'll be fun, Abebi!" Efia encourages her. "We'll make the altar under the tree with the squiggly roots." (It's a kapok tree.) "Can you think of another offering to go with the plantain and meat?"

"I could give him this," Abebi says, holding up a damaged shell, which she was about to discard.

"No! Your offering has to be something you value yourself. I'll think up something for you. You, meantime, think what you want to say to Gran Legbwa."

"I don't have to think, Mammi. I'm going to tell Gran Legbwa to beat the heck out of the bad boys!" As before, she pummels the air with bunched-up fists while Efia rolls her eyes in exasperation.

Misguided

West Coast of Africa

For the first time, Big Baba has undertaken to show Abebi around the masks and costume store and is now on his way to pick her up. He makes laborious progress up the hill from the Banyan to Thimba's compound. Baba can see before he arrives that Efia sits outside on a stool preparing ackees[67] for cooking. To do the job, she uses a knife to cut out the edible portions, which she piles on the ground at her side. It is important that she only use ripe ackees, whose fruit has split and is red.

Crouching, Abebi doodles with a twig on the ground. Efia is obviously lecturing, and Big Baba assumes his granddaughter isn't happy. She doesn't like the lectures that Efia delivers all too frequently, but it's none of his business. On arriving, Baba gestures to Efia - she faces him - that he will not be interfering and will wait until she's finished. Settling on the throne without Abebi noticing, Baba listens to Efia's sermon. She is explaining the rituals of the Gran Legbwa celebration, which - as Efia has told him - she wants Abebi to start attending. On previous occasions, the child has always spent the night of such ceremonies with Twenty-Eighth Wife in Big Baba's family compound, which is located well away from the poto mitan area.

Twenty-Eighth Wife is a nurturing soul, who always takes care of the young likely to be frightened by the fierce magnificence of the ceremony. Twenty-Eighth Wife was a surrogate mother to Efia, and she regards Abebi as her own grandchild. For her part, Abebi loves Twenty-Eighth Wife and always enjoys time with her. Baba realizes that it has never occurred to Abebi until now that she could actually attend a Gran Legbwa ceremony.

---

[67] Scarlet pear-shaped fruit with several big black seeds

Efia is telling her daughter how loas can speak inside the head of a devotee. Also, so she tells Abebi, during ceremonies, loas can speak to the entire community by taking control of the body of a person in a trance and using that body for their own purposes. Big Baba has to wonder if Efia is explaining the matter in a form suitable for a child, but seeing he has promised not to interfere, he remains silent.

Seeing that Abebi continues to doodle without comment, Efia says, "I've told you this before, child, but am now repeating it. By gathering around the poto mitan and singing Gran Legbwa's songs and dancing his dances, we attract his attention and invite him to join us."

As there is still no reaction from Abebi, Efia moves on to speaking of Gran Legbwa's *omniscient graciousness* and saying, "Although he is the greatest of our spirits and has direct access to Bondye, he is also old, humble, and kind and needs no big sacrifices. Grilled corn, ground nuts, and a little tobacco or coffee is enough for him."

At this, Big Baba is hard put not to interrupt. He wants to tell her to stop making Gran Legbwa sound like a wimpy Infana-type loa, who is small, peace-loving, and circumspect, the kind whose mask features half-closed eyes and a bulging forehead. Such drivel has nothing to do with the true Gran Legbwa, who is huge, fierce, horned, and phallic! Efia should concentrate on using her voice for singing instead of preaching such nonsense!

So as not to have to hear more of Efia's drivel, Big Baba closes his eyes, forgets about Abebi's education, and pictures a typical Gran Legbwa ceremony in all its high drama and ferocity. As the night falls, so he now sees it in his mind, the tribe is gathering in a circle around the poto mitan. He hears the drums as they find their voices. Then, as they come into their own, he watches the firelight flickering over a scene that features wild clapping, stamping, dancing, and singing. He has a clear picture of Thimba and Shamwari as solo dancers wielding their spears and, in the light of the fire, soaring above the crowd as they perform the Grand Leap. He hears - above the crazed drumming and the bellows, howls, and roars - the inimitable grandeur of Efia's voice, as she summons the unseen spirit, who explodes onto the scene with a triumphant shriek and takes possession of the apprentice's body[68], throwing it around like a doll. This is the real Gran Legbwa, very different to the way Efia portrays him for the sake of her daughter!

A real ceremony always leaves Baba short of breath. He has to rely on the drums to bring him back to normal. Losing intensity, they become light and playful with the log and base drummers allowing their fingers to skitter across the drumheads informing the tribe it's time to disband.

In the present, there are no drums to lead Baba back to normality. Sweating, he opens his eyes to see Efia digging her knife into the glistening flesh of the last ackee. "Gran Legbwa," she is saying, "offers us bridge to the realm of the spirits."

Looking at Abebi, Baba sees that her drawing is Gran Legbwa's vévé! She's not bored after all; she is merely engrossed in what she is doing. He'd maligned her.

Finished with the ackees, Efia stands up and inspects Abebi's artwork, which she praises lavishly. Abebi looks pleased at the praise. So, thinks Big Baba, all is not lost in spite of Efia's misguided efforts to present the ferocious and phallic Gran Legbwa as a weakling for whom a pinch of tobacco and sip of coffee suffice.

---

[68] Apprentice to the priest (houngan), who, in a trance, allows the loa to use his body to act and speak.

Mask and Costume Store

West Coast of Africa

As Big Baba, Abebi, and Inja proceed at an agonizingly slow pace toward their destination, Big Baba prepares his granddaughter for what lies ahead, telling her that the masks represent various loas - some personal like Infana and some accessible to all like Gran Legbwa.

"Big Baba, can I wear a mask?" Abebi asks.

Shocked, Big Baba replies, "No, child, certainly not! The masks are sacred, and the sculptors who carve them and the dancers who wear them are men, not women, let alone children and, most especially, not girl children! The skills involved pass on through generations."

Downcast, Abebi now asks, "Can children then do the things Mammi calls trances?"

"Child, you have a mind that jumps around like a cricket!" Baba complains.

Abebi persists, "Can children do trances, Baba?"

"No!" Baba tells her sternly. "Grown women can train as mediums but not youngsters like you. In a trance, the medium - whether male of female - hands over temporary control of his or her human body to an incarnate spirit to use as that spirit wishes. If the spirit in question serves the cause of good, all is well. The spirit will use the body briefly to say and do what needs to be said and done and then withdraw. With an untrained medium, an evil spirit can easily take possession of the medium's body without permission, not withdraw at all and wreaking all types havoc. It is a very dangerous situation."

Abebi is not sure she understands and feels Big Baba is starting to sound like Mammi in one of her sermonizing moods. However, because it is Big Baba and not Mammi, Abebi makes an effort to go on listening, as Baba continues, "*Houngans*[69] and their acolytes train to become mediums, and even legitimate loas don't treat the medium gently."

"Why?" Abebi wants to know.

With a self-deprecating smile, Big Baba says, "Child, like us warriors, loas enjoy flaunting their power and authority!" He then adds more for his own benefit than for Abebi's, "One has to wonder, if we modeled ourselves on our loas or if our loas modeled themselves on us!"

They have finally arrived at the storage hut. Unlike most of the round, windowless huts in Banyan Village, the mask and costume store is elongated and windowless but with doors at each end. As Big Baba has only unbarred one door, the masks hanging on all four walls are lit by a single shaft of light that serves to highlight no more than an eye, a beard, or a gaping mouth. The rest is in shadow and leaves much with which vivid imaginations can play.

As Big Baba walks Abebi systematically around the walls pointing with his staff and explaining various features on individual masks, Abebi sticks close to his side. Then as her eyes grow accustomed to the gloom, her innate curiosity takes over, and the masks no longer scare her. She loves the different materials used in their creation. Big Baba has told her the basic structure of a mask is usually wood, but she sees that other things are used for detail. She would like to study the matter more closely, but Baba doesn't give her a chance as he rushes on.

She sees only briefly in passing that one of the ancestors has hair made of straw and another a beard made of fur. She likes, too, the painted masks and knows the paint used is probably clay of the ochre type, but she doesn't have time to look more closely because Baba is already pointing out the broken tooth on the next mask. Normally she

---

[69] Priests

finds Baba walks too slowly, but now when she wants to linger - she just got an enticing glimpse of an earring - he doesn't give her a chance.

When she asks him to stop in front of a mask studded with cowrie shells, he says, "No, child. I don't have the stamina and am only doing this because your mother worries about you developing wrong ideas of your own."

Abebi doesn't understand the bit about stamina but settles for blaming Mammi. As they move relentlessly onward, Big Baba names some of the materials jabbing with his staff in the appropriate direction: wood, copper, straw, fang, bone . . . Abebi, meanwhile, tries to store the details in her head: eyelashes, tribal markings, chin shapes, noses, and slants of the eyes.

She is starting to understand that the facial features do not refer to what the ancestor looked like in life but, instead, tell of the person's character traits. The jabs of Baba's staff move from one attribute to the next but never touch the surface of the mask; they always stop a few inches short. He is now saying and jabbing, "You see by the protruding forehead that this guy was a wise person, and . . ." - he has moved on to the next mask - "by the large chin and mouth that this individual was strong and authoritative. The half-closed eyes of this woman show she was a kindly person, while the mouth and the fangs of the man here beside her indicate a fierce and aggressive nature like Gran Legbwa's."

As Big Baba speaks of Gran Legbwa's fierceness, Abebi sees he expects her to question this description of Gran Legbwa. Abebi while remembering Mammi saying Gran Legbwa was old and peaceful would prefer Gran Legbwa to be scary and so does not comment. Big Baba might not like her saying "if Gran Legbwa is fierce and scary, he'll be better at beating up the bad boys!"

With Big Baba still on the go, Abebi doesn't have much time to ponder the Gran Legbwa issue. She must make sure to remember that small round eyes mean humility and big wide eyes mean confidence. *Phew!* She'll need to comeback on her own to internalize this and pick up on the details that she hasn't had time for now.

They are almost back at their starting point by the door when, to Abebi's great joy, Big Baba stops in front of one of the rarer female masks. He says, "This is the mask of Twenty-Seventh Wife, your grandmother. She died in childbirth and is your mammi's loa."

"Ah!" Abebi gapes open-mouthed, then says in voice full of wonder, "She has a cornrow hairstyle like I want, and she's beautiful!" Abebi finds all the masks mesmerizing, but *beautiful* would not have been a word she would have used for any of the others. If she had the vocabulary, she would have been more likely to use such words as *fearsome* or *powerful* for the others.

"Yes, child, Twenty-Seventh Wife was beautiful," Baba affirms with a gentle smile as he reminisces, "but remember that the features depicted are symbols of attributes not depictions of how she actually looked. The almond-shaped eyes," - he points - "are not the way hers were. Eyes like that are symbols used to express all female beauty."

Far too soon for Abebi, they are at the door. They didn't even stop at the costumes; all she saw in passing was a raffia[70] skirt encrusted with mollusk shells, a beaded fringe, and headgear with horns. Now they are outside in the sun, where Inja greets them with enthusiasm. "He never goes in there anymore," says Big Baba, "because he's frightened."

"Of the masks?" Abebi is astonished. She isn't frightened of them anymore and always thinks of Inja as spunky.

"No, he's not frightened of the masks. He's frightened because he once peed in there, and I beat him."

---

[70] Strips of the raffia palm

"Oh!" Abebi is glad she would never think to pee there; she wouldn't like Big Baba to beat her! As they trudge back to Mammi's again - at agonizingly slow pace - she doesn't speak. Her mind is fully occupied by wondering how best to get herself back into the store without anyone knowing. She's often been told that is something she should *never* do but will be doing all the same.

Second Week of May 1800

From Job to Sickroom

Plantation, Louisiana

Tightening the reins, applying pressure with calf and heel, André coaxes Pégasse from a trot into a canter and heads for the farmyard. He encounters ahead - traveling in the same direction - three swaying wagons laden with cane. Although they are close to their destination, he overtakes using the path alongside the rutted track. Pégasse nickers greetings to his fellow equines while André remembers the time that - at a gallop - he unexpectedly encountered wagons around a bend. Only by a narrow margin did he avoid slamming into the wagons toppling them and killing himself, his fellow slaves, Pégasse, and the other horses. Those wagons have often killed people. His mother's broomstick husband was an example.

Bypassing a wooded area, André listens to the piercing songs of the cicadas. One part of him enjoys distinguishing the acoustic signals that compose the cicadas' songs; another part of him cringes at the shrillness. He believes the story of one of the slave women who maintains her son suffered permanent damage to his hearing by holding his pet cicada too close to his ear. Much to the boy's chagrin, she then threw the creature onto the red-hot grill along with others of its kind. The child never again ate cicada, although it meant sacrificing a nutritious and tasty item in the slave diet.

Now nearing midday, the sun beats down without remission. André wipes the sweat from his brow on his sleeve and longs to visit the master in the cool of the Big House. Pégasse, too, is wet and lathered but will find respite in the shade of a live oak in the farmyard.

The field slaves must continue in the murderous heat. Even while eating their midday meal, they must eat standing at troughs under the scorching sun. André knows that human sanity often succumbs under such brutal conditions. He knows, too, that some hold on to their wits against the odds thanks to his mother Agathe. She does her best to keep their African heritage alive for them passing on the type of tales passed on to her by her Africa-born parents. While featuring African stock figures, they also include countless improvised details drawn from the present.

The story about the loa Anansi, who sometime takes the form of a spider, is a favorite with Agathe's audiences, who offer suggestions for future exploits. André has to wonder at his mother's adeptness in weaving these suggestions - some quite ridiculous - into a cohesive tale that will amuse and help her fellow slaves deal with the tyranny to which their daily lives expose them. It is a talent that seems related to her ability to align their African ancestral faith with the master's Christianity. "Just think of the saints as loas," he once heard Agathe tell a fellow slave. "Think of the Holy Cross as the poto mitan, think of Jesus as *Gran Legbwa* and of God as *Bondye*, the Big Spirit."

Back in the farmyard, André strips to the waist and washes at a tub by the cookhouse. Meanwhile, the under-ten kiddies frolic around him and a white-aproned cook pokes her head round the door to wave her ladle in greeting. Refreshed, André sneaks into the Big House from the back porch and climbs the narrow staircase thus avoiding the eagle eye of the mistress, who is ensconced on the front porch.

Reaching the landing, André stops and lingers at the narrow window that looks out over the park and beyond toward the bayou. The sights and sounds of the bayou soothe him. He can still hear the cicadas although they are less intrusive from the distance. He loves the bayou with its vegetation and creatures. He and the master have often hunted deer there, just the two of them, each with a *fusil de chasse.*[71] He knows about the herons, egrets, catfish, frogs, and toads. His father taught him to respect the critters, something for which he is grateful.

Regular field slaves never get the time or opportunity to get to know anything about the place in which they live. Many spend their entire lives experiencing nothing more than the slave quarters where they spend their nights and the cane fields where they spend their days.

Agathe meets André outside the sickroom, and as they enter, she says, "Master has had a bad day, isn't speaking, but waits for you with his eyes on the door." From mounded pillows under the canopy of the bed, a wan face peers at them through rheumy eyes, then as recognition dawns, the eyes feast on André, and the parched lips move to exclaim in a rasping whisper, "My son! You're here!"

André clasps the proffered hand, gasps, "Master!"

It hurts him to see the mighty thus reduced. Composing himself, he settles on the bedside chair and feigns normality by embarking on a report of activities on the plantation in the past twenty-four hours. He starts by telling the master that the whipping post, stocks, and pillory have received their annual coat of paint. It's something on which the master insists, even though none of these instruments of punishment have been used since André took over the management of the plantation. The master feels though that their existence acts as a deterrent.

---

[71]   Hunter's gun

Moving on to speak of the sugarhouse, André reminds his father of the issues - a minor problem with one of the grinders and improved performances from the kettle and the condensers.

Wanting to stimulate the master's failing memory, André turns to the recent history of the sugar industry reminding the chevalier of how sugar became a major crop on the west bank of the Mississippi. He says, "Remember, Master, how this land was a general farm until Master de Bore discovered how to granulate sugar?"

He pauses, hoping the chevalier might continue the narrative, but he doesn't, so André continues himself saying that the discovery changed the general farm into one of the biggest sugar-producing plantations in the area. It is with pleasure that he sees his father's parched lips spread into a toothless grin. The master's pride in the plantation remains intact! It is a sign that gives André hope that recovery is possible. However, taking his leave as the master drops off to sleep again. He realizes he is grasping at straws. Yet apart from straws nothing else exists.

Hyde Park

London, England

Tom is in the southern area of Hyde Park. It's a place where commoners go to entertain themselves by watching the upper classes preen. He has researched the history of the royal park that King Charles I opened to the public in 1637, parts of it becoming fashionable with the upper classes. Riders on horseback used Rotten Row, while carriages used the adjacent drive, a situation that still persists.

Tom has been starting his days in London by using the opportunity to scrutinize the bigwigs. Seeing it is an accepted pastime, he has no scruples about ogling the beauty of dress, carriage, and horse, just as he might ogle exotic creatures in cages. However, as always conscious of time, he never allows himself more than half an hour for the frivolous pursuit of people watching. He needs to further his education. He therefore now heads off in the direction of the public speaking area. He has read about the Clapham Sect, a group of evangelical Christians that pursue the unpopular course of trying to abolish slavery. Today he discovers that the speaker he is about to hear is such a person.

Picking a spot near the front, Tom studies the man. He is small but stands on a tall box. As a result, the crowd clustered around must look up look up to him. Being close enough to see fanaticism blaze in this person's eyes, Tom considers leaving but doesn't.

"Do you know," the speaker thunders, "that our British banks give credit to those slave-based industries, which finance our industrial development? Sugar and cotton are examples."

"It's the job of banks to finance viable industries!" bellows Tom's neighbor, hands cupped around his mouth.

Paying no attention, the orator rants on, "Slave-dependent imports are driving our farmers from the land into factories, so we now don't have enough farmers to feed the inhabitants of our cities. Not even the toffs - they own most of Britain's land - can grow crops without labor."

"That is proof we need cheap slave-dependent imports!" shouts someone from the growing crowd.

Another remains fixated on the upper classes and bellows, "The toffs are to blame for the problem! If they didn't hold the general populace in feudal servitude, if they allowed us to make a decent living, we wouldn't be in this position."

Another snarls, "Sponges! Why don't they do something useful instead of whacking little balls around on a green all day?"

Cries of "Hear! Hear!" punctuate the comments.

The speaker tries to regain control and roars above the tumult, "The sugar we consume, the coffee we drink, the tobacco we smoke depend on slave labor."

Such a big voice for such a small man, Tom thinks. Yet his impressive voice is not helping him.

Tom's neighbor produces his clay pipe, holds it up, and shouts, "Are you saying we must forego these simple pleasures?"

The speaker thunders back his reply, "Does it not bother you that your 'simple pleasures' are unethical?"

"No!" comes the response from multiple sources, while the pipe smoker yells, "Ethics be damned!"

The speaker changes tack, says, "Slave-trade fortunes paid for many of our country's most prestigious buildings. The Bodleian Library is an example. I could name others . . ."

"Don't bother! We . . ."

The orator shouts down the heckler, hollering, "Does our greatness warrant the abuse of fellow human beings?"

A voice rises above the hubbub, "Blacks aren't human. They are beasts of burden and can work indefinitely. That's the way God created them, and there's nothing unethical about using them for their God-given purpose."

"Balderdash!" the speaker bellows amidst derision, scoffing, and boos.

"Bloody bleeding heart!" huffs someone.

"Soon he'll say we shouldn't be eating our domestic animals," a woman quips to the accompaniment of loud guffaws. "He probably thinks that plants have feelings and that we shouldn't be eating them either!"

As the speaker lifts a flask to his lips and drinks - his Adam's apple bobbing - Tom processes the opinions he has heard and formulates what he believes. He feels, if Britain needs slavery to retain its status as the greatest nation on earth, then slavery is acceptable. Both the king and Lord Nelson have made that abundantly clear. There is, however, a caveat as far as Tom is concerned. While on British schooners, slaves should receive humane handling! For this reason, he wants to become a writer, not for the abolition of slavery.

Glad to have straightened out his own position, Tom again listens as the orator continues his diatribe with the words "Slave-dependent fortunes drive this industrial revolution of ours, pay for the invention of machinery and tools, the building of roads, railways, bridges, and canals. Our wharves and harbors - the most advanced on the planet - depend on slave-generated profits, as do the mining of salt, coal, and lime. The production of building materials: lumber, rope, iron, and glass are no different. Our exports of high-quality nails and wrought iron to world markets are slave reliant. Above all, millions of hours of slave labor go into the production of cotton, which is better suited to our new industrial processes than is wool and . . ." The words get lost amidst jeering, hissing, and foot stamping. The orator - his voice now lost - can only croak, "Slavery is wrong, wrong, wrong . . ."

As the crowd embarks on a raucous rendition of "Rule Britannia," Tom sees the tears course down the little man's cheeks. Descending from his box, he sneaks away to the words that boom through the park, "Rule Britannia / Britannia rules the waves / Britons never, never, never shall be slaves!"

Only others should be slaves, thinks Tom with a twisted smile.

Better State of Mind

London, England

While staying with Aunt Stella in London, Sir George has chosen from her list of potential properties a house for his family in the West End. He has signed an Agreement of Purchase with a closing date for the end of October.

Although he doesn't want to buy a house in London and harbors resentment for having to do so, he likes what the West End was able to become after the Great Fire of London fortuitously destroyed the medieval urban sprawl. He also likes the house in question. It stands on a paved street with a gated garden and state-of-the-art lighting. The style is Georgian with the structural and ornamental detail inspired by the architecture of ancient Rome. The front door includes sunken panels, an ornate pediment, and pilasters with the number 19 affixed in heavy brass on the right-hand side. The inside of the house, too, leaves nothing wanting and includes crown moldings in the best classical tradition, modern lighting, and of course, wonderful bathroom facilities.

Having acquired the address that Jessica needs to enhance their daughters' matrimonial prospects, Sir George now is now enjoying his remaining time in London. He accompanies Aunt Stella to various cultural events and has bought her a George Stubbs's life-size horse portrait that had attracted her attention.

Most importantly, he manages to fulfill his own requirements by seeking out smaller forward-thinking educational institutions that favor the sciences. Keeping their advice in mind, he will be returning to Edinburgh with a better idea of how to proceed with his endowment, which he has come to realize has to be for the University of Edinburgh.

The project excites him. Taking his afternoon constitutional in Hyde Park, he hopes that, although he still carries the guilt for the unethical origin of his fortune, there will be room for forgiveness in the greater scheme of things. He is, after all, using his slave-trade-money for the good of his country. Enjoying the effusions of spring that surround him, he swings his cane with an atypical jauntiness.

His meanderings around the park take him past the area dedicated to public speaking. A rowdy crowd has just finished a rendition of "Rule Britannia" and is starting to disperse. Among the throng, a pallid young man with an amputated forearm catches his attention. Sir George speculates that he must have got in the way of a cannon ball in the French war, although with his pale face and delicate build, this lad looks more like a scholar than a soldier.

Fright

West Coast of Africa

Abebi has spent the week mulling over what she saw when Big Baba whisked her through the mask shed. Now she wants to look more closely on her own. She wants to check on the appliqued materials she saw: hair, horn, teeth, shells, seeds, straws, and feathers. The colors also interest her; she thinks they must be ochre, which comes from the earth and which can be either purple, red, yellow, orange, or umber.

As Mammi and Auntie Abena pound cassava, Abebi sits outside the hut picking at a scab on her knee. Although the mask and costume store is out of bounds, she wonders if any harm will be done as long as no one sees her entering and exiting the store. The problem is that both the back and front doors are always closed with heavy bars, but there are exceptions like today, when sculptors go in to take out masks for repair. She jumps to her feet and goes to take a look. If she's lucky . . .

She has never had any luck until now, but as she rounds the corner, she spots two of the sculptors entering the back door and leaving it open to let in light. When they emerge, both have a mask under each arm and neither bothers with closing the door. They leave it ajar, and Abebi, not believing her good fortune, squeals with delight as the men head back to their workshop.

She looks to the left and looks to the right and sees in the distance women at work in their family vegetable patches. She also spots a young mother washing a squalling piccanin[72] in a basin and an older woman swilling millet in a tub. (That is supposed to make it sweeter.)

Being sure that those in the distance are too busy to notice her, Abebi now turns her attention to Mammi and Auntie Abena, who are still standing on sturdy stools pounding cassava with the big pestle and

---

[72] Baby

mortar. Although they are closer, she doesn't consider them a threat. If the chatting, thumping, and singing stop, she will emerge quickly and do something innocent like running downhill to see Big Baba at the Banyan.

Sidling up to the shed, she enters through the open door, which - while letting in a certain amount of light - still leaves the interior dark and scary. Nonetheless, she's brave and knows the animal masks - gaping maws and ripping fangs - are nothing more than wood. As Big Baba has explained when the masks are in storage, they have no life of their own. A loa will only take up residence when the tribe gathers around the poto mitan and summons them.

Allowing her eyes to adjust, she lingers where the costumes hang on racks. She sees fascinating details - colored grasses and appliquéd shells of mollusks and cowries - but to see the costumes properly, she would need to take them down, and she can't do that.

She moves on to the masks hanging on the walls and, taking her time, notes jutting chins, protruding foreheads, and the differing shapes of the eyes: half-closed, big and wide, small and round, almond-shaped . . . The ancestral mask that she likes best is one she didn't notice before. It depicts a young woman with oval eyes, curved lashes, and ornamentation on her cheeks; unfortunately, though, she hangs too high on the wall for Abebi to identify the materials.

Engrossed in her studies, she is running her finger along the striations on the cheeks of a warrior mask when the shed door slams closed, and unearthly shrieks shatter the stillness. Now engulfed in total in total darkness, she sees nothing but feels herself surrounded by creatures that sneer, scream, and poke at her. She falls to the ground in abject terror, buries her face in her hands, and howls.

She is not sure how long the horror lasts, but she suddenly realizes the ear-piercing screeches of the loas have stopped. She hears an angry voice outside, then the door opens, and blinding light streams in. When she recovers her sight, she sees Big Baba stands outlined in the doorway saying to her in a stern voice, "Stop that caterwauling, Abebi, and come here!" She runs to him and clasp him around the hips and bawls even louder. He strokes her head and soothes her saying, "There, there, child, you're all right."

When she releases him, he takes her snotty hand in his and leads her to a nearby bench. They settle, and she, still sniffing, wipes her nose on her arm and presses herself into his side. He gives her time to recover, then looks down on her saying in a firm voice, "There is no need for you to feel sorry for yourself and to go pestering Infana or any other loa with your demands. Do you understand?"

She isn't sure she does but nods mutely, and he continues, "You deserve what happened, which was Kwame and Assimbola playing a trick on you. However, seeing it wasn't their job to punish you and they are skellums, I shall be the one to punish them, not poor little Infana!"

Third Week of May 1800

Forgetfulness

Plantation, Louisiana

With his head encased in an all-enveloping nightcap, the chevalier lies in his canopied bed. The breeze that wafts up from the Mississippi reaches him through the lofty windows of his upstairs bedroom. His lawyer and friend Olivier Girrard has spent time at the bedside reviewing the chevalier's Last Will. He has spelled out that Jacques, as eldest son, will inherit all on the condition that he provide generous stipends for Cécile and Jean.

Gathering his papers and getting ready to leave, Olivier says, "Let your mind be at rest, Guillaume. Your affairs are in order."

The chevalier, trying to collect the remnants of the authority he once possessed, raises his head from the pillow and says, "No, Olivier, they are not in order! What about André, Agathe, and the kiddies?"

Olivier, unimpressed by the remnants of authority, finishes storing the documents in his briefcase and says, "All you can do, Guillaume, is to place Agathe and her family in the hands of Le Bon Dieu and pray that he treats them kindly. We have no control over their fate. The law must not be broken."

The chevalier has always intended on looking into ways of bypassing the law that prevents slaves from owning property but has procrastinated believing there was still time. And who knows, perhaps there really still is time. He must just recover a little of his strength and will attend to the matter.

He slumps back into his pillows allowing the soporific effect of the breeze to carry him back to earlier times. On arrival from New Orleans, he would abandon the carriage at the jetty and full of youthful vigor cross the River Road. Avoiding carts, horsemen, and pedestrians, he would stand at the wrought iron gates and savor the joy of being home. In his mind, he now again strides up the avenue under the live oaks and the streamers of Spanish moss. Again, he mounts the steps to cross the porch and entrance hall to climb the split staircase and arrive in the room where he now lies. He is just a little tired after the long carriage ride from New Orleans and will attend to the matter tomorrow.

Feeling the breeze play around his bed, he suddenly realizes he can no longer remember the matter that so urgently needs his attention. As hard as he tries, his memory refuses to release even the tiniest inkling of its nature.

Increase the Dosage?

Plantation, Louisiana

Cécile lies in bed debating whether she should get up. It is earlier than normal, but she had a bad night and is restless. She doesn't want to stay in bed, yet she has nothing to do when she rises. She has to wonder if Jacques really wanted the arsenic to take so long to kill his father. He had only said that they didn't want the chevalier to keel over immediately with a large dose. She can't imagine, though, he'd want the smaller doses to take so long. She's been lacing his coffee since early April! She should perhaps increase the dosage, but it would be best to check with Jacques first. Suddenly more animated, she sits up. Checking with Jacques about increasing the dosage is a good idea! One that has never occurred to her before. She'll write him a letter and ask. That will give her a reason to get up.

She would like to get on with the job right away but first needs to do her ablutions and dress. She heaves her bulk to the side of the bed and swings her legs to the ground. *Grâce à Dieu* today is a short wash - a little dab here and there with a damp cloth will be enough. The pundits preach that too much bathing destroys the natural oils and opens the path to disease. Besides, for the short wash, she doesn't need to summon a slave to help. The pitcher of water left in the room the night before will do; it is tepid, but that's all right. She hates having any of the plantation slaves around her; she dislikes them all - especially the coffee-coloreds. She can't bear the thought that they are siblings of her own highborn sons.

In situations where she needs help from a slave, she insists on the services of the pure black slave Adrienne, who is no relation to her sons. For the recent weekly bath, she got Adrienne to bring a basin, bidet, extra towels, and two pitchers of warm water. The full bath, a monthly event, is by far the most labor-intensive. It requires a wooden tub and eight pitchers of warm water. With any luck, by the time she needs her next full bath, she will be back in New Orleans planning her departure for France.

She doesn't object to her New Orleans house slaves the way she objects to these plantation house slaves. She always makes sure that all female house slaves are past their prime and unlikely to catch her husband's eye. In addition, she sees that the slaves that cater to her husband's personal requirements are male, most especially those that look after the outdoor bathhouse that her husband uses to cool himself. He sits naked in the tub, and the slaves pour cold water over him. Here on the plantation, she sees no sign of such a building; therefore, when her husband is well, he probably has a tub in his dressing room with a bevy of nubile young slave-girls in attendance. *Grrr!* She can just picture the orgies!

After dabbing at her cheeks and armpits with a damp cloth, she pulls a clean shift over her head; it protects her outer clothing from bodily effluents. (Her husband wears a fresh shirt every day to conceal the sweat and prevent staining his waistcoat and frock coat.) He owns over sixty linen shirts!

Next on the agenda are teeth. Although she has always been conscientious about using a cloth and abrasive powder on her teeth, several are nonetheless giving trouble and rotting. She doesn't like the idea of having to let nature takes its course and, like most older people, end up with a mouth full of rotten teeth. The only other option is, like her husband, to brave the brutality of a dental surgeon and let him extract them all. That though would adversely change her facial features and make her look older.

She wriggles into her skirt, pats the pocket to ensure that the glass vial containing arsenic is still where it should be, and moves on to the tall window to open the drapes. It's a job normally done by Adrienne and as she now discovers is no mean feat; it leaves her breathless. Made from heavy brocade, the drapes hang from a ten-foot ceiling and puddle on the floor. Once she has them open, she finds the view over the farmyard a revelation - full of hustle and bustle. Because she normally gets up later, she has never seen the place so full of activity.

Her glance sweeps the area, then stops at the sight of a figure on horseback by the sugarhouse. It's her husband, yet that's impossible! He's been in bed since they arrived. She studies the apparition more closely. She is long way away, but she is long-sighted and the trousers, shirt, jerkin, and plantation-type hat all seem to be her husband's. This man though is younger, darker, and more handsome the way her husband was when younger. Blood rushes to her head. Anger and resentment roil in her chest as the realization hits her that this is the elusive André, who she hasn't seen till now, the one who means more to her husband than Jacques or Jean. Unable to tear away her gaze, she watches the pretender rein in the horse, a magnificent beast. A black slave on the back of a noble beast like that is unacceptable! Her husband of all people should know that overturning the given order is never an option. Slaves are slaves and can never be masters.

She realizes, too, that apart from possessing the same physical attributes as the chevalier, the imposter mimics her husband's mannerisms, his horsemanship, and his arrogant bearing. *Intolérable!* She feels she'll burst with indignation. How could her husband ever have allowed it? He deserves everything that is coming his way! Yet is it really coming his way? The arsenic dosages are too weak.

She still needs to put on her face, but then she'll write that letter to Jacques, and by the end of the week, they'll be able to up the dosage and put an end to this forty-year-old travesty of a marriage.

She sits down at her dressing table and stabs her finger into her rouge jar. Tight-lipped, she paints on the face she shows the world - that of a *grande dame* with impeccable credentials. Standing and smoothing her skirt, she notices she wasn't careful enough about wiping the rouge from her finger and has now stained her skirt.

Rouge Stain

Plantation, Louisiana

Since her conversation with Adrienne in the storeroom, Agathe has recovered her equilibrium. Due to the master's health - he has not improved in the interim - the worry about him making a move on Adrienne has abated. For now, the child will not need to follow through with the ridiculous idea of sacrificing her virginity to his lust.

At present, Agathe is in the scullery gathering the materials she needs for the master's sponge bath: hand basin, wash clothes, soap, and towels. She will have to come downstairs again for the jug of hot water because the girls are all otherwise occupied, but she doesn't mind. Climbing the stairs, she feels a curious sense of lightness and relief that she has not yet had to betray the master's trust, and that for the time being, she can enjoy nursing and pampering him. It is something that gives her both a sense of empowerment and tallies with her instinct to nurture too.

It has dawned on Agathe that the best solution to the Adrienne problem would be for the master to recover from his illness but for him to remain permanently impotent. She knows some illnesses have this effect and prays to both saint and loa that this be one of them. She would dearly love not to have to spend time thinking up ways to make him impotent without killing him. She is determined though that her beautiful daughter will not fall prey to the lust of a lecherous old man.

To hedge her bets, she has started to fashion a Vodun doll for the curse she will have to think up if the master is restored to his former self. She enjoys making Vodun dolls. She inherited the skill from her mother, who, like Agathe, kept stashes of fetish materials[73] hidden behind her cabin. Agathe's collection features at present a number of animal tails,

---

[73] Materials with magical powers

bits of skin and bone, a dried lizard, and the tusk of a wild boar. All possess the power of attracting the spirits.

Reaching the sickroom, she opens the door soundlessly - he still sleeps - puts down her load and draws open the damask drapes. The master once told her that's what they are and explained about contrasting colors in the warps and wefts. She likes such snippets of information and remembers them.

Although the morning light streams in through the tall window, the master continues to sleep, so she tiptoes out of the room again to fetch the water and the mistress's skirt. The mistress had earlier waylaid her to tell her she'd had left a skirt on her bed for cleaning.

On checking the skirt, Agathe finds a rouge stain and, in the process, feels something in the pocket. It's a small glass vial, a pretty little thing she has never seen before. It is now almost empty but had obviously contained a white powder. She removes the stopper, holds the container to her nose, and sniffs; it has no smell. A medication? Not one of the mistress's; hers are on a silver tray by the bed.

As Agathe stares at the powder, certain oddities start to fall into place. Questions that she has asked herself since the mistress's arrival now have an answer. Why is the mistress here for the first time when she has nothing to do and hates the place? Why does the mistress pay no attention to the master, except to insist on being present for his breakfast? Why does she insist on pouring his coffee? On the first day, when the master said, "You don't have to pour my coffee, Cécile. Agathe can do it," the mistress had snapped.

"There's no need for Agathe to do it. I'm capable."

Why does the mistress wait until he drinks his coffee and then leaves the room? Why is the master sick in the first place?

As it dawns on her that the mistress is poisoning him, a suffocating blanket of gloom engulfs her. She has been hoping that the master would recover minus his libido but now knows that he will not be recovering.

She holds her head and groans. Adrienne might no longer be in danger, but seeing the mistress's intention is to kill the master, the two *real* sons will take over and will not want their half siblings around, mocking them by their very existence. The likely outcome is that they will send the coffee-colored kiddies to the slave auctions, where they will be sold to different buyers. The *real* sons probably won't bother with Agathe, but how can she live without her children, without knowing what happens to them, without knowing about the children they might have? She would prefer death. Also, they will want Adrienne in their beds as did their father.

No sooner have these thoughts taken shape than a bell clangs in the distance. The master has used the bellpull, has woken, and needs attention.

She replaces the vial in the pocket in which she found it. The mistress need not know that Agathe has already been in the room and has handled the skirt; she must never suspect that Agathe has stumbled on her secret. Agathe will willingly take the rap for not cleaning the skirt, but with any luck, the mistress will not mention the matter again knowing she has had a lucky escape. When the skirt is no longer on the bed later in the day, Agathe can say, "Mistress, I'm sorry I didn't have time to pick up your skirt. Master needed me."

As she enters the sickroom, a rasping voice comes from the bed, "Agathe!" A big, warm, toothless grin accompanies the greeting.

The Kahve Bean

London, England

Tom has been pleasantly surprised to find that knowledge of coffeehouse culture acquired in Liverpool has now stood him in good stead in the capital. Although there are certain differences in how they serve the coffee, he feels as much at home in the Kahve Bean as he does in the Merchants' Coffeehouse; only Ambrose is missing. Today though will be Tom's last visit to the Kahve Bean because he will be returning to Liverpool tomorrow for *Spirit*'s departure.

As he enters the establishment, he notes as always the sign that features the harvesting of coffee beans by happy slaves in some distant land. Although he has never yet laid eyes on a happy slave, he desperately wants to believe that once they leave the filth and disease-ridden holds of the *Spirit of the Clyde* - provided they survive the journey - their situation improves.

Such is his thinking as he enters the coffeehouse, greets the proprietress, places his order, leaves his penny on the counter, and picks up the broadsheet he wants to read from the table by the counter. Settling himself alone at a table, he waits for the coffee boy to bring him a bowl. Yesterday it was a *barmaid*[74] doing the job. He had looked at her thinking that one day he would like to find a woman for himself. That though is unlikely to happen at a coffeehouse seeing that coffeehouses are men-only establishments. The only women that a person sees in a coffeehouse are barmaids or proprietresses, and even those are rare. On *Spirit*, he used to see plenty of slave women. They, through no fault of their own, were filthy and disease-ridden, which bothered Tom if not other members of the crew.

Tom's agenda for today is to study an editorial that he noticed in one of yesterday's broadsheets but was too tired to read at the time. It

---

[74] Although referred to as *barmaids*, alcohol was never served in coffeehouses.

concerned the roots of libertarianism mentioning the Enlightenment, the American Revolutionary War, the American Declaration of Independence, the United States Constitution of 1789, and the French Declaration of Rights passed shortly afterward. He looks forward to reading the article, but will wait for his coffee before starting on his reading and note-taking though. He has grown accustomed to the grittiness and bitterness of a drink that some describe as "gruel that tastes of oil and ink or of leather."

Watching the boy ladle the black liquid into bowls from pots by the fire, he thinks how some tout coffee as an effective medicine for dropsy, scurvy, gout, and scrofula. He has to wonder how much proof those people have when they make such sweeping statements. As science has not yet established a grip on the country, it is easy for anybody to claim anything.

When his coffee arrives, Tom thanks the boy in a mannerly fashion and takes his first sip. It was worth the wait. He would like to take another sip, but knowing he must pace himself, he starts reading.

Several hours later, he feels better informed about the exciting era in which he lives and about the seismic forces that are undermining the traditional power of the church and that of the upper classes too. The editorial that attracted his attention starts with the following sentence: "The eternal verities of church and nobility are starting to look tarnished and tawdry under the onslaught of science and individualism." Tom can only applaud the sentiment when he compares the tedious, moth-eaten verities with the euphoria he feels at hearing the words "All men are created equal and endowed with the unalienable rights to life, liberty, and the pursuit of happiness."

The biggest surprise of his afternoon's reading comes from the fact that Thomas Jefferson had worked hand in glove with General Lafayette on France's groundbreaking document - the Declaration of Rights - without which, there would have been no French Revolution. It amuses

Tom that French texts never mention Jefferson; instead, they give all the credit to Lafayette. Like most Englishmen, Tom enjoys taking jabs at the French. After all, the two nations are still at war.[75]

Swigging back the dregs of his now cold coffee, Tom feels it is wrong that there seems to be no British input in either of the two seminal documents of the new era: the United States_Constitution and the French Declaration of Rights. Surely, the greatest nation on earth must have contributed in some way!

Looking around, Tom sees an elderly amputee, a major, sitting alone. Tom had spoken to him a few days earlier discovering the soldier had lost his leg in the American Revolutionary War. However, in the past decade, having overcome his anti-American bias, he has become an avid student of events of the second half of the eighteenth century.

After returning the broadsheet to its place, Tom approaches the major, saying, "Sir, perhaps you can help me . . ." He buys the veteran a coffee and soon discovers that in 1791, when Jefferson had formulated the amendments to the United States Constitution, he had borrowed from the British Bill of Rights of 1689. That in turn had borrowed from Britain's six-hundred-year-old Magna Carta.

When the major finishes speaking, Tom grins and comments, "I knew the world couldn't do this without us!"

"I admit," the veteran adds, "that I, too, find the words and ideas of these documents intoxicating, but let's remember it is one thing expressing such lofty sentiments as all men are created equal, it is another putting such ideals into practice. Not many of us - even in libertarian circles - think these things also apply to Africans. We temper

---

[75] The War of the Second Coalition (1798–1802) was the second war on revolutionary France by the European monarchies to contain the French Republic and to restore the monarchy in France.

our liberalism with doses of nationalism and pragmatism not to mention racism!"

Tom leaves shaking his head in wonder at himself. While thinking that slavery per se is all right provided it serves Britain, it has never occurred to him that slaves too have an inalienable right to liberty. How can he remain a patriot at the same time as believing in the inalienable rights of every human being?

Salmon Beat[76]

Aberdeenshire, Scotland

The laird in his hip-high waders moves out into the current and, with expertise honed through a lifetime, casts his line toward the opposite bank. Reeling in, he watches the lure bounce back toward him across the water and feels unusually content. He believes that as the riparian owner of a six-mile stretch of a swift-flowing stream, he is among the most fortunate people on the planet.

On this fine spring day with water skittering in white and silver over the rocks and with an eagle in the sky, there is nowhere in the world he would rather be than here. Although the spring run for salmon is nearly over and is smaller than the autumn run, the catch rate is usually high throughout the summer, thanks to his meticulous maintenance of brae and water.

Wading back to the water's edge where he left his tackle on a large flat rock, he crouches down to change his fly for one he feels might be more suitable for today's conditions. With care, he opens a box filled with lures: his pride and joy, skillfully tied by his own hand over the past winter. What a sight! He marvels at the diversity of their patterns. The *stone fly* pattern, the one he has just used, was on the line from the last time he fished and was better suited to the early spring when the ground water was starting to thaw. The *hex fly nymph*, a favorite of young salmon, would be a better choice for now. The fuzzy *wool bugger* is also a good option for spawning salmon. The *wiggle minnow*, especially the blonde version of the pattern . . .

Heavy footsteps from the woods behind interrupt his study. Adrenaline floods through his body. No one has a right to be here but

---

[76] Stretch of river or stream that flows through a landowner's estate and to which he owns the riparian rights.

him! Outraged, he turns to see a big rough-clad man emerging through the oaks. He recognizes him as one of his tenant farmers.

"McCready!" he thunders, "This is outrageous!"

McCready stops a few feet from the rock where the laird wishes he could jump to his feet to assert his authority but instead is crouching. Getting quickly to his feet is no longer an option. Red in the face, fists clenched, McCready does not remove his cap as would behoove someone of lower status. Being no match for a man in his prime, the laird wonders if McCready is dangerous, but in spite of bunched fists, his hands hang at his sides.

With voice loud and harsh, McCready says, "I have something to say!"

"Then the estate manager is the person to whom you should speak," counters the laird.

McCready fires back his response, "Not when the matter concerns your unborn great-grandchild, who is due any day now!"

Banishment

Aberdeenshire, Scotland

From the drawing room window, Stanley sees the laird stomping up the path from the glen, sees him emerge from the woods, and hears him march through the hallway. Still wearing his waders, he bursts into the drawing room where the family is starting to gather for tea. He grabs Stanley by his necktie, "You! You!" he shouts speechless with rage. "You are not worthy of the lairdship! I want you off my property. Now! You are a disgrace to us all."

Stanley has to hold his grandfather by the forearms; otherwise, the old man would have punched him in the face. Barking furiously, Angus McCorm tries to join in the fray. Pontefract jumps to his feet, grabs the dog by the collar, and holds him. Frances more laboriously rises and tries to soothe the laird with her words, "What's the lad done, Father?"

The laird purple in the face splutters, "He's dragged our family name through the mud, behaved like a sewer rat. He must go! Now!"

Then running out of breath, the fight leaves the old man. Stanley lets go of his arms, and Frances, after helping her father to a chair, fans his face. As Pontefract helps Stanley smooth down his clothes, Stanley says to his father, "I guess McCready told Gramps, as he told me earlier today, that his daughter Donalda is soon to give birth and that I am responsible."

Pontefract takes a few steps back, stammering, "Is it true?"

"It could be," Stanley acknowledges.

"Go! Get out of my sight. Never let me see you again!" rages the laird with renewed vigor. Dangerously purple and leaning forward in his seat, he tries to rise but falls back as, with a groan and hands over her stomach, Frances slumps down into and chair. Pontefract rushes to the bellpull to summon help and then returns to Frances. Stanley would like to help his mother but doesn't know what men are supposed to do in such a case. He, his father, and the laird look on gormlessly as maids help Frances to the door.

With the mood now changed, Stanley turns to his grandfather and says, "Gramps, I shall be collecting a few things from upstairs and leaving never to return, as is your request. I hope to be leaving for Louisiana soon and . . ."

"Louisiana!" Pontefract exclaims, face pale.

"I'll give you the details later, Pops," says Stanley. "We can meet in Edinburgh." He feels a surge of relief that Louisiana issue is now out in the open. Turning back to his grandfather, he says "Gramps, you and I are responsible for Mums losing yet another of her babies. That's obviously what's happening now. This being the case, I would suggest that, instead of raging, you take Donalda into the house as a nursemaid and allow a baby of your bloodline to be born here. No one needs to know of a sixth little grave by the chapel. No one needs to know that I am the child's father. The newborn can be given out as Mums' and Pops' child, thus avoiding the stigma of illegitimacy and giving Mums a replacement for the baby she is losing too."

Stanley does not wait for a reaction. Slipping out into the hallway, he tells one of the kitchen staff to get a message to Wee Johnny to saddle the gray while he goes upstairs to gather a few items that he'll be needing for the ride ahead.

As he climbs the stairs, Stanley thinks how fortuitous it was that McCready had approached him earlier in the day. It gave him time to think up scenarios of how best to deal with his grandfather's likely reaction. That his mother should lose her baby at the same time was unforeseeable, but it offers the family a good solution for the future of the lairdship and for Mums' longing for another child.

Knapsack over his shoulder, he strides toward the stables, where Wee Johnny is finishing saddling the gray. He keeps his mind on the journey; he knows of an inn tucked away in the countryside. No one will find him until he is ready to reappear.

Interesting Encounter

Liverpool, England

Wanting to remain incognito, a down-dressed Sir George sets out on foot for the docks. The mirror has assured him that his plebeian attire will not be attracting attention. He enters the port from Water Street. There, an arch marks the expansion of the port at the time the slave trade with Africa and the West Indies took over from local trade with Wales and Ireland. From then onward, the port became a mecca for traders, businessmen, and titans of industry - Aaron Migu is an example - who belong here and not in the hallowed halls of places like the New Club!

Turning toward the river, Sir George sees *Spirit* in the distance. Along with other vessels, she is moored to the dock, waiting for the tide to turn, but seeing the tide is still rising, it will be a while yet. In the meantime, Sir George wanders around the wharves that serve both the Irish packet trade and too-battered trawlers from Stornoway, Uig, and Stromness in the north of Scotland.

Once back in the George's Dock area - the best place to watch *Spirit* depart - he spots an empty seat on a bench next to . . . he can't believe what he sees! It's the frail young man with the amputated forearm that he saw in Hyde Park a couple of days earlier! The lad now has a notebook in which he is scribbling away with a pencil and hasn't yet noticed Sir George.

Sir George wonders if he should move on but then realizing he is not going to get a bench to himself anyway, he might as well stay. When he asks the youngster if he can join him, the lad looks up, closes his notebook, and invites him to sit.

"I don't want to disturb you," Sir George says.

"I like talking," says the young man. "It's a nice change after life at sea, where there was no one with whom to speak. The crew was a rough lot, and I had no language in common with the slaves."

That, thinks Sir George, *was a lot of gratuitous information for a situation that only required a nod!* However, seeing the boy seems harmless, he joins him on the bench. Mention of slaves shows the lad worked on a slave schooner, a matter of interest to Sir George. It might even have been on *Spirit.* Many of those now in the area will be here to see her sail for the first time since her refurbishment.

"So you're a sailor!" Sir George exclaims. "I thought you might be a student!"

"Oh, I am that now, sir. Since I can no longer work as barber-surgeon. I am trying to educate myself. I want to become a writer, but without much money, it isn't easy." The lad looks off into the distance to the hills across the Mersey. When Sir George doesn't comment, he says, "I would give my lifeblood to use the power of the pen to write about my theories for improving the health of slaves in transit, but I don't have the necessary scientific training."

Sir George finds humor in the young man's volubility and to something endearing in the ardent pursuit of an unreachable goal. It is for people like this that Sir George intends endowing the Edinburgh University with a faculty of science.

The youngster is now standing up and apologizing, "Sorry, to gab away like that, sir! I won't bother you anymore. Before *Spirit* sails, I need to check on my new kitten."

Sir George surprises himself by feeling sorry that the boy is leaving and has a sudden idea. He says, "I'd like to hear more about your ambitions. If you let me buy you a coffee, we could meet later at the coffeehouse."

The lad's face lights up, "Oh, sir! Thank you!"

The Young Dandy

Liverpool, England

Migu has been waiting a long time for today's event. The refurbishing of *Spirit* in the Canning Dry Dock has taken longer than anticipated, but luckily, the wait is now over. He hates seeing a major asset sitting high and dry.

He approaches the port from Water Street and enters through the arch that celebrates the newer world - one that embraces industrialization; one where he has found his niche, feels at home, and prospers. Once inside the port, he heads for the dock where *Spirit* awaits the change of tide. He has arrived ahead of time wanting to check on her cargo and to make sure an earlier problem has been resolved. Once on board, in the company of the captain, he climbs into the holds to make sure they contain what they should: textiles from his mills and garish mass-produced items to bait the unwary. The error with the cargo has been rectified and all is now as it should be.

As he climbs out of the last hold, it occurs to him that while these holds now smell new, they will soon be bursting with men, women, and children lured on board from the African jungle. He's been told that the odors of human excrement and unwashed bodies will soon be so strong that the smell will be detectable from distance even on high seas. He refuses to think of such matters and leaves the vessel as quickly as he can.

Now standing on the dock with the sun peeking through scudding cloud, he checks his pocket watch, sees he has time before meeting Émile, so decides to take a walk. His cape billowing around him, he is striding along the promenade, when a gull dive-bombs a woman ahead of him, and she careens into two gentlemen coming in the opposite direction. One is a young dandy dressed in the Beau Brummel style; the other is someone he knows!

"Gadzooks!" he exclaims to the lemon-faced nobleman, "If it isn't Lord Richard!"

As the young dandy helps the woman regain her balance, his lordship throws Migu a look of loathing and stalks onward. The young dandy doesn't follow immediately; instead, he raises his top hat, gives Migu a pleasant smile, and says, "Good morning, Mr. Migu! Lovely day, is it not?"

This polite behavior throws Migu off balance but gathering his wits, he replies, "Indeed! *Spirit* will be a fine sight when she sets sail."

The young dandy says, "I look forward to the spectacle!" With another smile and deferential nod, he trots off after his mentor.

Émile's Transformation

Liverpool, England

Migu arrives too early for his meeting with Émile at the arch, so to pass the time, he takes another stroll this time outside the port along Water Street. As he goes, he thinks of his cousin whose entrepreneurial brain is constantly coming up with some bizarre, new scheme. He had recently mentioned that when the messy Revolutionary War with France ends, setting up a wine business in Britain could prove a profitable undertaking.

Sidestepping a dead gull in his path, Migu shakes his head. It is not that Émile's ideas are ill-advised; they aren't. In the Middle Ages, wine from France was imported through Liverpool with Ireland as the main market. Now the market would be much larger and more lucrative. What bothers Migu about Émile's schemes is that he expects Migu to invest in every one of them. Meanwhile, Migu feels he has enough on his plate with the plantation, worries about Betta's health, and Rose's marital plans.

Heading back to the arch, Migu arrives at the same time as Émile, and they head out on the tour of the port that Migu had promised his cousin. They start with the Salthouse Dock - a beehive of mercantile activity, featuring anchor smithies, block-and-sail-maker shops, pubs, and eating houses. They give a wide berth to the side streets - home to dens of vice, misery and prostitution - but no matter how wide the berth, the odors from filth and garbage are inescapable. Migu has to push aside the knowledge that the pristine *Spirit* soon will smell like this too.

Handkerchiefs to their noses, Migu and his cousin move on quickly. Back on the public walkway, they have a view of the open river where small boats ply the Mersey estuary. Some scud along with the wind; others are rowed with rhythmic strokes of oars.

"I was hoping to see one of the newer three-mast schooners," says Migu, "but we're out of luck. *Spirit* only has two masts."

Émile is more interested in real estate. "What are those buildings?" He wants to know. As his cousin points, Migu notices that Émile is no longer wearing his flashy rings. He thinks, *Can Émile be flirting with Beau Brummel's unadorned style? What a hoot!* He says, though, "Those buildings are the Goree Warehouses. They are named after a slave market in West Africa. The dock on which we now stand is the George's Dock, which is connected to the Canning Dock, where *Spirit* underwent her restoration."

On George's Dock, a new set of smells assault their nostrils - fish, salt, seaweed, and dung - all better than those at the Salthouse Dock. Nonetheless, they are none too pleasant, especially when the sinking and lifting of ships moored to the dock are enough to make anyone feel queasy. Thus, with Émile in tow, Migu negotiates a path through dockworkers, merchants, and sailors and bypasses horses and carts and piles of buoys, rope, canvas, and netting until they finally arrive at a place of relative calm. There are two benches close at hand. One is occupied by an elderly couple; the second is free, and they are able to settle with nothing more intrusive than the cry of the gulls and the sound of water slapping against the hull of a lone trawler.

The peace does not last. Shouts, bellows, swearing, and laughter suddenly erupt from within the trawler. It doesn't faze Migu or Émile but bothers the scavenging gulls that with battering wings and piercing cries explode into the air, frightening the elderly couple. The husband starts to shake uncontrollably, and she, recovering more quickly, strokes his arm, consoling him with the words, "There, there, dear! They were only birds, not cannons." Given that the British and French have been at war for years, the old man must have been involved in the fighting.

Good. He does not know Émile is French, thinks Migu.

The episode reminds Migu of his recent encounter with Lord Richard, which he now reports to Émile. When he is finished, Émile says, "Aaron, please repeat what you said to this Lord Richard."

"I said, 'Gadzooks if it isn't Lord Richard.'"

"I was hoping you had given up harassing the elite," says Émile, his tone more sad than critical. "I don't know what *gadzooks* means, but it doesn't sound like a polite way of addressing a nobleman."

"*Gadzooks* is a harmless exclamation, but I see no reason why anything I should say should bother you."

"Would it not be good and right for Rose to be proud of her father?" Émile asks, peering at Migu, his head tilted to one side in curiosity. "Surely, you don't want her to feel ashamed of you. I know that I should like to see her proud of her papa."

Migu is taken aback by the remark, and as they move on, he's not paying attention, he nearly gets hit by a load that swings overhead on the arm of a juddering crane. Not bothering to think he might have been knocked out or even killed, he wonders at the fact that it never occurred to him that Rose might feel ashamed of him. The thought though is immediately superseded by wonder at Émile's wording. *Would it not be good and right . . .* and *surely, you don't want her to . . .* do not sound like something a *Frog* would say or like something Émile would have said previously. The realization hits him that Émile's English has improved and that he is also acquiring inflections used by the British upper classes! Bizarre! He asks tentatively, "Émile, are you taking English lessons?"

"I am glad you've noticed!" Émile replies with a type of laugh that surprises Migu even more than his words. It is a polite upper-class chuckle, not his usual guffaw.

Migu needing time to digest this extraordinary turn of events reverts to his tour-guide mode. He says, "It's to this area we'll return to see *Spirit* sail, not exactly where we are now but over there." He points. "It will give us the best vantage point. Seeing though we still have time until the tide turns, we should continue our tour. First, let me show you a fine specimen of United States' naval architecture."

They are inspecting a detail on the hull of the frigate when a bystander says, "We taught those Yanks well, didn't we?"

Migu lets out a guffaw, and Émile repeats his upper-class chuckle. With that, it dawns on Migu that the sound is similar to the way Lady Abigail expresses amusement! With a triumphant voice, he says, "You've been taking lessons from Rose's governess!"

Émile, chin held high, replies with pride. "Yes, Lady Abigail is turning me into a gentleman!"

Migu collapses into paroxysms of raucous laughter with Émile joining him, no mannerly chortle this time! When they have finally wiped away their tears of laughter, Émile again reverts to his new persona, saying, "Lady Abigail is a lovely person, Aaron, and she admires you."

With an incredulous tone, Migu exclaims, "An upper-class dame admires *me*! No! No! Hasn't she taught you, Émile, that gentlemen must never lie?"

Émile replies in a stilted tone, "Aaron, Lady Abigail has taught me many things about polite society that you, too, would do well to learn."

Migu grunts and asks, "What other platitudes does Ms. Etiquette dump on you?"

Émile ignores the scorn and embarks on a list of what is vulgar and revealing of low-class origins. "If one doesn't understand someone," he tells Migu, "one mustn't say pardon. That is vulgar. One must say instead, 'I'm afraid I didn't understand what you said, sir. Perhaps, you wouldn't mind repeating it?' It's more polite."

"Sounds like groveling to me," Migu growls.

Unruffled, Émile continues, "One must never laugh out loud, instead just give a refined chuckle. One must never shout or assert oneself, instead, remain calm and collected, allowing others to do the talking."

"Lady Abigail should write a book on how to become the world's best ass-kisser," Migu comments. On seeing Émile flinch at the vulgarity, he says, "Pardon. Carry on."

Émile rushes on with gusto. "Never laugh at lewd jokes and never mention the slave trade, pretend to know nothing about the Middle Passage, or that schooners are made for anything more than to skip across the waves. One must only wear muted colors and prefer poetry to balance sheets. One must know about pianofortes and that the Austrian-made instruments are better than their English counterparts. It is necessary to hire famous architects to build a new wing on one's château, and the balustrades and mantles can only be of Carrara marble. One must commission large paintings . . ."

When Émile had started on his list, Migu decided to see how long it would take before he ran out of steam, but he now gives up. Holding his hands to his ears, he says, "Stop, Émile! Enough is enough! Besides, you didn't even mention sticking out your pinkie when drinking tea."

"I hadn't got to that bit yet. Besides, it's a pretentious habit," says Émile. He adds with his old grin and his normal French accent, "You know, Aaron, you do have to stop harassing the likes of Lord Richard."

Migu sighs. "I hate to admit it, but you're right."

Pretty as a Picture

Liverpool, England

Ahead, Sir George sees among the crowd on the pier not only Lord Richard and the young earl but Migu and the cousin too. He also catches a glimpse of the lad he will meet later at the coffeehouse and resolves to avoid all of them. The boy - so he notices - has found a good spot from which to watch the spectacle and waits with an air of stoicism.

As he takes a circuitous route to avoid all those he knows, Sir George recalls the boy saying he was pouring his *lifeblood* into the task of educating himself and smiles at the wording. When he gets to know the lad better, he must remember to point out that the elegance of understatement is preferable to hyperbole. Immediately, his irritating counter-voice tells him he is judging the youngster by upper-class standards that decry exaggeration and shows of emotion. Instead, he'd do better to give the boy the education that he needs.

The musings come to an abrupt halt as the band starts playing, and a sudden eruption of cheering alerts him to the fact that - sails swollen fore and aft - the *Spirit of the Clyde* is rounding the bend! As the wind tugs at his clothing, the scene - *Spirit*, the sun, blue sky, and water - startle him with their beauty.

As *Spirit* approaches Pier Head, miniature figures on board wave to the crowd while wild cheers and a brass band playing at full volume compete with the metallic *brrrrrs* of foghorns. The noise is such that Sir George must hold his hands to his ears to protect his hearing until, all too soon, *Spirit* is leaving the safety of the harbor to become a mere speck on the open waters of Liverpool Bay and the Irish Sea.

As he turns and joins the crowd leaving the pier, Sir George wonders at the scientific knowledge that culminates in the splendor of a two-master like *Spirit* skimming across the water under full sail.

Although Scots have an affinity for the ocean, Sir George possesses little knowledge of the relationships among mast, spar, rigging, and sail. He can only marvel at the refinements to an ancient science that enables a heavy wooden hull to skim across the water looking every bit as elegant as the terns that fly overhead.

Thinking these thoughts and not concentrating on his surroundings, Sir George gets closer to Lord Richard and the young earl than he would otherwise have done. Luckily, they don't notice him though. (There are definite benefits to being nondescript!) Aaron Migu, with his execrable cousin, has also spotted his lordship and calls across the crowd, "As pretty as a picture, was she not, Lord Richard? I'd commission a painting of her from dear old Reynolds, if the poor man were not already dead!"

Surprise for Tom

Liverpool, England

Although the gentleman he had spoken to earlier wanted to meet him at the coffeehouse after *Spirit* sailed, Tom doubts that he will appear. Why should this person find an out-of-work barber-surgeon of interest?

However, on the off chance that he will come, Tom is here. He sits alone in his corner by the window; he has a broadsheet published on Tuesdays and Fridays spread out in front of him. It features five top-to-bottom columns of dense print per page and is hard on the eyes. He has finished reading an account of a hanging at the Kirkdale Gaol, and instead of moving on to a report on the council meeting, he returns the newspaper to its assigned place and goes back to his table and picks up his pencil. Fair head bent over his notebook, he jots down strings of disjointed words pertaining to *Spirit*. His concentration is such that he does not notice at first when someone materializes at his side. Then jumping to his feet, he pulls out a chair, exclaiming, "Oh, sir, I'm glad to see you! Please take a seat."

"I don't want to interrupt you."

"No, you are not interrupting me, sir. I've finished reading the *Merseyside* and am now jotting down a few thoughts on *Spirit*. My friend Ambrose says if I want to be a writer, I must start learning to get my thoughts onto paper. I know though that I need a better education before I will ever learn the craft properly. I don't want to be just a reporter that writes the type of things I read in the *Merseyside*. I want to write articles that deal with ideas and can change opinions and promote debate."

"Good writing can certainly be used to influence public opinion and even government policy," the gentleman comments. "It does take a while to acquire the necessary skills though. Don't you think some type of tutor or school could help you achieve your aim more quickly?"

"Oh, sir, I could never afford anything like that! Besides, Ambrose says formal education in England is backward-looking and places more value on the classics than on science. Meanwhile, it is *now* that interests me and . . ." - his face registering his distaste - he adds, "I *hate* all those muses, goddesses, and heroes like Hercules, Achilles, and Perseus."

Tom sees the gentleman is trying to hide his amusement as he comments, "You must have looked into the matter to know their names. To what is it you object so strongly?"

"All that strength and beauty makes me feel insignificant," Tom explains. In a protective gesture, he clasps his stump to his chest.

"What does your friend Ambrose say about all this?" the gentleman wants to know.

"He thinks I need to get myself a good general education and should begin practicing writing my own material now."

"Sounds sensible."

"It's wishful thinking, sir, because I can't afford to spend more on an education than what I do already by buying notebooks, pencils, and a daily cup of coffee here at the coffeehouse. The latter gives me access to newspapers and to people who enjoy debate, but it's not enough to get me where I want to go." With a hangdog mien, he sits looking unseeingly into the distance.

The gentleman says, "You are right about a coffeehouse education not being enough, and I might be able to help you with your training. First, though, I need more details. You say your friend Ambrose has put thought into the matter, so he might know of suitable schools here in Liverpool. If I meet him, we can discuss the matter."

Tom's eyes fly open, like a bud bursting into bloom, as he exclaims, "Oh, sir!"

Lord Richard and William in Liverpool

Liverpool, England

Inviting smells of roasting beef emanate from a nearby restaurant. William's nose twitches, and he lingers.

Lord Richard says, "Hungry, are you? I am too, but we have to get out of the port. We can't risk another encounter with the oaf."

William doesn't comment but feels he would like another encounter with Aaron Migu. Lady Abigail has orchestrated several more *chance* meetings with Rose on Princes Street, which have only increased William's determination to ask for her hand in marriage. He knows though that for a successful outcome, he will need to get around her father. He has therefore been picking up as much information on Migu as he can and feels, if given the opportunity, he may be able to circumvent the bluster of the persona Migu presents to the likes of Lord Richard. He is pleased that his approach on the promenade did not meet with a rebuff or with the type of treatment accorded to Lord Richard.

Lord Richard, with William behind, walks for what William considers unnecessary miles to end up in an upscale restaurant with oak beams, low ceilings, and latticed windows. They settle at a table in a corner where candlelight picks up the gleam of mahogany and where the warmth from an open fireplace reaches their legs. The weather outside has turned cool and blustery.

As they wait for their order, William would like to turn the conversation to Aaron Migu, but Lord Richard is telling him how the flagstone floor dates back four hundred years and how the structure of the building incorporates old barrels and ship masts. He also points out the rare pewter-topped bar and the copper reliefs on the vaulted ceiling.

Their drinks arrive, and Lord Richard asks, "Do you know any good nautical toasts to help *Spirit* on its way?"

William has to drag his thoughts away from Rose and, after a moment, says, "All I can think of is 'Bottoms up,' which would hardly be appropriate!"

"Indeed not!" says Lord Richard with a thin smile. "I think we'll make do with 'Fair winds and following seas.'" Intoning the words, they raise their glasses and drink to *Spirit*, now on its way to the coast of West Africa.

Alternative Plan for Tom

Liverpool, England

The turn of events over the past few weeks has given Sir George a sense of accomplishment. The compulsion to prove himself to his peers is waning, and he is no longer allowing his guilt to debilitate him to the degree it has until now. He is determined to allow himself satisfaction in how he spends his ill-gotten gains. Taking on Tom Brown as a protégé - he is glad to be giving the boy the name written on his notebook - is his first undertaking of the kind, and he finds the personal contact with an individual beneficiary more rewarding than dealing with executives.

Over the weekend, he dedicated time to thinking about how best to handle the Tom project. He has come up with a couple of options, which he will present to Tom at his meeting with him and Ambrose in a few days' time. Meanwhile, he sits alone at a table in a corner of the Merchants' Coffeehouse looking through the papers. When he tires of that, he tunes in to various debates at nearby tables. He is still dressing down and enjoys the incognito status it lends him. No one pays him a whit of attention, and he prefers it this way, as opposed to previously when he wanted to be recognized as a bigwig and dressed for the part.

Across the distance, he hears fragments of conversations pertaining to libertarianism, the Declaration of Rights, and other issues of the day. Some of the debates he finds intellectually stimulating, like the subject of evolution versus creation, but others he finds disturbing and often downright provocative and illogical. How for instance can anyone believe that all men are created equal when that is obviously not the case? How can anyone justify the barbarism of beheading France's King Louis and his Austrian Queen while remaining loyal to Britain's monarchy? (Thankfully, all participants in that debate are at least monarchists!)

Sir George feels that while the Merchants' Coffeehouse cannot be described as a hotbed of dissent and rebellion, the general tenor of discussions around the tables tend too far to the left[77] for his comfort. For that reason, he doesn't feel the environment is suitable for his new protégé. He doesn't want to find himself nurturing another abolitionist like Wilberforce! It would be better to help a person who, while being capable of independent thought, opts for the middle.

He is glad to have gained this insight before meeting with Tom and Ambrose. He now will not be presenting Tom with two options but instead will make one grandiose offer!

---

[77]   *Left-wing* and *right-wing* stem from French revolutionary era and refer to seating in the National Assembly: aristocrats on the right; commoners on the left.

Preparations for Gran Legbwa

West Coast of Africa

At the first light of dawn, the hunters disappear into the forest, fishermen take to the ocean, and a small party of women and children armed with baskets leave for the forest to collect crickets, caterpillar, weevils, termites, and beetles. All are delicacies if correctly prepared. The majority of the women and children remain in the village making the necessary preparations there for the late-afternoon feast that will precede the evening's rituals. Efia's job will be to coordinate the efforts of this faction, but before she starts on her round of inspection, she must finish wrapping an offering of tobacco for Gran Legbwa.

Efia likes the smell of tobacco; she wouldn't mind a smoke now, but giving this tobacco to Gran Legbwa is intended as a sacrifice, so she resists the urge and feels virtuous for doing so. She hopes the invisible Gran Legbwa is watching and taking note! When it comes to offerings and sacrifices, all loas have their personal tastes, and tobacco is one of Gran Legbwa's favorites. That doesn't mean information of this type can't be adjusted to suit circumstances though, the way she adjusts it when she wants to make a point to Abebi for instance. To make sure the gift pleases Gran Legbwa, she has put thought into the packaging and now has a big leathery leaf from Big Baba's banyan. She feels it will do the job nicely. It has an attractive reddish tinge occasioned by the imminent onset of the rainy season.

As she sits on a mat in front of the family hut wrapping the tobacco, Efia wonders how Abebi will make out having her hair done in cornrows down at the Banyan. From the distance, Efia can see that her daughter has just arrived there. One of Big Baba's elderly sisters-in-law, Zainia, is doing the job. Although Zainia can barely walk, she still has agile fingers and a large clientele for the complicated hairstyles in which she specializes too.

In spite of the hard work, Efia loves all the preparations for these feast days; she finds them exciting with villagers bustling around in seeming chaos yet knowing their jobs, knowing they are contributing to a vital rite in the life of their tribe. Adding to the celebratory atmosphere are the overexcited children chasing about among the cackling, barking, and bleating of indignant chickens, dogs, and goats. The soundscape, while not as overwhelming as the parakeets at sunrise, has a piercing quality that intrudes on one's thought. Nonetheless, as Efia's fingers work on the tobacco package, she manages to run through in her mind the jobs and work parties on which she must keep an eye.

She starts with the granny group that must ensure that the large copper serving platters are removed from the storage shed and washed in the forest stream. She can see the women in their wraparound skirts carrying them in the appropriate direction. When they have done that job, they must provide an ample supply of individual plates in the form of leaves from the plantain palms.

Efia can also see the stew crew - another group of grannies - sitting on mats outside one of the huts. They are sorting through the black-eyed peas grown in family vegetable patches and requisitioned for the evening's feast. Because they have been harvested sixty days after germination, the leaves are still tender and can be used along with the pods, but they do need cutting into pieces, which the grannies will do after they finish sorting.

To have a good stew to accompany their fufu, Efia knows that it is very important to get the spices and thickening right. Today's thickening will be the grounded nuts that she, Abena, and several others grounded with pestle and mortar yesterday. As to the spices, Efia has decided that ginger, cayenne, and white pepper will accompany the essentials of tamarind and salt.

Shea butter - a treat only used on feast-days - and okra need to be added at different stages during the cooking process and can easily be forgotten. Chopped up and dried chimpanzee meat is also an important ingredient that should only be added just before serving. Adding a small amount enhances the flavor of any meat by making it richer. Last time when they forgot to add the chimpanzee flavoring, Thimba had said something was wrong with the stew and wondered if it was because they had used plantains as thickening instead of peanuts. Who would have thought that he knew anything about cooking, but he obviously does!

With respect to tamarind, it features in all Efia's recipes. There is a tamarind tree[78] not far out on the savanna that serves the tribe well. While the fruit is used for seasoning, the leaves, bark, and root have medicinal purposes. In the past, Efia had often fed Abebi and Infana tamarind fruit mixed with coconut milk. Traditional wisdom maintains that the beverage gives strength and wisdom to those who drink it. Poor little Infana didn't have time to prove, or disprove the theory, but Abebi is certainly strong, if not wise!

Having wrapped the tobacco to her satisfaction, Efia reaches for a coir[79] cord to secure the package. As she extracts a suitable length, she thinks of the fourth work group: the women preparing the cooking area with its pits and fires for the cauldrons. Most of the women are young and not yet trained in the skills of womanhood. They need to be reminded of general principles, such as boiling needs a quick, vigorous flame; stewing, a low flame, while frying or broiling require a bed of glowing embers.

Of the two cauldron fires in the main cooking area, one is used to boil water for fufu, and the other is for the cauldron that will contain the big stew, which must simmer for hours over a gentle flame. Of the two large firepits, the deeper one is for roasting chunks of meat, birds, and small animals on the spit; and the shallow one, for grilling insects, steaks, and fish on flat pieces of metal. For the latter, glowing ashes are better than flames.

---

[78]   A leguminous tree
[79]   Fiber harvested from outer husk of a coconut

It will be a while yet before Efia needs to look for the dugouts from the ocean or for the insect collectors emerging from the trees, but her glance is already scanning the edge of the forest for the hunters. It takes time for them to turn their carcasses into manageable sizes and for them then to cook. On the other hand, the fishermen while needing time for preparation - sorting, descaling, and gutting - don't need much time for cooking. The same applies to the insect collectors.

A fifth work crew is supposedly attending to the beverages. The millet and palm wine are done, and Efia has already seen the women transporting the urns to the stream for cooling. The nonalcoholic ginger drink is not yet ready. Grinding the ginger is labor intensive and entails the use of the waist-high mortar. To operate the pestle, two women have to stand on stools and work in tandem, often with piccanins on their backs. It is no mean feat, and they can only keep it up for a short time before having to hand over to the next pair. Yet as Efia cocks an ear, she hears neither the rhythmic thump nor the work songs that characterize the job. In other words, the women have not yet started. She clicks her tongue; she does not like chivvying them, but to have the drink ready in time, they will need to get going soon.

Having tied the last knot on the tobacco package, Efia holds it up, admires it, and gives it a pat. Gran Legbwa will be happy with the offering! Tidying up after herself, she then resolves to look in on the beverage women right away. She hopes they didn't get so enthusiastic about sampling the wine prior to taking it to the stream. It wouldn't be the first time!

Hairdresser

West Coast of Africa

As Zainia attends to Abebi's bush of black hair, Abebi sits on a low stool under the banyan; Big Baba sits on his throne watching. A cluster of women sitting on the ground on blankets de-husk coconuts provided by Abena's group, who brings them over in batches. Abena's son, Assimbola, visible from the banyan, is palm walking to harvest what is needed.

Abebi, her hair now long enough for a cornrow style, is starting to realize that she has let herself in for more than she anticipated; she finds the process lengthy and uncomfortable with a lot of pulling and jabbing. As a result, she fidgets and whines.

"Eeeh, Abebi!" Zainia complains. "Stop squirming around like a worm. You've seen this done before, so you know what to expect."

Indeed, Abebi has seen it done before; she has seen how Zainia divides the head into quadrants with a wooden pick before separating each quadrant into small squares. She then smooths the hair in each with shea butter before braiding it from top to bottom and securing the ends with beads and rings. Abebi hopes Zainia is not being too stingy with the shea butter. The nearest shea tree is a lone tree out on the savanna, and Zainia is too old to get there herself, so has to depend on Mammi to part with some of her precious stock.

While Abebi enjoys watching Zainia doing a braid or two on Mammi's head, she soon gets bored and runs off to play. On return, she will find Mammi with a complete head of beautiful braids. Having to sit through the intervening time herself is proving more difficult. She looks over to Big Baba, her eyes pleading for support, but all he does is smile and say, "You have to suffer for beauty, Abebi." Seeing no option but to resign herself, she sits as still and silent as an effigy for the rest of the tedious session.

On completion of the job, she returns to her own giggling self, especially when the women clap and ululate and call out, "Eeeh, look at Abebi; such a little beauty!"

In the distance, Abebi then spots Assimbola surrounded by a group of onlookers as he prepares to embark on his next palm-walk. This is something she must see! She has had her back to him until now. She takes off at top speed with nary a word of goodbye to those she leaves behind.

A naked, pudgy little figure with her new braids flopping around on her head, she barrels across the clearing toward the coconut grove. Thanks to her special toes, climbing trees is her area of expertise. She would love to show off her prowess along with her new hairstyle. She doesn't even need to be tied to the tree like Assimbola is.

Palm Walking

West Coast of Africa

Efia's friend Abena heads the contingent whose job it is to harvest the coconuts needed for the children's drink at the feast in the evening. Each child will receive a dehusked nut with two holes on top that make it easy to drink the *water* inside.

Abena and her crew - made up of a number of her peers and many curious children - stand around the palm, ready to gather the nuts as Assimbola starts his ascent. Even though her thirteen-year-old son must make his way to the top of an eighty-foot tree, Abena knows there is no cause for concern. She can rely on Assimbola's skill; he has been doing this job for a number of years and knows what he is doing. She also always checks and double-checks the knot on the length of cloth that will hold him to the trunk, and he is already pushing back and manipulating that cloth, as he starts on his *walk* into the sky.

Aware that there is no need to keep her eyes riveted to the tree, Abena looks around and sees the tubby little figure of Abebi barreling toward them. The dog Inja gambols at her heels while the new braids joggle around her head.

"Look at you!" Abena greets her on arrival. "Zainia has done you proud."

Others gather around clapping and ululating as Abebi preens and grins before turning her attention to the figure climbing the towering trunk with agility of one born to the task.

Abena returns her attention to her son. As Assimbola is now two-thirds up, she no longer sees him against the backdrop of land, but as a dark silhouette against the light. He and the tree are mere outlines against ocean and sky. The tree has a slight lean and rises from a swollen base to an elegant crown of long, feathered leaves with the nuts hanging clustered at the transition between fronds and trunk. It is a sight common in the village, one she has often seen, yet this time, it has taken on a transcendental dimension and strikes her as timeless, beautiful, and ineffable.

Laying the Fires

West Coast of Africa

On the way back from checking on the beverage crew - in spite of sampling the wine they are still compos mentis - Efia receives a message that one of the members of the cooking-fire contingent has gone into labor. Several of the women are attending to her; thus, the crew is shorthanded and needs help. The midwife apparently hurt her hand, and although she can give instructions, she can't do anything herself.

Efia therefore now finds herself laying the kindling for the two cauldron fires. What she needs for each fire is on hand: three suitable stones of the same height on which to balance the cauldron. For kindling, the women usually use small twigs, bark, dry leaves, or grass, but today the mask carvers have produced enough wood shavings to do the job. Seeing that the wood is seasoned and dry, the shavings will catch the first spark with ease, especially if aided by some gentle blowing. It's a job Abebi enjoys when she is present, which she is not at the moment.

Looking up to check on Abebi and expecting to see her at the banyan, Efia spots her instead arriving at the coconut gathering. However, seeing that Abena has taken her in charge, all is well. She can stay there for a while, and Efia can save her lecture on Gran Legbwa and the poto mitan for later.

With the flame now burning in the shavings, Efia starts laying down small bits of wood. As she does so, she thinks how Big Baba scoffs at her attempts to explain to Abebi matters pertaining to the tribe's rituals. He says she should leave such things to the houngan[80] or Babalawo, but she feels no one understands her child the way she does.

---

[80] Priest who looks after the rites and rituals and maintains the relationship between the spirits and the community

As she continues to feed wood of ever-increasing sizes into the fire, she sees out of the corner of her eye that the hunters are arriving. Thimba and his friend Shamwari emerge from the trees and now lead their fellow hunters eastward along the forest fringe toward the butchery - an open shelter at the top end of the village.

As expected, she is able to ascertain that the men have none of the larger varieties of game given that they are a small group and have only hunted in the forest and not out on the plains where the antelopes, buffalo, and elephants graze. The biggest animal the men have this time - visible from the distance because it needs two men to carry it - is a small forest antelope dangling by its legs from a stick carried by a hunter at each end.

With regard to the rest, Efia can't see more detail but does see from the hunters' distorted outlines that many carry smaller animals slung over their shoulders; the heads dangle, and the legs are tied together and point upward. Although she can't identify the individual species - except for a young tapir whose long snout is a giveaway - she can see no one will be going hungry this evening and that enough will remain for drying, salting, and smoking whether it be monkey, cane rat, pangolin, or porcupine. There are usually birds among the mix, but given their size, they don't contribute much to communal gatherings such as tonight's.

With water in the two cauldrons now heating, Efia decides to go down to the coconut grove and wrest Abebi away from the scene. As she goes downhill, she manages to catch Abebi's attention, so she stops, cups her hand to her mouth, and yells, "Come with me, Abebi!" She beckons to emphasize the point.

Abebi, clearly understanding the order, clasps her hands behind her body and probably pouting gives her head a vigorous shake. The message could not be clearer; she will *not* come! Looking at her daughter, if it were not for the disobedience factor, Efia would have laughed at the contrariness emanating from that small package of humanity; evident even over a considerable distance.

"You are to come *now*, Abebi!" she yells again. Abebi, now has her head tilted back and transfixed though, watches Assimbola ascend adjusting the cloth that holds him as he goes.

Grim-faced, chin stuck out, Efia storms down the hill bracing herself for the confrontation that must inevitably follow. She pictures herself dragging away Abebi, who would be shrieking and struggling like a goat led to the slaughter. Abena, however, saves the day by calling to Efia from the crowd at the foot of the palm, "Don't worry about her, Efi! I'll keep an eye on her."

Letting go of her irritation, Efia acknowledges the favor with a hand gesture and makes an about-turn. It is just as well Abebi isn't with her because that way she can go up to the butchery and see if the hunters need anything. Heading back uphill, she thinks of the first and last time Abebi accompanied her to the butchery. The child had stood at the side of the shed, trying to bat off flies with one hand and pinching her nose with the other. Meanwhile her expression had alternated between fascination and revulsion as her eyes moved from the hunters to dead animals in various stages of dismemberment and finally to the piles of meat crawling with flies. That's when she started heaving and vomiting and couldn't stop.

Falling Coconut

West Coast of Africa

Assimbola, now level with the clumps of heavy nuts, is freeing his chopper from its strap and is starting to hack at a clump. Abebi sees that onlookers are looking skyward and probably won't notice if she dashes forward to the palm and starts to shimmy up the trunk.

Starting to run forward, she doesn't notice that one of the coconuts at the place at which Assimbola has directed his axe is starting to hurtle earthward right above her. It is only thanks to Abena yanking her out of the way in the nick of time that it doesn't crash down on her head.

"I don't know what you were thinking!" the normally kindly Abena chastises in fury. "You could now be dead!"

"Auntie Abena, please don't tell Mammi," Abebi whimpers.

"I'll have to think about that," Abena says sternly. "You should now run along and catch up with Mammi. I can still see her heading for the butchery."

Abebi takes off at top speed but then slows down. She doesn't want to go to the butchery. She knows what she will be seeing there - frightening men drenched in blood and wielding axes, knives, and cleavers. She knows, too, that she would see things for which she has no name: haunches, shanks, ribcages, and worse, slithering piles of innards, frothing lungs, and hearts with severed blood vessels. She knows that the purple things Mammi told her are livers and would glisten with slime, and that things called brains would feature shiny white lobes packed into cavities to keep their convolutions, twists, and fissures in place.

Abebi cannot imagine from whence these horrors come and what purpose they serve. It only confused the issue when Mammi told her that the things she saw at the butchery were dinner. No food she has ever eaten looks like that, and she certainly wouldn't eat it if it did!

She realizes that the horrors have something to do with life and death and knows that live things move and dead things don't, yet her knowledge doesn't fit into a cohesive whole. She is confused about the relationship between life and death. Auntie Abena said she could have been dead. What would that have been like? Infana would know; he's dead.

Gran Legbwa Celebration

West Coast of Africa

The tribe is gathered in a circle around the sacred pole, the poto mitan. A night of high drama lies ahead. The celebration is in honor of Gran Legbwa whose symbol is scratched into the naked earth at the foot of the pole. By using the dances, songs, rhythms, masks, and costumes specific to Gran Legbwa, the tribe will invite their loa to join them and speak to them.[81]

As the houngan[82] gives the signal for the ceremony to begin, Efia initiates the singing and dancing while the drummers find their voices. This initial phase is low-key, and Big Baba has no compunction about allowing his mind to wander. Although his throne is part of the circle, he is the only person in the circle who isn't performing. That would have bothered him more a short while ago, but he is now becoming reconciled to the depredations caused by aging.

He is content to see by the light of the fire his tribe gathered in celebration. With a sudden surge of emotion, he feels proud of his people. They are a fine sight! Inja - he sits on Baba's lap to be out of the way of the dancers - senses his master's emotion and licks his face. Baba, turning his attention to the dancers, admires their masks and costumes. He especially admires a solo dancer who has now entered the circle. While performing the obligatory moves, the lad adds a personal touch. He is able to move his arms and body in a different rhythm to his legs. It is fortunate, thinks Baba, that the tribe has certain drummers who are capable of *marking* a dancer's feet and skilled enough to accommodate the improvisations by playing a four-beat rhythm over a three beat. From his vantage point, Big Baba can see one such drummer sitting on a stool among his peers. He has a *djembe* between his thighs, and his hands blur with the speed he needs to create the rhythms.

---

[81] The spirit uses the voice of a medium to speak.

[82] Priest

Extracting pipe and tobacco from where he keeps them tucked into his loincloth, Baba muses on how music and dance are as natural to his people as speech. It is not like that with the Arabs who he used to meet on the savanna; they reserved music and dance for special occasions, whereas for Baba's people, music and dance are part of everyday life. *Regardless of time or place,* thinks Baba, *music and dance are how we tell others who we are.*

The drumming, along with the singing, clapping, and stamping are starting to quicken. The smell of sweat and a shaking of the ground lend urgency to the proceedings. Big Baba shifts his focus and immerses himself in the ceremony. Soon Babalawo - Medicine Man - and the warriors will be moving into the circle and putting on their show. They were all clustered around Thimba on the perimeter of the circle but are now on the move. Babalawo, wearing a fierce mask, dances into the circle first and performs the appropriate moves with panache. Encouraged by clapping, stamping, and whoops from the crowd, he leaps ever higher into the air, twisting and turning to send the strips of fur tied to his waist flying away from his body.

After a few minutes, the warriors led by Thimba burst into the circle with their fierce war cries. Accompanied by frenzied drumming that sets Big Baba's heart racing, they stage the dance at whose climax three figures explode out of their midst for the Grand Leap. Wielding their spears and bending at the knees, they propel themselves upward, leaving the earth beneath and heading skyward. Lit by the fire from below, they resemble otherworldly beings.

Only when the drummers slow down and the warriors retreat does Baba's old heart stop racing. It needs a rest before the real climax that still lies ahead. In the meantime, he returns to reminiscing, to which his age group is prone. Apart from being useful to the tribe as a way of passing on their history, Baba also finds the process of reminiscing of benefit to himself personally. It soothes and stabilizes him, and he has come to see the tendency, as part of a natural progression that will soon return him to the world of the spirits from whence he emerged at birth.

Of the three dancers who performed the Grand Leap so well, Thimba and Shamwari were no surprise; they have done it for years. Surprising is the presence of the third dancer - Thimba's adolescent brother Kwame. He has joined his big brother and Shamwari for the first time, albeit with a stick to simulate a spear seeing he is not yet a warrior. Baba has sometimes seen Kwame from a distance as he practices the Grand Leap and knows from this and other observations that the boy will eventually challenge Thimba. It's a pity he's not older. The tribe needs someone of his caliber now.

When younger, Baba himself was no slouch, when it came to the Grand Leap. He was the best of his day. That type of athleticism though was one of the first things to go as he aged. Although he is now always tired, even when doing nothing, he had remained energetic for a long time. He had only recently become an observer instead of a participant. Prior to that, he had always played a role in ritual celebrations, even if only as a drummer and singer. Drumming is the gift closest to his heart and has proved the most enduring. Although his hands have lost their agility, he can still play with cross-beats and make the drums "speak."

Baba's present role as a listener and not a teacher allows him to follow in detail the innovations in the polyrhythms of this new generation. The way in which some of them divide the basic pulse with cross-beats amazes Baba. He also admires the skill with which they whip the crowd's emotions into a frenzy before guiding emotion down again by laying stress on the main beat and minimizing the counter beat.

Now relaxed, Baba waits for the culmination of the ceremony in which Efia and her voice will play a pivotal role. Even as a child of Abebi's age, he recognized that Efia was blessed with an exceptional voice. However, it was though only later that he came to fully recognize the magnitude of the gift. The thought of Abebi distracts him briefly, and he throws a glance in her direction. She is dancing alongside Twenty-Eighth Wife with unparalleled enthusiasm using the simplified dance steps taught to children. What a little skellum!

Returning to Efia, although song, dance, and rhythm are innate in his tribe, he had always known that systematic instruction could carry those innate gifts to new heights. With this in mind, when he retired as a warrior and became an elder, he started teaching both singing and drumming; the former to both boys and girls and the latter only to boys. That's when he first realized the full extent of Efia's talent and ever since has felt that getting Efia to sing to her full potential is among the greatest gifts that he has given to his tribe. All those pep talks!

"Flatten the diaphragm. Take in as much air as you can. Let it out in a slow steady stream. Let the notes ride on it like an eagle riding thermals . . ."

The climax approaches. Drums, rattles, clapping, and stamping are becoming faster and louder, their momentum permeating the jungle and shaking the ground beneath Baba's feet. To the roar of the crowd, fervor builds into a peak of ferocious splendor, crackling with supernatural energy. It's the moment that Efia lets loose with her glorious voice, sending it soaring into the night calling to the loa, telling him his people are ready.

In a moment of earth-shattering drama, the unseen spirit explodes onto the scene and with a triumphant shriek takes possession of the medium's body hurling it to the ground. That body - no longer under control of its owner - rises and, growing into gigantic proportions, speaks with a voice of thunder, "Beware! Danger lies ahead!"

Fourth Week of May 1800

Danger in the Bayou

Sugar Plantation, Louisiana

As the chevalier listens to André speak of the bayou, he allows his mind to drift like morning mist through cypress and palmetto; through gum, myrtle, and cottonwood. He loves the bayou and taught André to love it too. Often, they would watch long-legged herons fishing in the shallows, ospreys swooping in from on high, beavers and muskrats slaving away on their dams. He also took André on deer hunts and taught him to use the long-barreled *fusil de chasse.*[83] It is not something other plantation owners taught slaves, but then he was not the quintessential plantation owner, nor was André the quintessential slave.

He smiles as André speaks of the time that they saw a snake skimming across the water, its eye on an unwary bird.

"Remember, Master?" André is saying, "I was small at the time and shouted at the bird, which managed to escape! That was when you taught me that snakes that swim with their bodies on the surface are poisonous and that Louisiana has two types of venomous snakes: coral snakes and pit vipers like the copperhead, cottonmouth, and rattlesnake."

---

[83] Forerunner of the shotgun

The boy's mind is a sponge, thinks the chevalier, *he absorbs everything.* The chevalier himself does not remember delivering those snippets of information about the snakes, but he must have done so because as a slave André would have no other access to that type of information. The boy was and still is a delight!

André is now listing the creatures that live in the waters of the bayou. In the chevalier's mind, each name evokes an image. It is as though he is paging through a book of illustrations with one image giving way to the next: crawfish, shrimp, shellfish, catfish, frogs, and toads.

Birds now replace the water creatures: pelicans, egrets, ibis, ducks, vultures, hawks, owls, sandpipers, woodpeckers, wrens, quail, snipes, ospreys, sparrows, rail, bee-eater, guinea fowls, bustards, cormorants, herons . . . The chevalier stops listening as the list continues, but his mind's eye dwells on the image of a heron they once saw. It had a wriggling fish clamped in its beak and its long legs trod water as the bird struggled to become airborne with the extra weight. It amazes him that André can list so many species. The boy had a good teacher!

As André moves on to raccoons, opossums, and armadillos, the chevalier's mind begins to tire delivering unrelated filaments of thought. Word and image no longer have a context. He sees his cousin Émile's face, something he has never seen in reality yet knows it is not unlike what he sees in the mirror.

Émile with his wild black hair mutates into the chevalier's own son Jean splashing through the bayou at night. Lost and alone, he doesn't know where to turn until he finds a rock and pulls himself to safety. The sight of Jean lifting his eyes in gratitude to the heavens fades behind a vision of Cécile. She is in the water fighting for air as heavy clothing drags her down. He would like to help her but can't. As she sinks beneath the surface, blood-tinged bubbles rise and fade behind an image of the guillotine. The crowned head of Louis XVI - by the grace of God, king of France - is placed beneath a monstrous blade that with resounding clatter hurtles downward.

The final vision takes the chevalier back to the bayou. André is in the water floundering; he half swims, half wades as he tries to escape a snapping alligator. As he heads for the bank, blood darkens the water behind him. The chevalier wants to cheer him on, but then he sees what André cannot see. On a rock close at hand, Jacques stands surrounded by items designed for slave-castigation: shackles, chains and a branding iron. Like André warned the bird, the chevalier wants to warn André of Jacques but can't; he has no voice.

As André approaches, Jacques's smirk expands into a grin. Taking to hand his cat-o'-nine-tails,[84] he cracks it over André's head. The sound brings the chevalier back to the present. His heart racing, he opens his eyes to find Agathe and André hanging over him fussing. Agathe swabs his brow while André strokes his hand and peers into his eyes.

---

[84] Multi-tailed whip

"Stop Interfering, Maman!"

Plantation, Louisiana

The courier on horseback has come early today bringing a letter for Mrs. Cécile. Thus, when the bell clangs at the back of the house telling Adrienne that the mistress is ready to rise, Adrienne takes the letter up to Cécile's room on a tray. She hasn't forgotten the ivory paper knife - something for which she has received reprimands in the past. However today, in her eagerness to read the letter, the mistress rips open the envelope, not bothering with the paper knife.

For her part, Adrienne, who can barely read in the regular sense of the word, has become adept at "reading" the mistress, and now watching the emotions cross the mistress's face, she would dearly love to know what the letter says. The initial look of excitement and anticipation changed first into one of extreme displeasure but has now softened into one of guarded relief.

The letter starts in an angry tone. Jacques writes as follows:

Maman,

I know exactly what I'm doing. Stop questioning my judgment! I've planned for Papa to die around the middle of June, and I have my reasons. I *do not* want you interfering with the dosages and upsetting my plans! Continue doing what you are doing. You'll see how everything will fall into place. You need to be patient for a few more weeks. I know it is not easy for you, but it won't be long before Jean and I shall be joining you.

Cécile reads the missive with mixed feelings. The tone can hardly be termed either respectful or affectionate, but she understands Jacques is under pressure and probably didn't mean any harm. Like his father, he is controlling by nature and likes to have his way. He just sometimes forgets that he is addressing his mother and not his younger brother.

Also, while two weeks may sound like a long time, she is glad to hear Jacques has a plan, and the matter isn't as unpredictable as she has come to imagine. Knowing the time frame, even if she doesn't like the duration, is better than having the matter shrouded in uncertainty.

Phony Academic

Liverpool, England

Tom last saw Ambrose when they parted company in London and has eagerly anticipated today's meeting at the coffeehouse. He is now regaling his friend with the circumstances under which he met a Scottish gentleman whom he refers to as Esquire and who is prepared to finance his education. He tells of their meeting at the *Spirit* event and then touches on their interaction at several encounters since. Ambrose wants to know Esquire's name, but Tom isn't sure, saying, "He's well-educated, has a posh accent, and mentioned he's a retired academic."

Ambrose takes a puff from his pipe, then comments, "A retired academic wouldn't have enough money to finance the education of a young man whom he only knows from a brief encounter on a dock. Tell me more. Why is he interested in you? What do you and he talk about?"

"He asks a lot about *Spirit* and finds the poor conditions on board upsetting. He liked it when I said I wished I had scientific training so that I could help improve conditions in the holds. He doesn't think much, though, of libertarianism."

"Esquire sounds to me more like a member of the upper classes than a retired academic. He would have attended one of our old universities that specialize in delivering a classical education to the offspring of an elite who have no interest in seeing the common man as an equal. Such people are not meant to have the need to earn a living or to acquire practical skills of use in the modern world. They are meant to live on inherited wealth generated by ownership of Britain's land. Industrialization though has taken workers off the land, depleting the coffers of the upper-class landowners. They then have difficulty maintaining their lifestyle and staying afloat without another source of income. Perhaps Esquire is one of those and is ashamed to admit it, especially if the added source of income isn't of an honorable nature. That's why he needs to pretend to be an academic."

Tom looks doubtful, saying, "He doesn't dress like a toff."

"Perhaps that is a disguise. Let's work out what the source of his extra income might be. He came from Scotland to see *Spirit* sail and is taking an interest in you because you sailed on *Spirit*. Add to that our knowledge that - apart from Aaron Migu - the owners of the *Spirit* consortium are upper-class Scotsmen whose identities are clothed in secrecy. Esquire is most likely one of those. Perhaps, at heart, he's a decent person trying to assuage his conscience with good works."

Ambrose pauses for another few puffs on his pipe, then adds with a smile, "In his beliefs, he might be a bit like you and me, leaning toward the left with interest in new ideas but not sufficiently to the left to cut ties with the establishment."

New Mother

Aberdeenshire, Scotland

Frances loves babies; she would have had dozens - her own and adopted - if circumstances had permitted, but it is not a subject on which she now dwells. With the fragrance of spring entering through the open window, she sits on the nursery rocker singing a lullaby to the sleepy infant in her arms. The lullaby is one her mother used to sing, and Frances knows the tune but is not sure of the words, so she makes up her own, singing, "Let there be a hand-on-high to guide you, my darling."

For so many years, her arms have hung limp and empty, but now they are full. With the lullaby done, she sits staring into the face of the sleeping child that she holds in her arms. Feeling she might become gushy - her father hates sentimentality - she averts the danger by telling herself that Glen Orm's future laird will be a handsome man. She knows she is biased, but with Donalda McCready and Stanley Staymann as parents, Baby Adair has to be a looker.

Donalda, Adair's real mother, is unusually pretty with a head of red curls and delicate coloring. Frances had brought the lassie into the house before Adair's birth; thus, the future laird was born, where he belongs and where both his grandmother and birth mother will always be on hand to love him.

From the outset, Frances was determined to like Donalda, regardless of any failings, but she now finds she genuinely likes the girl and knows that, given the opportunities, Donalda could have made a good wife to Stanley. However, that being impossible, she is glad that the few people who know Adair is not her son but her grandson have received generous compensation and will remain silent.

On many levels, Frances couldn't be happier with the way things have turned out; nonetheless, two slivers of pain are lodged in her soul - the loss of Stanley and of the stillborn infant. The pain only manifests itself at night as she lies awake next to her sleeping husband. The laird is forbidding her all contact with Stanley, but when her father next visits his sister, she is determined to sit with her son one last time under the Scot pines among the graves of his deceased siblings.

The most recent grave is unmarked. Pontefract and the laird had gone out the night of the miscarriage and had dug the grave, said a prayer, and buried the child wrapped in a crocheted shawl. After filling the hole, they had concealed it with moss and pine needles.

These sad facts only surface at night; during the day, Frances enjoys Adair's presence to the hilt.

New Plan

Liverpool, England

Sir George, Ambrose, and Tom arrive within a few minutes of each other at the Merchants' Coffeehouse. Sir George - interested to see how Tom and his mentor will react to his proposal - dispenses with small talk.

He explains to Ambrose, "Since declaring myself willing to help Tom with an education, I've changed my thinking from paying for his instruction here in Liverpool and asking you, Ambrose, as Tom's friend and mentor, to find a suitable institution. Now I've thought of a better solution, and your role would be to help him decide whether he should accept the offer I am about to make or not."

Tom stares at Sir George with saucer eyes, and Ambrose says, "Certainly, sir. Having witnessed Tom's struggles for months, I couldn't be happier that he has found someone like you to help him. I assure you that you could find no worthier protégé."

Sir George wades in without further ado, saying to Tom, "What I am suggesting is that you join me in Edinburgh, where I can arrange for suitable instruction that - provided you prove yourself and work hard - will equip you to enter the University of Edinburgh. You'll have a place to live and a modest allowance."

As both Tom and Ambrose remain speechless, he continues to address Tom, saying, "I shall be leaving Liverpool next week for Edinburgh, but in the meantime, if you accept the offer, we'll meet a few more times to sort out details. I should have everything ready for you by the end of June, at which time, you would take the stagecoach up to Edinburgh. I'll be giving you the money for the fare before I leave.

Champagne in the Garden

Leith, Scotland

It's Sunday. Betta is not well; she is resting upstairs. Rose - she sports a bonnet of the latest fashion - and Migu sit in the back garden, enjoying the warmth of the sun.

Rose says, "I don't think our little garden warrants the attention of the likes of a Capability Brown,[85] but one day, I'll have a garden that does."

In mock indignation, Migu asks, "Are the roses I pruned with such care not good enough?"

"Oh, they are, Pa! Encouraged by Lady Abigail, I even wrote a poem about them. She liked it much better than the one I wrote today about the gardener digging up those baby mice."

"They weren't mice. They were moles."

"Oh dear! I was going to read it to Ma to cheer her up, but now I'll have to change it."

Migu is spared comment by the appearance of David, the footman, who says, "Sir, Mr. Staymann is in the hall. Should I bring him out here? He has brought a bottle of champagne and asks for glasses."

"The new crystal flutes, please, Davey," says Rose before Migu has managed to reply or work out why Pontefract thinks they should be needing champagne; Migu associates champagne almost exclusively with the launchings of the consortium's schooners. That being said, he would love to be celebrating something that Pontefract will definitely *not*

---

[85]   Lancelot Brown, 1715–1783, landscape architect

want to celebrate. Émile has received a letter from Louisiana accepting Migu's Offer of Purchase.

Migu is ecstatic about the development and wants to discuss with Stanley how best to tell the Staymanns and the old laird what is long overdue and will be bad news for them. Neither Migu nor Stanley wants to give Pontefract the opportunity of nixing the deal before the Agreement of Purchase was accepted. Migu, though, hasn't been able to find Stanley and therefore hasn't been able to share the news.

Pontefract now stands at the backdoor, his arms spread wide, and the bottle clasped in one hand.

"Time for a celebration!" he announces. "We have a son!"

Migu rushes forward to give his friend a bear hug. Rose is quicker; she gets there before him and rescues the Dom Pérignon before it lands on the ground as Pontefract staggers under her father's enthusiastic embrace.

"Wonderful news!" Migu exults, thinking how happy Pontefract, Frances, and the old laird must be. The cork pops under David's ministrations, and the crystal flutes, twinkling in the sun, are raised in a toast. As they settle, Migu says, "I'm assuming both mother and child are in good health. If it weren't so, you wouldn't be here with the bubbly."

"True, my friend!" Pontefract agrees. "Baby Adair is big and strapping, and both Frances and the laird are ecstatic. I haven't seen either so happy since Stanley was born twenty-two years ago." At the mention of Stanley, Pontefract's mien changes from exultation to concern as he adds in a sobering tone, "There is however a problem. Stanley has fallen afoul of his grandfather. The old man no longer wants him to inherit the lairdship and has banished him permanently from Glen Orm. Stanley had to leave Glen Orm immediately, and as he left, he said he would soon be sailing for Louisiana. I have no details though. All he said was that he'd tell me about it here in Edinburgh, but I now can't find him and am hoping he hasn't left already. Frances and I swing between exultation at the birth of Adair and devastation at losing Stanley. Such extremes of emotion are hard to reconcile!"

As Pontefract sinks into himself, he doesn't seem to notice Migu's expression, which shows a mixture of both disbelief and relief. For months, he has been agonizing over telling his friend about the Louisiana scheme that will rob Pontefract of his son and Glen Orm of its heir. Now his act of betrayal has become unimportant though because Stanley will be lost to the family anyway! Yet it slowly dawns on him that he is not entirely off the hook. When Pontefract finds out that Migu is financing the Louisiana project, he will realize Migu has been preparing to betray their friendship for months. It's an awkward situation that he'll have to sort out in due course. Meanwhile, he turns his attention back to Rose and Pontefract.

Rose has not spoken since Pontefract started speaking of recent events. Migu wonders if she is glad to be rid of Stanley in an even more radical manner than she could ever have imagined, but who can tell what Ms. Rose thinks? It turns out that she has not been thinking of Stanley at all. She is saying to Pontefract, "Lady Abigail has told me about Dom Pierre Pérignon and of how champagne was enjoyed by royalty and how it then became a celebratory drink. I've been looking forward to tasting it." She follows her words by taking a delicate sip from the flute, savoring it like a connoisseur.

Migu is horrified. He has never allowed her to sample alcohol, and he certainly didn't give her permission now!"

"Do you like it?" Pontefract is asking.

She replies, "I do, but I know Pa fears I might go overboard and spend my life in an alcoholic stupor, but he underestimates me. I shall not be going overboard and will always only sip champagne - or any other alcohol - in small ladylike quantities!"

Betta's Discomfort

Leith, Scotland

Betta rarely comes downstairs anymore. She was up earlier in the day, sitting in the bay window of the bedroom with her feet in a footbath. But now exhausted - even a footbath exhausts her - she is back in bed and is cold around the shoulders. Rose has gone off to see if she can find a lacy, crocheted bed jacket that her mother used to like and that always kept her shoulders warm.

Rose dedicates a lot of time to her mother, organizing the nursing schedules, doctor's visits, medications, and just chatting and making up nonsense poems to cheer her. Migu puts in his regular hours at work but comes home to check up in the middle of the day and makes sure to get home early in the evening. The servants go about their regular chores, and the governesses shorten their sessions to allow Rose more time with her mother.

With Rose out of the room, Betta sinks back into the pillows thinking how lucky she is to have such a caring family. She knows Rose loves her and is of a good and kindly nature, but the child has no inkling of how hard this business of marrying an earl is on her mother. Betta has nightmares of Aaron snarling at Rose's in-laws and - even if he makes an effort to do things their way - she can picture them smirking and looking down their long-barreled noses at him and at her. Aaron would no doubt find a way to fight back and would probably enjoy the drama of it, but how would she cope? She doesn't think she could. She could never feel comfortable in her daughter's home, nor would she feel comfortable having those people in her home. As to future grandchildren, what would they think of their low-class grandparents? She can picture them tittering behind their hands as she and Aaron - in their efforts to conform for Rose's sake - deliver one *faux pas* after the other.

Turning over in bed and facing the wall, she feels glad her failing body is offering her a way out of the problems that she sees ahead. She is a woman of faith, and if she can see Rose settled and happy, regardless of the circumstances, she would be able to embrace death with relief. Even in a haughty upper-class family, a deceased low-class mother-in-law could be touted as acceptable, and there would be no future *faux pas* to prove the statement inaccurate!

She is still smiling at her thought when Rose returns to the room saying, "I have the bed jacket, Ma, but the moths have got at it, and it has more holes than the crocheting would warrant." Seeing her mother is smiling, she too smiles, as she disposes of the item in the wastepaper basket. "I'll write an elegy to the bed jacket, so you won't feel too sad!" she says.

New Worries

West Coast of Africa

Big Baba - with tribal striations, bush of white hair, and naked but for a loincloth - sits enthroned under the banyan in the company of dog Inja, Big Billy, and the *hookus*. The carvers work out of sight but not out of sound as they chat and chisel in another area of the banyan's all-embracing shade.

Big Baba feels the tree is a dimension of his own being and never ceases to marvel at the reach of its shade and the ingenious method the tree uses to create that shade. From low horizontal branches, it sends out vertical shoots that - once they reach the ground - take root supporting the parent-branches as they become longer and heavier.

The mahogany, the kind of tree that Thimba chose for his altar to Masimbarashe, uses a similar system, but there, the problem is not heavy, horizontal branches; it is an unstable forest floor. This means that the tree, which needs to grow tall to reach the sun, requires buttressing around the bottom so as not to become uprooted and topple. It therefore employs aerial prop roots at the bottom of the trunk that thicken and hold the tree upright.

These solutions found in the natural world are a matter of great wonder to Big Baba, and in his years as an elder, he has always tried to act in a similar way by making sure he understands the nature of the problem before taking action. That is what he did with the Thimba problem even though that issue still awaits resolution.

Now as Gran Legbwa had intimated, a new danger threatens: one that is as yet impossible to define, but is starting to take shape in Baba's dreams. Thinking about it now, he realizes that those dreams receive substance from rumors passed on by Arab traders. Originally, the rumors concerned inland kings becoming wealthy by selling members of their tribes to foreigners, a scenario not applicable to Banyan Village.

More recent rumors, though, tell of the foreigners becoming bolder and of them moving along the coast into new areas where they no longer buy tribesmen but kidnap them. Baba realizes with a jolt that this item is the one on which he should focus. He is glad to have clarified the point, but doesn't know how to guard against a threat so ill-defined. How would the kidnappings take place?

Giving in to Inja's nagging for a swim, Baba gets to his feet, and together, man and dog head for the path down to the beach. On reaching the descent though, Baba realizes he is no longer able to negotiate it without aid. He therefore watches from along the ridge, as Inja scampers down on his own and plays in the shallows chasing the waves as they retreat and dashing back as they return to chase him.

Baba wishes he could see the beach from the banyan, but he can't. The drop down to the beach from the ridge makes it impossible.

Fifth Week of May 1800

Monsieur le Docteur

Plantation, Louisiana

The master sleeps while Agathe sits by the window and knits. The peace is rudely shattered as the mistress with Dr. Jules Le Blanc in tow barges into the sickroom. Agathe sets aside her knitting, stands, bows her head in greeting to the doctor, and makes her way to the door.

Dr. Le Blanc calls her back. "Agathe, is your master still having the cramps, convulsions, and vomiting you mentioned yesterday?"

"Oui, Monsieur le Docteur, c'est la même chose."[86]

"Thank you, Agathe. Go now but don't go far. I might need you."

Agathe departs, smiling to herself. She wouldn't dream of going far. As always, she will remain outside the door listening and watching through the keyhole. The keyhole is big, and the key never used; it lives in the drawer at the master's bedside.

As a consummate eavesdropper, Agathe's techniques have been in place since childhood; she doesn't miss much. Now she is able to watch

---

[86] Yes, Doctor, nothing has changed.

Monsieur le Docteur as he feels the master's forehead, takes his pulse, and pulls down the coverlet to poke and prod at his emaciated body. She feels like giggling as the doctor tries to make him stick out his tongue. She sees how the master is keeping his mouth clamped tight shut, although for days, it has hung open. This small act of rebellion confirms what she has long suspected: while the master might seem unaware of what goes on around him, it is not always the case.

Agathe notes, too, that Monsieur le Docteur and the mistress do not realize there is a possibility of the master understanding what they say to one another. If they did, they would not speak the way they are speaking now. The doctor has finished his examination and is washing his hands at the washstand. As he dries them, he says to Mrs. Cécile, she sits demurely and silently on the far side of the bed, "Madame, *Monsieur le Chevalier* is declining: lungs, skin, kidneys, and liver are failing. It's the normal progression, and there is nothing I can do except to recommend he eat lots of pork liver."

The mistress leans forward and asks, "How long will it be before he dies?"

"If I were to hazard a guess, I'd say about ten days. If your sons plan on coming, now is the time."

Cécile says, "Monsieur le Docteur, you mention 'normal progression.' For which disease, may I ask?"

As he thinks, the doctor strokes his pointed beard - he sports the Spanish style - then coming to a decision says in a solemn voice, "Madame, Monsieur le Chevalier's symptoms point to arsenic poisoning."

Agathe sees a look of shock pass across the mistress's face. She sees, too, that Monsieur le Docteur watches the mistress like a hawk and realizes that the doctor knows the mistress is the culprit! The question is, What will he do with that knowledge? Surely, he will not confront her; surely, he knows that people like the mistress do not pay for their crimes; they blame their slaves.

The mistress having regained her equanimity, confirms the point with the words, "I find it hard to believe, Monsieur le Docteur, that someone should be poisoning my husband. However, if it is true, only house slaves would have the opportunity."

As she speaks these words, three things happen simultaneously. First, Monsieur le Docteur suddenly, realizing he has disturbed a hornet's nest, starts to backpedal, saying, "No, madame! I was not suggesting human intervention. Arsenic poisoning can come from ground water or from exposure to certain wallpapers and paints. Also, some medications contain the chemical, even rice, because it is grown in flooded fields, absorbs natural arsenic that seeps from the soil into the water."

Secondly, the chevalier who has not spoken in days starts clamoring, "Agathe! I want Agathe! Where's Agathe? Bring me Agathe!"

Thirdly, Agathe does not wait for the doctor or the master to finish speaking. Fury flaring in her fierce face, she bursts into the room, takes her place at the bedside, but before picking up the cloth to swab the master's brow, she gives the mistress a ferocious glare. Mistress should *not* accuse slaves of the crime that she herself is committing! Although Agathe can never take on the mistress in any meaningful way, she has registered her protest, and it makes her feel better, especially as the mistress hasn't noticed the insubordinate glare; she is too busy dabbing at the beads of sweat that have sprouted all over her face.

Again, clamor from the master claims everyone's attention. This time no one but Agathe understands what he is babbling, and Agathe merely smiles as she continues to swab the feverish brow.

Dr. Le Blanc says, "Agathe, perhaps you can tell us what your master said. You are always with him and understand him better than we do."

Now Agathe's dilemma is how to tell the doctor what the master said, but not to tell the mistress. Thinking on her feet, she finds a good solution. She knows the doctor has served in the area for a long time and understands her slave patois. She uses that patois to say, "Master says no slave has the opportunity to poison him because he makes me sample everything first. His morning coffee is the only exception. The mistress sends me from the room and serves it herself."

The doctor raises his eyebrows but does not speak; he nods instead. Agathe hopes this means he understands that, while his suspicions about the mistress are correct, he should *not* mention poisoning again for fear of harming the slaves. She cannot be sure though if he really got the message.

The mistress, obviously feeling left out, says to the doctor, "What's the stupid woman jabbering about? Can't she speak a proper language? I have a right to know what my husband says, not that it is likely to make any sense."

Agathe holds her breath and waits for the doctor's reply. He is stroking his beard and taking his time. Agathe sends him a silent plea, *Please,* Monsieur le Docteur, *it's important you get it right!* The delay is making Cécile suspicious.

Tone testy, she asks, "What did my husband say? What are you hiding from me?"

The doctor rallies. "We're not hiding anything, madame. I was merely trying to think of a polite way of telling you that you and I are no longer welcome here. Monsieur le Chevalier told Agathe that he is tired, and she should get rid of us both, so he can rest. Perhaps we should take our leave."

Agathe then watches as Dr. Le Blanc assumes the role of the *gentilhomme*,[87] bows gallantly, offers Cécile his arm, and escorts her to the door. Agathe sees Cécile's facial expression soften at the polite treatment and hears the doctor say as they go, "There will be no more talk of arsenic. I should never have mentioned the matter." With the hand of his free arm, he pats Cécile's hand. "And you must promise me, madame, never to think of the matter again. Promise?" He bends his head to look adoringly into her face. Agathe sees Cécile nod; a small smile playing around her lips.

Phew! Agathe offers up a brief prayer of thanks to *Le Bon Dieu*. The mistress feels she is off the hook! If there is to be no more talk of poisoning, then there will be no need to place blame on anyone.

As the two backs disappear through the doorway, Agathe returns her attention to the master and gives him a wide smile; she has never once tested his food or drink! He acknowledges her thanks with a toothless grin of his own before his eyes close, his mouth falls open, and he returns to a semicomatose state.

---

[87] Perfect gentleman

Opening Up

Edinburgh, Scotland

Sir George is glad to be home. He has the window open; the sun shines in; and he feels pleased with himself. He is enjoying an afternoon cup of tea and blows on it to cool it. It's a low-class habit, but something he likes to do when alone; it's better than burning his tongue. He is starting to understand that he has lived an unnecessarily cramped life until now and feels the need to make changes. First though, he must address matters pertaining to young Tom not only with regard to education but also to accommodation.

During their brief interaction, the lad's irrepressible enthusiasm is a breath of fresh air and is an antidote to his own jaded, lackluster self. Besides, he is pleased that his plan to help Tom is easing the burden of his perpetual guilt. He is looking forward to setting up a plan for the boy's education. He will start by speaking to someone today about how to best to approach the matter.

After that, he'll begin restructuring his social life, and he won't bother any longer about pleasing or antagonizing the ultraconservative members of the club. He will just avoid them. Someone like Pontefract Staymann might prove to be more open-minded. People speak well of Staymann, who is said to move more fluidly between the classes.

He wonders if he should go to the club now, but sitting while enjoying his tea in the fresh air and sun from the window, he doesn't feel like going anywhere. Owning a fine terrace house in the New Town, he doesn't have to gallivant around the place the whole time. *Fine terrace house . . . fine terrace house . . .* The words jangle around in his head. How *fine* is it with all but his bedroom windows closed and shuttered and with the furniture swathed in dustcovers? Something is wrong; assets should be used to their full potential.

With his mind now on the domestic front, he reminds himself that he needs to put thought into how to house Tom. Startled, his eyes widen; he has an idea! He gets up and yanks at the bellpull, hearing its muted jangle somewhere deep inside the house. When Ms. Young appears, he says, "I've been thinking, Ms. Young. We should be opening the main floor of the house again and that you will be needing help. Perhaps you could speak to your niece about arranging for extra staff. From the end of June onward, we will be having company."

He sees her face brighten, and the dour old woman, who has served him for years smiles, and he sees she is not old at all!

"I'm delighted, sir!" she exclaims. "It's been like a morgue here."

Double Confession

Edinburgh, Scotland

Migu and Pontefract sit in the study at the New Club taking their midmorning coffee. Migu chose the venue to prove to Pontefract that he has given up behaving in an intentionally boorish manner toward the likes of Lord Richard. He therefore gestures discreetly to the server that they would like a fresh pot of coffee. Previously he would have shouted across the room but now feels virtuous for handling the matter correctly. Pontefract doesn't comment but would have noticed seeing that he has always cringed at Migu's excesses.

Migu's real reason for organizing the present meeting is to make his long overdue confession regarding his involvement in Stanley's Louisiana venture. As they wait for their fresh pot of coffee, Migu wonders if his lifelong friendship with Pontefract will survive the knowledge that Migu was prepared to willfully harm him for the sake of good business deal. He hopes the friendship will survive, but he also knows that he would do the same again if the situation required it. He is a businessman through and through, and a good business deal will always trump all else, even a lifelong friendship.

Spooning sugar into his fresh coffee, he thinks how business is his raison d'être and is the area that delivers him greatest thrills. He finds just looking at the crystals of sugar in his spoon exciting; they could have come from a plantation that will soon be *his* plantation, and they could have crossed the ocean in one of *his* schooners.

As Migu stirs the crystal into his cup and watches them dissolve, Pontfract asks, "How is Rose? Does she have someone in mind now that she and Stanley have decided they aren't suited?"

"Yes, and I don't like it, but the little vixen has twisted me around her finger, and I find myself falling in with her plans. An opportunity for me to meet the person she has in mind - by coincidence and without formality - is arranged for tomorrow."

"'Arranged for tomorrow' doesn't make it sound much like a coincidence!" comments Pontefract.

Migu ignores the remark and says, "I'm going to have to try to like him and get the matter settled as best I can. It seems important to Betta, and seeing she's ill, I want to please her." After a pause, he adds, "Although I've programmed myself to dislike all earls on principle, I have faith in Rose, who, as Betta's and my daughter, must have a few grains of common sense in her head and will not have made a choice that is too outrageous."

Not wishing to procrastinate further with his admission of guilt, Migu plunges into the deep end with the words, "If you remember, I once told you about Émile, a member of *the lost tribe of Israel,* who recently appeared in my life." Pontefract nods, and Migu babbles on, "Well, Émile, wearing one of his many hats, sometimes acts as an agent for real estate sales across the Atlantic and . . ." - he pauses for a gulp of his coffee - "back in January, he had a good prospect on his books. The seller was reliable, and Émile felt that Stanley and I would fit the bill. Landownership would give me a base for access to the expanding markets in the New World, and Stanley would be able to run a plantation as is his dream. Confirmation that the deal has gone through arrived a few days ago. Stanley and I realized we should have told you but were afraid you might have tried to prevent it." Out of breath with the speed on his delivery, he stops and peers at Pontefract.

Pontefract's face is pale and his expression unfathomable as he says, "Aaron, in due course, I'd like the details of what you and Stanley have landed yourselves in. Now I need to get back to work."

Migu starts babbling in relief, but Pontefract holds up his hand and says, "Stop, Aaron. I get the gist of the matter and see that you realize, it would have been best to have consulted the family before going ahead. However, now that it's happened, and the existence of the scheme will give Stanley a place to go, we'll overlook the rest."

Getting up, he adds, "If it makes you feel better, I, too, have a disclosure that I could have made earlier. Adair is not France's and my son, but our grandson, and there's another grave by the chapel."

Waving off Migu's garbled efforts at commiseration, Pontefract leaves, and Migu remains in the study to ponder the remarkable qualities of his friend. A similar situation with another could have ended in shouting and fisticuffs. In France, it could have ended in a duel. Émile, with his flair for drama might have liked that, but he'd have lost a sale. Migu is not a good shot! His musings end when he hears Lord Richard's voice outside, and remembering his resolve to behave, exits by the service door.

Encounter on Princes Street

Edinburgh, Scotland

"Gadzooks," begins Migu in mock surprise, "if this isn't Lady Abigail and my lovely daughter!" Then as he looks in the direction of William, the surprise becomes genuine, and he adds, "If I'm not mistaken, this is the young gentleman, who was with Lord Richard in Liverpool!"

Lady Abigail steps forward and makes the formal introduction after which William says to Migu, "I recently inherited certain shares from my grandfather, and Lord Richard has undertaken to teach me the nature of the relevant business. I understand that he is only one of five, along with yourself, who can do that."

Migu is not sure how best to handle the conversation at this point. Earls supposedly never talk about anything as low-class as business and money, so he settles for something noncommittal and says, "Yes, that would be correct," before moving on to safer terrain asking, if the *Spirit* event had been the young earl's first experience of the port of Liverpool. From there, the conversation becomes the type of casual masculine exchange to which Migu is accustomed: developments in the textile industry and the achievements of engineering companies such as Mr. Staymann's.

Migu is amused thinking, *The young devil has done his homework and is playing me along as the old laird plays along a salmon!*

Lady Abigail and Rose stand slightly to the side. Rose - while at her decorative best but at the same time demure and shy - follows the interaction without participating. Migu notices that the young earl - while embarked on his charm offensive - sneaks brief smitten glances at Rose as if asking for her approval for his performance. Migu knowing his daughter all too well can see she is proud of how her beau is handling her father. To his astonishment, he can also see that she is proud of her father for the way he is responding to her beau! Well!

On parting company with the trio, Migu notices a certain smugness in Rose's expression that seems to say "See, Pa, earls are not all as bad as you think."

Migu, heading in the direction of Leith Street, cannot help but think she might be right. An important point in the boy's favor is that he appears to be head over heels in love with Rose, which means money is not his only motive. The lad also has brains and interests beyond the noble blood that flows in his veins.

Hunters Depart

West Coast of Africa

In the gray light before sunrise, drums inform the villagers it's time for the hunters to set out for the giant eland hunt that will take place deep into the plains. As Efia, Abebi, and Abena (Abinti tied to her back) arrive at the place where the village meets the savanna, they find a crowd already gathered. The hunter-warriors - bodies and faces painted and carrying spears and leather shields - mingle with those who must stay at home: women, children, and the elderly, including Big Baba. He sits on a throne positioned by his younger wives and watches the warriors flaunting their magnificence.

Efia notices through the crowd that her father's eyes dwell more on Thimba than on any other. Furthermore, she notices that he does not seem entirely pleased with Thimba. Why? She turns her attention to her husband to find out the problem but notices nothing untoward as he organizes his boisterous trainees. This is to be the boys' first major hunt, and all are in a state of high excitement. Adolescents are always hard to handle, but Thimba is doing the job better than any other could, so why is Baba displeased? Perhaps, she misinterpreted his disgruntled expression. She says to Abena, "I think Baba is wishing he could still take part in the hunt."

"Maybe," says Abena. "It's hard on warriors whether old or young to have to stay at home on such occasions. My man always said he couldn't live without the hunt." Abena, now turning her attention from Baba to Thimba, watches Thimba putting on his helmet and exclaims, her face alight with admiration, "That man of yours, Effie, is the pick of the bunch!"

Efia glows with pride; she knows Abena speaks the truth. Helmet now in place, Thimba stands in incomparable magnificence well above all others. The helmets that the warriors wear add at least eighteen inches to their normal height. They are the manes of the lions, which each warrior killed in single combat prior to their initiation. Thimba's helmet is therefore the massive black mane Masimbarashe sported in life.

Efia, although her heart is awash with pride, also feels a jab of discomfort. She knows that, soon, Thimba will not be hers alone. When he returns from the hunt - so Big Baba has warned her - he must start taking more wives. She doesn't like the idea of sharing him but knows she must accept it. She comforts herself with the fact that no other woman can ever rob her of her status as first wife. She will always be the one that rules Thimba's *kraal*.[88]

Assimbola is standing among his peers gawping at Thimba with adulation. Abena draws Efia's attention to her son and says giggling, "Look at my Assimbola! He wants to be like Thimba but doesn't realize, unlike Kwame, he'll never end up that big."

The women have started to sway, clap, and sing as Thimba, having marshalled his forces, leads the way onto the path through the grasslands. Shamwari falls in behind him, followed by the other hunters. The bad boys, whose job will be to act as porters and factotums, bring up the end of the procession carrying camping equipment and supplies.

Efia, with her huge voice, leads the singing of those songs appropriate for the occasion. At times, she improvises and is now pleading with Gran Legbwa to watch over their men and see that no ill befalls them. She couldn't bear to lose Thimba!

Later, as Efia goes about her chores, her mind remains with the giant eland hunt that takes the hunters deep into the savanna. The giant eland is the biggest known antelope, and hunting it requires skill; yet even with skill, the injuries inflicted can be horrible. As Thimba once pointed out, danger and damage are inevitable when dealing

---

[88]   Used here in the sense of a family compound

with a stampeding herd of very large and very frightened animals. Efia knows that all warriors are addicted to the excitement, camaraderie, and bravura of the giant eland hunt, but she knows, too, that the prosperity of the village depends to no small degree on the large quantities of tender meat and high-quality hides that the annual hunt provides. By selling hides and meat on the spot at the local savanna markets, the hunters bring home a wealth of cowrie shells to use as currency later.

Efia puts away the broom and shoos a broody hen out of the storage hut. As she does so, she thinks how, - as a child, she had picked up more information about hunting than most girls do. Finding it an all-consuming topic, even though girls don't hunt, she would pick the brains of her male relatives guarding the information gleaned like jewels.

A surprising source of knowledge was Thimba himself. On the occasions that she had persuaded him to talk about the hunt, he had told her interesting things like how, when stalking prey, hunters become part of the circle of prey and predator and adopt a collective persona as defense.

Usually she listened closely when Thimba spoke, but there were occasions when she wanted to block her ears, For instance, he once told her about a roan antelope hunt when a small antelope - a duiker - had become mixed up in the fray, and the hunters had torn the live creature apart with their hands and thrown its testicles back and forth. Efia remembers saying she hoped Gran Legbwa had taken action against those disrespectful hunters, but she doesn't remember if Thimba replied.

Outward Trek

West Coast of Africa

Thimba leads the way into the savanna knowing he has seen the last of Banyan Village. Yet he feels no sorrow. He has long since prepared himself to slough off the place of his birth, like reptiles slough off a skin that no longer fits. Nonetheless, he looks forward to the next ten days, which will prepare him for his passage into the world of the spirit. While hunting, he feels part of the natural world and supremely equipped to deal with its challenges.

Although the morning cool has long since dissipated and the sun beats down on the plains, Thimba does not slow the pace, nor seek out shade until midday when he calls for a rest by a shallow stream. Here the water ripples over sunlit pebbles, and with no crocodiles in evidence, the group takes to the water to drink, wash, and frolic. Then while the adolescents continue to romp in the water, the men retire to the shade of an acacia for a smoke.

Thimba and Shamwari remain lolling in the sun on a rock and, seeing they are alone, Thimba tells Shamwari of his conversation with Big Baba and of his promise to choose a new wife on return from the hunt.

"I'm surprised this didn't happen earlier," says Shamwari, swotting at a fly and missing. "You should have started taking more wives of your own accord when I did."

Thimba gives his friend a fierce glare, says, "I didn't want more wives earlier, nor do I want more wives now!"

Shamwari glares back, saying, "I know you don't *want* more wives, but now that you've promised, you have to comply. If you don't, it will be the end of both of us and of our families."

With a grin, Thimba says, "That will not be the case seeing that no one, not even Big Baba, can expect a dead man to keep his promises!"

Shamwari's scowl deepens. "Stop talking like that! More wives and children might not be your preference. They are not my preference either, but I manage. The tribe needs children, a lot of children, so I do my duty."

Thimba, now on his feet, says, "I do my duty in other areas, but will *not* do it in this one. I'll move on while I'm still a hero."

Shamwari, too, stands and says, "You're sick. You wouldn't be talking like this otherwise."

Thimba grins. "No, I was sick but am no longer so. Soon I'll be free from the pretense of being what I'm not. Meanwhile, I look forward to the hunt."

Stolen Dinner

West Coast of Africa

Thimba has led his party to a camping spot in the jess[89] at the bottom of a rocky outcrop. They will be spending a number of days here before setting off for their rendezvous with hunters from three other villages further out on the plains.

They have reached the site in time to set up camp and to sit out the afternoon shower. Now it's time to find dinner. Thimba has decided it will be best for a number of hunters to go out separately each accompanied by a couple of the bad boys. Thimba will take out his younger brother Kwame and Kwame's friend Assimbola.

While as preteen boys, Kwame and Assimbola have always been encouraged to use simple weapons like stones, slings, knives, and bows and arrows to trap and kill small prey, this present outing with Thimba is out of the ordinary. In spite of the long hike behind them and in spite of having collected enough firewood to keep the fires burning throughout the night, in spite of thinking they were exhausted, they now bubble with enthusiasm. That there are lions in the area - they have seen dung and spoor close at hand - only adds an edge to their enthusiasm. They will be with Thimba, and no ill will befall them.

Only half an hour out of camp, Thimba and his little band, witness three young lionesses, although inept, managing to separate an equally inept young zebra from its herd and make the kill.

Thimba and the boys crouch in the long grass watching as the lionesses tuck in. Snarling, they rip at skin and flesh and crunch at bone. "Easy dinner for us," Thimba whispers to his young charges, "Let's see, if we can steal a haunch from the zebra."

---

[89] Thick undergrowth

The three boys look at their hero, aghast. While Thimba has his spear, they only have bows and arrows. "Don't worry," Thimba consoles them. "You don't need weapons. I hope I won't even need my spear. Those lions are young and inexperienced, and we are going to frighten them away. We'll creep forward until we are level with the acacia, then standing close together, we'll rise out of the grass and move forward slowly like one big creature. The moment they spot us, we'll start running toward them waving our arms and making as much noise as we can by shouting, bellowing, growling, and snarling like they do."

They are already close when one of the lionesses looks up with a blood-stained face, and seeing an unusual apparition steadily approaching, the lioness emits a deep-throated growl of alarm. At the same moment, with ear-splitting shrieks, the three hunters acting as one charge forward. The lionesses spring to their feet and scatter, leaving the prey unattended.

Thimba hands his spear to Kwame, and as the boys, yelling and shrieking, cavort around him, the lionesses prowl back and forth at a safe distance. Thimba, using the chopper he carries tied to his body, manages to sever a pristine, untouched haunch in the blink of an eye.

By the time the milling lionesses realize what has happened, Thimba and his boys are up and away with their booty. Looking over his shoulder as he runs with the dripping haunch, Thimba sees the lionesses are not following; they have resumed their interrupted meal. He calls a halt to their escape, and with panting and laughter, the group celebrate their victory before returning to camp.

Thimba hasn't enjoyed himself so much in years and sends up a thank-you to Masimbarashe for his support in this show of bravado that could easily have gone wrong but didn't. The village and his problems are so far from his mind as not to exist. This is life! So precious! He is glad to have given the boys this final gift.

On the hunters' last night at the camp, before setting out for the giant eland hunt, the waxing moon pours light over the land. Thimba and Shamwari make use of the brightness to climb the rocky outcrop above the camp and to look out over the plains. They are aware lions may be present and are careful, sniffing the air and listening for the slightest sound, but are confident there is no danger in their immediate environment.

However, looking down over the land, they spot a lioness low on the ground stalking a pack of hyenas. Around her, other lionesses are slinking into strategic positions, but before they get positioned, the hyenas detect their presence, take off, and are able to outrun the pride.

"No dinner for them tonight," says Shamwari of the lionesses. They have returned and flopped down, dispirited, having wasted valuable energy in a fruitless chase. Thimba doesn't comment but knows that many lions will be going hungry for as long as the moon is bright. He has factored the knowledge into his plans and knows that humans - they are easy prey - will be becoming more desirable than normal.

En Route

West Coast of Africa

As they cross the savanna toward the location of the big hunt, Shamwari strides along behind Thimba. He loves the wide-reaching grasslands dotted with lone acacias, silk-cotton trees and baobabs; they are different to the trees of the jungle. He sees in the distance giraffe and zebra heading for a waterhole and hears the bark of baboons before spotting them as silhouettes on the rocks of a granite outcrop.

As he goes, he reviews the days they have had at the camp: happy ones seeing that Thimba had sloughed off all tension and forgotten the nonsense he had spouted before they arrived at the camp. Hunting was always Thimba's cure. On previous occasions - none as bad as the most recent - he would return to the village rejuvenated, resuming his duties and managing to keep the darkness at bay, at least for a while.

Shamwari has faith in the restorative powers of the hunt. Although his peers never speak about such matters, he suspects it is something all hunters feel. It has something to do with a camaraderie that transcends the individual and, entangled with their prey, embraces them as an intrinsic part of the natural world.

Thimba yells out a warning before taking a leap over a trail of marching ants. Shamwari follows suit, barely interrupting his train of thought, which remains with hunting but now centering on the upcoming giant eland hunt. He knows a lot about giant eland; they are the king of antelopes both with respect to the quality of meat and of hide. Their size, too, is impressive: over five-and-a-half feet at the shoulder and often weighing more than a ton. Nonetheless, they can run at over forty miles an hour and are good jumpers, sometimes clearing obstacles of shoulder height.

Giant eland are not easy to hunt because to conserve water, they need to keep cool and have to spend the daylight hours resting in jess, only emerging at night to graze and browse. In order to hunt them, scouts must locate them at first light to know where they intend to spend the day. They can then chase them out of the undergrowth to where the hunters wait.

Thimba turns his head and says over his shoulder to Shamwari, "We're now in eland country." He points with the shaft of his spear to a pile of dung and close at hand to broken branches on an acacia - signs that the eland browsed here before going into hiding. The idea of the eland resting up in the shade fills Shamwari with envy, but he consoles himself with the fact that eland always like to be close to water, so there will soon be a respite. Thimba always stops for water.

First Week of June 1800

The Jetty

Plantation, Louisiana

Cécile, with bonnet neatly tied and cheek and lip rouged, sits in the moving carriage admiring through open windows the live oaks and Spanish moss that hang over the driveway. She approves, smiles to herself, and is happy. She can't find fault with anything, not even with the coachman, his livery, the horses, or their harnesses. The reason is she is excited to be on her way to the jetty to meet her sons.

The coachman drives out of the gates, crosses the River Road, and parks the vehicle in a lay-by that gives Cécile a good view over the river. Down at the *môle*,[90] she sees that a couple of slaves, luckily not coffee-coloreds, also await the boat's arrival. Her eyes scan the Mississippi to the south downstream, but she sees nothing. Then realizing she is wrong in trying to spot the vessel in the center of the river - that's where the water flows fastest - she shifts her gaze to the edge and, *voilà*, sees the craft hugging the bank.

With its rounded and upturned snout, it parts the muddy water in a courageous struggle against the current. The vastness of the vista has made it look smaller than she imagined it would be. Also, it is a

---

[90]   Jetty

strange-looking vessel. She has never seen anything like it; it isn't a keelboat, scow, or regular barge. None of those would attempt the journey upstream from New Orleans as this unwieldy apparition is now doing; neither would any of them have the superstructure and puffing chimney of this experimental steam vessel.

Cécile knows from what the chevalier told her during their wearisome carriage trip to the plantation that what she now sees is the prototype of a paddle steamer. It belongs to a company in which, on the advice of his French cousin, the chevalier has become involved. She was not listening properly at the time (she would rather have slept), but she heard enough to know that the top-heavy diamond-shaped superstructure on the boat that she now sees is a walking beam that moves up and down like a person striding. This beam together with a Watt steam engine and a paddle wheel at the stern (she can't see that yet) propel the craft forward.

The wooden shell of this vessel is similar to the hulls of the older barges, but those, after unloading in New Orleans, can't return upstream, so the company dismantles them and uses the wood as lumber. The hull of this new vessel will not meet with such a fate seeing it's already returning to its starting point and will continue to ply up and down the river, provided it doesn't sink in the meantime. The older barges that transport freight from the north to the south, but not vice versa, are a common sight on the Mississippi. Turning her head, Cécile sees one of those older vessels riding the current as it rounds the upstream bend. It sits low in the water so is probably loaded with sacks of sugar from the neighboring plantation.

The chevalier not only has a financial interest in the company that owns the prototype of the new steam vessel but he also has shares in the company that runs the old barges. He also uses the old barges himself to transport the refined sugar from his plantation downstream to the port of New Orleans. There the sugar replaces incoming slaves in the holds of the schooners, which then return across the Atlantic to Europe and Britain.

The chevalier often used the older type of barges himself to return downstream after his regular visits to the plantation. Cécile will do the same when her husband finally dies. He has made sure that the vessels have a small private area toward the bow that features a well-appointed cabin with a bench on the deck outside. When she becomes a widow, soon *s'il plait à Dieu*,[91] she can use that area without loss of propriety even if she is alone. Jacques and Jean will have to stay behind to cope with the plantation, and she couldn't bear having a plantation slave accompany her on her return to New Orleans.

Getting impatient, Cécile turns her focus back to the steamboat. It might be an amazing invention - "the transport of the future," according to her husband - but its upstream progress is *lentissimo*.[92] (The chevalier always tended to use musical terminology, regardless of the context.) A rip current might speed up matters but then again perhaps not. As her husband told her, the walking beam and chimney make the vessel top-heavy, and it can topple in unstable conditions. She wouldn't want that to happen with Jacques and Jean on board! She bows her head and says a little prayer, *Please, Lord, let no rip current topple the steamboat!*

As Cécile continues to wait, she reviews last week's events with Dr. Le Blanc. She is grateful that he seems to have lost the scent and no longer considers arsenic a valid diagnosis. For a while, she was concerned, and had he stuck to his initial diagnosis, she would have arranged for Agathe to take the rap, although she would have preferred to lay the blame on André. However, seeing he never comes into the Big House, he would be a less likely culprit than a house slave. Either way, it would have been a nuisance, and she's glad not to have to bother.

---

[91]   If God will

[92]   Very slow

As the boat continues to battle upstream, she turns her thoughts to more pleasant matters: she is looking forward to the gossip her sons will bring from New Orleans. For the past month, she has spoken to no one of her own standing. She doesn't count her exchanges with Dr. Le Blanc as conversation. He is not her social equal, although he can put on a good imitation of the *gentilhomme*. Besides, the exchanges with him always concern her husband's health. It's not a comfortable topic seeing that she wants the patient to die, and he feels he should keep the patient alive!

The steamboat has now disappeared behind overhanging trees, but she assumes it will reappear. Meanwhile, she returns her thoughts to New Orleans. As a white woman of noble birth, she is a rarity and is seen as a *doyenne* of all that is right and proper, a role she relishes and milks for all its worth. The lack of suitable white women in the city has given rise to a system, whereby upper-class Frenchmen enter into *marriages de la main gauche*[93] with women of color known as placées.[94] The system itself is known as *plaçage*.[95] The men involved in such relationships require that their substitute wives - some are slaves, some free blacks, some Creoles[96] - behave in a manner acceptable in upper-class French circles. They need instruction, and no one is better equipped to teach them than Cécile.

While enjoying the recognition of her authority in matters of etiquette, Cécile harbors a deep-seated contempt for both the colored girls she instructs as well as for the men, who - in exchange for sex - shower the women with unsuitable luxuries. She could tell these men that a sow's ear will never make a silk purse, but no one can tell a rutting stag about dignity and decorum!

---

[93] Left-handed or common-law marriages

[94] Women of color in a common-law relationship with white men

[95] A system whereby a European man enters into common-law marriage with a colored woman

[96] The children from common-law marriages

At their get-togethers, Cécile and her so-called friends amuse themselves on an ongoing basis with the gaffes of the *parvenus*.[97] The camaraderie in these events is what Cécile misses. Yet in spite of a frisson of anticipatory pleasure at news of recent social blunders, the subject of substitute wives and left-handed marriages leaves Cécile uneasy about the future of Jacques and Jean. Jacques, at the age of forty, should have found a suitable French bride by now, yet because - *Dieu le sait*[98] - it is no easy task, he remains single. She fears if he becomes impatient, he will acquire placées for himself and Jean too. She shivers at the thought. It must never happen!

She again plays with an idea she has had before of suggesting to the boys that they should accompany her to France to find suitable matches. She had put the idea on hold, knowing few French girls of suitable standing are willing to cross the ocean to live in a backwater like New Orleans. Yet there are exceptions; she herself was one. Others like her might still exist - girls willing to follow the man they love across the ocean. It is worth risking when placées are the only other option.

She cringes at the memory of once being madly in love with the chevalier, although back then, he was dashing and handsome and considered a good catch. Unfortunately, neither Jacques nor Jean has those advantages though Jacques does know how to behave properly - if he so wishes - and is capable of launching charm offensives. Also, when his father dies, he'll be wealthy, which will add to his allure.

Finding a bride for Jean will be more complicated. Now at thirty-three, he still relies on his brother Jacques to an abnormal degree in spite of having spent years at the university in Boston and achieving academic success in his chosen field of ethnomusicology. She and the chevalier had allowed him to go with Girrard's son - in spite of the abstruse subject - hoping that the separation from Jacques might cure him of his unnatural dependence. Hélas, the ploy hadn't worked. No

---

[97]   Upstarts, social climbers
[98]   God knows

sooner had Jean returned than he again became clay in Jacques's hands, shivering and stammering at Jacques's smallest frown.

She and the chevalier have never fully understood why Jean is so frightened of Jacques. The reason seems buried in early childhood. Jacques, like his father, is undoubtedly controlling and bossy - a bully in other words - but not violent, or at least Cécile hopes he is not violent. When Jean was still a *bébé* and Jacques seven, Jacques dropped his baby brother. He said it was a mistake, but the slave who cared for Jean at the time and was the only witness said Jacques didn't drop the *bébé*; he threw him! However, seeing that slaves always lie, Cécile never gave credence to the story. She accepts that Jean marches to his own beat and that separation from Jacques didn't change the situation. It just made it worse in that Jean returned from Boston with ridiculous libertarian ideas spawned by the French Revolution.

The steamboat is now making better headway and getting closer. Cécile winds up her thoughts on Jean, remembering that his difference has one very pleasant manifestation: he does not ogle slave girls like his father! She just wishes he were less effeminate in his ways and less flamboyant in his gestures. He also has a girlish giggle, but she realizes that's the result of nerves, seeing that it only manifests itself in Jacques's presence; otherwise he has an attractive laugh.

Ah! The boat is finally pulling in at the jetty. Superstructure and paddles are no longer of interest; her sons are all that matters. Opening her reticule, she extracts her makeup, powders her nose, and brightens her lips, and she would have applied a daub of cologne, except she now uses that vial for arsenic. She is looking forward to reclaiming it for its true purpose.

Watching through open window, she sees a crew member helping her boys off the boat; she watches as the coachman and slaves greet them. Now they start toward the carriage where she waits. She notes that, although Jacques is small, he has a masculine stride; Jean, on the other hand, takes the dainty little steps of a girl.

Cécile is delighted that the boys are finally here; she would have liked to give them each a broad smile but makes do with a tight-lipped version, not wanting to show her rotting teeth. Each son in turn kisses her hand before taking a seat in the carriage. "Maman!" Jacques effuses. "You look well! How is Papa?"

Cécile again represses what might have been a beatific smile. Soon all three of them will be partaking of such delicacies as paté de foie gras, walnuts, and truffles in the *petit salon*[99] of the family chateau in the Dordogne, France.

---

[99] Front room

SLAVES, MASTERS AND TRADERS 317

The Real Sons

Plantation, Louisiana

The chevalier in his ornate canopied bed and Agathe - she sits crocheting by the bedroom window - await the arrival of the *real* sons. The mistress will be accompanying them up to the Big House from the jetty. Agathe gives a disparaging sniff at the thought of the word *real* that she has overheard white men use for their legitimate children at some of the master's men-only gatherings.

Now as the crochet needle flicks back and forth and the ball of yarn tumbles around on her lap, Agathe ponders the changes that the new arrivals are likely to cause. She doesn't get far before she hears the distant crunch of the carriage pulling up on gravel at the front porch. It is something another would not have heard, but Agathe's ears are highly attuned to the sounds of her environment.

Knowing the mistress has arrived with her sons, she tucks her crocheting under the cushion and goes to the bed to adjust the master's nightcap. She had knitted it at a time when his head was bigger; now it barely dents the pillow and tends to droop over his eyes. As she pushes it back into place and puffs up the pillows, she says in an urgent whisper, "Wake up, Master! They're here."

As he opens his eyes, she steps back and waits by the bedside to see how the *real* sons will compare to her coffee-colored kiddies. Will they be big and handsome like her André? She'll reserve judgment until she sees them.

Agathe's words rouse the chevalier from his slumber. He hears the familiar voices in the corridor and, with a sigh of resignation, opens a bleary eye to see Cécile making a triumphant entrance followed by

Jacques - small and strutting - and Jean a step behind. With a sweeping gesture, Cécile exclaims, "*Voilà, messieurs! Vôtre papa!*"[100]

"Papa!" Jacques gushes. "We have come to be with you! How *are* you?" He lifts his father's hand and kisses it. The chevalier feels too tired to feign civility and doesn't respond; he wants to save his energy for André, who has not yet paid his daily visit. However, when Jean moves forward and lifts the limp, blue-veined hand, holds it, and kisses it, the chevalier reciprocates with a brief squeeze of his own. He has always preferred Jean to Jacques; he's a dear boy. If only he had more gumption and was more like André . . .

As Jean gently replaces his father's hand on the coverlet and steps back, the chevalier turns away and allows the nightcap to droop back over his eyes. As far as he is concerned, the visit is over. He will take his mind to other places and hope the boys and Cécile will retire to their rooms. They might well want to rest after their long trip in the new steamboat. Thinking about that steamboat, he would not have minded asking about that trip, but it's too late now. He proceeds with the original plan of getting rid of the *real* family as soon as possible.

Initiating feigned sleep with a few gentle snores - he has learned a thing or two from Cécile - he follows through with measured breathing. The technique had fooled him for a while, so maybe it will work now on the boys and even on Cécile herself. She has taken over Agathe's chair by the window and is reading a New Orleans broadsheet that must have come with the boys.

While keeping up the even breathing, his mind remains with Jean: this time not on the boy's fear-filled relationship with Jacques but on his eccentric habit of humming odd tunes to himself. Cécile blames the latter on the Choctaw slave whom Jean had adored as a toddler preferring her to his parents. Yet the chevalier does not agree with Cécile's theory because the girl was only with them for a few months

---

[100] "Behold, gentlemen! Your father!"

before Cécile got rid of her. Jean at such a tender age could neither have remembered either her or her ethnic tunes. The chevalier though remembers her, which is strange seeing it was thirty years ago and she was not even a good-looking girl. (Cécile never allows good-looking female slaves in their New Orleans home.) The girl's memorable feature was - as he remembers it - an aura of strength and dignity not common in slaves

In their late teens, Jean and one of Olivier Girrard's sons pursued the discipline of ethnomusicology specializing in slave music, the very thing that every plantation owner forbids! Olivier Girrard had not allowed the son in question onto his plantation for a decade because of it. The chevalier hadn't needed to go to that extreme with Jean because his *real* sons never came to the plantation anyway.

Over the years, the chevalier has tempered his opinion of ethnic music but has retained his preference for violin and chamber music. Bach and Haydn are his musical heroes. The sound of Bach's figured bass and the complexities of his counterpoint never cease to thrill him, while he finds Haydn's thinner texture and more defined melodies and bass lines equally enjoyable.

They're so small is Agathe's first reaction as she watches the two sons file in and approach the bed. It strikes her as unfitting that the master should have such small sons; neither is bigger than any of the early teenage coffee-colored kiddies on the plantation. The master though had once told her about Napoleon - a short man - and said size was not a reliable measure; she therefore withholds her judgment. Then she watches Jacques approach and greet his father. She watches him take the withered hand, kiss it, then step back, and dig Jean in the ribs hissing, "Go, *bêta!*[101] It's now your turn." Hearing this, Agathe decides

---

[101] Idiot

her instant and intuitive loathing for Jacques is justified and measured by any standard of decency he is loathsome.

Agathe also notes how the master acknowledges the sons' presence with only a nod before feigning sleep. He usually greets André with a grin and feasts his eyes on him until he leaves. Agathe knows that the satisfaction she feels at the master's favoritism is petty, but she can't help it.

Now as the two brothers settle on the chairs set up for them on the opposite side of the bed, Agathe is free to study their physiognomy. Both have pasty complexions that remind her of the grubs she digs up in her vegetable patch, and although both have a family resemblance, Jean has pleasant, nondescript features while Jacques has the weasel-like features of Mrs. Cécile.

Along with the differences in appearance, the brothers obviously possess different temperaments. Jacques wears a constant frown; Jean's expression is benign. Also, when Jacques turns away to study the master's medications, Jean gives Agathe a friendly smile. She likes that and responds in kind. She likes, too, that Jean is obviously not a sexual predator. Jacques is another matter, although Agathe assumes he will regard all coffee-colored girls - his half sisters - as off-limits. Adrienne, though, being pure black is not related to Jacques and will not be off limits when his father dies.

The mistress lays aside the newspaper and goes to the window that looks over the farmyard. Agathe sees the grim expression on her face as she turns and beckons to Jacques. He joins her, and although Agathe can't hear them, she knows they speak of André when Jacques comments loudly, "So that's the usurper! *Telle impertinence!*[102] A slave on horseback! Papa was obviously out of his mind long before now." As the pair turns back into the room, Agathe shudders at the hatred

---

[102] What a cheek!

written on both faces and at Jacques's words, "You'll see, Maman! The bastard will pay for this."

"*Bravo, c'etait vraiment bien!*" Cécile applauds before instructing Agathe to show the sons to their rooms.

Agathe leads the way down the corridor with the sons in tow. As they enter Jacques's room, gauze curtains between the open drapes flutter in the breeze. Jacques turns to Agathe and snarls, "Those drapes are to remain shut at all times! Is that clear, woman?"

Agathe acknowledges the words with an inclination of her slender neck and says, "I'll send someone up to close them right away, Master." Leaving Jacques to his own devices, she leads Jean along the corridor toward his room.

Catching up with her, he says in a pleasant manner, "My drapes can stay open, Agathe. I like the breeze."

Too Far Left?

Liverpool, England

The rain slashes onto the roof of Tom's attic. It streams down the window in a waterfall as it used to on the portholes of *Spirit* as she dropped and rose on the heaving ocean. Tom's kitten Fluff lies curled up on her blanket next to the sheet of writing paper that he has prepared for himself. That she purrs pleases him. It makes him feel wanted and useful. In spite of the horrors of *Spirit*, he had never felt useless, had always done what he could to help the slaves, and now misses that sense of purpose. He reaches out and strokes Fluff's head, saying to her, "Thank you, Fluff, for coming to live with me."

Gratitude is a subject on his mind. He wants to write to Esquire expressing his thankfulness, but doesn't know how to go about it. Closing his eyes for inspiration, his head drops to his chest, and he falls asleep. He dreams he is on board *Spirit* clinging to the rail in a howling gale that drives breaking waves over the deck. He feels *Spirit* bucking underfoot as she rises on a mountain-high swell with cross-waves breaking across the top. He tastes salt water as the vessel plummets into yet another abyss. Water streams over him filling his eyes, nose, and throat and forcing him to loosen his grip on the rail. As he slides down the sloping deck, he hears the mast crack and fall toward him. He is plunged into a darkness that gives way to a sunny room where Sister Angelique leans over him and Esquire stands at her side smiling. He is safe!

Filled with the notion that Sister Angelique and Esquire are embodiments of the same principle of good, he embarks on his letter. He writes as follows:

Sir,

While I feel I should thank the good Lord for what he is giving me through you, too, I have to wonder if he really sits in heaven or if he might not be among us as a principal of love that will manifest itself in whatever manner we are able to recognize him. What do you think, sir? Am I straying too far from dogma? Also, how far can a person go in rejecting a literal interpretation of the scriptures without becoming a pariah and heretic?

Reading what he has written, Tom remembers Ambrose saying, "With Esquire, you've struck gold, laddie, but you'll have to tread with care. You must realize that being a libertarian, you lean more to the left than does Esquire, and you'd do best not to express extreme opinions."

Tom therefore now asks himself if what he has written is extreme. He is not sure, but for better or for worse, he likes what he's written and resolves to take the letter to the mailbox when the rain stops.

Back in Circulation

Edinburgh, Scotland

Stanley has been out of touch for several weeks and is now again in Edinburgh; he and his father have caught up with each other. Seeing it is fine day, they are spending the afternoon at the Royal Botanical Gardens on Leith Walk. The Gardens came into being in 1670 as a physic garden for medicinal plants, but since has moved several times and expanded by adding plants from every part of the planet.

Both father and son are interested in botany, but botany is not the subject on their minds as they settle on a bench near a plot used as a market garden. They need to discuss recent events, but as neither knows where to start, they sit in silence.

While watching a gardener hoeing between rows of young carrots, Stanley knows he has to speak about the plantation, seeing he'd mentioned Louisiana on the day Gramps threw him out. Yet he doesn't know if Uncle Aaron has mentioned the scheme in the meantime. There are also other things he doesn't know: did Mums really miscarry the day he left and has Donalda given birth yet?

As his father still hasn't spoken, Stanley treads carefully by asking innocuous questions: How is Angus McCorm? How is Gramps? How is Mums? On being told all were fine and nothing more, he knows he must find a better approach.

He asks, "Pops, have you seen Uncle Aaron?"

That loosens the blockage, and he receives the answers he needs without prodding.

"Yes, son, I've seen Aaron," his father tells him, "and he told me about the Louisiana venture. He also told me that you and he feel guilty for having acted without informing us."

"What did you say, Pops?" Stanley asks, with caution.

"I was shocked and surprised," his father replies. "I pointed out that it would have been proper for you both to have consulted us before going ahead. I then realized though that - in view of recent events - recriminations weren't appropriate. It is because of what you and Aaron have done that you, son, now have somewhere to go."

Before Stanley is able to react fittingly, he sees a sudden radiance suffusing his father's face as Pontefract adds, "I still need to tell you the best news. Although Mums and I sadly lost our bairn the day you left, Donalda gave birth a few days later, and we now have Wee Adair as a substitute. It still amazes me how a deplorable situation and so much reprehensible behavior have suddenly turned into something quite wonderful!"

Watching the gardener moving on from the burgeoning young carrots to the beetroots, Stanley marvels at what has happened. His father is right! It is nothing short of a miracle that Glen Orm has its heir, and he himself will have slaves and a plantation that will not only grow sugar but also carrots, beetroots, and heaven knows what other exotic produce! His heart beats faster at the prospect.

Meanwhile, his father is saying, "Wee Adair is a priceless gift to your grandfather, your mother, Donalda, and me. We all dote on him and live in peace and harmony."

Hearing his father effuse in this manner, Stanley realizes for the first time what a disruptive presence he has been in the household. Now that there is another heir, his absence can only be an asset! It is a sobering thought seeing he was always the center of everyone's attention. Ah well . . . He will soon have slaves and a plantation to console him.

He turns his attention back to his father, who is now talking about his mother.

"She has returned to her art and is producing lovely sketches of everything around her: Wee Adair, Angus McCorm, the golden eagles, busy spiders, and dumpy hens. She is also illustrating a book featuring the giants, dwarves, dragons, and bulls that occupy such a prominent position in our ancient history. What I like best, though, are some beautiful sketches she has done of Donalda and of the cart house where Donalda told your mother Adair was conceived.

Stanley straightens and his eyes widen. "Donalda said that?" he asks in astonishment. He cannot imagine a conversation of that nature transpiring between his mother and Donalda! Things are changing on Glen Orm!

"Donalda is a lovely girl and gets on well with your mother," Pontefract says before adding, with creased brow, "One aspect though worries me about her - your mother not Donalda. She often slips out with the baby and sits for hours under the Scots pine doing I know not what. It bothers me."

"Don't worry, Pops," Stanley comforts. "It's harmless. She just talks to her dead bairns."

"What can anyone possibly say to dead bairns?" Pontefract wants to know, shaking his head.

Schools

Edinburgh, Scotland

Sir George intends writing to Tom outlining how he foresees the boy's immediate educational needs. He has now consulted with those in the know and has a good idea about how to proceed.

With this in mind, he sits at the writing desk he has had brought up from the downstairs and on which he has just finished arranging his writing paraphernalia: ruler, inkwell, quill, and quill-knife along with a pounce[103] pot, which resembles a saltshaker. It was quite a process getting the desk up the stairs, but it is now here, and Ms. Young and her nephews have withdrawn to the kitchen for tea, oatcakes, and honey.

Sir George surveys his new setup with critical eye. The desk has been a favorite since childhood. It is an elegant Sheraton mahogany writing table with a rectangular top, rounded projected corners, and tapering fluted legs, topped with carved tassels. The three frieze-drawers have brass fittings. As he gets going on the letter, he feels at ease as though reunited with an old childhood friend. The desk was a present from his grandmother when he first moved into his own room as a preteen. He will pass it on to Tom, when the laddie moves in at the end of the month.

Sir George has determined that Tom should start at an academy with leanings toward science. That will prepare him for a university-level entrance exam with one of his options being the new science faculty at the University of Edinburgh. Taking his quill to hand, he dips it into the inkwell, first telling Tom the plan, then giving him some insight into the background of Scottish academies.

---

[103] A fine powder, made from powdered cuttlefish bone used to dry ink

He writes as follows:

> Most schools in Scotland, until recently, looked like regular houses and had a single schoolroom, which could hold up to eighty pupils taught by a single schoolmaster. From the 1790s onward - thanks to sponsors using slave-trade money - dedicated buildings referred to as academies have begun to appear. Most are built in a classical style with a separate house in the same style for the headmaster.
>
> Academies have many more teachers than previous schools but also use the monitorial system, whereby competent pupils can volunteer as pupil-teachers and pass on the information to others. You might enjoy doing that, Tom.

Having written enough, Sir George sets aside his quill, and using the pounce pot shakes the fine powder onto the wet ink. He surprises himself by finding he is looking forward to Tom's arrival. He wonders what Jessica and the girls will think of the lad, if they decide to spend time in Edinburgh at the end of the summer as they often do.

Weaning of the Young Earl

Leith, Scotland

After a long spell of feeling poorly, Betta is more animated today, and wrapped in a shawl, she and Rose sit in the garden on cushioned wrought-iron chairs in range of a fragrant lilac. Under the eaves of the shed, a busy robin flies back and forth to her nest carrying tidbits to four voracious chicks with yellow beaks, open mouths, and pink gullets.

"Perhaps, I should write a poem about robins," says Rose, watching the mother robin leaning back to brace herself as she tugs at an earthworm that is getting ever longer and skinnier.

"What happened to the poem about the mouse that Pa said should have been a mole," asks Betta.

"It goes like this," says Rose.

> Today we mourn a mole / that the gardener dug out
> of a hole. / He picked up a shovel and killed a mother/
> leaving her pups / hairless and cold / bereft and unfed.

Betta never knows what to say about Rose's off-kilter poems, so merely tut-tuts and comments, "Poor little dears!' She then asks Rose to fill her in on events of the past week during which Betta was so ill. Rose starts with Migu's meeting with William. "Imagine, Ma, William talked about business and was well-informed!"

"And Pa? Was he up to his old tricks?"

"No, Ma!" Rose's face is pink with excitement. "Imagine! He didn't blunder, wasn't rude, and wasn't even wearing one of his appalling cravats!"

Betta smiles, says, "Heaven knows where he finds those ugly things!" As Rose gives a girlish giggle, Betta asks, "Was the slave trade mentioned?"

"Only marginally," Rose replies. "William is still feeling his way, and I am hoping Pa's money may help him understand he doesn't need his grandfather's slave-trading fortune. He is still under Lord Richard's influence, but I'm working on phasing both his lordship and the slave trade out of our lives!"

"Remember, Pa is also a slave trader."

"Yes, but like Uncle Pontefract, Pa was wealthy before he became involved in the slave trade, and the money that will go to William - through me - must come from the nonslave trade part of Pa's fortune. For the sake of respectability for William's and my children, the slave trade is best forgotten."

"You think the stigma fades with time?"

"Lady Abigail seems to think so."

The Giant Eland Hunt

West Coast of Africa

Trackers have located the jess,[104] where a herd of twenty-five of the huge antelopes is preparing to spend the day. Bulls - females and juveniles - are congregated in separate groups, but these groups, never far from one another, are still milling around as the sun starts to rise. Then one of the bulls, sensing the presence of the trackers, alerts the herd by giving a series of deep-throated barks. In panic, the herd bursts out of the jess and stampedes.

Bellowing in outrage, knees clicking, and hooves thundering, they stream past the waiting hunters. The air is thick with dust, and Thimba feels the ground shaking beneath his naked feet. His heart pounds as he draws back his spear and, with balance perfect, launches his ten-foot missile toward a young male as it passes. The projectile with the full force of Thimba's size and weight behind it flies straight and true.

A number of his companions have taken aim at the same animal, which stops in its tracks. Its side now perforated with spear-shafts, the creature bellows in pain and fury; its coat streaked with blood, it gives itself a vigorous shake, causing the colliding spear shafts to rattle in a manic arrhythmia.

Shouting in gleeful anticipation, the hunters swarm forward through the dust. Thimba manages to yank his spear out of the animal's resistant flesh, and remaining as close as he can while avoiding the horns, he repositions himself for another throw. He knows that for the spearhead to reach the heart, it must enter from behind the shoulder blade. It is no easy task on a moving target, but he hopes he has it right as he pulls back his arm and launches a second throw.

---

[104] Thick undergrowth

In spite of clamor and turmoil - dust, blood, and shouts and bellows - even Thimba, normally supremely confident in his own abilities, is surprised that he manages to do what needs to be done. The spear finds its mark, and a cheer goes up from his companions. Blood and saliva gush from the nose and mouth of the choking animal, and as the big head pulled down by heavy horns starts to droop, the hindquarters collapse.

The hunters, knowing life is mere clothing for a spirit that never dies, give thanks to Gran Legbwa in a wild dance and song.

Second Week of June 1800

Revelation

Plantation, Louisiana

Jean is visiting his friend Olivier Junior at his father's nearby plantation while Olivier Senior is in Philadelphia. As always at this time, Mrs. Cécile and Jacques have settled on the porch for their midmorning refreshment. Adrienne pours a glass of juice from a jug at the serving table and, on a small tray with a napkin, hands it to the mistress, who on taking a sip says, "Ugh, another tepid drink!"

Adrienne, on return to the serving table to pour Jacques's drink, whispers to Agathe, "Have you noticed, Mammi, how Master Jean always says 'thank you.' The mistress and Jacques never bother."

Agathe smiles and replies in a low voice, "Few white folks ever say 'thank you' to a slave. Your master Jean is an exception."

"*My* master Jean!" Adrienne huffs under her breath as she loads another glass and napkin onto the tray and takes it to Jacques. As she bends to place the tray on the low side table, he reaches out and tweaks her breast.

With a gasp, Adrienne jumps backward spilling the drink down her front. Agathe, watching from behind, doesn't see exactly what has happened. What she does see is the mistress suddenly sitting bolt upright and exploding into a reproof so loud that even the slaves dusting the hall come to the door and gawp.

"Keep your fingers to yourself, Jacques!" she bellows. "Gentlemen do *not* behave like that! Even your father would *never* have behaved like that in the presence of a lady. He has a sense of decorum that you would do well to emulate!"

Agathe and Adrienne, caught between outrage at Jacques's action and amusement at Cécile's reaction, retire to the pantry and collapse into laughter.

"She has her uses, doesn't she?" says Adrienne, wiping her eyes. "Did you see his expression?"

Not wanting to miss anything, both women compose themselves and return to the serving table in time to hear the mistress saying, "If your brother Jean manages to control his lust, why can't you?"

Jacques, leaning forward in his chair and with elbows on knees, says in a rough voice, "Maman, your namby-pamby son does not like women the way most men do." He pauses to let the comment sink in then adds, "He is a sodomist!" She gasps, as he elucidates, "That is a person that both society and church condemn in the strongest manner!"

Agathe does not know the word *sodomist* but can guess its meaning.

The mistress, for her part, loses her fire and whimpers, "No, Jacques! He's a dear boy. A bit eccentric, but he'd never act as you suggest. It's wrong to say such things!"

"Wrong, Maman, is what your son is probably doing at this moment with his lover. They are not inspecting the cane fields, I assure you."

"Ah! Ah!" sobs Cécile, patting at her pockets trying to locate her handkerchief.

Jacques continues without mercy. "You were telling me you want me to be like Jean! No! Never! You blame me for ogling slave girls. What do you expect me to do? I'm a red-blooded male. There are no suitable white women in the territory. Why shouldn't I take my pleasure where I find it? Would you prefer me to take a placée, Maman?"

If his eyes bulge any farther - thinks Agathe - *they will roll down his cheeks.*

The mistress, for her part, is backpedaling furiously. "No, Jacques, please! No placée! When your father dies, come with me to France. I'll find you a bride. I can't bear the thought of you living with a placée and producing more coffee-colored bastards. Let's keep our bloodlines pure," she pleads. "Please!"

With a harsh laugh, Jacques says, "It's too late for that nonsense, Maman! Your blood already runs in the veins of countless slaves. If I knew how many coffee-colored grandchildren you already have, I'd tell you, but I neither know nor care."

Cécile lets out a howl and asks in a choked voice, "Who knows these things?"

"If you refer to your colored grandchildren, I have no idea. If you refer to Jean and Olivier, only you and I know."

Agathe smiles at hearing Jacques thinking only he and his mother know about Jean. Seeing that Agathe and her peers now know, it won't be long before the entire slave population will also know. Agathe marvels at the way whites talk freely in the presence of slaves. The master and his guests always do it; now the mistress and Jacques are doing the same. They obviously don't see slaves as human in the way that they see themselves as human. However, as insulting as the attitude might be, it serves Agathe well by providing her with valuable insights.

The mistress is still having difficulty breathing and groans, gulps, and mops her face with fierce dabs. Meanwhile, Jacques eyes her with contempt. Although Agathe feels far from well disposed toward the mistress, she dislikes Jacques even more. There is no kindness in the man, nor any respect for his mother. Filled with revulsion for the little man, she approaches Cécile and places a hand on her shoulder and says, "Let me help you to your room, Mistress. You need to rest."

Change of Guard

Aberdeenshire, Scotland

In the crisp morning air as the sun rises over the glen, the old laird stands at the front door surveying his domain. From hooded eye, he watches the eagle take off from the precipice, and soaring, it seek out a thermal. With a sudden lurch of exultation, he feels some vital part of him explode out of his body to soar with the bird. At the same time, with a cry of agony, he falls to the ground, writhing and clutching at his chest.

The funeral and burial take place at the stone chapel among the Scots pines with their clusters of blue-green needles and peeling, orange bark. Frances, the sleeping baby in her arms, and Pontefract sit in the front row. The remaining pews are occupied by a sprinkling of friends, tenants, neighbors, and servants.

Frances' friend, the retired parish priest from Stonehaven, conducts the rites. Standing at the altar, he faces the congregation and receives the coffin reading from the scriptures, "Those who believe in me, even though they die, will live . . ."

As the priest further intones, "We are here gathered . . ."

Stanley slides in from the side aisle to settle by his mother.

"You are home!" she gasps.

"*Shh*, Mums," he whispers. She takes his hand and squeezes it as the service continues. After the final blessing, Frances says to Stanley, "Pops and I should be at the door to receive the condolences. Perhaps you could keep Baby Adair here with you." She places the sleeping child into his arms and leaves.

Stanley has never before held an infant and is assaulted by conflicting emotions, especially as this child is his son, although to the world he is a brother. The physicality of what he holds in his arms is more than a word, like *son* or *brother*, can convey. It has shape, weight, warmth, a beating heart, warm breath, and a nice smell.

Before he can sort out his feelings, he hears through the jumble of voices behind him a clear upper-class voice saying to his father, "William and I are here instead of my parents, who are unable to attend, due to the poor health of my mother." Stanley swivels his head and shoulders in a precipitous move that wakes the baby, who sets up a vociferous squall.

Frances, abandoning her station at the entrance, runs down the aisle to find out what is wrong. As she takes the child from Stanley and calms him, Stanley gets to his feet, takes the gloved hand that is graciously extended toward him, bows, and says, "Rose! It's been a while!"

Calton Hill

Edinburgh, Scotland

Sir George sits at his writing desk shaking pounce over the wet ink of his weekly letter to Tom. As he does so, he thinks of the word *pounce* and its origin; it comes from Latin for *pumice* via French. The English word though does not remind Sir George of the pumice stone, which he uses to remove the dry skin from his feet in a bathtub; it makes him think of what cats do with a mouse.

This circuitous route calls to mind the startling thought of Tom's kitten. He knows the boy loves the creature. Setting aside the pounce pot, he wonders what the lad will do with the animal when he takes the stagecoach up to Edinburgh in a few weeks' time. Might he want to bring the creature with him? No! Sir George holds his hands to his head in horror. Ms. Young feeding the dog is more than enough: this is a Georgian terrace house, not a menagerie! One of the best aspects of the New Town is that the streets and squares are purely residential. While there is a ban on *noxious* traders and animals, he now realizes that unfortunately does not cover pets. He harrumphs in frustration.

Realizing he needs to get out for some fresh air - he will deal with the kitten problem later - he reads through what he has written. It is a reply to the letter in which Tom wonders if he is straying too far from a literal interpretation of the scriptures. Sir George has written this:

> I personally believe it is acceptable to regard traditional beliefs as metaphors for one's own beliefs. I also believe though that to avoid running afoul of people with an unrelenting literal frame of mind, it makes life easier if one gives a semblance of compliance. No one need know what you really think.

Glad to get the job done and looking forward to his afternoon constitutional on Calton Hill, Sir George makes short shrift of addressing the envelope and affixing the stamp. Ms. Young's niece can take the letter to the mailbox later. If he were going to the New Club now, he would have done the job himself, but he hasn't been going to the club recently for lack of congenial company. Pontefract Staymann, so he hears, is tied up with Glen Orm, and no longer comes to the club either.

Given its history and the coexistence of human monuments with the natural world, Calton Hill is one of Sir George's favorite destinations. Today he has decided to visit the Old Calton Burial Ground, which is up the hill from a village that no longer exists. While climbing the hill and being out of breath - it's steep - he takes a break and admires the view. He sees the spaciousness and symmetry of the New Town as compared to the city's medieval core with its cramped housing, cobbles, alleys, and hidden closes.[105] The science and clarity manifested in the New Town are vastly preferable to his tastes. He regards himself as privileged to have been born into the newer and better world that replaces superstition and darkness with science and clarity.

Continuing to battle up the hill, his thoughts turn back to the New Club; he has never enjoyed the company of the members; he has only wanted the approbation of those, who had previously belittled him. Now though he no longer feels the need for their approval.

"To hell with bigots and bores and to hell with the club!" he exclaims in an outburst of spontaneous rebellion that leaves him feeling invigorated. Looking around he is glad there is no one within earshot to have heard him. Negotiating the last stretch of the climb, he feels he would much prefer the company of those with a scientific bent to that of anyone at the club.

Reaching the Burial Ground, he makes his way to the Hume tomb. David Hume, philosopher of the Scottish Enlightenment, is buried here

---

[105] A street that can only be entered from one end

in a mausoleum designed by Robert Adams, the person responsible for the elegant architecture of the New Town. Hume and Adams are a pairing of two of Scotland's finest sons! Staring up at the stout cylindrical tower, a David Hume quote occurs to him: "The great end of all human industry is the attainment of happiness. For this *(purpose)* were arts invented, sciences cultivated, laws ordained, and societies modeled."

Descending the hill - easier than climbing it - he mulls over the happiness quote. Since concentrating on science education for his charitable undertakings, he feels more at ease than previously, but happy? No; he will never be happy until he has sloughed off the slave trade.

Now on Princes Street, he asks himself why he should rob young Tom of his chance of happiness by not allowing him to bring his kitten to Edinburgh. He comes to the conclusion there is no real reason. When he gets home, he wastes a stamp and an envelope by opening the letter he had written to Tom and adds a postscript: "When you come to Edinburgh, bring your kitten if you wish." He addresses and stamps the new envelope feeling virtuous for having robbed his inconvenient conscience of a bit more of its leverage.

When Ms. Young brings him his afternoon tea, he says, "Ms. Young, the young man, who will be staying with us will be accompanied by a kitten. With that in mind, I've been thinking you might want to start bringing the dog into the kitchen."

Glowing with pleasure, she says, "Oh yes, Sir George, thank you!"

Betta in Bed

Leith, Scotland

Rose sits at her mother's bedside describing what she will be wearing for her next meeting with the young earl and then adds, "Now that Pa's met William, I want you, Ma, to meet him too, but you have to get better first."

Raising her head from the pillows, Betta says in an unusually firm voice, "Remember, child, the doctors say my condition is serious. You and Pa should be preparing yourselves for the worst."

"The doctors aren't always right!" Rose counters. "Besides, I have the feeling you are not even trying to get better. Please try! I want you to meet William, and I want you at my wedding!" She sticks out her chin.

Betta smiles inwardly; that strategy used to work in the past, but no longer! She says in a kind voice, "Lassie, I wouldn't fit in at your wedding. I might be confused with a servant! Nor would I ever feel comfortable in your home or with your in-laws. I am not as flexible as you and Pa are. In spite of all his posturing, he can change his stripes and will adapt. I would always remain plain old Betta."

Rose - eyes downcast, hands neatly folded on her lap - remains silent for a while. Then looking over at her mother, her expression both loving and fearful, she asks in a quiet voice, "Ma, are you asking me not to marry William?"

The unexpected question throws Betta off balance. She ponders before saying, "My only wish, love, is that you be happy. Do you genuinely love William, or is it only his title that interests you?"

Rose springs to her feet, saying, "Oh no, Ma, I love him!" She goes to the window and looks down into the garden before turning back to the bed and saying with a smile, "I've been fortunate. Had I not found

William, I might have taken someone like his old grandfather just for the title! Now I know that even if William had no title, I'd want to marry him anyway."

She stops because Betta, with a look of horror, is gasping, "You would have taken that old . . ." But she can't continue for lack of breath.

Rose backtracks and apologizes, saying, "Sorry, Ma, I was teasing, but I shouldn't tease when you're sick. I won't tease again until you're better, which must be in time for my wedding."

Now at peace with the situation, Betta relaxes into the pillows, feeling she will soon be able to let go of life in the knowledge that her nearest and dearest will be all right. Of course, they will grieve for her - she knows they love her - but they will manage. Lack of resilience is not among their failings.

Returning to the Camp

West Coast of Africa

After high-spirited celebrations, the Banyan Village hunters have parted company with the plain's dwellers. Seeing they can only carry a limited amount of meat, horns, and pelt, they have exchanged much of their share of the bounty with their savanna partners for cowrie shells and barter items to be delivered later.

Thimba has enjoyed his last hurrah to the full. As he leads his group back to their original camp by the rocky outcrop, they encounter the same hazards as on the outward journey - flooded rivers, mud, heat, and voracious insects - but they return with riches that will benefit the village as a whole. Big Baba will be well pleased - as is Thimba - that his tenure as leader of the warrior-hunter cadre is ending on this high note.

Thimba's plan is a good one. His death will no doubt throw Big Baba and the village into temporary turmoil, but they will recover, and unlike the corpse from Mbaleki village that landed up on the beach, Thimba's reputation will remain intact. His tribe will always fete his memory, and he will not be letting down youngsters like Kwame and Assimbola, who assign him hero status.

Striding across the plains, his following - especially the adolescents - straining to keep up, Thimba's thoughts turn from the outside world. He has done his job, must now eliminate distractions, and head for the goal. His plan is based on the knowledge that - although the moon is on the wane again - it is still bright enough to give the herds warning of predators on the prowl. Thus, now ravenous after days of unsuccessful hunting, the lions will take what they can. If available, humans are easy prey, and Thimba intends on making himself available. He is not certain how the end scene will play out, but he knows the time, the place, and the method. For the imponderables, he relies on Masimbarashe.

When the rocky outcrop above the camp appears in the distance, he makes a point of repressing all thought and feeling. He wants no messy emotions interfering; he needs to remain in full control to the end.

Shamwari Follows

West Coast of Africa

They have returned to the camp at the base of the rocky outcrop with its skeletal trees and sparse grass. Shamwari wonders if Thimba has forgotten what he threatened on the outward journey. He has been in top form, and Shamwari hasn't seen his friend so ebullient since their initiation. With any luck, he has overcome his malaise and will comply with Big Baba's requirements. It's not that difficult.

No sooner has Shamwari decided that he can let down his guard, he sees Thimba sneak away with spear, shield, and helmet and knows he must keep track of his friend's movements but without being seen. Instead of following Thimba, he climbs the rocky outcrop above the camp, and hidden by the scrub between the rocks, he finds a position by a stunted tree that affords him an overview.

He knows he must take care not only to keep out of Thimba's sight lines but also keep a lookout for lions in his own immediate environment. The previous week they had seen fresh dung and spoor in the area, and Shamwari knows that caution is vital.

With eyes sweeping the plains from his hideout, Shamwari spots Thimba in the open, spear in hand, walking with slow deliberation toward a nearby patch of jess. He assumes there must be a lion there but can't see it. As he watches, Thimba suddenly comes to a standstill. Helmet on his head, he stands straight and tall holding the shield strapped to his left forearm in front of his body. With the right hand, he holds his spear pointing upward at his side.

Shamwari steps back in shock. This is no posture for facing a lion! Or perhaps it isn't a Big Cat that Thimba faces. Shamwari's eyes sweep the area finding nothing of interest. Then a slight movement in the grass catches his attention, and there it is - a lion after all and not just any lion. It's a male in his prime - sleek and tawny with a massive black mane around its neck and shoulders. The creature - raw power, muscle, and energy - has no thought of ambush; instead it pads toward Thimba with supreme confidence. Just out of spear range, it stops, sits on his haunches, looks left and right, and gives a massive yawn.

When Thimba does not react, the creature becomes bored, gets to its feet, and trots a short way to the side. Then - in a surprise move - it swings around and with lightning speed attacks.

Shamwari sees Thimba still has time to launch the spear if he wishes, but with sudden insight, Shamwari understands Thimba has no intention of defending himself. He is smiling.

Family to Feed

West Coast of Africa

Shamwari does not witness the denouement of the drama below on the plains; he has let down his guard and is taken unaware.

Short tawny coat and tufted tail, a lioness keeps her first litter of three speckled cubs in a nearby den. They have just woken. All are hungry. She hasn't killed for days. She yawns, and with hindquarters in the air and forelegs parallel to the ground, she stretches. A night of hunting lies ahead, but she is getting weaker. Suddenly, stopping her stretch midstream, she holds her breath, pricks her ears, and sniffs. She hears something, smells something, and pokes out her head out of the den. Her senses do not betray her. The cubs, too, smelling something unusual, sit up on their haunches. Alert - soft ears pricked over baby faces - they fix their eyes on their mother.

She is an ambush hunter; she keeps her head low and body close to the ground. While not making a sound, she creeps forward over rock and tufts of grass and gets close and takes Shamwari from behind. Leaping onto his back - claws in his shoulders and fangs in his jugular - she pulls him to the ground and calls to her cubs.

Sequel

West Coast of Africa

It takes a while for the Banyan Village hunters to realize their two leaders are not in the camp. They must have slipped away and not yet returned, an unusual set of circumstances since it's been dark for a while and the stew is now ready. A cursory check of the environment reveals nothing.

It is only the next morning after an extensive search that they discover the two sites: one on the plains and the other on the rocky outcrop. All that remains are Thimba's helmet, the spears, a few splinters of bone, and the adornments that both warriors wore in their neck, wrist, and ankle.

The group, now without leaders, is confused and mills around without aim. Babalawo - medicine man - steps into the breach and organizes what needs to be done. The group has lost comrades before, and certain procedures apply. Gathering first at one site, then at the other, they lay aside their spears and sing the traditional dirges. At each site, they gather the adornments and fragments of bone to store in pouches for the afflicted families.

Return to the Village

West Coast of Africa

Lookouts spot the approach from afar, and now the whole village is assembled at the end of the path that leads into the village. Efia, Abebi, and Abena stand solemn-faced and wait. In normal circumstances, song and dance would have been the normal form of greeting. Now, though, the expectation is fraught with anxiety, and the crowd stand in silence not knowing what to expect.

During the night, the king of the forest - the mahogany where Thimba had his shrine to Masimbarashe - had fallen for no apparent reason. There had been no wind, no prior damage to the tree. It was the worst of omens. Hence the somber mood of those gathered.

Efia is starting to identify many of the familiar silhouettes: the hunters with small antelopes slung over their backs with the feet held together in front and those with the antelope slung over one shoulder. The larger antelopes are carried upside down on a pole with a hunter at each end. That is all normal. However, as the procession draws closer, Efia receives the confirmation she dreads; something is definitely amiss. Thimba is not leading the line of hunters strung out along the path, nor is it a rousing hunting song that the warriors sing. It is a dirge.

Efia groans and covers her eyes with her hand, and tears ooze through her fingers. Then feeling Abebi tugging at her skirt and seeing her child looking up at her with huge petrified eyes, she wipes away the tears and pretends she has dust in her eyes. She must protect her child from the truth.

Trying to act normally, she says to Abena, "Please, my friend, take Abebi to Twenty-Eighth Wife." To Abebi she says, "It's not going to be fun for you here, little one. You know you don't like dead animals.

Auntie Abena will take you to Twenty-Eighth Wife to play with the puppies."

Abena takes the child's hand, saying, "Come with me, Abebi." Abebi, although not sure if she should be leaving her mother, lets herself be lead but keeps looking over her shoulder as she goes. Efia, watching, manages a reassuring smile and waves until Abena and Abebi disappear behind the huts. Then feeling herself shredded by the ferocity of her love for Thimba, she lets out a howl of anguish, and with arms spread, she runs forward to the approaching column, crying, "Thimba! Where's my Thimba?"

Jacques Explains

Plantation, Louisiana

For the second time in the week, Jean is visiting Olivier Girrard Junior. Meanwhile, Jacques and his mother Cécile sit on the porch with their midmorning fruit drinks. Agathe and her house slave trainees wait in the shadows for whatever service might be needed.

Cécile takes a sip from her glass and makes a face; she says to Jacques, as she does now and then, "In spite of forty years in this godforsaken territory, I cannot accustom myself to lukewarm drinks."

"Well, Maman," replies Jacques, gulping down his drink with obvious pleasure. "Having been born in this country, I take it for granted. I know though that you had icehouses in France."

Agathe notes how the mistress perks up at the opportunity to speak of her homeland.

"Yes!" she reminisces. "Icehouses were usually underground, but ours was one built into a hill. In winter, servants would cut blocks of ice from the lake below the château and drag them up on sleds to the icehouse. Properly packed with straw, those blocks would see us through most of the summer."

Agathe following the conversation as always from the sidelines is full of wonder. Temperatures on the plantation, even in winter, rarely dip below what the master calls *zero*. Hence, the only ice Agathe has ever seen resembles a thin lid of glass on top of a bucket of water. She cannot imagine whole lakes covered with slabs of thick glass, nor, for that matter, can she imagine the countryside turned white for months on end with what the master calls *neige*.[106] The only *neige* she has ever seen came and went quickly.

---

[106] Snow

Jacques, as he beckons to Agathe for a refill, says, "Maman, you might be interested to know - even though I haven't mentioned the matter before - that off and on through the past seven months, I have been putting thought into the matter of transporting ice in winter down to the south of the continent from the north. Last December, while ploughing through Papa's letters from his cousin Émile in Bordeaux, I found references to a Norwegian cousin, who has made a fortune transporting ice from the northern countries of Europe to the warm south. Émile suggests to Papa that the two of them should perhaps look into the feasibility of establishing a similar business here. Although Papa doesn't seem to have shown interest, the idea intrigues me."

As Agathe returns to her post after refilling Jacques's glass, she notices the mistress is staring at Jacques, aghast. Jacques, too, notices and asks, "Why should you object to the ice trade, Maman?

"It's not the ice trade that shocks me, son. It's that you were entering your father's office months before he fell ill or before you spoke to me about the arsenic. If he had found out that you were there looking through his papers without his permission, he would have taken you to court and had you sent to prison. Imagine the shame!"

Jacques replaces his glass with care; he says, "You underestimate me, Maman. I would not have gone to prison. I had the law on my side. Even before I started entering his office, I already had full *pouvoir*[107] over Papa's business affairs!"

Cécile splutters, "How is that possible? We are talking about last year when he was still healthy and competent. We only started to talk about the arsenic mid-April, and I only administered the first dose toward the end of April. That means you were going through his papers for four months at a time when he was still *en pleine santé*!"[108]

---

[107] Power of attorney
[108] In good health

Agathe sees Jacques smirk. "Quite so, Maman," he replies, "but I'd already decided he would not be *en pleine santé* much longer. Not wanting to delay, I found a doctor, who after money changed hands took my word for Papa's mental incompetence and provided the necessary medical document. I then wrote to Cousin Émile saying Papa's mind was failing, that I had the power of attorney and would be looking for an overseas buyer for the plantation. I acted prematurely, but am glad I did." Pausing to underline the drama of what he is about to say, Jacques then continues with the words. "Because I acted when I did, I've found an overseas buyer for the plantation, which would otherwise not be the case."

Cécile gasps and raises her hand to her mouth. Agathe notes that the reaction is one of pleasure. Cécile's eyes sparkle as she inquires in honeyed tone, "Did I hear right, dear? Did you say you have an agreement to sell the plantation?"

Jacques gives a scornful laugh; he says, "I thought you'd be pleased, ma chère Maman!"

His tone is one of contempt, but Cécile doesn't notice.

"Tell me about it, dear," she urges. To Agathe's surprise, the mistress looks pretty. Her cheeks flushed, and her features pleasingly arranged.

Jacques explains the situation with Émile, and when he has finished, the mistress says, "I'm delighted, son, but I need to know how you could be sure that I'd cooperate. You only mentioned the matter when everything else was in place. What if I had not agreed?"

"Not for a moment did it occur to me, Maman, that you'd refuse the job!" With a smirk, he holds up his glass and mocks her with the words, "I drink to you, Maman! You're a good little poisoner!" He drains the glass and smacks his lips.

Beginning of the Third Week of June 1800

Adieu, Mon Père

Plantation, Louisiana

In the canopied bed, the chevalier's head rests on a mounded pillow. His face, under the floppy nightcap, resembles a death mask. Yet he is not dead; he still breathes in shallow wheezes.

Kneeling at his bedside, André prays the rosary, while opposite him, Agathe dressed in the long dark dress, white pinafore, and cap of the house slave swabs her master's brow. As André knows from his mother, the master's skin is cold and no longer needs swabbing; nonetheless, she does it. When still capable of communication, he had told her that he likes her doing it. "It's like a caress, Agathe. It gives me comfort," he would say. There is nothing the master could do, if she decided to stop, but André knows she'd never deny a dying man this simple comfort.

As André prays in silence - *Ave Maria, gratia plena* - Jacques and Jean stand close at hand in the formal dress of the ancien régime: big wigs, high heels, and long brocade jackets donned in the expectation of their father's demise. André knows that his presence at the deathbed irritates Jacques, knows that Jacques has resented the daily visits, knows that Jacques detests him, but knows, too, that as long as his father lives,

Jacques is unlikely to take action. What will happen with his father's passing, André can only guess and does not like the options.

As he continues with the *Ave Maria*s he hears that his father's wheezing is becoming slower and more sporadic. He hears Jacques whisper to Jean, "The end is near. Go and fetch Maman from the porch. I'll send someone to Baton Rouge for Dr. Le Blanc."

"He'll come too late," warns Jean.

"Idiot!" Jacques hisses. "That's not the point! We don't need resuscitation. We need a death certificate saying Papa died from natural causes."

"Just so, *mon frère*," babbles Jean, reduced to jelly by his brother's displeasure. The pair leaves the room as André continues the rosary, now praying aloud. The house slaves gathered as shadows in the background give the responses in Latin; the chevalier has trained them well: *Ave Maria, gratia plena, Dominus tecum / Benedicta tu in mulieribus.*[109]

Tears streak André's cheeks as he recites his lines; then, waiting for the response, notes his mother has stopped swabbing, and her head is bent in prayer. His father's eyes flick open one last time before the body lurches and falls silent.

---

[109] Hail Mary, full of grace, the Lord is with thee / Blessed art thou among women

Smiles

Plantation, Louisiana

Dr. Jules Le Blanc, mounted on Beau, canters up the driveway to halt at the steps of the porch, where the stable boy Gerald waits to take the horse. Dr. Le Blanc recognizes the twelve-year old as one of the chevalier's coffee-colored kiddies with Agathe's deceased sister.

As he dismounts and hands over the reins, he notices the lad has been crying and wears a black armband. He realizes suddenly how hard life will now be for the spoiled coffee-colored kiddies. Jacques is unlikely to appreciate the presence of so many half-cast siblings. He chucks the boy under the chin, says, "Cheer up, laddie!" Then, knowing that the boy has no reason to be cheerful, he delves into his pocket and comes up with a handful of silver coins. Handing them over he says, "Ask your Aunt Agathe to keep these in a safe place for you. Meanwhile, look after Beau for me."

As he takes the porch steps, two at a time, he remembers the time he mentioned arsenic poisoning to Cécile. He still smarts at his own *bêtise*.[110] Had he put thought into the matter, he would have known to stay well clear and not breathed a word. Since ascertaining the chevalier's problem was arsenic poisoning, it became obvious the wife was the culprit. Slaves would not have access to arsenic and had they wanted to poison their master, they would have used plants or poisonous creatures available in their environment. Yet being certain of both the diagnosis and perpetrator did not mean he should have tried to reveal the fact to the culprit. Mounting the stairs, he realizes his ego was to blame for the faux pas.

Pausing at the top of the stairs on the landing to watch young Gerald through the window - he leads Beau to the water trough - he reviews the problem with his ego. He loathes the likes of Cécile treating

---

[110] Stupidity

him like a country bumpkin when he is just as competent as are the French-trained doctors of New Orleans. He trained at the best medical college in France and had an amorous adventure with a highborn lady not antagonized her husband, he would now have an illustrious career in Paris.

As he walks down the corridor to the sickroom, he tells himself there must be no repeat of his thoughtlessness. Although it irks him that the likes of Cécile and her sons are rarely held to account for their crimes, he does not have the clout to take them on. He and the slaves would suffer if he tried.

Jacques greets him at the open door of the sickroom, "Ah, Monsieur le Docteur! Sorry, there was no one to meet you. You will realize we're upset and aren't thinking clearly."

They are thinking clear enough, the doctor notes five minutes later as Jacques shepherds him downstairs to the Gentlemen's Study and seats him at the Louis Quatorze escritoire, where the form he needs to sign, an open inkwell, a new quill, and a pounce shaker wait for his use. All he has to do is fill in the cause of death and sign; it is simple. He picks up the quill yet does not write.

It annoys him that he feels intimidated by having Jacques - in the full regalia of the ancien régime - hanging over his shoulder watching his every move. Perhaps, he should after all gather his courage and take on the family. He inspects the feather, determines it is a hand-cut swan's quill that has already been dressed and requires no further sharpening, although a quill knife lies close at hand. At home, he uses goose quills; wonders if he will like this pen better. Should he or shouldn't he expose the family? They are murderers and deserve to face the full force of the law.

Jacques's patience has reached its limit. In a manner far from civil, he snaps, "Do your job, Monsieur le Docteur! I can't wait here all day. Other matters need my attention."

Dr. Le Blanc dips the quill into the inkwell and guides the tip gracefully across the paper. He shakes on the pounce and replaces the quill in its stand; it is a good pen, better than his goose quills. Looking up at the glowering figure at his side, he says, "I have written, monsieur, that your father died of natural causes."

Jacques's nod of approval is so vigorous that his wig slips askew, and he has to turn to a nearby mirror to readjust it. "I'm glad we understand each other," he says. "Agathe will now show you to the door, and I'll return to my duties."

As Agathe opens the front door for the doctor, he nods at her by way of thanks; she in return gives him a lovely smile. He has never before seen that stern presence smile. As he descends the steps, he assumes she was listening at the keyhole and knows therefore that poisoning received no mention on the death certificate. His step becomes more buoyant. Although unable to bring down the high and the mighty, he has at least saved the innocent.

As he retrieves Beau's reins from young Gerald, the child stuns him by giving him the same lovely smile he has just received from the aunt! Mounting, he wheels the horse and, with a cheery wave, takes off at a canter down the drive and onto the River Road. As he passes through the deafening cacophony of the cicadas, he thinks that although the day had hardly been pleasant, two smiles had done much to improve it.

Whipping

Plantation, Louisiana

When André leaves the death chamber, two husky men whom Jacques must have brought in from Baton Rouge jump him, wrestle him to the ground, and shackle him. Dragging him down the staircase, they set him on his feet at the bottom while Jacques in the attire of the ancien régime, remains five steps up. André sees that Jacques has put thought into this setup, which allows him to look down on André.

"Bâtard!" snarls Jacque, pouring venom into every word, "Nine-and-thirty with the cat[111] will teach you your place. My men will take you to the whipping post. I'll see you there in a few minutes."

There is only one whipping post on this plantation, thinks André, *and that is several kilometers away.*

As Jacques moves down a step, André sees Jean - eyes scrunched up and wearing a pained look - has been sheltering behind his brother. In different circumstances, André might have smiled, but not now. He must prepare himself for the *nine-and-thirty*. He knows it will not be easy but is determined to neither bend nor beg. He has never received a whipping but has witnessed a couple and heard about many more. He knows that few manage to preserve dignity even though, with lashes delivered at a rate of one per second, the ordeal only lasts thirty-nine seconds.

The improvised whipping post turns out to be a strong horizontal branch of an old fig tree in the park that surrounds the Big House. The house slaves along with those that work in the farmyard, stand in clusters at a distance. Jacques still in the dress of the ancien régime stands close at hand. He holds the whip and rebukes his flunkies for dawdling.

---

[111]   Bastard! Thirty-nine lashes with the cat-o'-nine-tails whip

André, standing tall, does not resist even as the lackeys strip him naked, which is *not* the accepted practice. Realizing the intention is to deepen his humiliation, the insight only strengthens his determination to show no emotion. He also cooperates by holding up his tied hands to make it easier for the flunkies to feed through the rope that will pass over the branch lifting him onto his toes.

The scene thus set, Jacques hands over the whip to the bigger of the two men. André sees that Jacques does so with reluctance; he understands that Jacques would prefer to do the beating himself, but given that he's small and weak, he would not be able to deliver the lashes at the required speed, thus making himself a laughingstock.

The beating begins with Jacques calling out the lashes with zest. "One, two, three . . .," he counts at the top of his voice. With every stroke, the *cat* digs deeper into open wounds. In the fraction of a second that separate the strikes, André finds that he both dreads the zing that heralds the next strike, yet also wants it to come quickly, so the ordeal will end. Sinking his head to his chest, he closes his eyes and thinks of the Christian martyrs. Opening them again, he focuses on the flies that collect on the sweat and blood that pour from his body and puddle beneath his feet.

Meanwhile, Jacques continues to punch out the count, "Twenty-seven, twenty-eight . . ."

To André the numbers are starting to sound like orgasmic grunts. He knows Jacques is in his element and enjoying every moment.

"Thirty-one, thirty-two . . ."

Will thirty-three never come? He passes out and seems to leave his body for a moment. Looking down on himself, he sees his back engulfed in flame. Then he returns to the unrelenting count: *zing . . . zing . . .*

362   H. Ann Ackroyd

zing. The pain is beyond bearable. He tries to scream, but can't; he has no voice.

"Thirty-six, thirty-seven, thirty . . ."

It's over but not the pain, which continues in searing agony. Yet he still registers what is happening. He sees the lackey hand the blood-drenched *cat* back to Jacques and feels the release of pressure on the shoulders and arms as the rope is loosened, and he is set back on his feet. Unable to stand, one of the men supports him, while the other covers his nakedness with a horse blanket. Jacques then steps forward and pokes the whip-handle into André's chest, "Get yourself cleaned up, bâtard! Tomorrow you will be back at work, but don't imagine you'll ever sit on horseback again. Pégasse is mine, and only I shall ride him!"

Unable to lift his head, André sees the blood splatter on Jacques's boots and thinks, *That is the same blood, Jacques, that flows in your veins!*

On the afternoon after the whipping, André lies on his stomach on the back porch of his cabin. The mattress on which he lies is stuffed with gray moss and corn shucks and is normally pleasantly soft, but now rustles each time he winces in pain. Agathe, who is treating the gouges on his back, apologizes saying, "I'm trying not to hurt you, but I have to clean the wounds." She is using a clean rag and one of her secret muti[112]: the one that stings more and smells worse than any other!

Surprisingly, Jacques has given Agathe the afternoon off to tend to her son's wounds. As she winds up the job and replaces the cap on the bottle, she says to André, "I think Jacques is worried that he overdid it. Because you didn't cry out, he didn't realize how badly he had damaged your body until afterward. I suspect he might now even have a grudging respect for you. For us slaves, you're a hero!"

---

[112] Medicine

SLAVES, MASTERS AND TRADERS

"Jacques bloody well should be worried," grumbles André, who, thanks to his mother's ministrations, is starting to feel marginally better. "Who else does he think will run his plantation for him? He certainly isn't capable of doing it himself!"

André doesn't comment on the hero aspect, knowing full well he's a fraud. He would have screamed if his body had cooperated, but he doesn't say so to his mother. Instead, as she leaves, he drops off to sleep,

The moment his eyes fall closed, images crowd into his mind without chronology or order. His brain is obviously still trying to process the death of his father while at the same time is dealing with the whipping. One moment he is at his father's knee learning about the moods of the Mississippi, the fauna of the bayou, and the long and glorious history of France. The next, he is a young adult sitting late into the night with his father drinking Bourbon from a crystal tumbler and smoking a Cuban cigar.

He has no time to linger on any one scene, before another replaces it. The replacement this time is himself as a small boy kneeling next to his father at the *prie dieu*[113] babbling words that he does not understand in an effort to emulate the chevalier as he prays the rosary. That image forward him to this very day when he prayed the rosary at his father's deathbed. He sees himself kneeling in prayer - head bent over his hands, palms together and held at his chest in the way his father had taught him.

Now awake - his wounds niggling - he ponders the fact that his father taught him to be a good Catholic; even took him once to the church in Baton Rouge. The ceiling of a painted heaven remains with him populated as it was with saints, cherubs, and angels - all white-faced, of course. Also, his father allowed him to train as an altar boy for the times the priest came to the plantation.

---

[113]   Kneeling bench for praying; has a raised shelf for elbows and book

His knowledge of the Catholic faith has always stood him in good stead. Even now at the whipping, the thought of the stoicism of the saints and martyrs had helped him - albeit for only part of the time. He wonders if those brave people would have screamed had they had the physical energy to generate a scream. Might it also have been like that for the heroes of the stories his mother passes on from her parents? Those stories tell of their African forbears, whose status in the tribe depended on their ability - during barbaric rites - to withstand intolerable pain with equanimity.

Opening the House

Edinburgh, Scotland

With Tom soon to arrive, Ms. Young and her niece have spent the morning removing dust covers, opening windows, and cleaning Sir George's study on the main floor. Sir George could not believe how they jabbered away with one another. He always thought of Ms. Young as monosyllabic, but it turns out she and her niece are regular chatterboxes! Nevertheless, that didn't seem to stop them getting the job done, and he is now transferring his writing paraphernalia back to where he has a big slant-lid mahogany bureau and a sizable filing system. It is housed in a cabinet behind a well-nigh invisible door in the paneling.

Rifling through Tom's letters with the intent of filing them, he glances through one, which reads as follows:

> Sir,
>
> You know so much that I must wonder if you know about spiders. One lives outside my door, and I have watched her weave her web. Is it not amazing that a speck of a brain contains the template for such a complex construction? Is it not incredible that her tubby little body contains the tools to perform a feat, which seems to me nothing short of genius?
>
> Postscript: I wrote this initially as assonant verse, but then was ashamed of it and turned it into prose.

Continuing his sorting, Sir George surprises himself by finding a few Tom-like lines that he himself had scribbled on the back of one of Tom's envelopes. He must have read the letter it contained at breakfast, and Ms. Young would have brought it to him on a tray using good china. It reads as follows:

> My tastes are frugal
> No Wedgwood, please!
> Kitchen crockery
> best serves my needs.

Bundling the letters into a folder, he marvels at the degree to which the boy has helped him find more in life to enjoy. As he labels the folder, he even finds himself wondering if he should do a bit of writing himself. He thinks of Tom's obsession with obtaining an education that would qualify him as a writer. Meanwhile - so Sir George thinks - he himself is already educated and qualified to write and might well enjoy writing outrageous articles using a nom de plume, outrageous by the standards of his peers but not outrageous by the standards of more liberal thinkers. He could write from the point of view of a libertarian or of a dissenter; he could take digs at Lord Richard or at various dignitaries. He could create all types of mischief. A mouse of a man - like himself - would never be a suspect!

Outlandish Ideas

Edinburgh, Scotland

Sir George has just finished reading a letter from his eldest daughter, Isobel, who is now with the family in North Berwick. Strangely - although the acquisition of the London house is for her benefit - it is of no interest to her. As he sets aside the letter, he wonders about that disinterest. Could it be that she does not wish to be offered up on the London marriage market? Perhaps she would be happier just marrying a nice boy - no title needed - here in Edinburgh. It would be a lot cheaper!

As Sir George walks through the drawing room into the hall - he is readying himself for an outing - he marvels at the play of light throughout the house. With the curtains closed and the furniture swathed in dust covers, he had forgotten the inherent beauty of his surroundings and wonders anew at the doors Tom is opening for him. If the family comes to Edinburgh at the end of the summer, he wonders yet again how they will relate to the boy.

As Sir George sits to put on his outdoors footwear, an extraordinary idea occurs to him. Isobel and Tom are similar to one another in character - if not in background and upbringing - and would probably get on well together. What would happen, if . . .? He hardly dares think the thought but does. What would happen if in the course of time, they fell in love? Tom does have loveable attributes and an undeniable, eccentric charm. If he is well-dressed and well-groomed - as he will be after arrival in Edinburgh - and if he learns to behave in an appropriate manner, he could appeal to a young girl. As to the amputated arm, it might add allure. Lord Nelson had his arm amputated after he was hit by a musket ball three years ago and is considered a romantic hero. Further, if Tom sticks to his studies - the indications are he will - he has the potential of becoming a respectable citizen, and if not a son-in-law of whom Lord Richard would approve, he could well be a better husband for Isobel than the type Jessica has in mind!

At this point, Sir George has a major flight of fancy visualizing not only one protégé as a potential son-in-law but several of a similar type, i.e. students with the abilities to rise above the norm if given the chances he would give them. Five sons-in-law with a scientific bent would be a wondrous thing! He could pull out of the *Spirit* consortium and free himself from the slave trade. He could slough off his upper-class friends, and instead of the New Club, he could join a science club. He could . . .

Hearing Ms. Young coming up the back stairs, he pulls himself together. Banning all foolishness from mind, he puts on his top hat, and taking to hand his walking stick, he flees the house. However, by the time he reaches St. Andrew's Square, he is back to thinking that the notion of regarding Isobel and Tom as a wedded couple is *not* totally outlandish.

Christening

Aberdeenshire, Scotland

Only a week after the old laird's funeral, family, friends, and neighbors again gather at the stone chapel under the pines. Under normal circumstances, the christening would have been delayed, but Stanley will soon be leaving with Émile for Louisiana and the old priest too is failing and wants to officiate as long as he is still able to travel.

Stanley, standing at the font holding young Adair, notes that the old priest no longer uses the official wording but improvises. Gramps would have been fuming, but seeing he is not present, it doesn't matter. (If he is present - in spirit - one hopes it's in a more tolerant form than in life!)

As godfather, Stanley is dressed in the new style of formal Highland attire: the *small* kilt in the clan tartan and all the appropriate accessories: pins, belt, buckle, sporran, knee socks, garter flashes, and ghillie brogues. The younger men at the service are similarly attired while a couple of the older generation still wear the *big* kilt, which has part of the plaid pleated around the waist and part slung over the shoulder. Seeing the elderly are always cold - so Stanley thinks - the *big* kilt is a good choice.

Stanley hopes he has said the right things as a godparent, renounced deceit and evil in the name of his godchild, and undertaken to help the wee laddie take his God-given place in the world. (He doesn't know how he can do all that from Louisiana, but the good will is there and that's what counts. He has listened how - through baptism - the Lord promises to be with the child through joy and sorrow. He has seen, too, a candle lit that Adair may shine as a light in the world. Finally, he has witnessed the priest make the sign of the cross on the smooth little forehead telling the child, "Christ has now claimed you as his own and will never forget you."

To Stanley's relief, Adair gurgled and cooed throughout the ceremony and raised no objections. However, that changes when the priest's wobbly hand douses him with too much water; earsplitting shrieks ring up into the rafters. Frances has to rush round the font to the rescue.

Stanley now in the more comfortable role of observer lets his mind wander. He knows he belongs here in a way that he can never belong elsewhere and feels a twinge of regret to be leaving. Not only will he be leaving Glen Orm but also a son whom he has come to love in the past week. One look into that angelic face and he was smitten.

Now with Gramps gone, the initial impetus that set him on the path to Louisiana is no longer valid. Can he renege on the deal? Does he want to renege? He sees Émile eyeing him warily from the congregation. He obviously suspects Stanley might be tempted to stay and neither he nor Uncle Aaron wants that to happen!

Fulfillment

Leith, Scotland

Betta no longer gets up to sit by the window, and Rose dedicates more time to her mother. She organizes the nursing schedules, doctor's visits, and the medications, and she sits and chats when Betta is up to it. Migu puts in his regular working hours but comes home to check in the middle of the day and is home early in the evening. The servants go about their regular chores, and the governesses still come but shorten their sessions to allow Rose more time with her mother. This afternoon, Rose is using that time to search out a certain night jacket that Betta wants.

With Rose out of the room, Betta sinks into the pillow thinking of the enormity of the changes in the last little while. She finds it miraculous that Rose has found an earl she can love and is not merely taking for his title. The cherry on the cake is that Aaron has told her that he is giving up heckling and that he feels he will get on with his future son-in-law. He also said that the official Betrothal Agreement with the new earl is signed and sealed.

Feeling happy but tired, she closes her eyes and is nearly asleep when Rose returns to the room, saying, "I have the bed jacket, but unhappily the moths have got at it. It has many more holes than the crocheting warrants."

Betta smiles and tries to comment, but nothing comes out. She feels she will never speak again; some vital function inside her has ruptured.

What Next?

West Coast of Africa

Big Baba has spent nothing but restless nights since the night prior to the hunters' return. That night was the forerunner to the worst week in Big Baba's tenure as senior elder. The entire village had heard the thunder of a tree crashing to the ground. Filled with foreboding, the villagers had emerged from their huts and gathered in ghostly groupings in the moonlight.

"Could that have been Thimba's mahogany?" they had asked of one another.

Daybreak had confirmed the most ominous of portents; Thimba's mahogany had indeed fallen.

Tonight so it seems will be another sleepless night for Baba. As he lies on his mat with Forty-First Wife keeping watch by the fire outside, he listens to the distant wash of the surf and to the wind rattling through plantain and palm.

It was like this the night the tree fell and, as it occurs to Baba now, that tree not only smothered everything in its path, but it had also smothered the whole village. A miasma prevails with everyone performing their chores in a daze. Big Baba knows he should be showing leadership in this moment of crisis, but neither he nor his fellow elders know how best to move forward.

The tribe now not only lacks a headman but also its two top warriors. This means that of the three pillars needed for good governance - headman, warrior-hunters, and Council of Elders - two pillars are missing. The crisis is in urgent need of a resolution, yet sleeplessness makes Baba's normally agile mind slow and plodding.

The only thing that Baba and the Council of Elders have achieved in the past week is to appoint Babalawo as temporary head of the warrior cadre. Although not an ideal solution, it is better than nothing. Like all healthy male members of the tribe - as an adolescent - Babalawo had trained as a warrior and had fulfilled all requirements. Since then, he has always been available to the corps in cases of emergency, but while being competent as a warrior-hunter, it is not his principle calling. Everyone knows Babalawo to be a good medicine man - conscientious in caring for the physical and mental well-being of his fellow tribesmen. It has been the family vocation for generations. Neither the warriors nor Babalawo himself are comfortable with his sudden change in role, but accept it as a temporary stopgap.

Through a crack in the door, Big Baba sees Forty-First Wife's shadow in the flickering light of the cooking fire that she has kept burning for company. He wonders what goes on in her mind as she sits there alone in the night. Perhaps she is thinking up new stories to tell the children: happy and funny stories. Of that, he is certain. Baba envies Forty-First Wife's nimble mind. He used to have one too. Surely, it must still be hiding somewhere inside him; surely when a tree falls and blocks the path, there is a way to bypass it!

Five minutes later, a glimmer of hope presents itself. Perhaps - now with Thimba gone - it would be easier to instate Efia in a temporary capacity in the headman's position. That might help lighten the burden of grief that incapacitates her and would help the tribe by having someone cope with day-to-day issues.

Encouraged by having made progress with the headman issue, he moves on to the blow dealt to the warrior corps and wonders if revisiting an idea from the past might have potential for the present. In the past - through long nights around the fire - he and Mbaleki had often spoken of working together to create a benevolent yet dominant presence in the region. An aspect discussed had concerned training their warriors together, but they had never got beyond the talking stage. There had been no major crisis to warrant it. Now there is a major crisis, and Mbaleki would understand. He doesn't want a weak and vulnerable neighbor and would surely cooperate.

Forty-First Wife, knowing Big Baba is still awake, looks through the door saying, "Baba, can I bring you water? It might help you sleep."

She has a gentle voice and pleasant personality. He's pleased he chose her, gives her a wan smile into the dark, and says, "Yes, please. You're a good girl."

Waiting for the water, he feels that an answer to the present problem would be for Mbaleki, firstly, to allow the bad boys to finish their training with the savanna trainees and, secondly, to supply a top warrior as a stand-in for Thimba.

There is, however, one problem with his two otherwise satisfactory solutions. Would they satisfy the tribe? The tribe likes to consult its loas in times of crisis. Startled at this last insight, Baba sits up in bed. Why had he not thought of it earlier? While he himself might be happy to chat under the banyan with his loa Mkulu, the tribe needs a spectacle. Even though they had a Gran Legbwa celebration last month - given the new situation - they need another one now. He'll give them what they need and thereby affix spiritual approbation to his own solutions: Efia as headman and Mbaleki as key to the warrior dilemma.

Walking slowly, so as not to spill, Forty-First Wife returns with the water in a halved coconut shell. Pushing open the door with her shoulder, she hears Big Baba's gentle snores. With a smile, she drinks the water herself and settles on her mat knowing Big Baba is again in charge.

Kwame in Trouble

West Coast of Africa

With the blanket of gloom that has smothered the village, Kwame has fallen through the cracks. His family is so caught up in their grief that they don't realize the devastating impact the death of Kwame's idolized elder brother Thimba is having on him. People who might normally have noticed that he is in trouble are as dazed as everyone else. Normally, too, Kwame and Assimbola would have been a support to one another in coming to terms with the loss of their hero. Assimbola, though, is now ill; he is suffering from malaria and hasn't left his pallet in Abena's hut since the hunters returned last week.

Abena has been tending to her son both day and night. Kwame sees that she is now nearing the end of her tether but doesn't know how to help. He knows he would like to be in the tiny hut with Assimbola, but realizes he would be in Abena's way. Besides the few times he's been with his friend, they have barely been able to exchange a word because Assimbola is constantly plagued by alternating chills and fevers, by vomiting, diarrhea, and nausea. Sometimes he doesn't even know where he is and speaks as though Thimba were still alive.

Loitering outside Abena's hut, Kwame thinks how lucky Assimbola is to have such a nice mother. He likes Abena; she is a kind woman. When he'd been hanging around the hut yesterday, he'd felt so abysmally lost that he had buried his face in his arm against the back of the hut and howled. He couldn't stop, and Abena - he hadn't realized she could hear him - had come out and held him in her arms and comforted him. It had felt good. Today he feels like howling again but not wanting to inflict himself on Abena for a second time, he takes off in the direction of the forest. There he finds a suitable tree and again buries his face in his arm and howls until exhausted.

When he stops, he feels there are people watching him but knows it's impossible. Sniffing, he wanders around ending up by the fallen mahogany. He would like to speak to Masimbarashe, but without altar or offering, he knows it would not be right.

The creatures of the forest are becoming accustomed to him. Even the cobra that Thimba had told him about, no longer slithers away. Yesterday he'd found himself hoping - if he could get close enough - it might give him a lethal bite. He yearns for death. Today though he feels that a cobra bite might not be worthy of Thimba. Taking on a lion with a bow and arrow might be better. Tomorrow he'll discuss the matter with Assimbola.

Ackees

West Coast of Africa

Efia and several of Big Baba's younger wives - none older than Efia - have just returned from harvesting ackees. Efia didn't want to lead the trip; she hasn't wanted to do anything since Thimba's death. She feels weighed down with an all-consuming apathy and finds it difficult to put one foot in front of the other. Yet Big Baba forced her to do what she'd promised to do weeks earlier and hadn't done till now.

Standing by the ackee tree - it is a half-mile walk from the village - she had held a lecture on ackee trees. She had told the girls in a monotonous voice that ackee trees were evergreen and their fruit was available throughout the year. She had warned them, too, that great vigilance was needed in preparing them seeing that everything about the fruit - except the arils[114] in their ripe red pods - was lethal. "Only medicine men harvest unripe ackees for use in concocting poisons," she had added as they filled their baskets.

Then back at Big Baba's compound, she had shown the girls how to free the creamy edible arils from their lethal surroundings. The only time her voice showed any animation was when she told the girls to *always* use a lidded container to dispose of the poisonous parts, especially the shiny black seeds that attracted children. After demonstrating how to wash and drain the arils, she then left the girls with instructions to place the arils in boiling water, removing them the moment they turn bright yellow.

Now she is glad to be home on her own to prepare the delicacy for herself and Abebi. Abebi is still with Twenty-Eighth Wife, where she now likes to spend most of her time. Every so often she'll come and visit Efia and give her a brief hug, saying, "Don't cry Mammi," before scampering off again to be with Twenty-Eighth Wife and the puppies.

---

[114]   Seed coats

She does the same with Big Baba, visits him under the banyan, and says, "Don't be sad, Baba." After briefly nuzzling her head on his chest, she then scurries off again to Twenty-Eighth Wife's hut.

Although Efia has told her daughter that her father has passed into the spirit world and will be looking after them from there, she sees that Abebi doesn't miss Thimba in any meaningful way. She suspects that while Abebi is proud that her Baba Thimba is a hero - it gives her added status - she is also glad to have him out of the way. It's behavior that doesn't really surprise Efia. Although Thimba never touched her - either for good or for bad - he frightened her as much as the bad boys.

Making sure that the lid fits well on the container in which she'll be discarding the inedible parts of the ackees, she takes to hand a small paring knife and goes about the job in the manner just shown to Big Baba's young wives. She has nearly finished, when she looks up to see Abena running over from her hut. *Poor Abinti,* thinks Efia of the child bouncing around on his mother's back. Efia then quickly realizes something must be amiss for Abena to run. Abena with her full figure and a piccanin on her back is not given to running. Efia puts down her knife and goes to meet her friend. "What's wrong, Abena?"

Out of breath and puffing, Abena says, "Efia, I must get back to Assimbola. I shouldn't be leaving him. He is bad today, but perhaps you can help us. Assimbola just told me - even though he has difficulty speaking - that he is worried about Kwame, who has just left. He thinks Kwame might be planning to end his life on the plains like Thimba." After stopping to regain her breath and to adjust the howling Abinti on her back, Abena continues, "Kwame's parents should be told, but the baby grandson they were raising died in the night, and they are in turmoil. The next best thing would be to take Kwame to Babalawo, but I don't dare leave Assimbola." She starts to sob, saying through her tears, "I . . . I think my Assimbola is dying!"

Shocked, Efia hugs her friend and tries to gather her senses. She has been so immersed in her own misery that all else has passed her by. She hadn't realized that Assimbola was seriously ill, that Kwame was in dire need of help, and that a baby had died in the night. As Abena's sobs start to abate, Efia says in a businesslike manner, "I'll take Kwame to Babalawo now. Where is Kwame?"

"He shouldn't be far," sniffs Abena. "As I left, I saw him heading in that direction." She points toward the forest behind the butchery.

"I'll go right away," says Efia and starts off in the direction

"Woha, Efia!" Abena calls after her. "If that is ackees you are preparing, you shouldn't leave them unattended! I'll take them home and deal with them for you."

Chastised and mortified at the unforgivable oversight, Efia wonders if she is just as much in need of Babalawo's ministrations as is Kwame. However - so she tells herself - by now undertaking the Kwame job, she has taken the first step toward recovery. It shocks her to realize how selfish she has been and for how much she now has to make amends. She hasn't even been to commiserate with Shamwari's wives.

Babalawo and Kwame

West Coast of Africa

Efia, chin stuck out, marches an intimidated Kwame to Babalawo's compound. For the first time since Thimba's death, she feels that she is again in charge. She is determined to place the lad - Thimba's flesh and blood - back on his feet. She has obviously underestimated the hero-worship Thimba evoked in his young trainees.

On arrival at Babalawo's compound, Efia and Kwame find him seated in the shade in front of his hut, which is not small and round like most in the village; instead it is large and elongated. Although there is a big carved chair by the door, Babalawo sits on the ground with his back against the wall and his well-muscled legs stretched out in front of him.

From her childhood days, Efia remembers Babalawo's venerable father - Babalawo Senior - sitting in this same manner. It always surprised her to see the contrast between the terrifying role he played at the ceremonies compared to the unthreatening relaxed pose, which his son now also uses in daily life. For the frenzied dancing at public celebrations, the father would wear a leopard skin and a fierce eagle headdress with fringes of raffia[115] that dropped to the ground. The fringes would sway and lift with the jumps and twirls of the body to reveal adornments of stone, claw, copper, and bone.

Babalawo Junior wears as much of his father's gear as he can. It is a symbolic gesture acknowledging his indebtedness to his forefathers, for passing on the skills, mysteries, and guarded secrets that pertain to the vocation of a traditional diviner, healer, and herbalist. The calling has remained in the family for generations.

Efia and Kwame give Babalawo time to get to his feet before greeting him in the formal manner accorded to a person of his standing. Efia

---

[115] Fiber of the raffia palm

then hands him a portion of dried chimp meat, a delicacy to which she knows he is partial. He looks pleased, says, "What brings you, Efia and young Kwame, to my door?"

Efia replies, "Babalawo, Abena and I are worried about Kwame. Thimba's death has affected him badly - as it has everyone - but he is taking his grief too far. He now wants to follow Thimba into the world of the spirits."

Babalawo gives Kwame a piercing look and asks, "Is that so, Kwame?"

Kwame, in his adolescent gawkiness, drops his eyes, kicks at the ground, and does not answer. Babalawo suggests in kindly tone, "Why don't we step inside, lad, and talk about it, man to man?" He puts a big hand on the boy's shoulder, and as he guides him into the hut, he turns to Efia and says, "Efia, it will be best for you to stay in the background and out of earshot. That way, Kwame will feel more at ease."

Efia would have liked to have been within earshot but realizes the wisdom of allowing Kwame to pour out his heart knowing that she will not be listening. The lad was always shy in her presence. She thus chooses a spot at the back of the elongated hut and instead of sitting on the ground she crouches. She suspects the floor isn't swept as often as it should be. Babalawo's young wives are in need of instruction, or perhaps, she is maligning them. The reason might lie with Babalawo not wanting flighty young things moving among his treasures.

The gloom and indefinable smell of this hut have been familiar to Efia since her childhood visits with Twenty-Eighth Wife. The fetishes[116] hanging on the walls, mostly skeletal remains, might change every so often, but some are always there. Today, with knowledgeable eye, Efia picks out as recent additions the jawbone of a jackal, the skin of a large lizard along with the two-toed foot of an ostrich. Finally, her eyes alight

---

[116] Objects with magical powers inhabited by a spirit

on an item that, on recognition, shocks her to the core and precipitates a bout of shivering: Masimbarashe's black mane! Thimba, so she had been told, had been wearing the helmet at the time of his death.

Realizing that she is here with Babalawo for Kwame's sake and that she mustn't draw attention to herself, she manages to stop her shivering and is grateful that Kwame won't notice what she has seen because he sits with his back to it. She wrenches her eyes away from the helmet and forces herself to follow proceedings.

Kwame sits cross-legged on a mat in front of Babalawo, who now in his finery, also sits cross-legged but on a raised platform. A yellow gourd with a candle inside has become a lustrous gold delivering light to the surrounding gloom. With its flickering, it lends life to the statuary behind Babalawo: a human-size statue of Gran Legbwa along with representations of lesser loas.

Efia is glad Babalawo has not gone overboard with his costuming or other ritual accoutrements, which might have intimidated Kwame and prevented him from telling Babalawo how he feels. As it is, there are enough ritual props to command respect and emphasize Babalawo's ability to change persona, but not too many to intimidate Kwame and prevent him from opening up. Kwame has to be able to speak freely and give Babalawo insight into his state of mind if Babalawo is to help him.

At the moment, neither Babalawo nor Kwame is speaking because Babalawo has told Kwame to shut his eyes, calm his emotions, and collect his thoughts. He must say when he is ready and then present those feeling and thoughts to Babalawo in a coherent and cohesive manner. Efia knows from her own experience that this is how all sessions of this type begin.

As Efia waits, she lets her gaze wander over to the area where Babalawo stores his mutis[117] in an assortment of leather pouches, lidded

---

[117] Medicines

baskets, and packets wrapped in leaves. The leather pouches are seamless and made from the scrotums of eland bulls. As to the baskets, Efia made them to Babalawo's specifications using reeds, palm fronds, and grasses. One of Babalawo's wives uses lianas to make the string, which holds the leaf packages together.

The type of medicine in each container is a matter for speculation. The bigger ones probably hold lethal unripe ackee pods, bark-of-the-root,[118] and kola beans. The smaller ones probably contain hair, claws, splinters of bone, and samples of dung, while the leaf packets would most likely hold powders and medicinal compounds. Liquid samples like spittle or urine have their own miniature containers made of clay.

Kwame is now speaking. Words pour out of his mouth as though he is unable to stop them. Efia has never seen the boy talk so much; she has always only known him as monosyllabic and would now like to know what he's saying. She remembers though that Kwame doesn't want her to hear and for her to try would be wrong and intrusive. Babalawo, for his part, is listening intently and no doubt picking up clues on how to handle the matter.

When Kwame finally stumbles to a halt, Babalawo says a few words before preparing himself to enter that trance-like state that lies between sleeping and waking. It means draining himself of his own concerns and for him to fill the void with Kwame's problems. Reaching the necessary state, he speaks the incantation that will summon the spirit. Efia does not understand the words spoken but then feels an electrical charge in the air that signals the arrival of an otherworldly presence. Babalawo's mien indicates he is engaged in a silent interaction with the presence.

Finally, Babalawo breaks the loaded silence by addressing the unseen presence with words spoken aloud. He says, "Yes, I'll make sure Kwame understands that you are proud of him and that he has within him what he needs to become a great leader." There's a pause before

---

[118] Perennial rain forest shrub with mild psychedelic properties

Babalawo adds, "Yes, I'll also impress on him that there's no need for him to follow you before his time."

The words leave Efia in a state of shock. The spirit invoked was Thimba's! The essence of her Thimba was here - present, and she wasn't even given the opportunity to speak to him!

As Babalawo slowly opens his eyes and shakes his head to clear the mists, Efia must again exert self-control and remind herself this session is about Kwame and her spat of jealously was petty. Tuning in again to Babalawo and Kwame, she hears the former say, "Kwame, I'd advise you to spend the next few days out on the plains, alone, giving yourself time to heal. Meanwhile, I'll give you something that will help you when you feel low."

Turning, Babalawo reaches for a small earthenware container and hands it to Kwame saying, "This contains an ointment of spiritual significance. Use it sparingly by rubbing a little over your heart when you feel desperate. It's lion fat and will give you courage to carry on."

As Efia and Kwame take their leave from Babalawo, a bone-shaking cry comes from the direction of Abena's hut. All the village knows what it means; Assimbola has died. After a stunned silence, Babalawo places his hand on Kwame's shoulder, says, "You, Kwame, must now live the future that is denied to Assimbola. It is your obligation."

Last Night of Third Week of June 1800

Strangers on the Pry

West Coast of Africa

The three strangers are spies in the pay of others from across the Great River. For the past week, their mandate has been to learn as much about Banyan Village as possible but without revealing themselves to the villagers. They know very little about the whys and wherefores of their mission except that, on the first day of the fourth week of June, their light-faced employers aim to kidnap the entire population of the village with the exception of the old and infirm. The operation will involve landing on the beach in rowing boats that will be launched from a mother ship anchored offshore in deeper water. For the daring plan to succeed, they need to know as much as possible about the lay of the land and about the people, their activities, and their routines. The more information they are able to provide, the better their pay

Camouflaged by the trees, the trio has watched the villagers go about their daily lives. In spite of a pesky little dog that detects their presence when humans do not, they have accumulated many a detail that will serve their minders well. The lone banyan is a case in point. It will serve as a valuable landmark for the big ship sailing in from the northwest.

During their week of watching, they have come to recognize Efia, Abena, and their children. They have seen Kwame visiting Assimbola's sickbed and spending the rest of his time alone and howling. They saw Kwame and Efia leave the shaman's hut and heard Abena's cry broadcasting Assimbola's demise. Most importantly, they have observed the warriors; it is on their resistance that the mission could flounder.

The spies understand the local lingo and have been able to overhear conversations between the villagers. They have heard the warriors conversing at the butchery learning in the process that not only is the headman's post vacant but also that the warriors have lost their leader and are in disarray and demoralized. While aware that Babalawo now heads up the warrior corps, they also know that no one is happy with the situation.

As the watchers' spokesperson has pointed out to the minders camped in the forest, all this bodes well for the kidnapping. It means the cadre will not be the formidable fighting force, which it would have been under correct leadership. The fact that the warriors will also be imbibing spiked ale on the eve of the schooner's arrival will help. While remaining able to swim out to the schooner the next day, that is essential, they will not be thinking straight and will fall easy prey to skullduggery. The mission has had a lucky break with the impromptu Gran Legbwa celebration; it will make the ale-spiking easier given that all the containers will be gathered in the stream for cooling.

Kwame on His Own

West Coast of Africa

Immediately after leaving Efia and hearing Assimbola had died, Kwame had followed Babalawo's advice and taken off for the savanna. He has now found a cave in a granite outcrop that he feels will offer him suitable shelter for the night. Using all the survival and hunting skills that Thimba taught his trainees, he has built a fire at the mouth of the cave and has bagged a rabbit with a sling. After gutting the still warm body, he'd covered it with mud from a nearby stream and the bundle now lies in live embers.

Meanwhile, he sits on a nearby rock, letting his mind wander around recent events. He feels being alone here on the plains is helping him gain a better perspective. Hours pass before he starts noticing the clay around the rabbit starting to form a crust and to tighten. It is the aroma that finally tells him when dinner is ready.

As he removes the package from the ashes and waits for the juices to settle, he looks around. The sky to the east is starting to darken and he senses that nocturnal predators are beginning to circle in the shadows. He knows though that as long as fire continues to burn, they won't bother him, so he piles on more wood to get it going again. He will have to wake up every few hours during the night to keep the flames alive, but this had been one of his jobs during the giant eland hunt, so he is accustomed to it. Not long ago, he might *not* have taken the precaution of keeping the predators at bay; he might have courted death by allowing the fire to go out, but no longer. He now has a goal - leadership. That is what he is cutout for; Thimba had said as much to Babalawo.

With the rabbit now ready, he breaks open the crust and lets the pelt fall away with the baked mud leaving the juiciest and most tender meat imaginable. In his mind, as he pulls the creature apart with his fingers and rips the meat from the bone with his teeth, he imagines that Assimbola is sharing the meal. Thus, although out in the open under the stars, he feels neither alone nor frightened; he feels he is where he belongs - at one with the earth.

That first night is a scenario that has repeated itself for five nights now. In that time, he only once succumbed to bout of howling, but had fixed it quickly by rubbing the lion fat onto his heart, and like magic, his courage had returned. His determination to fulfill Thimba's expectations has taken root. He is determined to do whatever is required to qualify himself for a leadership role.

It is now the end of the week, and as the sun rises over the grasslands, he washes in the fast-moving stream wondering when it would be best to return to the village, not today though because tonight is the night that coincides with the Gran Legbwa celebration. He is not yet ready to face such a celebration without Thimba. That's not to say he doesn't like Babalawo, who will be taking over Thimba's role in the celebration. It is just that no one can replace Thimba.

With respect to Babalawo, Kwame had surprised himself by liking the way the medicine man had treated him during his recent visit with Efia. Babalawo had treated him not like a boy but like a man; he had encouraged Kwame to speak and listened closely without interruption. Kwame had never spoken about himself in that manner to anyone, let alone to an adult who holds rank in the community and interacts with loas and the world of the spirits!

Kwame realizes Babalawo seemed to know that Kwame might feel intimidated by someone who speaks to the spirits and had gone to considerable lengths to make Kwame feel at ease. He had put on his ceremonial gear in front of Kwame so that Kwame would know that, while he'd be in the presence of an emissary to the spiritual world, he would still be speaking to a human that he'd known since birth.

There is another advantage to postponing his return to the village by a day. It would give him time to put a few finishing touches to the carving of Masimbarashe that he has been working on during the week. He and Assimbola had learned a few woodcarving basics from Kayefi as part of their preinitiation training, and he had now discovered that he enjoys the art form. Although he is not yet proficient in the use of his knife and has cut his fingers a couple of times, he is nonetheless proud to have kept the blade so sharp. He is using Thimba's sharpening pebbles and knows Thimba would be proud of him for doing a good job.

After a few hours working on the carving, in the shade of an acacia, he feels he has done all he can. Standing the sculpture on a nearby rock and observing it from a distance, he is pleasantly surprised with the result. Elated, he feels the need to do a few Grand Leaps. Leaving his carving on the rock, he calls to mind Thimba's exhortation for practicing the Grand Leap: bend your knees and feel the ground beneath your feet propel yourself up into the sky.

Finding a sturdy stick to substitute for a spear and following Thimba's instructions, he soars up into the air. It feels good! He does it repeatedly until exhausted he flops down on his back on the ground. Looking up into the heavens, he says aloud, "Did you see those, Assimbola? I forgot to count, but there were a lot of them!

Bad Start

West Coast of Africa

Big Baba sits on his throne at the poto mitan. Not wanting to participate in the feast, he has taken up his place early. As night falls (it is to be a dark one in the lunar cycle), he sees that the feast is winding down and that the villagers, appropriately adorned, are starting to disperse and to collect around the pole. There, a fire bathes the scene in a flickering, unearthly light, setting the tone for the upcoming ceremony.

The warriors decked out in their war paint and finery look, so Big Baba thinks initially of what they are and what they have always been: big, magnificent young men in their prime. Pity that Thimba is missing, but in spite of the turmoil his death has caused, Baba has come to the conclusion that for Thimba himself, for his family, and for the tribe at large, his death as a hero and not as a sodomist was the best possible solution.

Suddenly words popped into Baba's mind, *Although the immediate future is bleak, Thimba's reputation will regenerate the tribe.* He jerks to attention: these are not his words! They are Mkulu's, and Baba hadn't even thought to summon Mkulu! Extraordinary!

In his private beliefs, Baba no longer needs rituals like others need them. He feels no need to ask Gran Legbwa to open the gate to the world of the spirit. He can speak to Mkulu and vice versa without an intermediary. Nonetheless, he does not want the rituals to fall into abeyance and is glad he has organized tonight's impromptu celebration. Rites and rituals go beyond a system of beliefs; they are how his people express themselves and are entwined with their very being.

Baba's introspection is interrupted by his acute hearing picking up the sound of Inja barking furiously from up the hill and near the forest.

He had noticed earlier the absence of Inja and had assumed he was begging for scraps at the feast. He had thought at the time it was lucky for the little devil that he didn't like ale because the ale that Forty-First Wife had brought him was not right. After taking a first sip, he had poured the rest onto the ground making a mental note to mention the matter to Efia.

Now along with Inja's unusual barking, he thinks he sees in the twilight three shadow-like figures gathered at the forest fringe; they are throwing rocks at his dog. He is, though, now not sure, if he can trust his own senses. Is what he sees accurate? The twilight can play tricks on the mind. When he looks over to where the warriors are gathering, he sees a slew of abnormalities. While the young men are togged up as they should be, their behavior is far from normal. Gone is the braggadocio. A droopy hangdog look has replaced the normal boasting and bluster. Babalawo - their temporary leader - is frantic in his efforts to stop them from slouching and to get them to hold their spears as they should. Unthinkable that such basic criticism should be necessary!

Baba has no time to ponder the matter as the elders start taking their places, and a couple of the houngan's acolytes help the old man to a seat near Big Baba. The priest has been physically frail for a while, but his mind has always been sharp. Now though as Baba greets him and is about to raise the question of the warriors, he sees the old priest looking around with a vacant stare and then suddenly lifting his arm.

The houngan lifting his arm is the signal to start proceedings, yet it is too early! The villagers aren't yet in place. Efia, who is meant to lead the circle into Gran Legbwa's signature tune, is not even watching for the signal; she is turned away engaged with Abena. The drummers are still fussing with their instruments. Confusion reigns. The women who saw the signal begin to clap and sing the Gran Legbwa anthem, but it is halfhearted and sporadic, as they turn to see others still making their way down to the poto mitan from the feast. This has never happened before.

Baba, turning back to the houngan, sees in the flickering firelight that he, who has guarded the tribe's *mysteries* for the past forty years, is staring with wild eyes and gasping for breath. With his mouth distorted, he drools as he tries to speak! Then falling from his chair and his fierce eyes still open and staring, he loses consciousness. The acolytes swarm over him, lift him, and push him back into the chair. There, propped up, and in the flickering light, he looks much as he did before. Baba knows though that the ancient has passed through the gate into the embrace of his ancestors, but, apart from the acolytes, no one else has noticed the drama, and the ceremony struggles on regardless.

Tears of an Old Warrior

West Coast of Africa

Since Abebi's first and only exposure to a Gran Legbwa celebration, the event has never been far from her mind. The raw emotion and wild drama transcended all description. Seared into her being are the frenzied drumming, dancing, and singing that had exploded into a glorious climax with Mammi's voice reaching into the heavens calling to Gran Legbwa. He had crashed into their midst with a shriek that pierced the eardrums. When he flung the houngan's dancer to the ground, Abebi had felt that her pounding heart might jump from her body.

Such is the memory that Abebi holds in her mind now, as she stands in the circle next to Twenty-Eighth Wife watching the tribe assemble as she had last time. That though is where the likeness ends. In the previous event, she had felt a prickle of excitement even at this early stage. Now, although not everyone has arrived yet, the singing has started and is thin and sporadic while Mammi, who is meant to be the lead singer, is standing on the opposite side of the circle looking around open-mouthed wondering what has happened.

The biggest shock for Abebi is the warriors. She remembers Baba Thimba's Grand Leaps from the previous month. He had jumped so high that he looked as though he might spear the moon. In his capacity as medicine man, Babalawo, too, had danced with an abandonment foreign to Abebi. He had leaped, twisted, and turned to the beat of wild drumming, singing, clapping, and whooping from the circle. This time, apathy has replaced drama and passion; Babalawo does nothing at all, and only one warrior tries the Grand Leap, albeit without accompaniment from the drums or the circle. It's a brave attempt, but he can't get off the ground, drops his spear, and falls. He is now crawling back to his comrades on his hands and knees. Abebi feels sorry for him and is desperate for Mammi to save the day.

The ceremony grinds on until it's time for Mammi to dance out into the circle and call to the spirit, informing him that his people are ready to receive him. Abebi waits with bated breath for that wonderful voice to reach up over the forest into the world of the spirits. Yet it doesn't happen. Mammi stumbles into the circle, and when she starts to sing, her voice is hoarse and flat. The circle and drums fall silent, and the houngan's apprentice, although he tries, is unable to dance himself into a trance. The spark does not ignite, and he ends up slinking away in shame.

Terrified, Abebi looks across the circle to Big Baba for comfort but finds none. The firelight catches the glisten of tears on his cheeks. It's too much for Abebi; she runs into the circle toward her mother, who struggles on. Tubby and naked, her arms pump and her pigtails bounce around her head. "M-a-a-mmi!" she wails as she runs. Then hugging Efía around her hips, she throws back her head and howls louder than Efía can sing.

Fourth Week of June 1800

Rip Current

Mississippi, Louisiana

Cécile has done her duty by attending the simple graveside ceremony that Jacques had arranged for his father in the small wooded area to the east of the Big House. The site is close to the tree used for the whipping of the usurper, or so she has heard. She would like to have attended the spectacle, but Jacques had not allowed it, seeing he intended stripping the upstart of every item of his clothing.

With the chevalier appropriately buried, Cécile is leaving the place she detests. She is the only passenger on a cargo vessel that is returning her to civilization - if that is what one can call New Orleans. The vessel is designed to transport bagged sugar from plantations upstream down the Mississippi to the port of New Orleans. There the sugar destined for the markets of Europe and Britain will be loaded into the holds of schooners recently vacated by slaves from Africa.

The company that owns the boat and many others like it now belongs to Jacques. It is a large flat-bottomed boat equipped with a small private area on the foredeck. Cécile is sitting on a bench outside the cabin door, but seeing the boat travels with the current and is riding the waves at a fair clip, she would rather be inside the cabin and out of the wind. However, the crew member, who accompanied her on board had told her that, for those prone to motion sickness as she is, the fresh air outside is better than the stuffiness inside. As a result, fresh air now abounds, and the wind threatens to whip her bonnet off her head; she has to reach up with her hand to hold it in place.

Feeling miserable, she reviews her situation. By rights, she should now be celebrating her freedom and planning her departure for France, but hélas, Jacques is proving more unscrupulous than his father. She now suspects that having disposed of his father, Jacques might also want to dispose of her. She knows too much and will only be a drain on finances for which he would have better uses.

With the wind getting stronger, spray now reaches her face. Normally she would worry about her rouge running or about her clothing, but with her very existence under threat, such issues no longer matter. Even if she is dramatizing by thinking Jacques will kill her, it is equally bad that he has told her he doesn't want her to return to France. She whimpers knowing none of the crew will hear her above the gusting wind and slapping waves.

Seeing Jacques refuses to let her return to France, what can she do with her life? After his revelations, she can never again show her face in New Orleans' high-society. How can she remain the doyenne of all that is right and proper when her noble blood runs in the veins of people of color? Every placée in the city will delight in her humiliation. She can picture them tittering behind jewel-studded fans; can hear them whispering, *All those airs and graces! Yet her son is a sodomist, and her grandchildren are Creoles just as we are.*

Sniffing, she lets go of her bonnet and opens her reticule to extract her handkerchief. Seeing there the vial containing an unused dose of arsenic, she knows she must throw it overboard. She is extracting the container when a member of the crew comes to tell her that because of the worsening weather, she must go inside.

With a gracious nod, she thanks him and says, "I understand, monsieur. I'll go in right away."

With the arsenic container in one hand, she starts to get to her feet, but the boat lurches, throwing her back onto the bench. She has to grab onto the armrest so as not to slide. The waves seem as big as they were all those years back when she crossed the Atlantic; yet this is just a river. Her husband had once told her about rip currents. Could this be a rip current? If he were here, he'd know.

She finds it strange that she thinks of the chevalier so often. She always imagined once he was dead, she'd forget about him. Yet since Jacques has proved the greater villain, she feels a softening in attitude toward the person to whom she'd been married for over forty years.

A second lurch, worse than the first, would have thrown her off the bench if she hadn't been holding on so tightly. She has to wonder if Le Bon Dieu is punishing her for killing her husband. Until now, she has never seen her actions in this light. She always saw her role as that of an avenging angel. How could she have been so shortsighted? She must pray!

While still gripping the armrest with one hand and clutching the arsenic with the other, she manages to kneel on the bucking deck. *Forgive me, Lord,* she sobs before embarking on the words of the rosary: *Sancta Maria, Mater Dei . . .* She has to stop as bile rises in her gullet, and releasing her grip on the armrest, she rises and totters toward the side but doesn't reach it. With the next lurch, she slips on the wet deck and slithers, feet first, under railing into the turbulent water.

Trapping air, her travel skirt keeps her buoyant as the current sweeps her away from the boat. She catches a brief glimpse of someone on deck shouting but hears nothing over the turmoil. She screams, and a wave, slapping her in the face, fills her nose, mouth, and lungs with muddy water. Chocking, her arms flail in a frantic attempt to get herself horizontal, but her clothing - now sodden and heavy - drags her down. No longer able to keep her head above water, her body fills with the frenzied shrieks of dying cells, which in spite of a desperate will to survive, succumbs and falls silent. Darkness ensues.

Stagecoach Terminal

Liverpool, England

Ambrose greets Tom as he arrives at the stagecoach terminal. The lad has a rucksack on his back and carries in his hand something that wriggles in a bag.

"Have you brought your sandwich on the hoof?" Ambrose inquires.

"It's Fluff!" Tom tells him as he puts down the bag and hands over his backpack to the coachman. "She'll be staying with me. I'm really happy that Esquire says it's all right to bring her. Imagine! I didn't even have to ask. He thought of it himself knowing I'd be unhappy without her. He writes that his housekeeper has a dog, and if Fluff and the dog don't get on, the dog can stay downstairs in the kitchen, and Fluff can live with me on the top floor. It sounds as though he has a big house!"

"I suppose he would have," says Ambrose, "but I also suppose anything would seem big to you after spending so much of your time in the restricted accommodation of a slave schooner!"

Wanting to leave, the coachman is chivvying his passengers to board.

"What happens when you arrive in Edinburgh?" Ambrose wants to know as they move toward the door of the vehicle. "How will you know where to go?"

"Esquire said he'd meet me with a hackney."

"Are you anxious?"

"Maybe a little, but I trust Esquire. He has warned me it might take me a while to adjust to my new surroundings, but now that I have Fluff with me, I hope I won't have a problem. You, Ambrose, are the only thing I'll miss of Liverpool." Before he is hustled into the carriage, he adds, "Do you think you would be able to visit me some time?"

"Who knows," Ambrose replies as Tom's face reappears at the open window. "In the meantime, you can write to me."

"I'll write weekly," Tom announces grandly. Esquire is the only other person to whom he has ever written letters until now.

The coachman climbs into his seat, takes up the reins, and with whip in hand, shouts, "Giddyap, my lovelies!"

Émile at Glen Orm

Aberdeenshire, Scotland

Émile has been staying at Glen Orm since Wee Adair's christening, which he attended in lieu of Migu and Betta. Seeing that Émile mentioned early in his visit that he'd like to become proficient at a gentleman's sport, Pontefract has spent the intervening week teaching the guest the ins and outs of salmon fishing. Émile has proved himself a good pupil and now knows how to cast with a fly rod and how to play and land a fish. He has also learned how to tie various types of lures and where to find the materials needed to do so.

Meanwhile, Stanley has been helping his mother, Frances, who wants to run Glen Orm herself. Together, they have acquired the modern agricultural equipment that Stanley had always wanted and have visited Hugh Watson in Keillor, where they bought an Angus bull of impressive pedigree. In accordance with the principles of selective breeding, this majestic creature will now be introduced into a herd composed of doddies[119] carefully chosen from Glen Orm's own existing stock. The doddies must be black, broad of chest and have well-padded rumps. These are to be the defining characteristics for the new breed. Within a decade, if all goes according to plan, Glen Orm could have a pedigree herd of Aberdeen Angus cattle capable of outperforming every other beef producer in Britain.

With so much to do, the regular afternoon gatherings have fallen by the wayside. Today is the first time that Émile is sitting down for afternoon tea with Frances, Pontefract, Stanley, and Angus McCorm. Baby Adair is in the nursery napping under the watchful eye of Donalda.

Émile, speaking of Migu, says, "As Rose is marrying a person of her choice, Aaron hopes she will soon settle and be happy. At that point, he would like to join Stanley and me in Louisiana."

---

[119] Polled cows hornless by nature

Stanley squirms at the comment. He has been wondering all week if he should try to back out of the Louisiana commitment but is still not sure if he should or shouldn't.

Frances is asking Émile about Betta accompanying Migu to Louisiana, when she is supposedly seriously ill. Émile wiping his mouth on the napkin - carefully as per Lady Abigail's teachings - says, "As far as Aaron is concerned, she'll be accompanying him. He assumes this is a temporary malaise that will soon be over. He feels they will fit better into the New World than here. He says Britain with its class distinctions and social niceties is too small for people of his kind."

"To what type of social niceties does he refer?" Pontefract wants to know.

"The type about which I'm learning from Lady Abagail," Émile replies and starts listing the items with obvious relish. "One must say *table napkin* not *serviette* and *sorry* not *pardon*, one must laugh in a refined manner and never show emotion or wallow in sentimentality like the Americans. One mustn't use a fork facing upward with the left hand, one mustn't . . ."

Pontefract interrupts the litany, saying, "Those are things Frances taught me, and I used to tell Aaron those when I still thought I should try and improve his manners. You obviously are a better student than he was because I've never seen him put any of it into practice!"

"Sir, you might find he's changing since Rose is determined to marry into the upper class, and he doesn't want to shame her."

Looking skeptical, Pontefract asks, "Are you sure he is serious? That doesn't sound like Aaron!"

"He hopes he won't have to keep up the charade for long. Once he sees Rose settled and Betta well again, he'll pack his bags and revert to his old self." Émile ponders briefly before continuing. He's now addressing Stanley with the words, "Seeing we're talking about Aaron, I should mention that he worries that with the new situation here on Glen Orm, you might want to back out of the Louisiana deal."

Frances snaps to attention; "Oh no!" she exclaims. "He would never leave you the lurch, nor" - she turns to her husband - "would Pontefract or I allow it, would we, dear?" Pontefract nods in agreement as she adds, "Besides, I'm looking forward to taking over the running of the estate while Pontefract continues to run his own business."

Stanley is stunned by his mother's outburst. So much for believing that he had an option! As an only child, he grew up thinking he was special, but now his infant son seems to have ousted him! Angus McCorm sensing the change in mood licks his master's hand, wherewith Stanley tells himself, *If I'm not wanted here, then I certainly don't want to stay.* He wishes he could take Angus with him because Angus seems to be the only one that will be missing him!

He tunes in again to hear Émile talking about the Louisiana plantation: the size, the number of slaves, and the potential for development. Turning to Stanley, Émile says, "Here in Britain, there will always be a struggle to hold on to land with the peasantry rising to the middle class and demanding both land reform and taxation of the wealthy. There is none of that nonsense in the New World, where masters sit high in the saddle. Not many here get the opportunity that Aaron is giving you, Stanley."

Tom's Arrival

Edinburgh, Scotland

The lad has just arrived with his kitten. Sir George met him with a hackney, fearing a luxurious carriage might intimidate the boy. Nonetheless, the ride back to Queen Street isn't proving comfortable. Sir George's conversation sounds stilted, even to himself, while Tom sitting next to him remains tense and monosyllabic. The kitten, meanwhile, mews pitifully in its sack. That changes though when they arrive and enter the kitchen from the area entrance. Ms. Young and her niece, obviously ready for the worst, take charge of the animals.

Surprisingly as Sir George and Tom look on with anxious mien, there is no snarling or hissing, and after a few minutes, the kitten is strutting around with its tail in the air, and the dog trying to snuffle at it. At this point, Sir George withdraws, and Tom remains in the kitchen for tea, oatcakes, and honey; after which, Ms. Young shows him to his room on the top floor. She then accompanies him to the study on the main floor and leaves him with Sir George, who pours them each a wee dram of Scotch. To Sir George's relief, that loosens the awkwardness of the situation, and they talk about the countryside through which the stagecoach passed on its journey northward.

Later in the evening when Tom has had his dinner downstairs with Ms. Young and the niece and has retired to his room upstairs with his kitten, Sir George summons Ms. Young to his study. "What do you think, Ms. Young?" he asks. "Do you think the lad and his cat will settle in all right?"

"I think so, sir. I was worried about Fluff and Coo, but am relieved that they get on fine. After we fed them, Coo lay down on his mat and Fluff joined him, snuggling into his neck."

That the dog actually has a name is news to Sir George. He has a feeling that the Gaelic word for dog sounds something like *coo,* but he is not going to get involved in that now and asks, "What about the laddie, Ms. Young?"

"I don't think there will be a problem, sir. He is amenable and should be easy to spoil."

Sir George is touched by her unusual wording of the situation. He is not accustomed to conversation with his housekeeper. He says stiffly, "I am grateful to you, Ms. Young, for your kindness. If this works as I hope it will, I would like to bring in a few more students. If you remember, I once mentioned the matter to you, and you said you'd be glad to cooperate, provided we hired whatever help you felt was necessary. I'm now wondering if you still think that might work for you."

"Oh yes, Sir George!" she replies, all smiles. "I miss having young people around me."

Beginning of the Fourth Week of June 1800

Goodbye, Betta

Leith, Scotland

Rose and Migu sit at Betta's bedside. By the flickering light of an oil lamp, they have listened to her shallow breathing throughout the night. Now although the streetlights still burn outside and dawn approaches, Betta's intake of air starts to slow and falter. Migu leans forward, and taking his wife's unresponsive hand, he pleads, "Don't go, dear! We need you!"

Rose has herself under control; hands clasped on her lap, she sits pale, poised, and upright. She listens to the breathing, counting the intervals between each breath, until one final gasp lifts her mother's body from the bed, then drops it back into stillness. Betta has left.

Migu covers his face with his hands and shakes in silent sobbing. Rose puts her hand on his arm, but says nothing. Then as the flame in the oil lamp flutters and dies, Rose, with a delicate finger, closes her mother's eyes, kisses her on the forehead, and pulls the sheet over her face.

A few days later at their local parish church in Leith, Migu sits in the front pew with Rose and her fiancé on one side and Émile on the other. Pontefract sits immediately behind them. He doesn't think he has ever seen the huge Migu look quite so diminished. It upsets him; his friend is normally so full of *piss and vinegar* - Migu's terminology - but one has to remember Migu is resilient and will bounce back.

Pontefract wonders if he made a mistake in dissuading Stanley from attending Betta's funeral. Stanley had wanted to come - has always liked Betta and Aaron - but Pontefract had said, "Stanley, there is only a week until you leave, and I think you should spend as much of that time as you can with your mother and Wee Adair on Glen Orm. You must realize that while we know Louisiana is what you want, your departure is hard on us."

He doesn't follow through with that line of thought because he can't help but overhear - he sits directly behind them - what William whispers into Rose's ear, "If it suits you, Rose, when we marry, we will have the service at the family chapel." Rose composed and looking intimidatingly beautiful turns to him and nods with a small smile. Pontefract sees that young William is totally smitten with Rose and that Rose, too, is happy, in spite of the somber occasion and the loss of her mother.

First Day of the Fourth Week of June 1800

Schooner

West Coast of Africa

Exhausted by the tumultuous emotions of the previous evening, Big Baba had fallen asleep immediately and now wakes to the breeze rustling through palm fronds and to the distant swish of the surf. A sudden cry (is it Efia?) startles him, and so he gets to his feet. As he looks out to the distant ocean, an odd sight meets his eyes. Is it a ghost ship manned by spirits of the drowned? He has heard such things exist, but this doesn't look ghostly.

For her part, as dawn breaks, Efia slips out of her hut, and with the sun sending shafts of light through the forest, she splashes water onto her face from a pot at the hut's entrance. Looking through dripping fingers, she freezes; something strange has appeared on the ocean. Transfixed, she sees the silhouette resolve into a ship with a red flag and bulging sails that is skipping across the waves toward her.

Action is needed! Hands to her mouth, she uses her huge voice - it has come back after last night's debacle - to send out the alarm, "Come see! Come see!" The village springs to life: dogs bark, fowl scatter, and huts spew out occupants blinking and trying to make sense of the apparition.

The warriors take to hand their spears, but without a leader, they dither until Babalawo, appearing in the nick of time, takes charge and leads them along the edge of the forest toward the beach.

Efia watches them move with stealth against the backdrop of the trees, and once at the ridge, she sees them creep into the north end of the elongated hollow, which offers those that hunker there a view of the beach without exposing their presence. The villagers know that, if strangers land, they should be given to believe that the village is deserted. This means the elderly - with exception of the elders - remain in their huts. All others - mostly younger women and children - make for the south end of the hollow, which is farther back from the drop and without a view of the beach.

Efia does not join the latter group as they stream down to the ridge behind the warriors. Instead, she heads uphill in order to pick up Abebi from Twenty-Eighth Wife. On the way though, she meets Big Baba with Abebi, who pleads, "Can I go to the beach, too, Mammi?"

Uncertain, Efia turns to her father and asks, "Baba, would these be traders?" There is excitement in her voice. The arrival of traders on the plains had brought untold benefits to the entire region.

"They're probably traders," Baba agrees, "but we'll be cautious. The beach is too far for me to walk, but I'll watch from the banyan. If you wish, Abebi can come with me, and you can pick her up later.

Babalawo

West Coast of Africa

Babalawo has led the warriors and the adolescent trainees - minus Kwame - down the slope to the ridge, where they now crouch in the north end of the hollow. From here, they have the benefit of height and a good view of the beach and ocean.

Babalawo hopes that he has the situation under control. *As long as the newcomers are traders and unarmed, nothing much can go wrong,* he tries to reassure himself. *It was like this on the savanna, when the camels - ships of the desert - appeared on the horizon for the first time, and everyone's worries proved unfounded.* Nonetheless, he can't help feeling concerned that he and the warriors might not have fully recovered from last night's debacle.

As the big ship draws closer, Babalawo wonders, if those who man her might come in too close and ground the vessel. He has little time to process that possibility before the ship makes a sudden turn into the wind and comes to a stop at a suitable depth. What next? The wait is brief.

The moment the ship drops anchor, rowing boats detach themselves from the mother ship and head toward the beach. As they draw closer, Babalawo sees that men with light skins, untidy beards, and bulging biceps handle the small craft with expertise. None carry spears, and the warriors outnumber them.

Now happier with the situation, Babalawo watches as the men jump into the shallows and pull their boats onto the sand. After checking their surroundings with a cursory glance, the strangers produce sacks, which - when unpacked - reveal a vast array of textiles and all kinds of baubles. After laying out their wares on lengths of cloth, they stand around smoking and chatting.

Babalawo feels vindicated in believing the foreigners to be traders but wants the opinion of the elders, who minus Big Baba now hunker in the beach grass farther along the hollow but without a view of the beach. Signaling to his fellow warriors to stay in place, he joins the elders reporting the presence of the rowing boats, the light-skinned men, and their wares.

"Are they aggressive?" one of the elders inquires.

"Do our warriors outnumber them?" another wants to know.

"Do they carry arms?" asks a third.

Babalawo gives the appropriate replies then poses the question, "Should we assume they are traders and reveal ourselves without challenge?" He looks to each in turn for agreement and seeing he has a consensus he thanks the ancients and returns to the warriors.

Abena

West Coast of Africa

Abena, with her infant son Abinti tied to her back, is with the village women and children in the hollow behind the ridge. Although unseen from below, they don't have the view of the beach that the warriors have, seeing their part of the hollow is even farther back from the lip than is the part of the elders'.

Abena still suffers from the inner paralysis caused by the death of her son Assimbola the previous week; nonetheless, she is becoming caught up in the sense of adventure that characterizes the mood around her. She participates in the whispered exchanges:

"What is happening on the beach?"

"Are we in danger?"

"Can Babalawo handle the situation?"

"Have the warriors recovered from last night?"

"Where is Kwame?"

"Why is Big Baba not with the elders?"

As Babalawo comes over to consult with the elders, the women fall silent hoping to overhear the conversation, but alas, the sound of wind and surf make it impossible. With big eyes, they watch Babalawo return to the warriors and see that a whispered order passes from one to another of the men. Then to the amazement of all, Babalawo, with the roar of a lion, leaps out of hiding into the air. Simultaneously, the entire warrior corps, spears pointing upward - a nonthreatening stance - rise as a unit from behind the ridge to stand tall and magnificent, silhouetted against the sky.

The unexpected action shocks and unsettles baby Abinti on Abena's back. He cries out in high-pitched protest, worrying Abena that, in spite of wind and surf, those on the beach might hear him and reveal their presence. Immediately, it becomes clear though that subterfuge is no longer needed. Babalawo from on high is exchanging hand signals with those below. After a few minutes of his strange antics, the entire warrior corps clasping their spears starts to slither down the slope through sand and tufted grass to the beach.

After a moment of stunned silence, the women assume they, too, can reveal themselves and therefore move along to a place that offers a full view of the beach below, and what a view it is! The boats are pulled out of the reach of the surf and lengths of bright cloth stretch across the sand to display arrays of undreamed-of treasures: glittering mirrors, bright textiles, glass beads, necklaces, bangles, earrings, headgears, umbrellas, and kerchiefs.

Abena shakes her head as she watches the warriors - fathers, brothers, and husbands - laying aside their spears to hold up some small trinket and guffaw at its novelty. She exclaims to her neighbor, "These men of ours! Just look at them! One moment, they inspire fear and trembling, the next, they behave like children!"

Efia

West Coast of Africa

Efia delays longer than she anticipated, as she and Twenty-Eighth Wife chew over the catastrophic events of the previous evening. When she finally leaves to fetch Abebi at the banyan, she sees that the ship has anchored and that the warriors remain crouched in the hollow peering over the lip. Villagers and elders are now in the hollow, too, but are in some distance away from the warriors. She'll pick up Abebi and join them.

Halfway down to the banyan, something extraordinary happens at the ridge. With the roar of a lion, Babalawo springs out of hiding in a sky-high leap. Landing back on earth, he assumes an erect posture, spear pointing upward. At the same moment, the entire warrior corps rises as one and stands lined up with Babalawo - their stance mimicking his - along the edge of the ridge.

Efia's heart misses a beat at the splendor of it. Even Thimba - so demanding of those under him - would have been proud of this moment, especially so soon after the inexplicable events of the previous evening. With the real action starting, Efia runs toward the banyan. She sees the warriors slithering down the slope and sees the women moving out of hiding to the edge of the ridge.

By the time Efia gets to the banyan, the women are jostling down the path that leads to the beach. To her surprise, Abebi is no longer with her grandfather.

"She and Inja went to join Abena," Big Baba explains. "She's all right. I told her before she left that she has to be my eyes and ears and come back to tell me what's happening down there." Before Efia can comment, he continues, "Daughter, I'd like you, too, to do a job for me by going to the elders and asking for their opinions. They've moved, so will now have a better view."

Efia takes off at an easy sprint across the beach grass of the hollow. Joining the elders at the top of the ridge, she looks down and sees the beach teeming with villagers. There is only a sprinkling of light-skinned strangers among them. She sees, too, that the strangers' rowing boats are strung out along the surf line, while the village dugouts remain above the high-tide mark. By this time, the fishermen should be out where the big ship lies anchored, but instead, they frolic on the beach decked out in exotic apparel!

The air is festive with everyone marveling at what they see and handle. Where are Abena and Abebi though? Inja is the giveaway. Efia spots his wagging tail next to a child swamped in a big red scarf. It takes Efia a moment to realize that the child must be Abebi and the woman with a towering turban in blinding yellow must be Abena. All the villagers egged on by the strangers are helping themselves to the items on display. Efia sees Babalawo pick up an object that catches a sunbeam and can be used to blind someone. With shouts of laughter, the warriors pass it from hand to hand.

The women have discovered a similar object wherein they can see themselves the way they do in forest ponds. They, too, laugh uproariously. One of the warriors picks up a red scarf - like the one Abebi has wrapped herself with - and winds it around his head. After doing a wild dance, he removes the scarf, and spotting Efia on the ridge, he tries to throw it up to her, shouting, "Come and join the fun, Efia!" The scarf lands halfway up the sandbank draping itself over a scrawny clump of beach grass. Abebi only now realizing her mother is up on the ridge with the elders also yells for Efia to join them.

Efia still has to report to Big Baba, so she yells back that she will be coming soon. As she does so, she notices the strangers are handing around blobs on sticks. They have started with the warriors, who stand clustered around each holding a stick and sucking on a blob. Their facial expressions leave the observer in no doubt that the blob is good! Before Efia directs her attention toward the women, she notes that Babalawo and the leader of the traders have initiated a further exchange of gestures, which involve pointing at the mother ship and making swimming gestures. What can that mean?

Seeing that the women and children are closer to where Efia stands, she is able to follow more easily what is happening with them. She sees how a trader demonstrates how to hold the stick and then to suck the blob.

With a rapturous expression on his face, he says, "*Mmm*! Yum-yum! Tre-e-acle!"

No one needs to understand his language to know that the blobs are exceptionally good and that there are not enough of them. With everyone clamoring for more, the foreigners show their empty boxes and point to the ship to indicate there are more blobs out there.

Efia's eyes return to the warriors, sees they have laid aside their spears and have taken to the water. Feeling a jolt through her body, she is starting to understand what the women do not. They - now noticing what the men are doing - stare wide-eyed as the warriors reach deep water and start to swim in a flurry of arms and bobbing heads.

Meanwhile, the traders are pulling their boats back into the water, and all smiles and solicitude, they jolly the women along. With gallant gestures, they invite them to wade through the surf and come for a ride. Efia sees her peers demure and knows what they think: *if our men have gone, can it be wrong for us to go too? Even without spears, they can protect us. There are so many of them, so few of the outsiders.* Women, with children scampering ahead, start to move toward the boats.

Efia is relieved to see Abena is not convinced and is keeping a hold on Abebi's hand. For her part, Abebi wants to go and struggles. The leader of the light skins approaches and, saying something to Abena, picks up Abebi, and Abena has to let go of her hand. With Abebi giggling in his arms, the man starts carrying her toward a boat. As he goes, he turns back to Abena and, smiling, encourages her to follow.

Efia, her mind in disarray, slithers down the ridge and runs. The boats are already pushing out into the surf, including the one with Abena and Abebi on board. She stumbles into the water, arms spread, and screams, "I want my child!" The leader of the light skins grabs her by one of her outspread arms and pulls her onto the boat.

Indaba[120]

West Coast of Africa

For Big Baba, the first indication that something has gone awry is when he sees the flotilla of boats loaded with passengers returning to the mother ship. Efia has disappeared from the ridge, and the elders, now at the far end of the hollow, are looking out at the ocean.

If he wants to see what is happening, he has no option but to get at least halfway down the path, and so, taking his staff, he sets out. He is only a short way down the path when he meets his dog Inja struggling up the slope; he is hurt and in pain. How could that have happened? Settling down at the side of the path, he rests and tries to comfort the animal. When he is ready to go again, he is unable to get to his feet so abandons his staff and continues down the path on his tail end.

When he finally reaches a point from where he can see the beach, what he sees mystifies him. On the side of the slope, a red cloth has caught on a clump of grass, while the sand below is strewn with all manner of glittering and colorful debris that has attracted a lot of squabbling gulls. Out on the water, the ship has raised anchor and is ready to go. In no time, wind in her sails, she is skimming across the ocean toward the distant horizon. Drained of all emotion, Baba clasps his arms around his shins, allows his head to fall to his knees, and he sleeps.

He only regains his senses when Inja licks his ear, and he looks up the path to see the elders. Slowly, very slowly, they pick their way down the path toward him. On arrival, they get him to his feet and, without a word, take him in their midst and drag him and themselves back up the path to the banyan. They are big men, ex-warriors one and all, but now age has taken its toll, and they are stooped and scrawny. They

---

[120] Meeting

have no teeth; their feet are splayed and creviced; their striations lost in folds of skin.

Progress is barely perceptible, yet they persevere, and finally on arriving, they are able to shoo away the goats and chickens and establish Big Baba on his throne with Inja on his lap. They tell Baba that Inja was hurt by a light face lashing out at him with an oar when he tried to jump into the boat with Abebi.

As they settle into the traditional circle, those who had found it too arduous to get down to the beach struggle downhill from their huts to the banyan and join the circle. With everyone accounted for - Kwame is the exception - Big Baba holds an indaba and presents a plan that finds general acceptance.

Masimbarashe

West Coast of Africa

After his last night alone on the savanna, Kwame wakes as a first shaft of sunlight enters the cave. He feels elated as he heads first for the stream and then on toward Banyan Village. His intention is not to enter the village immediately; instead, he'll bypass it and revisit the place where Thimba's mahogany fell. In his suicidal phase, he had visited the site often with no particular purpose. Now though, in spite of the fallen tree, he wants to restore the shrine dedicated to Masimbarashe. He has his new carving as an offering along with a rabbit whose warm carcass is tied to his body.

Back in his home territory, he picks his way through the trees focusing awareness on sights, sounds, and odors. Thimba impressed on all his trainees that harnessing the senses was as important as learning how to throw a spear or do the Grand Leap. Kwame, therefore, now makes a point of noting not only the presence of flashy creatures - monkeys and parrots - but also the presence of small things, such as fungi, moss, herbs, and insects.

Kwame's shrine to Masimbarashe will be more modest than Thimba's. For his altar, he chooses a middle-sized tree that is obviously progeny of the fallen giant and, which - like Kwame himself - will take time to become worthy of the old guard. Retrieving from the hollow of a tree the undamaged objects of spiritual significance - a gold-streaked chunk of quartz, an irregular-shaped pearl, a shark's jawbone, and an eagle's skull - Kwame cleans them and arranges them on a mat. He then stretches out the rabbit on the low table that Thimba used as the centerpiece of the altar. On a rock close at hand, he places Thimba's sculpture of Masimbarashe along with his own new carving of the loa. Clearing a space at the base of the altar, he scratches the appropriate vévé into the ground. Then standing back to observe the fruit of his labors, he grunts in approval.

The next step is to introduce Masimbarashe to the new shrine. Thimba had taught him how to proceed, and acting in accordance with those instructions, he bows his head, closes his eyes, and calms the noise inside himself. Then holding his hands together against his chest, he asks Gran Legbwa to draw back the curtain and allow Masimbarashe to pass.

"I need to ask him to become my loa," Kwame explains.

Thus prepared, he waits in silence. Not practiced in wordless exchanges with invisible entities, he is not sure what will happen next. What does happen is unexpected and leaves him wanting to laugh. It is the loud, rasping purr of a contented lion. He wishes he could tell Assimbola!

Kwame to the Rescue

West Coast of Africa

At the place where the forest gives way to the village clearing, Kwame stops in his tracks. Eyes wide with shock, he tries to digest the fact that the village is deserted. Except for a few foraging chickens and the puppies bunched together looking morose, there is no living thing in sight. Moving forward a little, he looks first to the left and then to the right before running another glance over the huts and gardens, over the butchery and work shelters, but still sees no one.

What he finds most unnerving is the eerie silence that has replaced the sounds of daily life in Banyan Village. The sounds that he now realizes have been a constant since the day he was born - those of laughter and chatter, of women sweeping and working, of children at play, and of the pounding of pestle in mortar - are missing.

Turning away from the village, he glances over to the ocean and notes that the boats are not out on the water. Ominous! Then shading his eyes from sun, he takes a closer look at the banyan and spots a group of the elderly camouflaged in the speckled shade. The relief he feels quickly dissipates as he realizes that the elderly never hold indabas on their own and, most especially, not without Big Baba, who is absent. He again wants to blabber but pulls himself together; he tells himself sternly that blabbing is something he doesn't do anymore. He thinks of using some of the lion fat but finds just thinking of it has restored his courage.

Moving forward with caution, he is startled to catch a glimpse of Big Baba supporting himself with his staff making his way around the huts in Babalawo's compound. The dog Inja is with him but, like his master, moves with difficulty.

What happened to the dog? Kwame wonders. He hopes one of his peers - *Where are they now?* - didn't kick it in the ribs. When overstimulated, he and his comrades were capable of such *childish acts*, Thimba's words for punishable behavior.

Kwame stays where he is, his eyes following Big Baba, who on arrival at Babalawo's main hut enters without a knock and walks in. Strange! No one in the village intrudes on the private domain of another without first announcing his presence.

Waiting until Big Baba is inside, Kwame approaches Babalawo's hut and peers through the open door into the darkness of an interior he remembers well. The bones, masks, and horns are all familiar; so too are the smells, pouches, leaf packages, and baskets. It is with the latter that Baba seems to find what he seeks. With a grunt of satisfaction, he tries to lift a basket but hasn't the strength. Kwame is about to step forward and offer help when Baba turns and spots him in the doorway. The fierce face lights up.

"Kwame!" he exclaims, "I just asked Mkulu to send me help, and here you are already!" He grins adding, "You, son, are our tribe's salvation!" Then with Kwame carrying the basket of ackee seeds, man and boy make their way back to the banyan, Baba filling in Kwame on the day's events as they go.

Instructions

West Coast of Africa

With the afternoon shower threatening, those present - with the exception of Big Baba and Kwame - return to their huts to don their finery. When the rain stops, they will return. Meanwhile, Kwame moves Big Baba's throne deeper into the shelter of the banyan, where they can keep dry in the company of Inja, the *hookus,* Billy, and his harem.

As rain batters down splashing up the mud around the banyan, Kwame crouches in front of Big Baba, who tells him what to do when the rain stops, what to do at dawn the next day, and in the long run, what he must do to resurrect his tribe and village.

Kwame, his mind threatening to erupt into chaos, has to draw on as yet untapped strength to keep his wits about him. Baba aware of the magnitude of what is required, says, "Son, I know I'm asking a lot of you, but I also know you are of Thimba's stock and have it in you to do what is needed. When the rain is over, you will get yourself to Mbaleki Village as quickly as you can. You will tell Mbaleki everything that has happened and what is about to happen. You will also place yourself in his hands and ask to train with his warriors."

"Will he allow that?"

"Yes. He'll also allow you to receive our tribal markings, although you will be swearing allegiance to those with whom you train. In the past, Mbaleki and I considered joining forces to create a more powerful unit and often discussed such details as tribal markings and training our warriors together."

"But I'd be the only one receiving our markings."

"Only at initiation. Then you'll start bringing our tribe back to life by choosing as many wives as you can from girls who carry our bloodlines. My sister was Mbaleki's first wife, so her manifold progeny carries my bloodlines, and that is only one example of many ties. You'll have ample choice."

Kwame, struggling to cope with all this, doesn't comment, so Baba says, "You have to trust me, Kwame. If you place yourself in Mbaleki's hands, he will see you through the next five years. You will take him my insignia - necklaces, armbands, and anklets - and he will understand the significance. He will also help with the immediate needs here tonight and tomorrow."

"What immediate needs, Baba?" Kwame wants to know, his tone suspicious.

"He will know that he should send guards here tonight to keep watch over our bodies. He will also know that he should come and take charge here tomorrow morning, while you perform tasks that only you can perform."

Baba watches the village as he speaks, and when Kwame turns, he sees that the rain has stopped and that the elderly - decked out in their finery - are emerging from their huts and gingerly picking their way through the mud.

Baba keeps on speaking. "Death is always messy. Remember though you are chosen and have been charged with a sacred trust that requires more courage than can be expected of someone your age. If you succeed with your job for tomorrow, you will earn the respect that adolescents normally only receive after killing their first lion. Mbaleki will see in you what I've already seen that you have the potential to become a warrior of the highest caliber. Have no fear. Mbaleki will make you welcome."

Pleased at the compliment, Kwame smiles but not for long, as Big Baba reveals the nature of tomorrow's test. When he is done, Kwame in solemn silence helps Baba remove his insignia - fetishes made from bone, stone, and copper - which in their tribal world signify top-ranking.

After moving Big Baba's throne back into a more open area of the banyan's shade, Kwame runs up to Babalawo's hut and finds the seamless giant eland pouches that he will need to transport Baba's regalia to Mbaleki Village. With the job done, he returns to the banyan.

The remnants of the tribe now sit in a circle, ready for what lies ahead. It is time for Kwame to leave for Mbaleki Village, yet he lingers. Big Baba eggs him on saying, "It's time, Kwame!" Kwame drops to his knees, and Baba places a hand on his head for the blessing. Then getting to his feet and slinging Inja around his shoulders, he leaves.

At the place where the village borders on the savanna, Kwame wipes tears from his eyes, then turns to take a last look at the remnants of his tribe: a small group of ancients gathered in a circle against the backdrop of tree, sky, and ocean. All are adorned. Only Big Baba sits unembellished, yet such is his bearing and dignity that no outsider would mistake him for anything but what he is - a great tribal leader. Kwame knows that - in his personal ranking of people - he must place Big Baba alongside Thimba as a measuring stick for his own future actions.

Turning back to the savanna and taking off at an easy lope, Kwame knows that this final image of his tribe passing around the tray of lethal seeds will remain with him until he too must negotiate the passage through the divide to that other world.

Final Thoughts

West Coast of Africa

Baba watches the platter pass from hand to hand, watches each person take as many seeds as fit into a cupped hand before starting to chew - action that releases the poison. He himself delays; he wants to make certain that everyone is still prepared to embark on this final journey. He also has to wonder how to deal with the matter should someone have a change of heart. However, as the tray moves around the circle, it becomes clear no one will be stepping back from the brink.

Nonetheless, Baba continues to wait a while before chewing his seeds. Having attended to the needs of others, he now withdraws into himself. Tapping out an edgy little rhythm on the arm of his throne, he reviews events of the day. He wonders how things would have turned out if he had kept Abebi and Efia with him and not asked for their input; or what would have happened, if Efia had got down to the beach sooner? She might have recognized the danger in time.

The business with Inja also bothers him. Had he looked into the matter of the dog's unusual barking, the presence of strangers might have come to light earlier. Changing his rhythm, Baba wonders, too, about his handling of Thimba. Had he not pushed Thimba with his demands for further marriages, Thimba might still have been heading up the warrior corps, and under his leadership, the warriors would never have behaved so irresponsibly. Yet, if, as he'd sometimes wondered, Thimba's death had been preplanned, that possibility would not apply.

Changing the rhythm to something slower and more soothing, his mind turns to Kwame. Everything about the lad pleases him, but he has to wonder how a mere adolescent will cope with what he will have to do tomorrow. He has to wonder, too, if he himself - from the other side of the divide - will even know what transpires here tomorrow, but he hopes he will. He hopes, too, there is some system in place that will allow him to guide the boy in the future. Nothing though is certain.

The night is closing in, and Baba is ready to leave. He starts chewing on his seeds, laboriously seeing he doesn't have many teeth with which to chew. Then before the seeds start doing the job, he rises from his throne and hobbles a few steps toward the ocean. There he lets himself down to the ground and stretches out on his back. Looking up at the stars, he listens to the breaking waves, and as he feels his essence leaking away and moving to a distant place, he allows his last conscious thoughts to turn to those on the ship. Wherever they are going, the tribe will live on and who knows what wondrous seeds they will sow in worlds beyond his ken.

Second Day of the Fourth Week of June 1800

Circle of the Dead

West Coast of Africa

Kwame, with Inja slung across his shoulders, returns to the village at first light. As he goes, he runs through Baba's instructions to make sure he does the job properly. He is traveling in the company of Mbaleki's warriors and Mbaleki himself, who sits on a throne carried on poles.

On arrival at the village, the entire cortège - joined by those, who Mbaleki had sent to keep watch overnight - gather by the circle of the dead. Mbaleki, with Kwame at his side, speaks a prayer after which the warriors - spears upright and shields at their chests - sing a dirge. Their deep voices carry the sound out to the empty ocean, forest, and plains.

Mbaleki and his following then adjourn to the previously inhabited part of the village, which Mbaleki will be running as an outpost until Kwame becomes adult and can take over for himself. Those who kept watch overnight disperse to gather fuel for the funeral pyre. Meanwhile, Kwame remains alone with the dead.

Resisting the temptation to procrastinate, he embarks on a task that only he can perform, because only he can name each individual correctly. Big Baba had warned him that it would not be an easy task and had mentioned the messiness of human death. Baba had told him to remember that while corpses are detritus - something the owner no longer needs - it is nonetheless incumbent on the living to treat the discarded shell with respect. Baba had ended his speech by reminding Kwame - yet again - that the way in which he performs his duty will determine the respect others give him and contribute to his future status as a great leader.

In a mindless state and following Baba's protocol, Kwame works methodically around the circle. He makes sure each individual is dead and sets the corpse to rights. He then speaks the person's name: "Zainia, Twenty-Eighth Wife, Mammi, Ife, Aunt Aziza, Madzimoyo, Uncle Ade . . ." and follows the name with the words, "May you be delivered from evil and rest in peace." To finish, he covers the corpse with a palm frond and moves on to the next.

Leaving Big Baba to last, he does the same for him as he has done for the others; then bending over the corpse beneath the spiky leaves, he whispers, "Baba, did I pass the test?"

"You're a skellum, but you'll do!" are the words - tinged with amusement - that pop into Kwame's mind.

Fifth Week of June 1800

André Scores

Plantation, Louisiana

Now that Jacques no longer allows André to ride Pégasse or any other horse, André spends his days in the farmyard mostly in a *bureau*[121] that he has set up for himself in a central area. From here, sitting at an old Louis Quatorze desk, he starts the day by assigning workloads and getting the gangs and their overseers off into the fields. Today having watched the dust cloud of the last cart dissipate, he updates the plantation journal.

What's next? He looks around checking his surroundings. Seeing Gerald filling the water troughs at the stables, André feels a stab of longing for Pégasse. He would love to visit his friend, but it would be unkind. It would raise hopes that he would not be able to fulfill. He shifts his gaze to the cooks, who are already starting to prepare the hominy,[122] meat, and a vegetable that will serve both dogs and field slaves as their midday meal.

His thoughts now with the dogs, André looks forward with pleasure to his training session with the puppies. It entails teaching them to

---

[121] Office
[122] Grits; cornmeal porridge

pursue whatever moves by getting them to chase a handful of kiddies around the yard at top speed. It is a glorious game with the puppies yipping and the kiddies shrieking in pleasure. It usually ends with the participants in a tangle on the ground and the defeated kiddies succumbing to the slobbering and licking of the victors.

What is now a game used to be an activity needed to teach young dogs to catch runaway slaves. The master, though, has not used dogs in that role for a long time; nonetheless, the game persists affording much pleasure to participants and observers alike. The event will only take place in the late afternoon just before the field gangs return. Meanwhile, now that André has more or less recovered from the injuries sustained during the whipping, he will do a job that he should have done earlier in the month - inspection of the storage area used for slave clothing and the one used for slave rations.

All slaves receive an annual allotment of clothing. Male field slaves receive a couple of coarse linen shirts with one pair of matching trousers and a jacket. In addition, they get a pair of thicker trousers for winter along with a pair of stockings and shoes. An overcoat, boots, and woolen cap come their way every few years.

The storage shed used for slave rations contains mainly bags of cornmeal along with boxes of dried fish, which give the space its distinctive smell. The weekly ration per adult is seven kilograms of cornmeal and a kilogram of dried fish. (Vegetables, fruit, and fresh pork are provided as available.) Due to the long interval since André's last inspection, the rats are back in full force and flit like shadows among the bags. Action is needed. He adds the word *rats* to his list not because he needs reminding - he remembers everything anyway - but because he is proud that he can read and write, and keeping lists was something the master always did.

Since the whipping, André finds that he tires easily and now heads back to his bureau. It is an open-air shelter featuring a throne to match the desk. Both items were acquired from a storehouse used for surplus furniture. Jacques has not yet seen André's bureau, because he and Jean only returned last night after attending to matters pertaining to the death of their parents. When Jacques does visit the farmyard, he will undoubtedly complain but will have to realize that André can't do a job that no one else can do without either a horse or an office. With the latter, André knows he has overstepped the limits, but he can't resist inciting his nemesis.

André is on his way back to his bureau, when a message comes from the Big House. Jacques wants Pégasse saddled and taken to the front steps in half an hour. This is something new and should prove interesting! Jacques has never asked for Pégasse before, and since André is no longer allowed to ride him, Pégasse badly needs exercise and is frisky. The only time André visited him he could almost hear the horse telling him in the chevalier's voice, "Accordez vos violon, mon ami![123] Let's go for a gallop!" The chevalier often used the violin idiom as a mild chastisement for the kiddies.

André arranges for the saddling of Pégasse and watches as Gerald leads the horse toward the Big House. When the pair disappears around the corner, André returns to his desk. He has barely settled when a kerfuffle breaks out from somewhere out of sight: wild whinnying, shouting, and barking, followed by a riderless Pégasse galloping flat out into the farmyard. The stallion holds his head high with his mane and tail streaming out behind him. The reins trail on the ground.

"Merde! He'll break a leg," shouts André, running - arms spread - into the path of the oncoming horse. "Whoa, boy!" he calls as they approach each other at top speed. Pégasse could have galloped right over André, or could have avoided him and carried on. Instead snorting and foaming at the mouth, tossing his head and stamping, he pulls to a halt nose-to-nose with the one he regards as his master. André manages to collect the dragging reins, soothes his agitated friend, and leads him

---

[123]   Pull yourself together, my friend! Literal meaning: tune your violin, my friend!

back to the stables. He then sends one of his *demi-frères*[124] to find out what happened.

The lad returns with the news that the house slaves are all giggling in the kitchen. It appears that when Jacques tried to mount Pégasse, the stallion objected. He reared up hauling Gerald off his feet and landing both him and Jacques floundering on the gravel. Gerald is all right, but Jacques landed on his tailbone. At present, Agathe is examining the injury on the porch while Jacques pours out vitriol onto his brother Jean, who supposedly frightened Pégasse although no one present saw anything of the kind.

André and his demi-frère share the fun with gales of laughter. André had forgotten the salutary effect of laughter; he hasn't laughed since the chevalier returned to the plantation for the last time in April.

---

[124] Half brothers

Nascent Plans

Plantation, Louisiana

The pleasure afforded by Jacques's encounter with Pégasse sustains André throughout the day. While gloating over the mishap, he knows this is only a minor victory. The real war against Jacques lies ahead, and while André already has a long-term plan, he must deal with it piecemeal. Keeping Adrienne out of Jacques's bed is the immediate need.

As the shadows lengthen, André finishes recording the overseers' reports of the day's events in the leather-bound journal and then stores it in one of the desk's deep drawers. As he locks the drawer, his thoughts return to Adrienne. It was one thing for her to consent to gratifying the master's lust; Jacques's lust is quite another kettle of fish!

With respect to the master, André had felt it best that Adrienne should sacrifice herself to prevent repercussions for the family. Besides, André had often thought that he himself would not exist if not for the master's lust! He had therefore often wondered if it could be so completely contemptible. He laughs remembering the look on his mother's face when he had once expressed this opinion!

Before the mistress left, her presence had protected Adrienne, but now that she is gone, and Jacques is uncontested king of the castle, he will not be having any qualms about Adrienne. The family needs to act quickly, but thanks to Pégasse, they have a few more days of grace! As dusk settles in, André wends his way homeward. He will arrange a visit with his mother to discuss the issue. Meanwhile, he will enjoy the only time of day he has to enjoy Andréa's company.

Opening the gate, he resolves not to mention to Andréa that he is itching to go after Jacques. She is now five months pregnant, and he does not want her to worry. She miscarried with the master's child, and it mustn't happen again!

It is unusual that Andréa does not appear at the cabin door to greet him. He hopes she is all right, but then one of his demi-frères from two cabins along the road puts his mind at rest by shouting that Andréa has gone to help with a birth in the field-slave quarters. It is something Agathe might have dealt with, but she is probably still dealing with Jacques's *derrière*. André hopes she is using her most malodourous and stinging muti and hopes that the injury will take a l-o-n-g time to heal!

Ravenous after the long day, he is quick to strip and wash off the day's dirt with the soap and bucket of water that Andréa has left for him in the backyard. Back in the kitchen, he dollops a serving of Choctaw mush[125] onto a dish from a pot still warm on the hearth. Andréa makes the mush with liver, pork brains, and eggs; it has always been one of his favorites. *Mmm!* Dish and fork in hand, he settles on a chair on the back porch and scrapes the plate clean in no time. Then, given the back porch overlooks their vegetable patch, he is able to wander between the plantings snacking on berries, tomatoes, and peas. He likes this part of the meal as much as the mush.

Returning into the cabin, he stretches out on the conjugal bed. It is his and Andréa's prized possession. Although just a mattress laid on planks supported by puncheons,[126] Andréa has covered it with a quilt, which she made from high-quality clothing handed down to André by the chevalier. It is highly decorative, but more important to André is that the item seems to have retained something of his father's essence. Tonight, the moment André's head hits the pillow, he falls asleep to find himself wrangling with the brooding presence of the chevalier. *Master,* he complains, *I wish you had tried to understand your kiddies better. You said you loved us, yet you never understood what it's like being trapped between irreconcilable opposites: master and slave, black and white,*

---

[125] Cornmeal and water, or milk, with additives,

[126] Poles driven into the wall

Catholicism and Verdun. You could have helped us; instead, you left us in Jacques's hands.

Woken again by the twinges in his back, André turns over onto his stomach and chastises himself for whining. He needs to accept the situation as it is and concentrate on how to escape it. He has already formed a long-term plan, but the details are sketchy and much depends on future events.

The plan revolves around what he knows from Agathe eavesdropping on conversations between Jacques and Cécile concerning the future of the plantation. He knows Jacques had found a buyer for the plantation even before his father became ill. André also knows from Agathe's most recent report of a conversation between Jacques and Master Girrard that the takeover is not yet imminent, and most importantly, the inventories provided to the buyer are only approximations. Excellent news! Only he - André - will be capable of providing precise details concerning slaves, animals, and equipment. Judicious omissions and adjustments might well be possible and go unnoticed.

On the Way

Scotland

Three days ago, Stanley with Baby Adair asleep in his arms had sat with his mother on the bench under the Scots pine. Two days ago, he had felt Angus McCorm's wet snout on his cheek as he bent to say goodbye. A few hours ago, after a miserable night in Edinburgh, Pontefract and Migu had waved goodbye as Stanley and Émile had clambered into a stagecoach bound for Glasgow. Tomorrow, they will board the packet that will take them from Glasgow to Liverpool.

Meanwhile, in a cold gray drizzle, Stanley and Émile sit side by side in silence in the lurching coach. Stanley feels an unsteadiness inside himself but forces himself to keep his mind empty and not to look back. Scotland and his life to date now lie in his past. Feeling neither excitement nor sorrow, he notes the smell of wet horses and listens to the pounding hooves and the splashing of wheels punctuated by the light snores of Émile slumbering at his side.

In spite of not wanting to look back, every time he lets down his guard, he finds himself wondering about Frances and Baby Adair. What might they be doing now? What about his father? Had he decided to spend a few days in Edinburgh or might he have decided to return to Glen Orm immediately? He might even have tried to persuade Migu and Rose to join him for a break at Glen Orm; they have not yet met Wee Adair.

Again Stanley reprimands himself for his nostalgia. It is not good enough! An exciting life lies ahead. He forces his thinking back to the journey. From Liverpool, they will sail south of the Azores to thirty degrees north in order to avoid the westerlies and to pick up the north-easterly trades - winds that have the ability to propel a ship across the ocean at top speed. The slave schooners use those winds when leaving for the New World from the west coast of Africa. Nonetheless, depending on conditions, it could take up to a full month to get from Liverpool to New Orleans. Stanley hopes he will have got over his homesickness by then.

Another Barber-Surgeon

West Coast of Africa

Although never on *Spirit* himself, he has done the job of barber-surgeon on several of the *Spirit* consortium's slave schooners. After years on the job, he has a jaundiced view of the world and would dearly love to earn a living in another way. Baiting simple people using cheap industrial goods as he is now watching from the mother ship is not worthy of Great Britain, but what can a man do? He can't take on those who have propelled his country to greatness, the captains of industry. Besides, how can he be sure that all those lords and sirs don't know better than he does? Perhaps in the greater scheme of things, it is written that life should be harder for some than for others.

Since dropping anchor, he has watched the action on the beach using a telescope. The warriors are now setting aside their spears and striding through the surf to deeper waters, where they start to swim using a powerful crawl. He watches mesmerized as the bobbing heads and flailing arms approach the ship and are directed to the far side. There they clamber up the ropes that the crew has thrown down for them, and they now stand gathered on deck, water streaming from their naked bodies and skin gleaming in the morning sun. In wonder, they look around absorbing their surroundings. With the vessel heaving gently underfoot, they swivel their heads this way and that taking in the stretches of deck both fore and aft. Lifting their eyes, they peer up at the mast and rigging, marveling at the unfamiliar patterns against their own familiar skies.

Watching, the surgeon knows this image will leave him no peace depicting as it does the last minutes of freedom for those, who along with their children and grandchildren, ad infinitum, will never again know what it is to be free living according to their own laws and in their own land.

He sighs as the hold is opened and the men take in the rank odor that billows forth. He sees in their faces how wonder turns into sudden and certain knowledge that they have been duped, but it's too late. Gone are the honeyed tones and *bonhomie* of the sailors, who have whipped out guns, batons, and scourges from under tarps and are yelling orders. Faces grim and voices harsh, they herd the warriors stumbling over one another down the drop into the hold. Some manage to escape the herd and jump back into the water where marksmen with deafening blasts from their guns take aim at the bobbing heads. Those that resist on deck meet with a similar fate.

Now in his cabin, the surgeon sits cross-legged in his hammock reviewing a long and arduous day. What he has witnessed leaves him feeling helpless and hollow. When his oil lamp starts to sputter, he tries to sleep, but all he can think of is the warrior - he had the markings of a medicine man - that put up the most resistance. By grabbing the barrel of one of the guns and wresting it away from the sailor, he had swung it around his head putting a number of the crew out of action before being shot and pitched overboard. It was a brave and desperate act. His corpse and many more will wash up on the shores of the land of their birth.

Lamb to the Slaughter

Plantation, Louisiana

Adrienne stands with her mother at a table at the back of the porch preparing slices of mango for Jacques and Jean. Due to Agathe's ministrations, Jacques has recovered from the mishap with Pégasse quicker than they hoped. Thinking of the contradictions woven into her mother's divided soul, Adrienne giggles as she peels the last mango. On the one hand, Mammi as a healer had felt obliged to nurse Jacques back to health as best she could. On the other hand, she is plotting with the family how best to dispose of him!

"What's so funny, child?" Agathe asks, as Adrienne bends to pick up a sliver of mango skin that has fallen to the floor. Adrienne does not have time to reply because at that moment, Jacques enters the porch from the house and pinches her bottom. She reacts with a gasp, and her knife clatters to the floor. He continues onto the porch, and nothing more is said or done for the rest of the day.

After dinner though, when Masters Jacques and Jean usually adjourn to the gentlemen's study for liqueur and a cigar, Agathe overhears Jacques say to his brother, "Mon frère, I'm tired. I shall go straight up to bed." Soon after, the bell clangs in the service area, and as is her job, Agathe goes to attend to her master's needs. She climbs the stairs to his room, where he tells her, "Agathe, when the slaves leave for their cabins tonight, you will ensure that Adrienne stays behind and joins me in my room."

As they wind up their chores, Adrienne says to her mother, her face a mask of misery, "I have to go, don't I, Mammi?"

Agathe grinds her teeth and replies, "Yes, child. We aren't ready yet but soon will be."

With head down, Adrienne nods, accepting her fate. She knows what will be happening to her; it happened to her mother and to many others besides. It is what happens to so many fifteen-year-old female house slaves.

The house now dark and quiet, Adrienne drags herself across the hallway, lighting her way with an oil lamp. As she starts climbing the stairs, she catches a glimpse of a figure by the window. It doesn't frighten her; she knows it must be Jean and carries on. Reaching the landing, she starts to shiver uncontrollably and stands at the closed door of Jacque's room for a full five minutes before knocking. Her teeth are now jittering so loudly that she can't be sure if she heard him call or not. As she tries desperately to control the jitters, the door is ripped open, and Jacques stands there in his nightshirt bellowing, "What's wrong with you, *Salope*? Can't you hear? I said come in!" He grabs her arm and pulls her into the room. Looking into her face, he says, "Stop that shivering, girl. It isn't necessary. You'll be doing that for which *Le Bon Dieu*[127] created you, and you'll enjoy it! That's an order."

---

[127]   The good Lord

Efia on Board I

Atlantic Ocean

After the confusion of the first days on board has subsided, certain routines are falling into place. In the women's hold, Efia has managed to work together with her fellow sufferers to negotiate for themselves and for their children the best conditions possible under the given circumstances. Not all the women are from Banyan Village; some of them are from villages along the coast - enemies in the past - but now everyone is working together to develop strategies that benefit all.

By being as pleasant and as tractable with their captors as possible, they have been given permission to spend most of each day up on deck. There the children can play, and the women wash themselves and their children in seawater. (Fresh water is rationed, and thirst a constant.)

The women's hold is place of horror infested with rats, cockroaches, and biting bugs. With only a couple of small portholes, there is never enough air or light, and the overpowering stench of excrement is unavoidable even when they are able to empty the buckets when up on the deck.

Seeing that use of the deck is a blessing of the highest order to the women and children, it hurts Efia deeply - one more wound to a sorely damaged soul - to know that their men in a neighboring hold are deprived of access to the outdoors. Further, they are manacled in twos and threes, can barely move, and must spend their time lying in their own excrement. Punishment for the rebellious - along with whipping and beating - includes depriving the entire group of both water and the gruel that is normally their only sustenance. At such times, the crew throws down into the hold an inadequate number of hard tack biscuits, which incite ferocious fighting among the starving men, an activity which amuses their handlers.

The women know about the warriors' plight from a young woman in their midst who is from another village. She understands a little of the light skins' lingo and has been able to liaise with the medico, who is of a kindly disposition. The news of the warriors' situation explains the sounds of pain and fighting that the women sometimes hear through the divide even above the noise of wind, wave, and water.

Efia often thinks of the warriors preening with their spears and headdresses and of how they would launching themselves into the sky with the Grand Leap. To now know of the unspeakable indignities that they suffer hurts Efia to a degree that she feels the knowledge might destroy her. Yet that is something that she cannot allow to happen for the sake of either Abebi or her companions, who look to her for leadership.

Second Week of July 1800

Vodun Dolls I

Plantation, Louisiana

It is late, and Adrienne is just back from one of her nightly visits to Jacques. She and Agathe sit cross-legged on the floor of their cabin. Each of them is fabricating a Vodun doll by the light of an oil lamp and of a pine torch, which young Gerald is holding up for them.

The dolls are for two different customers: one for a house slave and another for a field slave. Both customers are women whose broomstick husbands have wandering eyes. The purpose is to frighten the errant spouses back into a semblance of faithfulness. Initially, Agathe hadn't wanted to accept the commissions but then felt the work might help distract Adrienne from the abuse she must suffer regularly at Jacques's hands.

Agathe is seriously worried about her daughter who has lost her joie de vivre and become stiff and uncommunicative. Worst of all, she no longer sings when going about her daily chores. Since Adrienne was tiny, there has never been a time when she has not sung. She even managed to sing during the time when the mistress forbade it. Since the mistress died, Jacques has never forbidden singing, but it seems as though Adrienne no longer wishes to sing.

Mother and daughter have surrounded themselves with an assortment of buttons, pins, remnants of cloth, and a host of small found objects: sticks, roots, animal teeth, and slivers of bone. Agathe - with a sturdy fish bone needle - has made a long horizontal stitch for a mouth then small verticals for teeth. She holds the doll up for inspection.

"What do you think of that?" she asks her daughter.

Adrienne does not reply, and looking over at her, Agathe sees Adrienne has laid aside her doll and silent tears roll down her cheeks.

She says, "Mammi, would you mind if we finish the dolls some other time?"

Old Methods and New Allegiances

Plantation, Louisiana

The occupants of the cabins in the houseslave quarters have closed their doors and are settling in for the night. Agathe's door is closed, too, but André nonetheless enters holding his lantern and clutching his jar. Although Elise and Gerald are asleep in the cabin, and Adrienne would still be with Jacques, he assumes that his mother will be waiting on the back porch. A few hours earlier, he had sent a message with Gerald for her to expect him. Although for the past eleven days, Adrienne has had to visit Jacques nightly, André and Agathe are finally ready to free her from the ordeal.

Mother and son had started with two options for disposing of Jacques and had agreed to use whichever was ready first. Agathe said she would try an unfamiliar recipe for a lethal toadstool powder that the new Opelousa[128] slave had passed on to her. She has managed to locate the necessary fungus among rotting logs and, as instructed, has dried, pulverized, and soaked it in wood alcohol available on the plantation. Unfortunately, the final drying is taking longer than expected. Due to damp weather, the concoction is still moist and not yet ready for use.

It is therefore lucky that André is ready. His option was to provide a live female black widow, a formidable spider that he now carries in a tightly sealed jar along with her egg sac and a sticky tangle of web. The egg sac is an unexpected bonus. The plan is to transfer the contents of the jar into one of the silk stockings that Jacques will be wearing tomorrow. Agathe has smuggled out a pair for the purpose. Rolled together, the two stockings will trap the spider inside. Agathe will replace the stockings in Jacques dressing room - the stockings he will be wearing tomorrow - before he gets up in the morning. The manner in which Jacques's stockings return from laundering lends itself to what they have in mind. He will notice no difference in appearance in

---

[128] An indigenous American tribe

tomorrow's stockings, will unroll them, and on putting them on, will receive a bite from an irate *araignée*.[129] This is the hope.

A harebrained scheme indeed, thinks André, as he stands inside the door, hearing the regular breathing of Elise and Gerald and allowing his eyes to adjust. Yet harebrained or not, there are no alternatives. They don't have access to the type of sophisticated poison used by Mrs. Cécile.

André started with precious little knowledge of black widows, but one of the retired field slaves born in Africa - the one who loves Pégasse and now runs the orchard and vegetable garden - told him to look for the web under ledges, rocks, leaves, and debris. That web - so the old man told him - is a shapeless, sticky affair that protects an egg sac containing hundreds of eggs. He knows, too, that the female spider measures three centimeters and has a red hourglass design on her globular body. The old man made it clear that only the females - not males or juveniles - have enough venom to kill a person.

Armed with this knowledge and a lantern, André and his stepbrother Gerald, the one with the big smile, tried a number of times to find the elusive female. At a time when they should have been sleeping, they searched the mosquito-infested swamps of the bayou without success. Alligators, cottonmouths,[130] and lethal insects abounded, but the spider was nowhere to be found. This evening though their luck changed. They quickly found a nest and managed to transfer the female spider plus the egg sac and web into the jar that he now carries. The fact the sac is gold in color and not white is an added bonus. It means that the eggs are ready to hatch and might hatch in Jacques's stocking!

As André closes the door behind him, he hopes there will be no blame meted out for Jacques's pending affliction. Jean as the only

---

[129] Spider
[130] Poisonous water snake

remaining immediate member of the family is unlikely to suspect foul play or to apportion blame.

Picking his way through the cabin toward the back, André gives a grunt of surprise as he hears voices from the porch. He was expecting to find his mother alone. It irritates him to discover that she is not alone. She should be more circumspect given the sensitivity of the matter. He opens the back door and is squinting into the dark when something careens into him and nearly bowls him over.

It turns out to be Adrienne wanting to give him a hug.

"Adrienne!" he protests, "I wasn't expecting you! I could have dropped the jar! You would then have been living with this spider and her family," - he holds up the jar - "for a long time!"

"Ooh! Sorry!" Adrienne exclaims, hands to her mouth and eyes bulging as the light from the lantern picks out the whites of her eyes.

"Don't worry," he comforts. "I didn't drop it, besides I'm glad to see you in such good spirits." Adrienne's present exuberance is at odds with her behavior of the past eleven days with Jacques. Only yesterday, Agathe said to him, "It breaks my heart, to see her so crushed and silent. It's as though one of your spiders has sucked her dry." (André recently told his mother how black widows suck the liquid out of the insects they catch and sometimes even suck their mates dry.) Adrienne, babbling away now, is definitely not crushed, silent, or desiccated. She is saying, "Gerald told us you had the spider, but we no longer need her! You can throw her out!"

"What!" André is suddenly full of foreboding. *What has the silly girl done now?* Probing, he asks carefully, "I hope you haven't done anything stupid, Adrienne, like cutting off a certain piece of Jacques's anatomy." Adrienne shakes her head and giggles. André says, "*Grâce à Dieu!*" and crosses himself, before asking. "What *have* you done then?"

Voice jubilant, she proclaims, "Nothing! That's the beauty of it. Jacques is sick, and I did nothing to make it happen! His symptoms are chills, fever, rigors, and breathlessness. Master Jean told me Jacques caught malaria years ago and has periodic recurrences ever since."

"Does he want Dr. Le Blanc?"

"No, he doesn't like Dr. Le Blanc. He says he prefers Mammi's mutis: the one with Saint-John's-wort and the other with foxglove. As we know, nothing works anyway. The disease has to run its course. Either the patient dies or gets better. Master Jean says . . ."

Agathe interrupts, saying to André, "I've been noticing, son, how Master Jean favors Adrienne. He confides in her, enjoys her company, and depends on her. I don't know what to make of it.

Strange! thinks André. Turning to Adrienne he asks, "Do you, *ma petite sœur*,[131] like him too?"

Her voice soft, she replies. "It's nice not being treated like a slave. Master Jean likes to hear me sing, and he never shouts at me like Jacques does. He says please and thank you and tells me that I mustn't be afraid of him. He says that he is not like Jacques and that he'll never abuse me like Jacques does." She pauses before adding, "I feel safe with him." Then adding - her voice now challenging - "What's wrong with that?"

"Nothing, child," Agathe responds, "provided you don't forget slaves are always slaves and masters always masters. Besides, remember that although he's not stupid - he's not normal either. He is not like other masters."

"*Grace a Dieu!*" Adrienne fires back. "Besides, when Jacques is not present, no one would notice a problem. Master Jean told me that he has always been afraid of Jacques thinking he would hurt him."

---

[131]   My little sister

"He must trust you if he tells you things like that!" exclaims Agathe.

André says, "This is the second strange relationship that has developed since Master and Mistress died. Young Gerald tells me that Jacques has been favoring him by giving him small presents and getting him to do special jobs."

"Yes," Adrienne confirms. "Tonight, Jacques even wanted someone to fetch Gerald to sleep on the mat by his bed, but then Master Jean said he would sleep on a cot in the room instead."

Agathe chimes in, "I can't understand how it has happened that Jacques should have taken a liking to Gerald. The *petit gars*[132] hasn't been in the Big House since Jacques arrived. I keep the kiddies out knowing Jacques hates Master's children."

"You forget, Mammi," André says, "that, as a stable hand, the *petit gars* delivers Jacques's mounts to the Big House. On such occasions, he would have no qualms about milking the maximum advantage out of his smile." As Adrienne giggles and as André retrieves his spider and lantern, he adds, "Mammi, while Jacques would never have seen you smile, Young Gerald uses his smile constantly!"

"I doubt if Jacques has ever seen you smile either!" Agathe fires back.

Picking his way around the cabin, André hears the laughter that he leaves behind and likes it.

---

[132] Laddie

First Letter to Ambrose

Edinburgh, Scotland

Tom writes as follows:

I have only been here ten days, and already I feel at home - both upstairs, downstairs, and at the academy. I'm starting to feel like a proper person. Esquire has brought in a tailor to measure me up for a suit, and although it has not yet arrived, I've already been given some new items that give me pleasure. Also, Esquire had his barber cut and style my hair better than I can do it myself with only one arm!

Fluff has also fitted into the household. She has the run of the house and has even seduced Esquire with her winning ways. The dog Coo refuses to come upstairs, although there is nothing to stop him. The creature has a broken tail and a rib that sticks out. He loves Ms. Young, the niece, and Fluff and will also wag his broken tail for me, but he's frightened of Esquire and keeps his distance.

When I come home from the academy in the afternoon, Ms. Young and her niece ply me with tea, oatcakes, and honey while I tell them what I learned. I then go to my room on the top floor, do my homework, and study until Esquire summons me to accompany him on what he calls his constitutional. After that, I return to my studies until the niece comes to tell me if I'm to be eating in the kitchen with them or upstairs with Esquire. Both scenarios suit me fine.

When I eat upstairs with Esquire in the dining room, I find myself copying his table manners. That is a whole subject on its own. He never tells me what to do; I just learn by watching and copying him. He seems to like me trying to do things in what to him is the right way. I now, therefore, spread the napkin on my lap the way he does instead of tucking it in at the neck. I've also stopped buttering my bread in the air and first put the butter on the side of the plate - with the designated piece of cutlery - then take it from there with my own knife.

When I eat downstairs with Ms. Young and her niece, I eat their way, which is more like what I'm accustomed to. I also try to speak their way, and they tease me about not getting the *burr* right, which involves a trilling of the *r* at the back of the throat. The *ch* as in *loch* is another example. Esquire tells me it is a common sound in German. Ms. Young and the niece get me to practice words with these sounds and we all laugh when I get it wrong. When I'm with Esquire, I try to speak his way. Upper-class speech is easier and does not have so many strange sounds!

Conversation with Esquire is always interesting and contributes to my widening horizons. It's usually about ideas, history, and cultural matters, but never about the slave trade. As you know, he is conservative in his views, but he does have a curiosity about more liberal thinking, and provided I don't go overboard, I can offer smatterings of my own liberal ideas. My coffeehouse experience and your methods, Ambrose, allow me to handle my divergent opinions more skillfully than previously.

As you see, this letter is about a different type of education to the one that I'm receiving at the academy. Next week, I'll write about the academy.

Before signing off, I must say how grateful I am to whatever power it might be that determines the trajectory of an individual human life. That my unpropitious start should have led to this wonderful new situation fills me with a need to make my life count - as a force for good - in the greater scheme of things.

Tea with the Countess

Edinburgh, Scotland

Lady Abigail, at Rose's insistence, gave Migu lessons in the skills that would be required of him for the invitation extended by his daughter's future mother-in-law. It would be a first encounter and was to take place at William's swanky New Town address. Wanting to get the ordeal behind him quickly, Migu proved a good pupil, even mastering the unlikely skill of correctly handling fine bone china teacups! Apparently, sticking out the pinkie is not a requirement; only the pretentious do it, while those with true breeding refrain.

Sitting in the carriage with Rose on their way back to Leith, Migu is relieved that he seems to have withstood the test without offending anyone's sensibilities. Nonetheless, he does *not* wish to be exposed to many more such events. If only he could get away sooner! Although he doesn't say so to Rose, he wants to free himself of the constant reminders of Betta as well as removing himself from Rose's new circle of family and friends. Alas, he'll have to wait for the wedding, and it will not be immediate.

The countess had said, "Rose, dear, you and William probably shouldn't be marrying while you are still in mourning for your dear mother, but we can start planning and getting to know each other better in the meantime."

Besides the need to wait for the wedding, Migu realizes he'll need time anyway to put his affairs in order. His plan is to keep his investments in the slave trade as seed money for new business undertakings in Louisiana. He will hand over the rest of his business empire to Rose and William. The legalities will take time - especially as safeguards are needed to protect Rose, if the marriage should go awry. Although he is going to miss Rose, he very much hopes nothing does go awry with the marriage and knows that Rose will be better served without his ornery presence.

As he thinks these thoughts and the carriage moves at leisurely pace along Leith Walk, Rose asks, "What do you think of the countess, Pa?"

"I thought she'd be snooty, but she wasn't. I was also surprised to see that she seems fond of you."

Rose laughs her old laugh. "Why were you surprised, Pa? Do you think it is so difficult to be fond of me?"

Efia on Board II

Atlantic Ocean

In her determination to defuse the bitter and destructive hatred she feels for her captors, Efia has decided that - for the benefit of herself and her companions - she must milk her present surroundings for everything that can help counterbalance the unspeakable horrors of the situation.

Normally she would seek comfort from the tribe's loas, but they sensibly seem to have stayed at home in their familiar surroundings! She has no sense of them here. She turns instead to the only manifestations of the natural world available: wind, sky, and ocean. They - in their power and beauty - are keeping her all-consuming resentment in check. They give her access to a bigger picture and enable her to offer an escape to her companions from the evil, filth, and pettiness of their present environment.

Today, Efia and her companions are sitting on the deck watching from a distance as the cooks prepare the daily meal. They use two big cauldrons stationed on the bow: one for the slaves and one for the crew. The situation exacerbates the loathing that Efia tries to fight because today they have managed to determine the difference between the contents of the two cauldrons. The one for the slaves contains unidentifiable bits of root, leather, and fibrous leaf that float around in a thin gruel of millet. The crew's fare features yams, beans, peppers, and salted meat in gravy.

As Efia spoons the vile gruel first into Abebi's mouth and then into hers - it is their only meal of the day - she notes the bitterness on the faces of those around her. Feeling she must distract her fellow sufferers, she says, "I wonder what sorts of fish swim in this ocean. Could they be the same as ours at home? Maybe there are barracuda or . . ." The suggestions come in fast and thick: swordfish, marlin, tuna, cod, flounders, sailfish . . .

"Or they could be eels," says Abebi, standing up to move her arms and body in the undulating motions of an eel.

"Or octopus," says another little girl, wiggling her fingers like the legs of an octopus.

"We could make a new game for others to guess what fish we are mimicking," Abena suggests.

"Or make up a dance and a song," comes another suggestion.

"Or tell stories giving the fish voices and opinions and grouping them into families with mothers, fathers, and naughty children that bother the oysters," and so it goes on.

Efia's attention wanders. She feels pleased with herself for the animation her comment has generated. Now the minds of her companions are in a better place. She feels that the intensity of their hatred damages them while having no impact on those to whom it is directed.

Studying the ocean, she notes its different manifestations, wondering how to express them in an art form. The sounds of the words themselves often suggest their meaning: *heaving, surging, undulating, swelling* . . . One can also sing those words, altering the volume and speed though. One can add gestures and dance steps. She thinks of more words: *lapping, crashing, swooshing, thundering* . . . She is quite breathless thinking of it and would like to try some action but needs to swallow more of the revolting gruel to keep up her strength; they won't be getting any more so-called food until tomorrow.

As she forces down the liquid, she tries to think of something pleasant and what comes to mind are the colors of the sea around an island they had passed yesterday: turquoise, sapphire, black, blue, purple, gray . . .

They were all there. The medic had apparently told the person who speaks a little bit of his language that the ship would soon be reaching its destination. Could the place they are going be as beautiful as that island? Birds like those at home in Banyan circled above it. If they were going to such a place, what would they do there?

Third Week of July 1800

Good Riddance

Plantation, Louisiana

For a week now, Adrienne has watched the drama of Jacques's illness unfold from the sidelines. When instructed by her mother, she runs errands but otherwise stays in the shadows.

At the given moment, she stands by the closed drapes out of Jacques's line of vision. Seeing that he has an aversion to air and light, the room - originally the old master's - is now not only dark and stuffy but also smells of illness and sweat. No matter how often Mammi changes Jacques's night shirt, it becomes drenched again in minutes; no matter how assiduously young Gerald swabs his brow, his hair remains stuck to his skull in dark, wet clumps.

Adrienne watches as her mother tries to cajole him into taking his medicines, but he brushes it away and turns to Jean who sits by the bed. He says in a cracked voice, "Jean, call the priest. I won't be recovering this time and need to confess."

Jean, staring wide-eyed asks, "Are you sure, mon frère? You have always recovered before. It's difficult to imagine the world without you."

"You'll manage, Jean. I have always babied you unnecessarily and that is the least of it. The worst lies in a past. You don't remember, but I fear the Le Bon Dieu is not so forgetful. Now obey me one last time and call the priest!" When Jean hesitates, he adds, his voice querulous, "For God's sake, do what I say! I need absolution. I don't wish to face the fires of hell like Maman, who had no access to the last rites."

Jean jumps to his feet saying, "As you wish, mon frère!" Before leaving the room, he turns to Adrienne and beckons. She follows him from the room and - as they descend the staircase side by side - he says, "Help me, Adrienne. He wants Father Joseph. How do I summon him?"

It surprises Adrienne that although he's asking for help, he is showing no signs of an emotional collapse, as she feared he might. She replies, "I'll get André to send a message to the priest, Master."

She leaves the house and is glad to find André ensconced on his throne at his Louis Quatorze desk and says, "Master Jean is asking for you to send someone for Father Joseph so Jacques can confess before he dies." Adrienne sees that, like her, André is trying to repress his jubilation. Both know from their old master that it is not seemly to show pleasure at the death of even an enemy.

Jumping to his feet, André announces, "I will not be sending anyone. I'll saddle Pégasse and go myself!" Brother and sister exchange a smile worthy of young Gerald and go their separate ways.

Absolution

Plantation, Louisiana

Agathe is much relieved to hear Father Joseph arrive. She can see Jacques is holding on to life with his last reserves. He is determined not to die before confessing and receiving absolution. She feels that he has many sins and finds it encouraging that he recognizes the fact and wants to leave life clean.

As Agathe waits for Adrienne to accompany Father Joseph up the stairs, Agathe takes over the swabbing of Jacques's brow from young Gerald. While wringing out the cloth in a basin at the bedside table, it occurs to her that Jacques might not see his sins in the same light that she does. He would not regard his embrace of slavery nor his treatment of slaves as sinful, but judging from what he said before sending Jean to get the priest, he does realize whatever it was that he did to Jean was wrong. Also he realizes it was wrong to murder his father as proved by not wanting to die like his mother without the opportunity to confess. Agathe feels that recognition of at least some wrongs is better than nothing.

As Adrienne holds open the door for Father Joseph, Jacques's facial expression shows a palpable relief. As the priest dons the ritualistic apparel, Jacques fixes his eyes on him, begging him to hurry - or so Agathe interprets the look.

When the ceremony begins, Agathe moves back from the bed to the window to join Adrienne and the other house slaves in the shadows. From there, Agathe sees that Jacques has difficulty couching his confession into suitable wording; Father Joseph, hand cupped to his ear, has to lean forward to hear him. Finally, as Agathe now hears clearly, Jacques speaks the words required of him, "I regret these and all the sins of my past life."

Father Joseph stands and, making the sign of the cross, pronounces the words of absolution: "Ego te absolvo a peccatis tuis in nomine Patris, et Filii, et Spiritus Sancti. Amen."[133]

Agathe and all the slaves hear Jacques's sigh of relief at the *Amen;* it seems to coincide with the departure of his spirit. After that, Agathe sees no further sign of life and assumes he was dead even before the priest administered extreme unction.[134].

---

[133] I absolve you from your sins in the name of the Father and of the Son and of the Holy Spirit.

[134] The final sacrament of the last rites wherein a sign of the cross is made on the forehead with anointing oil.

Second Letter to Ambrose

Edinburgh, Scotland

I write this sitting in my attic with Fluff. It is a different type of attic to the one I had in Liverpool, which resembled my cabin on *Spirit*. The desk at which I now sit is an elegant Sheraton mahogany writing table. It has a rectangular top, round projected corners, and tapering fluted legs that are topped with carved tassels. Esquire is a stickler for detail and insists that I note such stylistic features, feels a discerning eye is essential for those like me who aspire to the ranks of the educated.

The academy I attend is designed to give basic education to those students heading for careers in science and engineering. Esquire thinks that, when I've completed my time there, I should be ready for the new science faculty that he is endowing at the University of Edinburgh. I'm much older than the other students at the present academy but seeing I am small and look younger than my age, it doesn't matter much.

For good conversation, I rely on Esquire. I walk with him daily when I get back from the academy. Today he me took me to David Hume's mausoleum on Calton Hill and filled me in on the history of the place. Then after we got home and I had done my preparation for tomorrow, Ms. Young came and told me I would be having dinner with Esquire in the dining room tonight and that before dinner I should go to his study. There over a wee dram of Scotch, he told me about David Hume and Adam Smith. He then lent me a book on both, which I'm looking forward to reading. During dinner, he told me that I could have free access to his library and that he would be interested in hearing my thoughts on what I read. I am excited about that and want to look into Scotland's practical form of humanism as manifested in utilitarianism and consequentialist thought.

I also mentioned to him that I was interested in those thinkers who looked into the relationship between science and religion. I am hoping that it's not too liberal a subject for such a conservative gentleman, but seeing he didn't say anything, I hope it passed muster. He does have curiosity for off-kilter subject matter as long as it is not too radical.

Before my sheet of paper runs out, I want to mention what I like best about the academy: it has managed to free itself from the compulsory curriculum that features the classics. I'm so grateful to Esquire that, along with everything else, he bothered to find such a suitable school for me.

PS. My new clothes have arrived! When I look in the long mirror, what I see is someone who could almost be a person of consequence, in spite of being of small stature and missing half an arm!

Abebi on Board

Atlantic Ocean

Abebi and Efia stand by the railing as Efia points out the different types of clouds. Abebi has the feeling this might be Mammi's new version of education - a subject she hated when they were still at home. For now, she is not complaining. She has come to like clouds. Mammi has fancy names for them, but Abebi just sees them as high, long, and wispy; as low, white, and puffy; or as dark, heavy, and threatening. The latter occurs when they bank up over a green sea.

A good reason to like clouds is that although they constantly change shape with the wind, they always remain pure and clean. That is why Mammi tells her to think of them at night when she tries to sleep in the dirt and stench of the hold.

Another advantage of clouds over loas is that loas need offerings, altars, and prayers; clouds do not. Clouds though would not be any good at beating up the *bad boys*, but then Infana wasn't good at that either. That is why she had to ask Gran Legbwa to beat them instead.

Mammi breaks into her musings by tapping her on the head with her forefinger and saying in a kindly manner, "Child, you're not listening to me! Your mind is miles away. What are you thinking?"

"I'm thinking about the bad boys," replies Abebi. "When I told Gran Legbwa to beat them up good and proper, I didn't mean that he should beat them so hard that Assimbola should die and Kwame vanish!"

Efia frowns and says in a shocked voice, "Child, you should *never* have spoken to Gran Legbwa like that!" She pauses a while, then adds, "Nonetheless, I don't believe that is what happened to Assimbola. As to Kwame, we might find him back at the village when we return."

Abebi has no chance to comment. The red-haired sailor - the one that picked Abebi up on the beach and took her to the rowing boat - is beckoning to Mammi to follow him. It is something that happens quite often, and as usual, Mammi calls to Abena, who with Abinti in her arms comes to sit with Abebi, while Mammi is gone. That is all right with Abebi because she can now tickle him and make him giggle, which she could not do a few days ago before the medic cured him.

Abena on Board

Atlantic Ocean

As Abena walks toward Abebi holding Abinti in her arms, she grinds her teeth at the sexual abuse so many of the women must endure in silence at the hands of the crew. The first sailor who had met with resistance had dragged his victim to the railing and pitched her overboard. Her head remained bobbing in the wake as the schooner skipped onward across the waves. After that event, the women had decided that for the sake of their youngsters, they must not resist.

Like Efia, Abena feels they should try to counteract their anger and hatred with creative endeavors. Using the sounds and sights of the sea to make up songs, dances, and stories helps. With this in mind, Abena settles down on the deck, patting the ground at her side for Abebi to join her.

Today, though, Abebi is more interested in Abinti than in songs and stories, which are just as effective in distracting her. Giggling and laughing become the order of the day and Abena thinks - with gratitude - of the ship's doctor, who had cured Abinti's diarrhea with a remnant of muti that had long since run out. He had held back a little for the very young.

With the youngsters suitably entertained, Abena returns her mind to her present project of making mental lists of the images, colors, movements, and sounds of the ocean. She stores these lists in her memory and consults them as needed. Every so often she runs through an entire list so that none of the items fall by the wayside. Now as she watches the children entertain one another, she runs through a list that contains such words as *swelling, splashing, crashing, murmuring, swirling, foaming; breaking, roaring, pounding, rumbling,* plus some she has made up.

When Abinti starts to get tetchy, Abena takes him back into her arms and rocks him. Abebi, too, is tired and says, "I am going to find Mammi."

"You are *not!*" Abena replies in panic. Her abnormally sharp tone stops Abebi, who sits down again. Abena apologizes saying, "Sorry I shouted at you, Abebi, but Mammi will be back soon. Meanwhile, I've been wanting to tell you about my dream. Big Baba was sitting on his throne with Inja on his lap, and they were waiting for us to come home again, when . . ."

Abebi interrupts, wanting to know, "Was Old Billy in your dream, too, Auntie Abena?"

"He was, and so were you running along the beach with your pigtails flying in all directions!"

Abebi giggles and claps her hands to her head, exclaiming, "I love pigtails!"

At that moment, Efia reappears, saying, "Look what I have!" She carries three treacle blobs on sticks.

Fourth Week of July 1800

Post-Jacques

Plantation, Louisiana

As Agathe and Adrienne settle on the back porch of their cabin, the colors of the setting sun are spread across the sky. The spectacle is a treat for them; something they are not accustomed to witnessing. Under the old master and Jacques, house slaves worked until after dark, and seeing that old-growth trees surround the Big House, sunsets never feature in the lives of house slaves. This morning though, Jean told Agathe that he does not need to keep the house slaves working until after dark to give him an evening meal that he doesn't want. If they put out a few ginger cookies for him to nibble before bed, it would be enough.

The light has almost faded when André joins his mother and sister. In the half-light, Agathe studies her son as he settles on the top step and extracts a cigar from the breast pocket of his leather jerkin. It will keep the mosquitoes at bay and is one of the Cuban cigars from a box that the old master gave André when he married Andréa.

Agathe marvels at the confident manner in which her son lights the cigar and blows out a stream of smoke; his mannerisms are identical to those of his father. She marvels, too, at how well he has recovered from the whipping along with the multiple stresses inflicted on him during

Jacques's brief tenure. Being back to riding Pégasse and running the plantation as before has helped with his recovery. Looking into the distance, she says wistfully, "Wouldn't it be nice, if we could carry on like this with Jean as our master?"

"You forget, Mammi," André reminds her, "that Jacques arranged the sale of the plantation even before the old master died."

"Couldn't that be changed now?"

"I doubt it," says André as he blows a smoke ring into the night air. "Besides, Jean as a half portion wouldn't want to own a plantation or know what to do with it if he did."

"He is *not* a half portion," Adrienne bursts out, glaring at her brother.

"You speak as though you have fallen in love with him," Agathe teases.

With Adrienne on the verge of tears, André apologizes, saying, "I'm sorry, little sister. I shouldn't have spoken like that. With Jacques gone, Jean will probably become more normal. An entire life spent alongside Jacques would be enough to set anyone off balance." André stubs out his cigar and gets up to leave before he offends Adrienne further by expressing his true feelings about Jean: that he finds Jean weak and effete, not worthy of the chevalier's superior bloodlines that Andre himself carries.

Third Letter to Ambrose

Edinburgh, Scotland

Oh, Ambrose, I'm so happy here. As I said in my last letter, since I have my new clothes, I feel as though a new person is emerging from its cocoon. I find myself doing things that I had never have thought of doing before. Today for instance on my way home from the academy, I passed a pretty young girl selling flowers on the street and seeing that Esquire gives me a little pocket money, I bought a bunch of dahlias, which I gave to Ms. Young when I got home. Imagine! Her eyes went all teary. It's something I'd never have thought to do before.

It is nice to be among people, whom I trust and with whom I don't get shy and flustered. Esquire took me once to the opera and once to an art exhibition, and I didn't feel out place. I can now even joke with Ms. Young and her niece, and we often laugh together at Fluff's high-spirited capers and at the dog chasing his broken tail. One has to wonder at how the poor creature broke it.

When I am so happy here, it makes me sad to see that Esquire is not happy inside himself. He suffers from some sort of disorder that robs him of pleasure. I think you, perhaps, pinpointed the nature of his malaise by saying it has to do with guilt and the slave trade. Since I have been here, he has never once mentioned *Spirit* or the slave trade.

I continue to write daily and a funny thing has happened: Esquire, too, has started to write! Imagine! He writes articles on erudite subjects that get published. He has never said so, but I wonder if my desire to write might have encouraged him to do what he is so well-equipped to do from the start. Isn't it extraordinary that Little Tom Brown should have unconsciously influenced someone like Esquire? Imagine, too, if sometime in the future, we both wrote under pseudonyms and exchanged opposing ideas in a public forum without realizing with whom we interact!

One of the articles Esquire wrote defended the classical curriculum of the likes of Oxford and Cambridge. I find that strange seeing that I know he also resents the old universities' disregard for sciences that would better serve our new industrialized world. He wrote this:

> The classics assimilate information from various areas creating a cohesive whole, which by disciplining the mind and making it more agile, train it to accept other types of learning.

To me, that seems fatuous seeing that science probably does as good a job of disciplining the mind as do the classics. Seeing Esquire is prone to guilt, maybe he feels - by putting science above the classics - he is betraying his background and this is his way of making amends. What do you think, Ambrose?

First Week of August 1800

Vodun Dolls II

Plantation, Louisiana

This evening, Agathe and Adrienne are putting the finishing touches to the Vodun dolls that they started during the time Adrienne was still visiting Jacques. Agathe, after snipping off her thread with her teeth, admires the mouth that she made with one long stitch and small vertical stitches for teeth.

Meanwhile, Adrienne is telling her mother how Master Jean is adapting well to the death of Jacques. As Agathe lays aside her doll and stands up to stretch, Adrienne continues with the words, "And you know what, Mammi? This afternoon, he asked me to accompany him to the graves of his father and his brother in the park. When we arrived, he explained how he wants to mark the area with two special headstones: one for the old master and one for Jacques. He wants the stones, plus a plaque for Mrs. Cécile, grouped in a small garden-like setting."

Agathe curtails her stretch to look over at her daughter in surprise that only increases as Adrienne adds in a breathless voice, "And, Mammi, you know what he did next? He asked me how he should get the project done!"

Agathe sees in the lamp light the wonder in her daughter's face that their new master should ask her - a mere fifteen-year-old slave girl - for advice!

"What did you say, Adrienne?" Agathe asks with caution.

"I said he should make a drawing of the area the way he wants and then discuss the matter with André about getting it done."

Agathe says, eyebrows lifted in surprise, "I'm proud of you, child! You answered well." She then picks up her doll and tweaks its hair first one way then another. (The hair is the fluff from the undercoat of an animal.) "That makes it look scarier, doesn't it?" she says finally satisfied.

Adrienne's mind is elsewhere; she has more to say. "Mammi, I haven't yet told you the best part," she continues. "Master Jean also wants to build a slave chapel!"

"Oh!" Agathe exclaims in shock. "Where?"

"Near the field slave quarters." The words pour out of Adrienne, as she tells how Jean wants to postpone the closing date for the sale of the plantation in order to get the two jobs - family gravemarkers and chapel - completed. She then continues with the words, "In meantime, he wants to use - this is how he phrased it, 'slave input on how to decorate the chapel using African motifs and crafts within a Christian framework!'"

Adrienne interrupts her extraordinary report by commenting, "By the way, Mammi, it surprises me that Master Jean knows so much about *African motifs and crafts*. I've noticed, too, in other conversations that he knows more about *African culture* - his words - than we know."

Agathe pauses then says, "It doesn't really surprise me. I'm only now realizing the implications of a conversation I once overheard at one of the old master's dinner parties. He was telling his guests how Jean had finally received a degree in Boston in ethnomusicology, which meant he was now an expert in *primitive caterwauling.* Without understanding what that meant, I had a feeling it had something to do with Africa, which is proved correct by what you now say."

"That long word you used, Mammi, is also helping me to understand why he always wants to hear me sing and why he knows so much about our music. He says that - in the new slave chapel - the music can be of *our type*, and we can use our own rhythms and body movements to sing Christian songs!"

"Oh!" is all Agathe manages to say before Adrienne continues, "He also says we can have images of a black Christ and black saints. He believes Christ is in everyone - whether black or white - and that Christ can take on the appearance of anyone, who is of goodwill and carries love and peace in their hearts. As to the saints, he thinks they are the embodiments of different aspects of good and that it is all right for us to depict them with dark skins and African adornments. He says white Christians make the mistake of laying too much importance on the historical and physical aspects of Christ and his followers. For him, they can take on different guises depending on the time and place."

"That is a lot to digest in one go," says Agathe, "and I am surprised you managed to repeat is so coherently, child! We need to put a lot of thought into these matters, but for now, let's finish the job on hand." She again holds up her doll for inspection and asks, "Do you think it's scary enough?"

"I don't think it is in the least scary, Mammi!" says Adrienne, inspecting the work. "If it weren't for the mouth and teeth, it could just as well be Baby Jesus in his crib! Even the teeth aren't that scary. Perhaps you should leave a couple of empty gaps between them."

Agathe looks at her daughter aghast before both erupt into gales of laughter. They do not hear André on the porch and look up startled, when he opens the door and enters.

"What's so funny?" he asks. Seating himself on a chair, he takes in the scene and comments, "Nobody can find Vodun dolls funny. It must be something else that's funny."

"Nothing else," says Adrienne with a mischievous grin. "Mammi and I are going to decorate Master Jean's chapel with Vodun dolls!"

"I have no idea what you are talking about," says André sternly. He picks up Adrienne's doll and examines it. It has a podgy figure, stubby legs, and a huge head. The hair is string. The eyes are snail shells, and the mouth - *pièce de résistance* - is a *smiling* fish bone stitched over the rouge-red of a desiccated tomato skin. He laughs out loud and says, "I was wrong. Vodun dolls can be funny!"

Adrienne pouts. "It is not meant to be funny! It's meant to scare a faithless husband!"

André takes out his cigar and, while dealing with it in the appropriate manner, says, "If the intention is to scare, I'm not sure it will fulfill its purpose. What I *am* sure of is that Master Jean would *not* appreciate Vodun dolls in a chapel, although how a chapel fits into the picture is beyond my comprehension."

Fourth Letter to Ambrose

Edinburgh, Scotland

Esquire's family is here! Imagine, Ambrose, Esquire's wife fell ill in North Berwick, so all the family and staff have come back here to Edinburgh! Lady McCallum is now in the royal infirmary for diagnosis and the girls - there are five of them - are here and at a loose end. If Lady McCallum does not recover soon, Esquire might send them to their grandparents in Glasgow. I'd though prefer them to stay; I enjoy their curiosity and joie de vivre.

Isobel, the eldest daughter, will soon be fifteen, and she and I get on well. We both have an enthusiasm for the *Encyclopedia Britannica*. It was first published in Edinburgh with two volumes, but its fourth edition will have twenty volumes! For the time being, Esquire has the third edition in his study, which - did I tell you? - has wall-to-wall bookshelves.

Isobel liked the idea, when I told her that - to improve my writing skills - I write a short article every day on a subject I research in the encyclopedia. Now she does the same, and we swap articles the next day. Her article today is about the history of bathing, which seems strange for a polite young girl. She though resents the fact that a girl's education is limited to polite accomplishments like music, art, needlework, literacy, and numeracy with piety as a desirable adjunct.

Her article is full of snippets about soaps mixed with herbs and spices, about scented rags used to rubdown the body, and heavy perfumes and fragrant powders to mask stench. Louis XIV supposedly only had two baths in his life: one on the day of his birth and the other on the day of his wedding day. According to a Polish ambassador, one could smell him from a long way off. In England, Queen Elizabeth found a bath a month befitting for a virgin queen, even if she felt she didn't need it.

Isobel didn't get further than that, but she encouraged me to read more myself and when I did, I found out about Roman baths. Mention was made of one such place where the dark-blue water reeked of sulphur and supposedly cured rheumatism, gout, and arthritis. I'm wondering if that is the bath in Somerset. Interesting, too, were the communal baths in monasteries and the large public baths that survived in Britain until the Black Death. That is when public bathing ended, leaving common folk - the great unwashed - with no options other than water and a rag.

As a postscript, Esquire's terrace house has running water with indoor taps in the kitchen and all four bathrooms! It does not yet have the flushable water closets that exist but are not yet widespread. Esquire is obsessed with modern conveniences.

As a second postscript, part of me feels guilty for living in all this luxury while another part of me - my commitment to giving slaves a voice - has to clamor to survive. The problem is that so many things interest me that I can only make my commitment to the miseries of slavery a part of the mix and not exclusive.

Second Week of August 1800

Proposal

Plantation, Louisiana

Jean sits on the porch, and Adrienne stands in front of him with a jug now empty from having replenished his glass. He says, "I'm going to ask you a personal question, Adrienne. Do you mind?"

"It's all right to ask, Master," she replies, wondering what will happen next.

"Adrienne," he starts, hesitates, and then looking up into up her face, continues with a rush, "I know that before his death, my brother Jacques was taking advantage of you."

She nods mutely as the black cloud that was Jacques engulfs her. She turns away to put down the jug as he asks, "Is there a possibility that you might be carrying his child?"

She cannot imagine where this is leading but turns back to him and answers truthfully, "I'm not yet sure, Master."

He tells her, "I should be happy if you were, Adrienne, but even if you are not, it won't change what I'm about to say." He leans forward and peers at her, trying to gauge her reaction, then continues with the words, "As you know, the plantation will soon be sold along with all the slaves, but before that happens, I should like you to come and live with me in New Orleans as my placée. I explained to you about placées. Do you remember?"

Her mind whirls, but she manages to say, "Yes, Master, I remember."

"You would remain a slave, but not a slave of the new owner. You would be *my* slave, but I wouldn't treat you as a slave. I would treat you with the respect accorded to a white wife. I also undertake never to touch you with sexual intent." He waits, obviously expecting a reaction, but she accepts the statement with equanimity. She has known about his preference for men since the day Jacques told the mistress that Jean was a *sodomist*.

Jean is still watching her, and even though she hasn't spoken, he *reads* her and his look changes from concern to satisfaction. He relaxes back into the chair and says with a smile, "Sing for me, Adrienne, that song with the clicks for thunder and rain. You said some of the clicks are made behind the front teeth and others by pulling the tongue back from the roof of the mouth."

She laughs that he should remember but doesn't comment as he continues, "I've tried it myself and have to wonder if my tongue is the right shape!"

Adrienne giggles and launches into the rain song. "You speak to my soul, Adrienne," he says when the last note has sounded. "Now sing something of your own choosing."

She sings a lullaby familiar to her since birth. Setting aside her uncertainties, she pours into the song her love for him and for the child she hopes - indeed believes - she carries in her womb.

New Horizons

Plantation, Louisiana

At dusk on the day of Jean's proposal to Adrienne, André wends his way through the deserted farmyard to Agathe's cabin. In the twilight, the familiar buildings of the yard are turning into threatening hulks reflecting his fears for the future. Pégasse's greeting - a low whinny as he passes the stables - reminds him not to become fanciful. He must keep his mind clear and concentrate on shaping a realistic future for himself and those who depend on him. His yearning for escape and the plan he is hatching run counter to rational thinking!

Nonetheless, the thought of his plan - he has come to think of as *Le Grand Plan* - sends a thrill coursing through his body. It is a plan of great daring and hinges on the fact that he is the only person capable of giving Master Girrard the updated figures for the inventory the new owner will need. André can therefore make certain adjustments that won't be noticed. He can omit from the list many of the lower profile coffee-colored kiddies. He can report a lower number of horses, goats, and dogs along with reduced quantities of tools, building materials, and equipment. This would provide him with the basics needed to 'seed' a new free-wheeling settlement in the wilderness. Unbeknownst to the master race, small colonies of escaped slaves already exist in the thousands of acres of the neighboring bayou. It is an area inaccessible to those not in the know.

While the *Le Grand Plan* could deliver on such a settlement, not all the coffee-colored kiddies could participate. He, for instance, and many of the house slaves could never be omitted from the inventory seeing that Master Girrard knows them. The same applies to Pégasse.

André has now arrived at Agathe's cabin. No one is on the back porch, so he stands for a while in the garden, watching the stars appear. The sensible course of action would be for him to start now by smuggling out items piecemeal at night. Lower profile coffee-colored kiddies could start disappearing too. Jean would never miss them. Meanwhile, he and his immediate family would carry on as usual and see how the new owner turns out.

Agathe and Adrienne, having noticed André's presence, come and join him, and they all settle on the back porch. There André tries out the corncob pipe that he had made for himself that morning. Most slaves smoke such pipes, and the plantation grows a small amount of tobacco for their use. Seeing the new pipe is still slightly damp, it produces more smoke than normal. Both Agathe and Adrienne vigorously fan their faces with their hands while Adrienne exaggerates her coughing and says, "We'd hoped you had given up field-burning!" She refers to the practice of setting fires in the cane fields in order to burn away the leaves and make harvesting easier. At such times, black foul-smelling smoke billows over the plantation raining down ash that clogs the lungs and burns the eyes of humans and animals alike.

André obligingly extinguishes the new corncob pipe and turns to Adrienne saying, "Well, *ma petite soeur*! Mammi tells me life will be changing for you. She doesn't seem sure about it, but how you feel is more to the point." As Adrienne takes her time in commenting, he says, "I find the new situation full of potential. I also have the feeling that - what with placées and freed slaves - barriers between slaves and masters are laxer in New Orleans than they are here."

Agathe stares at André wide-eyed, exclaiming, "Freed slaves! Can such things really exist, *mon fils?*"

"Yes. Andréa says they do, and she has more experience of the outside world than we have. She tells me many things the old master hid from us. Adrienne will be discovering such things in New Orleans, and Adrienne - so we hope - can pass them on to us."

Turning to Adrienne, André reaches out and gives her a friendly pat on the knee, saying, "But you, little sister, haven't told me yet how you feel about Master Jean's proposal? Do you like the idea of living with him in luxury? You'll have all the rouge and clothing that girls your age supposedly crave!"

Adrienne gives a guilty grin, then points out that while she'd enjoy the opportunity to adorn herself, she would also receive other opportunities like learning to read and write properly. She then adds, "Master Jean also says that he would like to arrange for some of his friends to hear my voice!" Even in the fading light, André sees her eyes sparkle.

Agathe choses the moment to comment, "I know that good thing will come your way, child, but you also need to remember your master Jean is a sodomist."

Adrienne replies, "But, Mammi, I don't think it is wrong that he won't be using me like Master used you and like Jacques used me. It's good!"

Agathe snorts and grumbles as André points out to this mother, "Mammi, if Adrienne has Jacques's child, and it will be given out as Jean's that should help quash rumors about sodomy. Besides - even if she doesn't have Jacques's child - we can smuggle in another coffee-colored newborn that can be given out as Jean's and Adrienne's child. We can even follow through with a child every year! All would share bloodlines with Jean through the old master. I am sure Jean would be genuinely happy with them, apart from the protection they would give him against gossips. Adrienne, too, seeing she loves all *bébés* - would be happy, wouldn't you, *ma petite soeur?*"

"Oh yes!" Adrienne exclaims all smiles.

André ends the topic by saying, "In general, people of color would benefit because Jean would provide his coffee-colored kiddies with the best of educations thus creating potential leaders for those of our kind!" It's a win-win situation for all.

Fifth Letter to Ambrose

Edinburgh, Scotland

Today, when I discovered among Esquire's books the two volumes of *Zoonomia*, I told Isobel about Erasmus Darwin. I then managed to find for her the passage suggesting that millions of years before the beginning of human history, warm-blooded animals could have arisen from a living filament, which the Great First Cause had endowed with the power of acquiring improved parts. I find these words exciting, especially as Darwin postulates that the living filament could be continuing to deliver improved parts down through posterity in a never-ending stream.

While I was holding forth about all this, I suddenly felt guilty about inflicting such radical ideas on a fifteen-year-old brought up on Adam and Eve, so I moved us quickly away from the subject, and instead, we each wrote a verse using rhyming vowel sounds. She wrote the following for her father:

> I like history, Papa
> Don't you?
> It tells us why we live in the world
> in which we do.

She pointed out that apart from *you* and *do*, she had used assonant rhymes internally as in *I*, *like*, and *why* and also in *history*, *it*, *live*, *in*, and *which*. I was impressed. At her age, I was scrubbing decks and not thinking about rhymes, assonant, or otherwise!

Third Week of August 1800

Arrival

New Orleans, Louisiana

It has been seven weeks since Stanley and Émile left Glen Orm at the beginning of a cool damp Scottish summer. Today, they disembark in New Orleans in the sweltering heat of Louisiana's hottest month. Olivier Girrard, a lawyer, has met their packet boat, and now after helping them retrieve their luggage, they are in his carriage on the way to the house that Girrard has leased for them.

They drive through the outskirts of the city but have little time to absorb their new surroundings as the lawyer informs them that the chevalier's son Jacques - with whom Émile had corresponded and made all the arrangements - had died in the interim."

"Oh!" Émile exclaims. "I was looking forward to meeting him. He was my cousin! Will Cousin Jacques's death have an impact on our agreement?"

"Changes will be minor," Olivier Girrard assures him. "The plantation now belongs to Jacques's younger brother, Jean, who, of course, is also your cousin. With two minor changes, he accepts the arrangements already in place."

Tone guarded, Émile asks, "What are these *minor changes?*"

"He wants the closing date moved to the end of October and also is asking for some small adjustments to the inventory list that Jacques gave you. As you know, the figures you were given were mere approximations seeing that only the chevalier had the exact numbers, and he was ill at the time."

Émile continues to look suspicious and probes, "Could you give me an example of a small adjustment?"

As the carriage rattles on over the paving stones, the lawyer tells them that Jean wants to keep one of the young house slaves for himself. "He intends on bringing her here to New Orleans with him as a placée, but you don't need to worry about it. You will still have ample choice of breeders from the young girls that remain."

As the mention of placée meets with blank stares from both Émile and Stanley, Girrard adds, "I'll explain the plaçage system to you later. Meanwhile, I'd like to draw your attention to what you are about to see out of the window."

He goes on to explain how, after a couple of major fires during the past century, brick was used as a replacement for wood. "As you see from what we will now be passing, the results were often amazing. Here," he says as they reach a large square, "are three impressive examples of formal Spanish colonial architecture. The two matching structures on either side of the church are the presbytère and the town hall, the one with the Spanish coat of arms. The basilica in the middle is St. Louis Cathedral."

Nine bays and an open arcade of elliptical arches with pilastered corners is as much as Stanley can absorb before the scene changes. The buildings that line the street now - some of them are multistoried - feature decorative wrought iron balconies and large arched entrances to courtyards filled with bright potted plants.

As the carriage continues to rattle on over the cobblestones, Stanley's thoughts turn back to the plantation. "Monsieur Girrard," he asks, "what is happening on the plantation at the moment?"

Olivier Girrard replies, "André is running it, as he always has in the chevalier's absence. Jacques probably mentioned André's existence in his original letter. André is an eminently capable mixed-race slave, but I'll tell you more about him later. We have now arrived at your new home. As you see, it comes with a full complement of slaves, and they are all standing outside to greet you!"

Stanley very much likes what he sees - so many subservient beings, all well-nourished, clean, neatly dressed, smiling, and ready to serve.

Several days later, Stanley and Émile are at Olivier Girrard's office, where they will meet Cousin Jean for the first time. The purpose of the meeting is for Jean and Émile, as Aaron Migu's agent, to sign certain legal documents. After that, Émile and Stanley will adjourn to Jean's house for lunch.

Stanley and Émile have arrived early at the office and sit listening to Olivier Girrard. He is seated on a gilded throne at a Louis Quatorze desk and is lecturing them on the ins and outs of the plaçage system. It seems to be a form of common-law marriage between a male, normally a Frenchman of high ranking, and a woman of color who might or might not be a slave. Then, addressing Stanley, Girrard says, "In case you, Stanley, are considering a similar type of situation for yourself, I feel I should mention the plaçage system is more common in urban surroundings than in the country. Plantation owners, like the chevalier and myself, never bothered with placées, who are more like wives than mistresses and are not so easy to discard. Plantation owners have many more slaves than city dwellers and therefore have a greater choice of fecund young colored girls for breeding purposes."

"So Émile's Cousin Jean is taking on a plantation slave as a placée and bringing her here to New Orleans?" Stanley asks, wanting to make sure he fully understands the situation.

"Just so," Girrard confirms as the appearance of Jean terminates the plaçage conversation.

A funny little man, thinks Stanley of Jean, and it amuses him to see the look of shock that passes across Émile's features. He was obviously expecting a cousin of his to have the large stature and wild black hair that characterizes the Migu-look. Nonetheless, Émile rallies manfully and greets Jean with the exuberance that Stanley knows so well from his Uncle Aaron.

For his part, Stanley notes something kind and diffident in Jean's manner and feels well disposed toward him in spite of his obvious eccentricity. Another point in Jean's favor is that he speaks good English. It makes for more relaxed conversation than trying to participate in the gibberish that Girrard and Émile fire at one another in French.

Lunch at the house in which Jean grew up confirms his eccentricity. After saying grace, "Pour ce que nous allons recevoir, que le seigneur nous rende vraiment reconnaissants,"[135] Jean settles them at a formal dining room table attended by a bevy of well-trained slaves, both male and female.

As they start their meal with *soupe à l'oignon* - a slice of a three-quarter-inch thick baguette floating in each bowl, Jean says, "This will be a simpler meal than either my parents or Jacques, God rest their souls, would have served. Compared to them and to most others, my tastes are frugal. Maman and Papa favored an obscene number of

---

[135] For what we are about to receive, may the Lord make us truly thankful.

courses centered on large roasts." He turns to Stanley, saying, "The cook at the plantation though will be able to do the same for you, if that's what you like. Or will you be introducing the Scottish cuisine?"

"No, not at all!" Stanley replies, but then remembers Rabbie Burns' night and adds, "The one exception will be on January 25, when haggis will be served. That's a type of sausage served in a sheep's stomach. I have my mother's recipe." He then launches into an explanation of the recitation of the "Ode to the Haggis" and of a bagpiper marching around the dining room table. He adds, "The latter though rather depends on whether I can teach one of the slaves to play the bagpipes in the intervening months!"

"You're a musician!" Jean exclaims, face aglow. "I, too, love music, especially ethnic music."

Although Stanley, too, likes ethnic music, he remains silent noticing that Jean, who only had a spoonful of soup, has now barely tasted the seafood quiche that seems to be the main course. *It is no wonder that he is so small and skimpy,* thinks Stanley before turning his attention back to Jean, who is elucidating his love of ethnic music.

"My affinity for that type of music," he is saying, "is why I have already started on the construction of a slave chapel on the plantation. The plan is to have it completed before the sale closes at midnight on October 31. Inauguration would be on that same day with both of you in attendance. I have formed and am training a slave choir for the occasion. Father Joseph has supplied me with suitable anthems and hymns."

As Jean deigns to take another small mouthful of his quiche, Stanley wishing to ensure that he has understood this bizarre information correctly, asks, "Jean, could you confirm for me, please, that you have created a slave choir that will be singing in their African way within the framework of Christianity?"

"Exactly that!" Jean acknowledges with verve. Abandoning his quiche, he explains, "I've always believed that, as white men, we should embrace what is beautiful and right in other cultures instead of scorning and rejecting them. I also think it would make slaves happier if they could find common ground between their beliefs and ours."

Émile intervenes with the remark, "I would have thought that the majority of whites would *not* consider the happiness of their slaves important."

"You're right," Jean agrees, "but their happiness is important to me, and their chapel will be decorated with African motifs. Also, Christ and the saints will be depicted as people of color."

"Does Father Joseph agree?" Stanley asks.

Jean gives a crooked little smile and says, "Father balked at first, but when I increased my donation to the church, he came to agree that the looks of the historical Christ are unimportant. When I made a further increase, he admitted that I might be right about Christ being in us all, whether we be slave or master. Papa, Maman, and Jacques would not agree, but . . ." He shrugs, the gesture indicating that their opinions no longer count.

"What about Olivier Girrard and those of a similar mind-set? Do their opinions count?"

Jean is now tucking into the chocolate mousse with more enthusiasm than was the case with the other items on the menu. He says between mouthfuls, "I'm now living life according to my own dictates and not according to those of others. I am enjoying the chapel project and shall be returning to the plantation tomorrow to continue work on it. I also look forward to forming a slave choir here in New Orleans when I return from the plantation with Adrienne at the beginning of November. Adrienne is the slave from the plantation that I shall be making my official placée. Apart from having a wonderful voice, she is a kind and lovely girl. I want to raise her to her full potential by educating her and equipping her for polite society, aspirations that would not have met with parental approval!"

As they move on to the cheese board - Brie, chèvre, and Roquefort - Jean says, "I have an idea. Perhaps, Stanley, you would like to take part in the inauguration of the chapel by playing your bagpipes. It'd be a way of introducing you to the entire slave body at the same time."

"Get them dancing to my tune?" Stanley asks with a grin.

In the carriage going home, Émile says to Stanley, "Of the many cousins with whom I've dealt, I've never encountered one like Jean! He not only looks different to the rest of us but also seems to inhabit another planet. Jacques couldn't have been like that, too, could he?"

"No!" says Stanley with emphasis, although he doesn't know how he can be so certain about Jacques except that he can't imagine anyone else being like Jean! He then adds, "Jean does though make sense in a way. I find the idea of the chapel interesting, and there is something appealing about the idea of taking a slave girl as a placée and grooming her according to one's own requirements too. I am wondering if I should try that. I would though prefer my placée to come straight from Africa and not be plantation-bred. That way, she'd be an empty vessel ready for whatever I care to pour into her." She'd also be a more reliable and uncontaminated source of the true, *noble savage*."[136]

"One has to wonder if kidnapping and transportation might not have created their own type of contamination," Émile ponders aloud.

---

[136] Concept propagated by Jean-Jacques Rousseau that glorifies uncivilized man as symbolizing the innate goodness in those never exposed to the corrupting influences of civilization.

Slave Auction

New Orleans, Louisiana

Stanley and Émile have arrived at the slave market half an hour before the auction begins. The place is a hustle and a bustle with men in their long-tailed coats and wide-brimmed hats. Many smoke cigars, carry crops, and strut around full of self-importance. The auctioneer - his gavel ready on his desk - stands chatting with a justice, while a newspaperman tries to strike up a conversation with a potential bidder. The latter sits on a chair with his legs crossed, jiggling his foot and refusing to answer.

As Stanley and Émile move through the crowd, Stanley notices that he and Émile attract attention. A banker and clergymen interrupt their conversation to stare as does the clerk standing at his lectern - quill and leather-bound ledger at the ready. On a placard nailed across the front of the lectern, stark black letters spell out the words *Public Sale of Negroes*.

The slaves themselves are behind the podium, where potential buyers cluster around testing the *wares* with pinching, poking, and prodding. The slaves recently arrived from Africa; they are easy to differentiate from the ones that are up for resale. In the latter case, the women wear long dark slave dresses with wrist-length sleeves, white slave caps and pinafores. The men wear clean but poor-quality cotton shirts, trousers, and jackets. Those recently arrived from Africa - both men and women - are bare-chested and bareheaded. Men in both categories are shackled while guards with whips keep watch over the scene.

"I don't like it here," Stanley tells Émile. "It smells. Let's go." He then casts a brief glance over the recent arrivals. He sees in their midst a woman with a long neck and a child at her side. She stands straight and silent, her hand resting lightly on the child's head. The woman's head is turned slightly toward the person at her side, who is smaller, dumpier, and cradles an infant in her arms.

"Such serenity," says Stanley of the woman with a long neck. "She seems to live in another world."

"Perhaps her thoughts are back in her native village," suggests Émile. "They can't be in this hellhole!"

They walk over to the woman, and Stanley greets her with a nod and says, "Hello!" Choosing to remain aloof, she looks past him. The child though looks up and smiles. Taken aback at the sudden beauty of the gesture, Stanley responds in kind, saying to Émile, "We'll stay for the auction after all."

Foreign Contraption

New Orleans, Louisiana

Efia and Abebi find themselves bundled into one of the many luxurious wheeled contraptions that feature in the outdoor space. They have never before seen wheeled vehicles, nor have they ever seen the magnificent creatures that pull them. They are animals that resemble zebras but have no stripes, are bigger, and not frightened of people.

The wondrous wheeled contraption takes them past places with sights, sounds, and smells never before experienced: crowded shops, buildings, monuments, streets, traffic . . . All are of hypnotic interest to Efia; all are to be added to her stash of sensual input, which began the moment she stepped onto the dock and saw the groaning cranes, the stacks of miscellaneous cargo, the different types of vessels . . .

Her mind is in a state of turmoil, but she'll have to process the new information later. For now, as she clutches a wide-eyed Abebi to her chest, she needs to make sure to keep her back straight and her neck long. The two ghost-faced men who share with them the small interior of the vehicle must never guess at her insecurity.

As the vehicle sways along the road, one of the two men, reaches over and taps her on the arm saying, "You can look at me. I won't hurt you." She doesn't understand the words, but his tone tells her that he won't be harming her or Abebi, not yet anyway. Having learned a lesson or two on board, she resolves to oblige and not to follow her instinct to rebel.

The ghost-face taps his chest and says slowly and clearly, "I'm Master Stanley." Then pointing his finger at her and briefly touching her lips, he says, "Now you repeat. *Master Stanley, Master Stanley . . .*"

She understands that *Master Stanley* is his name and that he wants her to repeat it, which she tries to do a couple of times before getting it right. At that point, Abebi joins in singing out with exuberance, "Master Stanley, Master Stanley . . ." which amuses the strangers. One claps, and the other exclaims, "Bravo, little one!

The one called Master Stanley then points at Efia again and says, "You are now Bertha. Repeat, Bertha, Bertha . . ." She repeats the name with Abebi following suit.

They are already arriving at the house by the time Stanley gets around to chucking Abebi under the chin and saying, "You, little cutie-pie, are now Annie! Repeat Annie, Annie, Annie . . ."

Abebi is still giggling and singing out, "Annie, Annie . . ." as the conveyance turns in through a massive gateway that closes firmly behind them.

Fourth Week of August 1800

The Voice

New Orleans, Louisiana

The house that Olivier Girrard has rented for Stanley and Émile is two-story high and is built around an internal courtyard lined with arcades onto which the rooms open. The facade is flat and stretches along the street, giving access to the courtyard through the wide gate that closed so firmly behind Bertha (Efia) and Annie (Abebi). Bertha had noticed immediately on arrival that all the outside windows of the house feature decorative wrought iron work, which, while looking good, would prevent escape.

A French woman with a harelip - relation of an absentee landlord - runs the household and with a watchful yet benign eye rules over the handful of slaves. The slaves include a laundress, a cook, kitchen helpers, a seamstress, and a number of housemaids. All are of African descent but being Louisiana-born, they only speak a French patois, which, during the past ten days, Bertha and Annie are picking up rapidly. Master Stanley is also teaching them new English words and phrases every day, which both Bertha and Annie are good at remembering.

Now as Bertha puffs up cushions in the salon, she realizes that she and Annie have come a long way in the past ten days since Masters

Stanley and Émile had stuffed them into the foreign contraption. She feels an approximation of pride and satisfaction at the way she and Annie are adjusting to surroundings so dramatically different to those of Banyan Village. The difference reminds her of the tales of the Arabs at the savanna markets. In those days, she had yearned to experience foreign places. Had she realized the horrors that can accompany new experiences, she would have tempered her enthusiasm!

Beneath the surface, the anger she felt on board continues to simmer unabated, and she vows never to let it die until she and Annie can return home, if not physically, at least in spirit. Even so, as she moves on to dust an ormolu singing-bird clock, she has no idea what it is; she knows that to brood on the past would be wrong, and it is a duty she owes to herself and Abebi to glean what she can from the present.

Going out into the arcade to shake out her feather duster in the courtyard, Annie plays there happily with other slave children. Bertha turns her mind to the new experiences of the past ten days. She tells herself she needs to be thankful for the improvement of their present condition, as compared to conditions on board, and in spite of herself, she feels genuine gratitude for the good food, for the pleasant environment of the house, for the courtyard, and for the availability of the facilities needed for personal hygiene. The companionship of the slaves that come with the house is also an asset.

As to Master Stanley, well . . . in accordance with the philosophy she developed on board, she accepts his authority and obeys him, although it goes against the grain. To be fair, he is never rough with her and his nightly sexual demands are an improvement over her experiences with the sailors even though sex is *never* of her own volition. She concedes to Master Stanley's demands knowing that for the sake of Annie, she has no option. That her daughter is enjoying herself here as much as she did in Banyan Village is a major payback for all sacrifices.

Annie, at this moment, has not even noticed her mother shaking out the feather duster. *One can only marvel at the resilience of children,* Bertha thinks, as she returns to dusting yet another unidentifiable object. As she winds up her assigned chores, the housekeeper comes to inspect the work done, praises her, and as a reward, gives her the job she likes best: the watering and tending of the plants in the courtyard.

Once Bertha is in the courtyard with the watering cans, Annie abandons her friends and comes to help. They are watering a large potted camellia - it has glossy dark leaves and double yellow blossoms - when Annie asks, "Mammi, why don't you sing anymore?"

"I'll sing again when we get back to Big Baba and Banyan Village," Bertha replies.

"Please, sing *now*, Mammi!" Annie begs. "*Big* singing, like you used to sing for Gran Legbwa."

Caught off guard by an attack of nostalgia, Bertha sets aside the watering can and closes her eyes. She is again at home gathered with her people around the poto mitan. The drumming is building to its frenzied climax, Big Baba sits on his throne and flickering firelight captures Thimba and his companions soaring into the sky as they perform the Grand Leap. Now it is her turn and opening her mouth, she sings as never before, allowing the huge sound to soar over the forest into the realm of the spirits. Returning to the present, she opens her eyes to see all the slaves have emerged from the house and stand staring. Masters Stanley and Émile, who have just returned home, stand in their midst with stunned looks on their faces.

Decision

New Orleans, Louisiana

In the heat of the early afternoon, Stanley and Émile sit in the shade of the arcade sipping lemonade and looking out into the courtyard with its huge pots of angels' trumpets, bromeliads, camellias, and bougainvillea. Hanging baskets and trellises drip with color: purple, gold, white, and magenta.

"Drinks like this would be better with ice," says Émile, holding up his glass. "Bringing in great blocks of ice from the north will be one of the new businesses I'll be suggesting to Aaron when he arrives."

Stanley doesn't comment. He is thinking about hearing Bertha singing earlier in the day. Who would have thought that a woman with such an incredible voice should belong to him? He had paid for her and Annie with his own money, not with Migu's. The sight and the sound of Bertha standing among the camellias singing her heart out had left him stunned and knowing that he had witnessed something of the highest order.

As Émile moves on to wondering aloud how Cousin Aaron would react to the idea of investing in steam technology, Stanley's thoughts turn to Jean - he is now on the plantation - and to Jean's area of expertise: ethnomusicology. That is the area where Bertha would find a fit, along with Jean's future placée. Stanley turns to his companion, asks, "Émile, what did you think of Bertha's singing this morning?"

Émile replies, "It gave me goosebumps."

Stanley is glad to hear Émile echo his own enthusiasm and says, "So you don't regard that type of singing as *primitive caterwauling*?"

"Of course not!" counters Émile. "The public needs educating. Voices like Bertha's would captivate the audiences of every opera house in Europe."

"Why Europe? Why not here? It'd be simpler to arrange suitable exposure here."

"You forget that the biggest slave owners in Louisiana are the plantation owners, and they do not allow their slaves to sing, dance, and drum. The wildness frightens them." Émile swigs back the remains of his tepid lemonade and gets to his feet, saying, "It's time for a siesta."

As they get up to leave the courtyard, Stanley says, "I'm going to write to Jean at the plantation and tell him about Bertha and suggest I send her to train with him and his choir."

Thirty-First of October 1800

Sixth Letter to Ambrose

Edinburgh, Scotland

Tom writes as follows:

This has been an eventful time. That's why you haven't heard from me since August. Lady McCallum, whom I never met, died a while back at her parents' home in Glasgow. Esquire and the girls then all adjourned to Glasgow, leaving Ms. Young, her niece, and me alone here in Edinburgh.

Now that the family is back, the house swarms with governesses bent on turning five clever little girls into suitable bait for men of noble birth on the marriage market. Lessons in French, Italian, art, music, dancing, and stitching are the order of the day. Any mention of science would be considered obscene!

Although the traditional education for upper-class lassies supposedly runs along those lines, all Esquire's girls are demanding a 'proper' education, alongside the traditional ones. Isobel quotes from the writings of

Condorcet, who writes that the education for both boys and girls should be identical. Isobel also scorns the rites of passage that high society inflicts on young girls. She equates them with the trade of merchandize: parents putting their wares on the market looking for takers.

All this is music to Esquire's ears, and I suspect he has been planting the seeds for such opinions for years! I believe the expense involved in providing an environment conducive to attracting highborn bridegrooms has been the root cause for his misery. As a result of Isobel's attitude and without her mother here to try to change her mind, Esquire is canceling the purchase agreement for the London house and is selling the houses in North Berwick and Glasgow. These decisions have made him into a different person. He seems to be enjoying life for the first time! It's a pleasure to behold. I believe he now sees a way to rid himself of dependence on the slave trade.

I'd not be surprised to hear that he is in the process of withdrawing from the *Spirit* consortium. If that turns out to be correct, I hope he will still have enough money left to continue sponsoring me! I think so, though; because he speaks of bringing into the house others of my kind and grooming them to his liking, as he is doing with me; let it be said with my compliance!

On the subject of the consortium, rumor has it that Aaron Migu will soon be pulling up stakes and leaving Britain. He is supposedly placing all his business interests - excluding the slave trade - in the hands of his daughter and her fiancé.

I must admit that I, too, have fallen victim to the talk about overseas opportunities and often play with the idea of taking the plunge myself. If - when I am a qualified - Isobel will marry me, perhaps we'll be able to find our niche over the ocean in a country more open to the new and less hung up on class.

Inauguration Day

Plantation, Louisiana

The plantation will change hands at midnight tonight prior to which Stanley and Émile will attend the inauguration of Jean's last hurrah: the slave chapel. Having hired a carriage for themselves and their luggage, Stanley had spent the previous night in Baton Rouge. Now in a state of high anticipation, they turn off the River Road and pass through the plantation's wrought iron gates.

They like what they see as the carriage proceeds up a long avenue under live oaks dripping with Spanish moss. The avenue takes them to the Big House where they see the house slaves neatly attired in uniforms lined up at the top of the steps of a wide porch with classically themed pillars. Jean stands at the bottom of the steps. As the coach comes to a stop, a mixed-race youngster runs forward to hold the horses while the coachman opens the carriage door and lowers the steps. Jean greets the new arrivals with a smile and asks, "Would you like to come in and refresh yourselves with some slices of mango?"

They accept the offer, and as they mount the steps, Jean says, "I'm going to have to leave you to your own devices for an hour or two. I still need to put the finishing touches to arrangements for the inauguration. In the meantime, Agathe and Bertha - Agathe is training Bertha - can give you a tour of the house. Then if you so wish, Gerald can take you to André, who will give you a tour of the farmyard." He points to the youngster who is holding the bridle of one of the horses and who, at the mention of his name, looks up and gives Stanley and Émile a glorious smile.

Mounting the steps to the level of the house slaves, Jean introduces Agathe, who moves forward, from where she was standing next to Bertha and Annie. Hands clasped, she inclines her head and says, "Welcome, Master Stanley."

Bertha follows suit, copying Agathe to the nth degree and repeating the words, "Welcome, Master Stanley."

For her part, Annie runs forward and, giggling, clasps Stanley around the legs. He pats her on the head and says, "I'm glad to see you again, Annie!"

An hour later as Gerald leads them from the side porch toward the farmyard, Stanley feels a jolt through his whole system as a big man of color saunters toward them. Except for a darker complexion, he is the spitting image of Émile and Migu!

André - that is the person this man must be - gives a small bow and says, "Good morning, Master Stanley. I am at your service."

Stanley is not sure what he was expecting but certainly not this confident and well-spoken person, who looks exactly like two people with whom he is familiar! Nonetheless, he rallies saying, "Glad to meet you, André. Seeing this is not a suitable time to get down to business, if you come to the Big House tomorrow at 9:00 a.m., we can start then."

"I shall be there, Master." The enigmatic presence bows and leaves.

Seeing Stanley had not asked André for the tour of the farmyard, Gerald wants to know if Stanley and Émile would like to see the horses. They accept and follow him in the appropriate direction. The slaves going about their work in the yard stop to gawp, and each time, Stanley gives them a nod in passing. Émile though, as Stanley notes, is in no state of mind to pay them any attention. His normally ruddy complexion is unusually pale, and he seems to be in shock. "What do you think of André?" he asks Stanley in a shaky voice as they pass the vegetable garden.

"His uncanny likeness to you and Uncle Aaron is indeed shocking," Stanley replies.

SLAVES, MASTERS AND TRADERS 509

"Such a person should *not* be a slave!" Émile bursts out. "I can't imagine what Aaron will think when he realizes that he owns an enslaved member of his own family: one that is the spitting image of himself and looks as though he is the son for whom Aaron has always wished."

Continuing on their way toward the stables, they make a brief stop to take in a view of the sugar mill at the far end of the yard. Then before arriving at the stables, they pass the craft shed. There Stanley catches a brief glimpse of a beautiful young woman - perhaps of native extraction - and he wants to tarry, but alas, she immediately moves out of sight, and his thoughts return to André on whom he will have to depend.

In the past ten weeks, he has been learning what he can about the production of sugar by speaking to plantation owners and visiting various plantations. Nonetheless, he is a long way from knowing how to run the plantation on his own and will have to rely heavily on the unslave-like André.

He has put thought into how to treat his slaves and intends on treating them well, provided they obey. He will not use corporal punishment for intransigence; instead, he'll send troublemakers to the slave market. However, that is not an option with André. Ergo Stanley will be stuck with a slave who has power over him. That is not the way he imagined his situation!

They have arrived at the stables. Gerald points to a splendid stallion grazing at the far end of the paddock and says, "That is Pégasse!"

Stanley remembers something Olivier Girrard said when they first arrived but had forgotten until now. Girrard had remarked, "If you wish to learn the ins and outs of running the plantation, you would do well to tolerate André's airs and graces." Olivier had then given as examples

André's *office* and added, "Let him use the wretched Louis Quatorze desk, along with the stallion, although both are totally unfitting!"

If even Olivier Girrard thinks he has to tolerate André's high-handedness, there can indeed be no other option.

Slave Chapel

Plantation, Louisiana

Stanley and Émile walk with Jean around the chapel inspecting its distinctive design. Stanley runs his hand over the siding. "Would this be Louisiana's red cypress that I've read about?" he asks.

"It's from the bayou," Jean confirms. "My father must have set aside a stash years ago to air-dry, and it's now ready. The person who designed this chapel was ecstatic. He's an anthropologist friend of mine who spent time in West Africa and now lives in Boston."

"You brought him here all the way from Boston?" Stanley wants to know.

"I did. He has returned now, but I'll bring him back once I decide on the type of building that I want for my New Orleans choir."

"This chapel and its choir are then a pilot project?" queries Émile.

"I suppose one could say that," Jean concedes.

Stanley notices how Émile towers over Jean, who has to tilt his head at an uncomfortable angle to see Émile's face. It was obviously like that with his father as well. Turning to Stanley, Jean adds, "If you, Stanley, allow the chapel to flourish, I'd like to see the two choirs affiliated. You could send Bertha to New Orleans every so often, and on return, she'd be able to pass on her expanded repertoire to your choir members. Like Adrienne, she is a splendid singer, and such voices should not remain hidden under a bushel."

The field slaves are starting to gather from their nearby quarters. Jean has obviously given them a day off, which is probably not something they have ever experienced before. In the distance, Stanley also sees a convoy of horse-drawn carts that bring the house slaves and those who work around the farmyard to participate in the ceremony. To his surprise, he also sees a rider on horseback pull out from behind the convoy and gallop at top speed toward the chapel. It is a fine sight with the rider leaning low over the horse's neck and with the tail of the animal streaming out behind.

"André on Pégasse," Jean tells Stanley. "I would advise you not to try riding that horse! André is the only person who can cope with him. Jacques once attempted to mount him and regretted it!"

As the slaves clamber out of the carts, the discrepancy between the new arrivals and the field slaves shocks Stanley. The new arrivals laugh and chat in excitement; they look healthy, clean, and are neatly dressed. In contrast, the field slaves, dirty and dressed in tatters, gather in silence. Their facial expressions remain uniformly bleak without a single smile to be seen, let alone ones like Gerald's or Annie's!

Another strange thing edges into Stanley's mind. With the entire slave population gathered in one spot, he sees very few light-colored faces. He expected to see a lot given the chevalier had a reputation for being a *prolific breeder*. He supposedly prided himself in his ability to pass on his superior bloodlines to an inferior race. Yet Stanley can only count five mixed-race slaves: André, several young house slaves, and Gerald. Five children over four decades would not qualify anyone as a prolific breeder! What then has happened to all the chevalier's other coffee-colored kiddies? Looking over to where André is handing over Pégasse to Gerald, Stanley feels André may well have the answer to that question, but what should be done about it is another matter.

He reaches no conclusion to the quandary before André saunters over to confer with Jean on a matter pertaining to the carriage that Jean and Adrienne will be using to leave the plantation after the ceremony. Observing André's get-up, Stanley has to wonder how Jean can tolerate it, yet Jean seems to neither notice nor care. André's jacket, breeches, shirt, and cravat are all of excellent quality, and he also wears expensive riding boots. As he speaks to Jean, he playfully slaps the crop he carries against the shaft of his boot.

When André has left, Jean turns to Stanley broaching the subject of Bertha and her amazing gift. "I'm glad you sent her to me for instruction," he tells Stanley. "Hearing that voice for the first time blew me away. I regard it as a privilege to work with voices like Adrienne's and Bertha's. They have no problem coping with my arrangements of traditional Christian music and of treating it in an African manner. Father Joseph, on the other hand, has had a problem accepting the new sound, but another sizeable donation to the parish won him over, and I now think he is starting to genuinely understand where I'm coming from!"

Listening to Jean, Stanley is gaining insight into why Jean has never found a good fit for himself either within the ranks of the snobby French elite of New Orleans or among the wealthy plantation owners and their racist views! However, he doesn't comment as Jean continues, "It is fortunate for us all that you found Bertha. I often wonder how much talent is lost in the drudgery of the cane fields. I'm hoping to save some of it."

A member of the choir - already clad in her bright African-themed choir robe - emerges from the chapel and, approaching Jean, says, "Master, we are having a problem with . . ." Stanley doesn't listen to the nature of the problem knowing it is time for him to assemble his bagpipes. He left his case on the back pew of the chapel and needs to fit together the bits: blowpipe, chanter with its reed, drones, and their reeds and caps. His job will be to stand outside, where they are standing now near the entrance to the chapel, and play his Scottish airs before the service begins.

Eureka Moment

Plantation, Louisiana

After playing his bagpipes outside where the field slaves were his principle audience, Stanley enters the chapel. With the exception of the first two rows, the pews are chockablock with slaves of higher ranking. Stanley takes his place next to Émile in the front pew where he and Émile exchange remarks in whispers as they wait.

Jean will join them, but he and Father Joseph are in the sacristy fussing with the censer and with the resin beads that will provide incense for the service that is about to begin. It is a service that, so Stanley heard Jean telling the field slaves outside, will celebrate the opening of *their* chapel using *their* music. The slaves have responded in silent bewilderment!

André will be sitting in the second pew behind Jean, Émile, and Stanley, but like Jean, he has not yet appeared. Meanwhile, on entering the chapel, Stanley had discovered that the pretty girl, whom he had seen briefly at the craft-shed, is the same one who now sits in the second row behind him. There is an empty seat at her side; she is therefore André's broomstick wife. The sleeping infant in her arms wears a long white christening robe in readiness for the baptisms that will take place after the inauguration.

When Stanley first saw the girl, he'd had a fleeting thought that she might be a suitable candidate for his bed. Now it occurs to him that by taking André's woman into his bed he would be proving to André who is the master. However, the fact that a child is involved causes Stanley a pang of nostalgia for Baby Adair, whom he had to leave behind at Glen Orm. It makes him think that he should probably find a more honorable method of putting André in his place.

"I enjoyed your playing, Stanley," Émile says sotto voce. "Do you think your audience also appreciated it?"

"I think they did," Stanley replies. "I have a suspicion that there is nothing in the lives of those poor wretches that gives them any pleasure. When I started playing, their empty faces suddenly became animated. Imagine how much better it will be for them when they hear Bertha, Adrienne, and the choir singing in their own African way!"

"If their families have been on the plantation for several generations," Émile points out, "they probably retain very little of their African culture and won't even recognize what they hear as *their way*. I've been told plantation owners forbid African singing, dancing, and drumming on the grounds that such things could lead to revolt."

After a moment of reflection, Stanley says, "We know that by definition slaves are not free, do not receive pay, and have to obey. Nonetheless, in all my years of wanting to own slaves, I've always assumed that, if well-treated and healthy, there would be room for content and happiness and they wouldn't want to rebel. I never thought of them as being without anchor or rudder. The house slaves in New Orleans and those we saw at the Big House seemed well nourished, clean, and content. Also the ones we saw getting out of the carts were laughing and chatting."

"They certainly stood in stark contrast to the abject misery of the wretches from the field slave quarters," Émile agrees.

"Exactly," says Stanley knowing suddenly he does *not* want responsibility for the untold numbers of unfortunates gathered outside. Yet as of midnight they will be his responsibility. Given their large numbers, it would not be feasible to start giving them everything they need. The plantation would lose its sustainability, and Uncle Aaron wouldn't like that! His interest is business, not a charity.

Stanley cannot believe his own naivete in thinking that all slaves under his watch would be of the healthy, well-fed, and well-treated variety. He had always imagined his slaves would honor and respect him for all the good things he would give them in exchange for loyal service and obedience. He now sees the attitude for what it is: a benevolent feudal paternalism as practiced by Gramps and his class in Britain. Shifting on the hard cushion-less pew, he suddenly understands that paternalism has no place on this large rambling plantation, where he will be forced to rely on the uppity slave André.

He would rather have a smaller and more manageable property: one in his own area of expertise, which he could manage without the financial help of the likes of Uncle Aaron. A modest undertaking of the kind he has in mind would require only a limited number of slaves. He could then afford to teach and treat them well.

In the house, alongside Bertha, who as his placée, would play the role of First Wife in African society. He would have just a sufficient number of women house slaves to give him a choice in bed companions.

This wonderful scheme would free him of the uppity slave André! Yet he is committed to Uncle Aaron and Émile and wouldn't feel comfortable letting them down. Could there be a way around this dilemma?

At this point, he interrupts his musings and sniffs. He smells something sweet and spicy.

"Ah," exclaims Émile, "that's incense! They have finally sorted out the problem with the censer! The service will start soon."

The arrival of André in his pew behind confirms the assumption. As André and his wife whisper to one another and their baby joins in with gurgles of pleasure, Stanley has a eureka moment: the perfect solution to his dilemma pops ready-made into his mind!

It's a solution that will serve the interests of Uncle Aaron, Émile, André, and Stanley himself. It hinges on what Émile had said earlier, "I can't imagine what Aaron will think when he realizes that he owns an enslaved member of his own family: one that is the spitting image of himself and looks as though he is the son for whom Aaron has always wished."

Ergo, Uncle Aaron does *not* need Stanley to run his plantation! He has a member of his own clan who already knows how to run the plantation and has done so successfully for years! With glorious African voices singing *hallelujah, hallelujah* . . . Bertha's voice separates itself from the choir and soars up and out of the chapel and over land, water, and time.

Vodun[137] Vocabulary

The traditional West African belief system known as Vodun is central to the lives of those depicted in this work prior to their enslavement. As an animist faith, Vodun is one of the most ancient belief systems on the planet, and one which is still practiced in many forms and many locations on both sides of the Atlantic.

Seeing very little was ever recorded, it is difficult to know how the faith was practiced in a specific location in AD 1800. Here the subject is treated in a basic manner focusing on its essence rather than its detail.

I lay emphasis on the following Vodun beliefs

- everything has a spirit that exists independently of the material world
- the divide between the spiritual and material worlds is flimsy, and interaction is a constant.

With regard to the different names used in Vodun for the same entities, I use those that African slaves in the French Colony of Saint-Domingue - now Haiti - translated from varying African languages into their French slave-patois during the seventeenth and eighteenth

---

[137] Also referred to as Voodoo, Vodou, Voudou, Vudu, or Vodoun, all of which come from the Fon-Ewe word for *spirit*

519

centuries. From there the words would have found their way for the first time into a written form. Some of them are listed below.

Babalawo—A diviner, healer of mind and body, herbalist, medicine man, shaman.

Bondye—Corruption of the French *Bon Dieu,* meaning "Good Lord," the Supreme Creator, unreachable and unknowable to humans, without the intervention of the spirits/loas

Gran Legbwa—Fusion of two Vodun spirits: Papa Legba and Gran Bwa, elemental power of nature, gatekeeper to the spirit world, and intermediary to *Bondye.* The name *Gran Bwa* is a corruption of the French *grand bois* (big wood), which refers to "the wooden pole, poto mitan, in the center of the ritual dance circle."

Houngan—Priest, who tends to the rites and rituals and maintains the relationship between the spirits and the community

Poto Mitan—Corruption of the French words *poteau mitan*, meaning "center pole," which refers to "the wooden pole in the center of the dance circle during a Gran Legbwa celebration."

Loas—From the French *lois* meaning "laws;" spirits of ancestors, animals, or natural forces

Vévé—Graphic representation of a loa's symbol

African and Louisiana Words

Cat-o'-nine-tails—Multi-tailed whip

Grits—Cornmeal

Hominy—Grits made with a treated type of corn

Hookus—Chickens

Kaier—Hut, house, home

Machete—Large knife used for harvesting sugarcane

Muti—Medication

Picannin—Baby

Rascal—Used as a term of endearment for a mischievous child

Shooper—Trouble

Skellum—Bug

French Words and Phrases

Ancien régime—Social and political system prior to the French Revolution

Bâtard—Bastard

Creole—Mixed-race offspring of common-law marriages

Demi-frère—Half brother

Dieu le sait—God knows

Fusil de chasse—Shotgun

Grâce à Dieu—Thank God

Hélas—Alas

Hors des limites—Beyond the limits

Le Bon Dieu—The Good Lord

Mariage de la main gauche—Literal: left-handed marriage

Common-law marriage between a black woman and a white man

Môle—Jetty

Placée—Black woman in a common-law marriage with a white man

Plaçage—A system whereby white men enter into a common-law marriage with a black woman.

S'il plait à Dieu—If God so pleases

West African Vegetation

Ackee Tree

- approximately fifty feet tall
- fruit: three-inch-long pods
- seeds: three per pod; big, black, and lethal
- seeds embedded in a cream-colored aril[138]
- aril is an edible delicacy when ripe
- turns bright yellow when cooked

Banyan Tree

- related to the fig
- branches spread out laterally
- uses aerial prop roots to support them
- mildly psychedelic

Jess

- thick undergrowth

Kola Tree

- approximately forty feet tall

---

[138] Seed coat

- fruit is star-shaped
- the seeds are referred to as beans or nuts
- contain more stimulants than Arabica coffee
- are chewed fresh or drunk in beverages
- taste bitter at first but sweetens upon chewing
- are used as a currency and for gifts

Fictional Characters

Aaron Migu—Born 1754; Leith, Scotland
 Captain of industry and slave trader

Abebi—Born 1794; Banyan Village, West Africa
 Daughter of Efia and Thimba

Abena—Born 1779; plantation, Louisiana
 Village woman and Efia's friend

Adrienne—Born 1785; plantation, Louisiana
 Agathe's black daughter

Agathe—Born 1763; plantation, Louisiana
 Chief African house slave
 Mother of André and Elise with the chevalier
 Mother of Adrienne with a broomstick husband
 Aunt and guardian of Gerald

Andréa—Born 1782; Louisiana
 Choctaw slave
 André's broomstick wife

Angus McCorm—Stanley's old deerhound

André—Born 1778; plantation, Louisiana
Mixed-race slave
Eldest son of Agathe and the chevalier
Married to Andréa

Assimbola—Born 1787; Banyan Village, West Africa
Abena's son
Kwame's friend

Babalawo—Born 1760; Banyan Village, West Africa
Medicine man

Big Baba—Born 1739; Banyan Village, West Africa
Father of Efia
Grandfather of Abebi
Senior tribal elder

Betta Migu—Born 1754; Leith, Scotland
Wife of Aaron Migu
Rose Migu's mother

Cécile—Born 1739; France
Wife of the chevalier
Mother of Jacques and Jean

Chevalier—Born 1730; France
New Orleans businessman and plantation owner
Father of Jacques and Jean
Father of all the coffee-colored kiddies, including André, Elise, and
Gerald

Efia—Born, 1779; Banyan Village, West Africa
Daughter of Big Baba and Twenty-Seventh Wife
Wife of Thimba
Mother of Abebi

Elise—Born 1783; plantation, Louisiana
Daughter of Agathe and the chevalier

Émile Migu—Born 1755; France
Cousin of Aaron Migu

Frances—Born 1761; Scotland
Daughter of Laird of Glen Orm
Wife of Pontefract Staymann
Mother of Stanley

Girrard, Olivier—Born 1733; New Orleans, Louisiana
Lawyer and plantation owner

Gerald—Born 1788; Banyan Village, West Africa
Slave of mixed race
Agathe's nephew

Gryphon (old Earl of)—Born 1720; Scotland
grandfather, slave trader

Gryphon (new Earl of)—Born 1777; Scotland
grandson William

Infana—Born 1797; Banyan Village, West Africa
Died 1799; Banyan Village, West Africa
Efia and Thimba's son
Abebi's brother and loa

Jacques—Born 1760; New Orleans, Louisiana
Legitimate son and heir of the chevalier and Cécile
Brother of Jean
Half brother of André and all the coffee-colored kiddies

Jean—Born 1767; New Orleans, Louisiana
Younger legitimate son of the chevalier and Cécile

Brother of Jacques
Half brother of André and all the coffee-colored kiddies

Kwame—Born 1787; Banyan Village, West Africa
Thimba's younger brother

Laird of Glen Orm—Born 1732; Glen Orm, Scotland
Father of Frances Staymann
Grandfather of Stanley

Lord Richard Castleton—Born 1740; Scotland
Scottish nobleman and closet slave trader

Masimbarashe—Thimba's lion-faced loa

Mbaleki—Born 1743; West Africa
Senior tribal elder of Mbaleki Village
Big Baba's friend

Mkulu—Big Baba's loa and in life his grandfather

Pontefract Staymann—Born 1754; Scotland
Captain of industry
Husband of Frances
Father of Stanley

Rose Migu—Born 1785; Leith, Scotland
Daughter of Aaron and Betta Migu

Shamwari—Born 1775; Banyan Village, West Africa
Thimba's warrior-friend

Sir George McCallum—Born 1748; Edinburgh, Scotland
Closet slave trader

Stanley Staymann—Born 1777; Glen Orm, Scotland
Son of Pontefract and Frances Staymann
Grandson of the Laird of Glen Orm

Thimba—Born 1775; Banyan Village, West Africa
Warrior-hunter
Husband of Efia
Father of Abebi
Tom Brown—Born 1776
Ex-barber-surgeon on *Spirit of the Clyde*

Zainia—Village hairdresser

Printed in the United States
By Bookmasters